W9-AZH-572

The Dark and Bloody Ground

Roberta Webb

THE DARK AND BLOODY GROUND
PUBLISHED BY TURNKEY PRESS
2100 Kramer Lane, Suite 300
Austin, Texas 78758

For more information about our books, please write to us, call
512.478.2028, or visit our website at www.bookpros.com.

Printed and bound in the United States of America. All rights reserved. No part of this book may be reproduced in any form or by
any electronic or mechanical means including information storage
and retrieval systems without permission in writing from the copy-
right holder, except by a reviewer, who may quote brief passages in
review.

Library of Congress Control Number: 2005907538

ISBN-13: 978-1-933538-08-2
ISBN-10: 1-933538-08-2

Copyright© 2006 by Roberta Webb

*This book is dedicated to my husband,
children and grandchildren, whose
love and support are my greatest joy.*

ACKNOWLEDGMENTS

Pam Brink, my editor and friend, pulled my sometimes-meandering manuscript into a book. To you, Pam, my everlasting gratitude. My thanks to Lois Tanner, my typist, who had to struggle through hundreds of hand-written pages.

A special thanks to the Texas Tech University Library, an unlimited source of information in every field. From government documents on Kentucky to day-to-day accounts of that state's involvement in the Civil War, it was a Mecca for information throughout my writing.

CHAPTER 1

"Please don't go, Morgan," Ingrid begged again. She had arisen each morning for the past week with a desperate sense of foreboding. Morgan's departure date was nearing, and despite her begging and pleading, she had been unable to persuade him not to make this journey. She knew he would never return, and she would never see her favored son again.

***

Stinging frost hung heavy in the air, cloaking everything with a sparkling white blanket of ice crystals. Leather bindings stiffened and refused to close as Morgan Collier swore to himself. Reflections of a sun rising orange bounced off the icy covering, creating a blinding glare, but no aggravation could dissuade him from continuing the job at hand. He checked the large, sturdy wagon again, as he had done a hundred times, and could find no flaw. His father and brothers had helped him in crafting a vehicle that would cover many tortured miles over rough and rugged trails.

Morgan's restless soul soared with excitement. The year was 1840 into the waning days of March. They would depart at daybreak and begin their trek into the wilds of hidden valleys and mountains in southeastern Kentucky. He had sharpened huge double bit axes and sturdy saws with voracious teeth before securing them in the wagon. Extras hung on strong rawhide loops on the wagon sides. In many places he would have to cut a trail for the wagon. Calvin Kelly had told him so.

***

Morgan Collier's father, John, had worked as a blacksmith apprentice in England before coming to Boston where he soon established himself as a master craftsman. There he met and married beautiful, fearless Ingrid Thorsen, and they migrated west to establish their dynasty in Ohio.

As a deprived orphan, John Collier craved land to bolster his income, along with his expertise in blacksmithing. His stoic, plodding, brute strength and endless determination were in stark contrast to his firey, young, six-foot Norwegian bride who charged headlong into the fray with him. Pregnant with a succession of six sons, Ingrid nevertheless helped to fire the forge and constantly replenished fuel for the ever-burning fires. She even hefted a heavy hammer over the anvil when John was rushing to fill overdue orders as his business increased.

The boys were taught early on to fill in, in every way possible, with Ingrid ever watchful for their safety. She was tall enough to look her husband in the eye and they worked shoulder to shoulder through the rough years.

Settling in Chillicothe, they gloried in the event that marked Ohio as a state in 1803. They watched with pride as their healthy and robust sons excelled in blacksmithing, farming, trading, wheelwrighting and wagonwrighting. Morgan was the last born in 1808, and he was his mother's golden idol. Ohio exploded with trade and commerce as the westward movement swept through the state over Zane's trace from the East. The family profited mightily by being in the right place with the right resources in the early 1800s.

***

Morgan, a strapping six feet and three inches, knew he had to make this move now or never. He grew up hunting and exploring in Ohio but always with the yearning to travel into the fabled mountains of far southeastern Kentucky, where high rising peaks mingled with those of Virginia and Tennessee. Calvin Kelly had paved the way for Morgan's dream.

Calvin, with his bushy red eyebrows meeting over the bridge of a large nose, was a rugged Irishman and long-time friend of the Collier family. Kinky red hair receded slightly from a sharply defined widow's peak unaligned with his prominent nose that threw his face somewhat off kilter. A wide mouth stretched a heavy mustache almost across the lower part of his face, covering it completely with a dark red fringe. His beard was cropped short. He liked to button his deerskin shirt up there. He barely scraped five feet and ten inches, but his huge, barrel chest projected a greater height. A heavy mat of light auburn hair curled over his entire body, and when he occasionally bathed in the cold mountain streams, the bears almost considered him one of their own. He was Morgan's hero.

***

In 1825, Liddy Kreiger's family moved to Ohio when Morgan was seventeen years of age, and he knew instantly he could never go anywhere without Liddy. Liddy's thick, shining mane of honey-colored hair was the first thing Morgan noticed about her as she sat on the high seat of their overland wagon. It was lustrous in the late afternoon sun, and he circled around the Kreiger's wagon to get a better look at her. Liddy had been very shy under Morgan's bold stare. For the first time he felt his trickle of Viking blood stir, and he wanted to yank her off the high seat. Her two older brothers standing close by had better plans and invited him to help unload their wagons. Morgan was only too happy to help Liddy and her family settle into the area. Herman Kreiger had traded a thriving grist mill business in Pennsylvania for a farm whose owner wished to return to the East. There was much to be done in early May, and Morgan even enticed his five older brothers to assist on several occasions.

Calvin Kelley returned for his annual visit just after Morgan's eighteenth birthday in 1826 and knew immediately that Morgan would not be leaving Ohio. Kelly had felt a keen sense of loss when he saw Morgan with sixteen-year-old Liddy. He had almost married on two occasions, but the lure of tall canebrakes and the "long knife hunters" had won out in the long run. Now, in his early seventies, he couldn't help but ponder what might have been as he watched the large Kreiger and Collier clans with their easy comaraderie.

Late in 1828, both families smiled on the union of Liddy and

Morgan. Now, twelve years later at age thirty-two, Morgan was realizing his long, sought-after dream. Not only was Liddy still beautiful at thirty, she was extremely strong and Morgan's mainstay. Their three young daughters, ages seven, nine, and ten years, had been sorting and choosing what they would carry on their journey for several months, and all was in readiness.

***

Calvin Kelly had made the trek from his beloved Kentucky mountains every year since Morgan could remember. He had filled Morgan's mind with the glories of an enchanted forest since he was big enough to sit on Calvin's knee. He spoke of canebrakes so high and so thick buffalo and deer could hide in them while large bears and panthers faded into a forest so dense the sun could barely penetrate the foliage. Magnificent rainbow trout, speckled trout, bass and perch crowded every stream and pond. Kelly had collected many black bearskins as large bears scooped up flapping fish from the water to abate their ravenous hunger. Morgan was all ears as his friend related the many close calls he had encountered when mortally wounded bears would turn on him.

"You always need to carry a rifle, Morgan," he told his young friend. "Big black panthers roam the mountains, and they can make a bear seem like a pet. It is their scream in the night that can scare the hell out of you. They won't come near a fire, and I have never seen one close to my lean-to, but they are out there. I have seen them dragging fish from the creek, and some will measure at least seven feet long and weigh over 300 pounds." Young Morgan shivered.

Calvin Kelly had been the Collier's most frequent and valued customer during the years of 1805 through 1807. Napoleon marched through Europe and demanded that his grenadiers wear pompous hats made from the best black bearskins in Kentucky. Eight thousand bears fell from the onslaught of hunters and trappers anxious to collect the great sum of four to five dollars for each skin. The best of the shiny, thick fur came from the Big Sandy Valley and the steep sides of Pine Mountain. The bears feasted on nuts, berries, and overflowing fish ponds, growing to enormous size. Kelly designed special bear traps that John Collier forged into massive jaws that would clamp onto even the largest bear. The traps yielded so many pelts that Kelly was traveling to the river ports every three months to sell his bounty. He always visited briefly with the Collier clan before returning to the mountains.

"Can I go live with you, Calvin?" Morgan asked many times.

The answer was always the same, "When you are old enough."

***

Ingrid Collier was disturbed by her youngest son's fascination with the wild mountains so far away. The week before their planned departure she had arrived at their farm to try again to change his mind.

"Morgan, it is too dangerous to take Liddy and the girls into that place," she said again, repeating her constant objections, but today she was on the verge of tears as their departure date grew near.

"Ma, you know Liddy can shoot a rattlesnake at thirty-five feet, and she can handle a gun as well as any man."

"You are a fool, Morgan Collier, leaving a fine farm for God knows what. It is all Calvin Kelly's fault, and I wish I had never let him set foot in my door."

"We are going, Ma," Morgan answered quietly.

Ingrid glared at her son and stomped into the house to talk to Liddy. Ten-year-old Sarah rushed to Ingrid, hugging her about the waist.

"It's all right Grandma, Papa has shown me and Ellen how to load and shoot the guns, and we do it really well, don't we Mama?"

Morgan had followed his mother into the house and was mortified at Sarah's announcement. He and Liddy had cautioned Sarah and nine-year-old Ellen not to tell anyone about their experience with guns.

"See to it you take care of your parents, girls. I'm not sure they can do it themselves," she hissed at Morgan.

He was dumfounded by his mother's reaction. He had expected her to be irate because he had exposed the girls to firearms.

Sarah strongly resembled her Norwegian grandmother with extremely long limbs and pale coloring, something Ingrid Collier had not missed, and she would always be her favorite granddaughter. White-blond hair fell below her waist and light-colored eyelashes curled just before reaching her cheeks. Long legs and a reed-thin body were rapidly spurting upward, and she could easily have passed for a twelve-year-old. With her mother's deep-set, blue-gray eyes, Sarah possessed a solemn look for one so young. Both Ellen and seven-year-old Rebecca inherited Liddy's honey-colored hair along with Morgan's vivid blue eyes. Neither would ever be as tall as Sarah, but there was a resemblance among the three.

Calvin Kelly's visits from the mountains had lessened in the years after Morgan and Liddy married. The three-day trip by horseback, and leading two-pack mules was beginning to aggravate his arthritis. He decided to double the load on the mules and make the painful trip less often. They were always delighted to see him, and Morgan was still his most attentive audience.

As Kelly left their farm in 1834 for his trek back into the mountains, Morgan worried about him. He was well over seventy. Stiffened joints jerked his movements, and Morgan noticed swollen lumps on his knees beneath his deerskin trousers. Huge rope-like veins had surfaced on his gnarled hands, and Morgan feared an accidental, lethal rupture in the wilds.

"I brought my best batch of bearskins yet, Morgan. They feed on them big piles of acorns under all them big oak trees, and it makes fer just about the purttiest skins a body could hope to peel."

The two men laughed, and Morgan knew Calvin's mind was still razor sharp.

"Them fish still jump out on the creek banks fer a breath of fresh air cause it's too damned crowded to breathe in the water, and I still got a yard full of animals corvortin' all night long. I get up between two and three in the morning jest to watch them critters. They come so quiet you don't hear a sound. Makes a body wonder if you're seein' things that ain't really there. The deer are the purttiest; them ole bucks are nuzzling up to them does, and he takes her right there. They just move on, not seein' me. Coons come up to me, sniff and go on; reckon I must smell like one of them by now."

Morgan again felt a strong urge to sit with Calvin and watch the profusion of animals, to climb mountains where huge trees stretched skyward increasing an enormous girth, to swim icy rivers and wade into cold streams, picking up dinner from the array teaming of fish.

"No," he told himself, "I have everything here," and his nights laced with Liddy were the greatest any man could hope for. Things were hectic on the farm, and Morgan had little time to dream about faraway mountains.

"Ohio is getting to be one of the busiest states in the Union," his oldest brother Seth allowed one day. Seth was more or less the over-seer of their family business. "Pa is gonna have to get more help in the smithy. A lot of folks are heading west, and we have orders backed up for wagons and parts."

Their farm products were being shipped back east and their well-built wagons were headed west. Pioneers moving westward could ride the Ohio River to the Mississippi, then depart to overland trails where the wagon trains were increasing in size each week. Some continued their trip down the Mississippi River to the rich bottomlands spreading all the way to New Orleans, and others stayed to enjoy the booming economy in Ohio.

"Morgan did you know Ohio has got almost a million people now?" Seth asked, as they worked shoulder to shoulder in the blacksmith shop.

"That's too damned many people," Morgan answered.

"You are still the wild buck in the family, Morgan. It's a good thing you have Liddy and the girls to keep you rooted."

Liddy and the girls helped Morgan with the farm chores, and Sa-rah became adept at watching out for her younger sisters. Morgan's long hours were beginning to reap excellent profits from livestock and corn, along with his work in the family business. By 1838, they were close to making the last payment on their farm.

"This is the longest time Calvin Kelly has gone without visiting," Morgan fretted to Liddy. "It has been almost four years, and I am afraid something has happened to him."

"How old is he?" Liddy asked, and Morgan hazzarded a guess of about eighty. "He didn't look well the last time we saw him. Could we send someone to find him?"

"It would take a month or more, but if he doesn't show up by fall, I need to do something."

It was as though Calvin had heard their worry. One week later he appeared on their doorstep and both young people were shocked. The haggard, shriveled man before them seemed to have lain down his former self and assumed a borrowed body. The blueness had been leached from his eyes and a rheumy discharge curdled in the corners. His constant blinking was a futile attempt to clear away a creeping film threatening to totally claim his eyesight.

"Morgan, I got me a chest full of phlegm, and my lean-to burnt down almost on top of me, so I decided to hightail it out of there and come on here."

Morgan embraced his old friend and had to blink back tears when he felt the bony structure beneath the buckskin.

"We are so happy to see you, Calvin," Liddy said, kissing him on the forehead when Morgan moved aside. "We have a room waiting for you, but first off you need some hot soup and milk."

"Thank you kindly, Liddy. I can't remember fer a fact when I had my last eats. Ain't got no appetite no more."

Taking Calvin's arm, Morgan led him to the table. "If it's got a mouth, Liddy feeds it," he announced, and Calvin laughed.

His trembling hand slowly emptied the soup bowl, streaking his beard in several places. Morgan half-carried him into the spare room. Removing his clothes, he slid a nightshirt over his old friend's emaciated body, and Calvin slept before Morgan could even leave the room. Holding the reeking clothes at arms length, he threw them out the kitchen door and walked back to Liddy.

"He is too sick and too tired to take a bath right now. I'm sorry, Liddy, I know he smells awful."

"It's alright, Morgan. He is so old and feeble."

Calvin rallied for a few days after Morgan had bathed him, cut his shaggy hair, and managed to rid him of his unkempt beard. Liddy filled him with nurturing foods, and the girls gave him constant attention. He was clearly basking in the love and thoughtfulness of the whole family. Calvin knew the trip had been worth it. He told the girls stories about the beautiful mountains. They gathered around him to hear more, and Liddy had to shoo them away at times when it was obvious his strength was depleted.

"Mama, did you know there is a big rock on top of Calvin's mountain?" seven-year-old Ellen asked.

Sarah was not to be outdone. "Calvin says Kentucky is called 'The Dark and Bloody Ground,' and the Indians won't live there. The Indians fought so many battles there, the ground was soaked with blood and they are afraid of the ghosts."

Liddy was about to reprimand Sarah when Morgan came to her rescue.

"That is true, girls. I have heard this many times. All the old-

14

timers tell the same story. The Indians used Kentucky as their hunting grounds but would leave as soon as they had collected all the game they could carry. The land is so rich that the grass grows waist-high. Chestnut, walnut, beech and oak trees bear so many nuts you can walk on a blanket of them on the forest floor in the fall. Animals of all kinds roam through the forest feasting on the plentiful food, and it has always been a paradise for hunters and many Indian tribes. It is still there, though the Indians have long since been driven out."

"Papa, could we go to visit Calvin's mountain?" wide-eyed Rebecca asked.

Liddy saw Morgan's body tense and a flash of burning excitement leap into his eyes. She felt something akin to a chill sweep over her, raising the hair on her arms.

"Maybe sometime, Rebecca," he answered vaguely.

Even after ten years of marriage, Morgan's unusual eyes could still hold Liddy spellbound. His heavy shock of white-blond hair had darkened somewhat in the past few years and curled slightly around his face and collar line. A strong jaw would have appeared jutting had it not been for his huge, heavily muscled shoulders and arms. Liddy's first impression of Morgan was not that he was handsome, he was truly beautiful. Many nights as they lay together, she would trace his face with her finger tips and marvel at his handsome features, and even in the darkness feel the strength embedded there.

Calvin's breathing was becoming more labored, and Liddy could hear him struggling for air during the night. Morgan had fetched old Dr. Wright shortly after his friend arrived, but his pronouncement of old age did little to relieve the symptoms. The girls tried to coax more food into him, but it was all to no avail. Two weeks after his arrival, Calvin asked Morgan if he could spare a few minutes.

"There's something I need to be telling you, Morgan. I got no kin left, and you are as close as a man can get for a son. You did the right thing in marryin' Liddy, and them girls are the salt of the earth."

He had to stop, letting his chest heave with raspy sounds and appearing to have dozed off. Momentarily, his heavy eyelids lifted halfway, attempting to focus on Morgan.

"There's some papers there in my ole saddle bag and you need to be seein' them. They done been fixed good and proper at a court-house. Look in the very bottom, and they'll be rolled up there."

Finding the papers, he carried them to Calvin's bedside. They appeared to be old but well-preserved in a deerskin pouch.

"Read them out loud, Morgan."

Morgan quickly scanned the first lines and was stunned by what he read.

"Cat got your tongue?" Calvin grumbled.

Morgan felt a great lump in his throat and had trouble grinding it away. "I, Calvin Kelly, do declare that all my land and belongings be give to Morgan Collier at my death. There be three hundred acres, more or less, that runs along Elkhorn Creek on both sides. I put three notches and my initials on big oak trees and walnut trees to mark the right spot. The line will go up a way on Pine Mountain and will be three miles downstream from the headwaters of Elkhorn Creek. The fish were purttier there, so I staked my claim. Long time ago I paid for the land with my buckskin and bearskin hides. The trees will be notched at every hundred paces. I didn't have nothin' else to do after huntin'. I am sixty-three years old and in my right mind. Your friend, Calvin Kelly."

The deed had been notarized and entered into court records when Morgan was only ten years old.

"Calvin, I don't know what to say. You did this so long ago."

"All the trips I made to your home all those years was because of you, Morgan. A body likes to have one person who will listen to him. From the time you could walk you would come runnin' to me the minute I set foot on the place. You would sit on my knee for the longest time, and I would tell you about the animals, the fish and them beautiful mountains. You always wanted to hear about Raven Rock again. How you could stand on top of that big cliff, looking down on Kentucky and Virginia and even see Tennessee on a clear day, you remember that?" Morgan nodded. "I built me a good lean-to and come to get you when you turned eighteen, but once I saw you with Liddy, I knowed you needed to be here."

Calvin looked about and appeared to be disoriented as a wracking cough almost convulsed his weakened body.

"Morgan," he wheezed, "just get on the Ohio and ride it down to where the Big Sandy River pours into it, and then head north through Kentucky on ole Sandy, and them streams feedin' her. Keep goin' till you come to the headwaters of Elkhorn Creek, and you're gonna bump right up against Pine Mountain. It is the most beautiful lay of land on God's green earth and Raven Rock will be settin' right there on top of it. It's a sight to behold, and you'll know you are home."

Calvin stopped talking and began to snore immediately.

Morgan quietly left the room and found Liddy in the kitchen. As he walked by her with tears streaming down his face, he dropped the deed on the table by her and fled to the barn. She read the document three times before she could fully comprehend the contents. Two days later, Calvin Kelly died peacefully in his sleep and was buried in the family graveyard.

For a long time Morgan did not want to talk about the gift from his friend and benefactor but his mind was racing. After three months of soul searching and agonizing, he knew what he wanted to do. He took the girls to Grandma Collier for two days while he laid out his plans to Liddy.

"Before I start Liddy, I want you to know that I will abide by your decision, but I want you to hear me out first."

She nodded in agreement, and Morgan placed a sheath of papers on the kitchen table on which he had sketched plans and detailed information. Liddy was amazed by his calculations and minute details. In the end she agreed to the venture, but then Liddy would have walked through fire for Morgan.

Both families were completely shocked by their announcement. Ingrid Collier was vehemently opposed to their moving into the wilds of Kentucky.

"Just where will my granddaughters go to school?" she demanded of Morgan.

"Liddy will teach them, and they are looking forward to seeing the many beautiful things Calvin has told them about."

"You can take a boat across the Ohio River and see it all right there," she argued.

"It isn't the same, Ma."

Morgan's brothers leased the farm with payment up front and preparations began for the journey. Morgan marked his projected departure for no more than two years hence, the spring of 1840. The girls would be older, and he especially felt that five-year-old Rebecca would tire less with an added two years. A first priority was to build a superior wagon for the trip. He carefully chose the best-seasoned white oak for the wagon bed and wheels. The Collier family excelled in wagonmaking, and Morgan's wagon would be their most precise production. He honed each spoke of the large wheels to the exact same size and weight for correct balance and used black cherry for the hub. He mortised each spoke into the hub so tightly it could not be pulled out. Seth, working shoulder-to-shoulder with Morgan, grunted, "These damned spokes are in to stay, Morgan." A six-inch wide felloe was fitted around the spokes and awaited the iron tire. The spokes inclined outward from the hub at just the right angle for maximum resilience and strength. Mortises in both the hub and the inside felloes were cut with an exactness that was the test of any wheelwright's art.

John Collier, now in his early seventies, was still the master blacksmith. Fitting the iron rim was his job. He shaped two curved sections out of the iron, one-half inch thick, perfectly tailored to the size of the wheel, then welded together at both joints. John built a hot fire around the tire and waited. When he determined the iron was hot enough, he lifted the tire off with a pair of tongs, slid it over the wooden wheel, and knocked it into place with a mallet. Dousing the hot iron with cold water, it shrank to fit the wheel. If the iron was too hot, it would char and weaken the wood. If the iron was not hot enough, the fit would be loose. If the iron cooled too quickly, it would split the rim. Even after half a century, John still smiled when he produced a perfect specimen. He then slid metal axles into the hubs, well-oiled bearings, and the wheels were complete.

Each of the brothers had their own say about the construction of the wagon bed, and the final product was superior in every way. The dovetailing connecting each board was so tightly fitted that not even a drop of water would penetrate. Morgan had always saved tallow when he butchered cattle, and now he mixed the fusible fat with wood ashes to spread beneath the wax canvas that would line the bottom and the sides of the entire wagon. When the tallow and ashes hardened, they produced an added watertight seal. Their trip upstream through Kentucky could be a wet one, but their supplies would remain dry. Morgan also installed strong, slender metal strips supporting the canvas wagon covering with special bolts. When the bolts were loosened the entire covering could be folded back. Massive overhead limbs in the wilderness would be formidable barriers to the tall wagon. Morgan would have to saw and chop many of the lower hanging limbs away, but being able to lower the canvas top would be a tremendous help. He chose two of his largest and strongest workhorses to pull the well-ordered wagon. The Collier brothers took turns pulling the wagon by its tongue to test the balance and maneuverability, and each was pleased to announce that it moved with great ease and smoothness.

The next decision was choosing which color to paint their production. Sarah, Ellen and Rebecca won out. The wagon would be painted a bright red. Morgan furthered their adventure by allowing them to put on old clothes and paint to their heart's content. He and Liddy smoothed over the rough spots and finished up when the girls tired out. Liddy's two favorite hooked rugs padded the bottom of the wagon and they gathered only essentials to take with them, with the exception of their brass bed. Morgan would disassemble the headboard and place the treasured bars in the wagon. While the twenty-foot vehicle sat on blocks in the barn to dry out, the family chose logs for the raft. A solid forty-foot log was placed on the ground with logs on either side, decreasing in length until the last end logs measured thirty feet. The wedge shape would help in poling upstream. The logs would wait in storage in Portsmouth on the Ohio River until just before departure, then be notched and secured together.

Essie Krieger arrived on a bright September morning to keep watch over her granddaughters while Morgan acquainted Liddy with wagon driving.

"In case you have to take up the reins, Liddy."

You are in for a surprise, Morgan Collier, she thought to herself. While Morgan closed gates to the pasture, Liddy climbed to the high seat and, taking the reins, drove expertly to meet Morgan latching the last gate. She gave out a lusty "haw" and the horses immediately turned left, offering the passenger side to Morgan who stood open-mouthed while Liddy giggled with delight.

"How come you got so good, Liddy?" he asked, mounting the seat by her as she expertly turned the horses right with a loud "gee."

"I aim to please my passengers," she said with a wicked look at Morgan.

"There, let's head down by the river, Lady, since I won't have to teach you how to drive."

To his utter amazement, Liddy snapped the large whip that had been cached by the driver's seat with ease and expertise over the horses' heads, and they left the barnyard at a full gallop.

"I didn't walk from Pennsylvania," she shouted over the loud hoof beats, and Morgan slid his long thigh as close to Liddy as possible without unseating her.

Each week Liddy hooked up the team and drove the girls about the farm, letting each one take turns with the reins. By November, snow descended on Ohio and did its best to bury the state completely. The wagon was stashed in the large barn, and Morgan meticulously began to load essential supplies for their departure, scheduled for the last of March. He sealed a large stash of ammunition with materials to produce more in watertight canvas bags and corn seed in boxes beneath the padded tops.

"Liddy, our seeds will ensure our food supply for years to come, and the ammunition will protect us. You never know when a hungry bear or stealthy panther could accidentally stumble onto our property," Morgan commented.

Liddy's look of alarm caused Morgan to explain quickly. "Calvin said they were in the area but never came near his lean-to. I just want to be able to protect you and the girls if the need arises." Still, Liddy shivered.

Morgan also loaded numerous blankets and heavy clothes, along with dried and preserved food. They would need flour, sugar, salt and cornmeal until they harvested their next crop.

Ingrid Collier became more depressed as the departure date approached, "John, can't you talk Morgan out of this foolhardy adventure?" she begged.

John shook his head in resignation, "It is something Morgan will have to get out of his system. He has always wanted to live in the mountains, and the girls are all fired up for it. Liddy doesn't say much, but she will back them up. I figure he will be back here in a couple of years and settle down on the farm for good. Remember, Ingrid, we both left our countries as teenagers to settle in a new world."

"It's different, John. You were a wandering orphan and my father was very poor. Morgan has everything here."

"He has his own reasons for leaving. Morgan is our last born, and he has had to struggle against bossy older brothers who took turns either pounding on him or trying to protect him in scraps he could have easily handled on his own. He is well prepared for the trip and knows what to expect, since Calvin Kelly never talked about anything else. He always talked to Morgan like he was all grown up, and it was what our son needed."

A cold hand of fear closed around Ingrid's heart as her golden boy proceeded with his plans.

Morgan loaded numerous pieces of flat metal into the wagon that could be shaped into extra hoes and shovels. The metal took up a small amount of space, and his expertise in smithing could quickly fire them into needed shapes. He stashed seeds of every description into all available corners along with seed potatoes and sweet potato slips. As a muddied path to the barn continued to deepen in the gradual thaw, the wagon became outfitted for the journey. Morgan bolted down a water barrel and tool box within easy reach of the driver's seat, and strapped on a large, tightly-rolled tent to shelter them at night. Calvin Kelly had cautioned Morgan of explosive walls of water that could roar through docile creek beds without warning. Torrential rains in the spring could send an avalanche of water hurtling into the narrow valleys from steep mountainsides, and they dared not risk traveling or sleeping on board the raft after nightfall. Morgan had made frequent trips to the Ohio River from Chillicothe in February, and now a strong raft lay in wait for them. He had chosen six young, strong and sturdy river men to bind the logs securely together and contracted them at a hefty wage to pole the raft upstream through Kentucky.

***

On March 27, they climbed onto the wagon that was overflowing with baked goods and prepared food to last them at least a month. It had been packed and jammed into space that wasn't there and still friends arrived with more.

A reluctant sun rode low in the sky and warmth was short in coming. The horses' nostrils flared as they snorted steam while stomping on ground that was still hard and frozen. Tearful good-byes to families and friends left Liddy and the girls weeping as the wagon finally moved forward.

Bessie, their milk cow was herded along behind the wagon by

their two cowdogs. By late afternoon they reached the river and were loaded aboard the raft and headed upstream. Morgan and the river crew nailed large blocks to the raft to hold the wagon steady and tethered the animals evenly about to distribute the weight.

Four days later, they had covered many miles up the Big Sandy River and had become seasoned travelers. Each night was an adventure for the girls as they traveled farther into the wilderness. At night, huge fires warmed the campsite, even when spitting snow came with the cold darkness.

The Big Sandy Valley was everything Morgan had dreamed of and even more. In places where the river narrowed and deepened, giant limbs laced overhead forming a canopy. Sunlight drifting through bare branches created a lattice on the quietly flowing water. On several occasions, Morgan had folded down the canvas wagon covering rather than hazard a tear by the jutting limbs. Dry cane stalks with long, brown, withered leaves stood high into the trees, while tall, thick grasses, turned pale by winter, clogged every space. Bushy tail beavers scurried along embankments, steering clear of an encroachment into their territory. The ring-tailed raccoons, with bright eyes continued to spy out fish on outer edges of the water, paying no heed to the visitors.

"Them coons must weigh at least forty pounds," one of the river men said. "I aim to bring my hounds back up this way and have me a good hunt."

As twilight deepened, inhabitants of the forest meandered to the river for a last drink of water before nightfall. On seeing the raft, bears quickly galloped back into the maze of a dark forest, while graceful deer sailed from the shore in fear, their bodies arching into the air with great speed. Fat porcupines waddled along the shoreline, secure in their quilled coverings, sniffing for buried worms and beetles in muddy banks.

The previous night Ellen had stepped ankle deep into a black puddle of goop that clung to her boots and socks.

"That doggone black stuff is everywhere," one of the river men said.

Not only did oil puddle throughout the valley, but natural gas seeped through rock fissures indicating immense deposits. Strata of black, glistening coal jutted from numerous embankments where millions of tons lay beneath the surface. Unfathomable fortunes lay encased within the living forest. For centuries, Indians in their fringed moccasins trod over incalculable riches, harvesting the plentiful game. Early settlers were equally oblivious to their mineral surroundings. Abundant game, fish, nuts and fowl supported them for years on end without them drifting out to civilization, and the riches lay undisturbed.

At night, the family tethered the animals in tall grasses, and the dogs bedded down near them. Frequently, their ferocious barking awakened the travelers, but whatever predator had approached the camp disappeared amid the uproar.

The young rivermen also took turns guarding the campsite, and Liddy was grateful for their presence. They kept the fires piled high with dry logs and the campsite well illuminated. Rebecca, taking one last look through the tent flap one night, shrieked in terror when an Indian ghost sailed over the outer edge of the bright fires. Morgan finally convinced her the apparition had been a great horned owl in search of his nightly meal. Each day the travelers hauled in more than an ample supply of fish and feasted on trout and bass encrusted in cornmeal and cooked in heavy iron skillets.

Three nights in a row, Morgan had brought down large wild turkeys with well-placed arrows. A river man quickly plucked the feathers and buried the bird in hot coals until morning. Turkey was an unusual breakfast treat for the girls, and after a few bites, they insisted that Liddy never again use an oven to bake a turkey.

Seven days had elapsed since leaving their farm, and Morgan was elated with the progress. The river ran smooth and wide. Runoff from heavy snows broadened the shoreline, and the husky men stayed close to shore, pushing off in shallow waters. Morgan knew he was racing with time. Plentiful spring rains were appreciated by almost everyone, except those bucking against the tide. By the middle of April, sweeping rains cascading down the mountains would swell the river to dangerous levels. Huge logs would be nothing short of battering rams. Morgan had calculated their time on the streams to the last ten days, leaving a few days' leeway before the heavy rains began. He needed to start clearing a garden spot by April fifteenth and readying the soil for planting as soon as the frosts receded. He would start work on their cabin as soon as the fields were laid by, and they could manage in the wagon and tent until then. On the night of April fourth, as usual, the crew had secured the raft with heavy ropes to large trees on shore. Morgan had attached extra ropes to the wagon resting on the raft, winding and tying them to the strongest trees. They had found a comfortable campsite on a level area topping a high incline above the river. It had obviously been used as a camp before, and the clearing that had to be done was minimal. The river men were grateful for small blessings. An extended week of poling had produced aching backs and very tired arm and shoulder muscles. After a quick meal, and except for the first guard, the group snuggled into warm blankets and slept almost immediately. At midnight a thunderous roar exploded the stillness, rousting the entire group from their beds. Excessive runoff from heavy rains in the steep mountains upstream sent torrents of water hurtling downstream. A half-moon illuminated an enormous wall of water frothing and rolling toward their campsite. Fortunately, they had climbed the hill to a higher level, but water rose almost to the campsite and they quickly carried supplies to higher ground. A wildly tossing raft heaved and bucked in the flood waters, slamming it into trees on the river bank. Everyone watched anxiously as the wagon remained in place on the battered raft. Morgan and the river men quickly hitched both horses to ropes, securing the bouncing wagon, and only in the nick of time. Outer logs connected to the raft began to separate first and within minutes it had totally come apart. Men and horses pulled with all their might and the wagon gradually left a stream that had turned wild. As the wagon was dragged to shore, the canvas was ripped in several places by low-hanging limbs, but damage was minor and the strong, well-made wagon remained intact.

Morgan was weak with relief. He did not dare think what could have happened had they camped closer to the river. His meticulous waterproofing in the wagon had kept supplies dry and seeds intact.

"Liddy, are you alright?" With light from the campfire, Morgan could see she was badly shaken.

"Yes," she answered, and he knew she was on the verge of tears.

"The rains have started early, Morgan. Will we ever be able to work our way through the forest?" Though shocked by the catastrophe that had almost befallen them, Liddy's mind was racing ahead.

"Liddy we need to move the camp farther uphill in case of more flooding, then we will talk about it. I promise you, it will be alright."

Taking strength from Morgan's words, Liddy and the girls helped to move supplies even farther from the river bank. They had to shout in order to be heard over the roar of the water booming its way north.

"Just be glad we've had dry weather so far," a river man said as he heaved another dry log on the new campfire.

Morgan volunteered to stand watch and Liddy sat with him. "I think we are very near the Breaks of the Cumberland Mountains, Liddy. Calvin Kelly told me about it before he died. When we get to the Breaks, we will travel along Elkhorn Creek to its headwaters and to our farm. Someday we'll come back to see the Breaks, but right now we need to get to our farm as quickly as possible. Russell Fork Creek has cut Cumberland Mountain in half, and who knows how many centuries it has taken. Calvin said that the walls rise at least sixteen hundred feet upward from the stream, and that it is truly a wonder."

The river men agreed to stay one more day to help Morgan forge a path for the wagon. Liddy shivered as she realized they would be on their own in the wilderness. A light snow fell during the night, but roaring campfires kept them warm. At daybreak, Morgan and five of the men loaded with axes, saws and shovels forged into the wilderness. The one remaining river man stayed to keep the fire going and was lucky enough to bring down a young buck that he promptly skinned and set to roasting over a slow fire. As the day progressed, Morgan was even more grateful for the strong wagon. It would be slow going but the large, sturdy wheels would be able to maneuver over fallen logs and large boulders.

He would have to fold the canvas down, and he hoped the rain would hold off for a few more days. He was disappointed in not being able to reach the Breaks before the river men departed but was relieved to see the flood-waters subsiding.

Calvin had told him that land along the Elkhorn Creek bed would be level enough for a wagon, but he would have to do some clearing.

Early the next day, the river men departed downstream on a quickly constructed raft and the Collier family headed toward Pine Mountain with Liddy on the driver's seat and the girls walking. They slowly crawled over large moss-covered logs with guidance from Morgan, and the wheels stayed steady.

After a late supper, Liddy and the girls bedded down in the wagon as Morgan added logs to the fire and crawled into a bedroll beneath the wagon. Liddy was apprehensive. They had sighted retreating bears along the way, and she had overheard the men talking about huge panthers that roamed the area.

"Liddy we will be safe, the dogs will be on either side of me, and I have two loaded rifles. The horses and Bessie are staked here by the fire."

Liddy finally drifted into a light sleep with her hand across another rifle. They awakened to a cold mist hovering over the forest, chilling them to the bone. Warmed by a large campfire and hot breakfast, the family began another day of forging into the forest. Numerous times they came to a standstill, while Morgan and Liddy sawed, chopped and hacked away underbrush and trees. Progress was slow even though they continued until almost sunset.

By daybreak the next day, Morgan, loaded with a saw and an ax, headed into the forest to ferret out the best trail. He returned a short time later and was jubilant. A large forest fire, probably caused by lightning, had destroyed several miles of forest and their trail was completely cleared. By the end of the day, they arrived at the "Breaks of the Cumberland Mountains." Though Calvin Kelly had told them many times about the incredible spectacle of nature, it was still overwhelming. Craggy rock walls, looming hundreds of feet above them, pushed against a cloudless sky as Russell Fork Creek frothed and crashed down the narrow gorge. Through eons of time, the stream had gradually cut a passageway through the mighty mountain, creating a gateway into the valley beyond.

To the right of the opening, Morgan saw what he had dreamed of for years: Elkhorn Creek flowing into Russell Fork as it left the Breaks.

"Liddy, girls, behold Elkhorn Creek."

A cheer went up from the group, and the girls joined hands to dance in a circle. Morgan instantly recognized the markers Calvin had told him to look for, and he knew that within twenty five miles they would find their new home, but by three o'clock in the afternoon, the sky had begun to darken and Morgan knew what they were in for. Quickly climbing the hill, he looked for any semblance of an area where they could park the wagon to escape the high water and finally found a rocky ledge that would have to be shoveled out deeper to accommodate their needs. They removed small saplings and underbrush to move the wagon to the shelter. Morgan accomplished the task in short time with Liddy and the girls dragging the limbs and underbrush away to clear the lane. The whole family dug into the pungent earth to enlarge the ledge, and by dark they had wedged the wagon into a tight space high above Elkhorn Creek. Lopping large limbs from towering pines, they staked the animals beneath them. The girls quickly set about collecting dry wood to stack beneath the wagon and throwing smaller pieces inside.

Morgan and Liddy had barely latched the canvas in place when the first large drops of rain began to pelt them. A vicious spring storm lashed the hills, with thunder and lightning hovering over the wagon. Sheets of driving rain closed a curtain about them, and Morgan worried about the rising creek that was beginning to roar.

"Our roof won't break, will it Papa?" Rebecca asked as she sat wide-eyed, listening to the constant drumming of heavy rain overhead.

Morgan hugged his youngest daughter to him, "Rebecca, this is the best wagon ever built, and the canvas is very strong."

The tough, heavily waxed canvas, peaked in the center with strong steel braces, adjusted to allow for rapid runoff. Liddy and the exhausted girls slept soundly, but Morgan barely closed his eyes.

If he dozed, the dogs wakened him with frantic barking, and he would crawl from beneath the wagon in boots and oil skins to check the livestock. Elkhorn Creek continued to rise, and Morgan was filled with dread. The animals were wet, but the thick evergreens sheltered them from the misery of pelting rain.

By midmorning the rain had lessened and Morgan built a roaring fire from the dry wood. The girls would always say it was the best breakfast they had ever eaten. Buckwheat pancakes, frying in a large iron skillet, bubbled with drops of rain sliding from the evergreen boughs, and the family feasted on their first hot meal in a day.

By nightfall the rain had completely stopped, and the next morning Morgan set out with an ax and saw to clear a path for the wagon. The trail they had planned to travel along Elkhorn Creek was completely under water, and Morgan knew it could be covered for days, so the family hacked, chopped and sawed their way though the dense forest. Liddy's arms ached at night from holding onto one end of the crosscut saw.

"We are almost there, girls," Morgan kept saying as the tired children slipped and fell numerous times on wet, slick leaves. Rebecca sat on the driver's seat while the rest of the family heaved, pushed and lifted the sturdy wagon wheels over endless boulders and large moss-covered logs.

After three days, they awoke to a much diminished stream, and the family was elated. Morgan immediately hitched the horses to the wagon, and they traveled the original trail, eating canned food for breakfast while riding in the wagon. By late evening, having traveled nonstop, they arrived at their destination. It was April fourteenth. Though several days later than their original plans, they were grateful to have reached their new home.

CHAPTER 2

Pine Mountain appeared to scrape the sky, beautiful beyond belief. An early spring fostered new leaves, cascading the length of ancient limbs, welcoming them to another endless cycle. Raven Rock, sitting atop the mountain with jagged edges extending outward, was the only break in a forest so dense it was almost impregnable. Gigantic trees crowded the steep sides of the mountain as smaller trees struggled for a foothold wherever possible. Dogwood blossoms were beginning to break bud, and in a few days their glorious flowers would adorn the entire area. Long, glistening, green leaves decorated huge mountain laurel trees, nurturing fat nodules that would shortly become large clusters of flowers: purple, pink and white, erupting in every direction. Logs and boulders lined a sparkling stream where small sprays of crystalline water shot over rocks large and small.

Morgan caught his breath as he watched large bass and rainbow trout gliding through the water, swimming around large rocks to circle beneath moss-covered overhangs. Thick, dark green moss covered everything along the banks, and dry, thick grass, waist high, spread along the entire valley.

Morgan immediately spotted Calvin's old burned-out lean-to and was grateful to park the wagon without using an ax and saw. Darkness was descending. The family barely had enough time to eat a cold supper and collect dry wood for the campfire.

"Papa, could we hike up to Raven Rock in the morning?" Rebecca asked, taking one last look at the towering cliff before climbing into the wagon.

Her sisters groaned just hearing about another walk. Before daylight, Morgan had piled dry logs on the low-burning campfire, and set the coffeepot to boiling for him and Liddy. As she emerged from the wagon, he held his arms up to her, lifting her to the ground.

"Liddy, we are camped on our land. Can you believe this? This valley is ours and in two weeks there will be flowers and leaves all over the place." Clasping her to him, he kissed her as he had not kissed her in weeks.

"I will build a paradise for us in this valley, and I am so proud of you and the girls. My women are the strongest," he said, and Liddy could hear a quiver in his voice.

"Right now I'll just have hot coffee and you can build a paradise later. I am freezing."

Morgan laughed and carried her to the large logs he had placed around the fire pit for seating. By the time the girls awoke, Morgan had crafted a rustic table with benches and erected the large tent. He could hardly wait to savor the flavor of their fish, and breakfast was, indeed, a feast. Hotcakes with honey, and sizzling, crusted trout. Bessie's milk was beginning to dwindle, and the girls would miss her sweet foaming milk each morning. Her swelling girth was expanding each day, and Liddy knew the arrival of a new calf was only weeks away. The girls held their tin cups close to the fire to warm the milk even more. Cold, crisp air tingled their cheeks and numbed their fingers.

"Papa, I can't see Raven Rock," Rebecca said. The top half of Pine Mountain was shrouded in damp, chilling mist that was beginning to creep slowly to the summit. As the sun melted away the last wisps of the soft mass, smoke from the large campfire also rose upward.

Elkhorn Creek was beautiful to behold. This was even more than Morgan had dreamed of. He decided immediately to build their cabin on a high bluff overlooking the stream. He had already seen what a heavy rain could do to a peaceful, meandering creek.

Sarah Collier had never seen anything as tall as Pine Mountain. As she squinted upward in the morning sun, she could not know the integral role this mountain would play in her life and that of her descendants.

The girls began exploring their new farm with shrieks and shouts of joy. Rebecca pulled thick moss from a log in one long piece and was ready to build her own shelter with a moss- covered frame. Sarah lay on her stomach by a moss-covered overhang on the creek bank and nabbed a large crawfish by the back as it swam by. Ellen and Rebecca screamed with fear when Sarah teased them with its large, flailing pinchers, waving and grasping.

"Girls, we are in a new place, and until we become better acquainted with it, you should stay close to the wagon," Liddy said and Morgan nodded in agreement.

Liddy, at Morgan's suggestion, carried a rifle, and Morgan kept his Colt-45 strapped on his hip.

"If a stranger comes by, call us at once and do not talk to them."

"Are we in danger, Mama?" Sarah asked.

"We just need to be careful until we know more about our farm."

Morgan began extending the burned area surrounding Calvin Kelly's demolished lean-to. The fire had burned numerous trees and stumps, and with any luck, he would have a large garden spot by next week. Liddy and the girls dragged limbs and sections of tree trunks to the blazing fire as Morgan waded into the timber with a razor-sharp ax.

Three miles away, Dan Edwards smelled the smoke before he saw it.

"Albert we best saddle up and ride over that way; looks like we got company. Get the rifles and tell your Ma and Daniel where we're going."

Fifteen-year-old Albert hurried into the cabin. Hearing the news, young Daniel popped from the doorway like a cork.

"I want to go too, Pa. You might need an extra gun." Dan laughed inwardly at his tall, gangly, twelve-year-old son.

"It's probably some traveler stopping for a rest. Your job is to stay and protect your Ma." A disappointed Daniel sulked back into the cabin.

Sarah raced from the newly chopped trees to the giant fire. Her heavy clothes soon became much too warm. Climbing into the wagon, she changed quickly.

Dan and Albert could hear voices before they could see anyone and were immediately beset by two large barking dogs.

"Friends coming in," Dan called at the top of his lungs.

Their horses were trying to turn for home as the snarling dogs advanced. Morgan gave a shrill whistle and both dogs began to head back toward camp, still barking viciously.

"Fine watchdogs you got there, neighbor," Dan said, as he and Albert rode into the clearing.

"Morgan Collier," Morgan said, offering his big hand to the tall, lanky stranger.

"Dan Edwards and my son Albert."

"Hello, Albert, this is one fine horse you have here." Albert beamed with pride and liked Morgan immediately. The two dismounted, and Morgan motioned Liddy to meet the newcomers. She was standing close to the wagon with her hand on the hidden rifle. Dan and Albert removed their hats and shook hands with Liddy. She was warmed by the kindness in Dan's eyes, and impressed with the husky Albert whose "Howdy, Mam" was spoken softly. She was suddenly conscious of her disheveled hair and the rough clothes that she and the girls had donned for the trip.

"That is Ellen and Rebecca dragging limbs to the fire, and Sarah is somewhere about. Do you live near us Dan?"

"Sure do, Morgan, about three miles northeast of here. Been here a little over two years. Brought my wife Ruthie, and twelve-year-old Daniel along with Albert here over from Virginia, and we've settled in pretty good. Where do you folks hail from?"

"Chilloette, Ohio. We left there on the twenty-seventh of March and got here about dark last night."

Albert was shocked, "You brought that big wagon all the way from Ohio?"

Liddy laughed at the young man's disbelief. "It surprises me, too, Albert, now that we are finally here."

"Ruthie is going to be mighty happy to know that there are other women folk on this mountain. It has been a mite lonely for her. If it's alright with you folks, I'll send Albert to the house to bring Ruthie and Daniel over here with some food, and I can start swinging an ax with you, Morgan. It looks like you are after a garden spot. What do you think, Albert?"

"I'm thinking maybe we could get our heads shot off by whoever is holding that rifle on us from the wagon."

Morgan shouted immediately to Sarah to put the gun away and come out. Sarah clamored down from the wagon and gave Albert a defiant look.

"Our new neighbor, Sarah," Morgan said.

"Morgan, I don't think you need them dogs with such a brave young lady guarding you," Dan said.

Sarah smiled at Dan and thought perhaps he looked sad. A huge handlebar mustache appeared to pull his long face downward. Albert didn't look at all like his father. His shoulders were already wider then Dan's, and she wasn't sure she liked his square jaw.

Albert galloped for home, and the two men headed for the tree line with axes.

Ruthie rushed about getting food together, while the boys hitched up the wagon. "Tell me about the Colliers, Albert," Ruthie said the minute he came back into the house.

"They seem to be nice people, Ma, except for the long-legged, skinny one that held a rifle on us. I think she could be a pest."

"You shouldn't say that, Albert, she was probably afraid for her family out here in the wilderness."

"Well, Mrs. Collier is really nice, and wait until you see Morgan. He is even taller that Pa, and he really has muscles."

"Three girls? You would think they could have just one boy," Daniel said. Ruthie smiled to herself. It was an answer to her prayers.

Liddy was astounded by the amount of food Ruthie had put together so quickly.

"Ruthie, how can we ever repay you for all of this?" she asked surveying the bountiful meal at mid-afternoon.

"You already have, Liddy. You are here."

Each morning the Edwards family arrived just as Morgan and Liddy began their hectic pace of sawing trees, clearing away limbs and removing rocks. There were happy shouts of laughter as the girls rushed to greet Ruthie, exchanging hugs with their new friend. She had become the aunts and grandmothers they had left behind, and Ruthie glowed with happiness. Their presence was like a ray of sunshine.

Dan smiled at the greetings and was delighted that Ruthie finally had the companionship of another woman and three beautiful girls. The Edwards family marveled at the story of Calvin Kelly. They knew he had lived on this land for many years, but had no idea what had happened to him. He had left the mountains just before they arrived.

Each day the forest gave way to more clearing, and the friendship between the two families became steadfast. The clearing was now ready for planting, and a cabin-site designated. Exploring the bluff high above Elkhorn Creek, they discovered a large area of very flat rock on which to build the cabin. Liddy's two scatter rugs would be beautiful on the stone floor. No one noticed the very fine hairline crack that traveled the length of the rock. Ruthie could hardly wait to get started back to the Collier's place each morning.

"What did we do before the Colliers moved here?" Daniel asked one morning as Ruthie was hurrying him to finish breakfast.

She smiled sweetly at her son, "We were waiting for the Colliers to come."

She and Liddy were already close friends. It was as though they had always known one another.

"Your father noticed you were teaching the girls to use sling-shots," Ruthie said to Daniel.

"Well, they are sort of fun and Sarah's tough, but I would still like to have a boy to hunt with."

"You have your brother Albert to hunt with."

"Ma, he is so taken with Morgan and helping him that he wouldn't go with me all week to check our traps," Daniel complained.

Albert was fascinated by Morgan's strength, energy and his excitement for their future on this mountain. He marveled at the way a huge ax appeared to come alive in Morgan's hands as he swung demonic blows into enormous trees.

"Girls, we need to make our onion beds now and have them ready to plant as soon as it is warm enough," Liddy said.

"Ruthie says we can find wild onions all over the mountains," replied Ellen.

"That we will, but we will also plant the onion sets we brought with us. They make larger onions than the wild ones."

Ruthie loved talking to the girls, and they hung onto her every word. Her thick, dark chestnut hair was beginning to gray prematurely and laugh lines at the corners of her eyes were beginning to deepen. A constantly smiling face helped the process. She stood only five feet, two inches tall next to her husband whose six feet, one inch dwarfed her, but Liddy felt Ruthie was the stronger of the two. Her energy was endless, and her short, stumpy legs and small feet never seemed to stop. Both Albert and Daniel wore her thick crown of chestnut hair, but the resemblance ended there. Daniel, with his long, thin body, was the opposite of Albert's powerful stocky frame.

Morgan constructed two large wheelbarrows to cart rocks from the garden and rapidly developing fields. Albert and Daniel bent strong backs and shoulders to move the loaded wheelbarrows to a dumpsite. The girls helped to fill them with the many rocks their father uncovered as he plowed deep into the new ground, many times breaking or denting the plow points. The two young brothers worked diligently to help Morgan reshape the plows.

As the first week of May ended, the mountains underwent an incredible transformation.

"Mama, look at all the flowers blooming," Sarah said, as the early morning sun sparkled on blossoms, still damp from the morning mist.

"The trees are so much bigger with leaves, and I can't wait for the mountain laurel to bloom. We are going to be buried in blossoms."

Dogwood trees were completely shrouded in blooms the size of a saucer, and many were tinted with the most delicate of pinks, while an equal number of trees were embellished with brilliant white blossoms. Liddy could not believe the height of the willow trees. The same trees bordering the stream running through their Ohio farm reached about forty feet, but the willows meandering up hollows and along Elkhorn Creek rose to at least one-hundred feet.

A rude cabin now covered the flat rock, and the family moved into their new home.

"Dan, I want to do payback time," Morgan said, as the men backed off to survey the finished product.

The ceiling rose to seventeen feet, and Morgan planned to convert the attic into a large bedroom for the girls when winter descended upon them. Large chestnut shakes extended well over the edge of the roof, affording protection from the rain, and the front porch was large enough for a swing.

"You mentioned another barn the other day, Dan, and I am signing on as your helper," Morgan said.

"Consider yourself hired," and the two men laughingly shook hands.

"Your boys have outdone themselves, and we could never have moved into the cabin this quickly had it not been for their help."

The boys had used Morgan's horses to drag large stones into place for a huge open fireplace. The girls carried many pails of red clay to use in chinking the logs and sealing the fireplace. On one occasion Albert dipped his fingers into the pail of clay and teasingly spread it the length of Sarah's forearm. He was astounded by her instant reaction, as she immediately grabbed a handful of clay and plastered his face with it, and the clay fight was on — Sarah and Daniel against Albert, Ellen and Rebecca. Finally, the young people washed away the muck and sat down to another mouth-watering meal prepared by Liddy and Ruthie.

Liddy and the girls planted large kernels of corn they had so carefully hoarded on the trip. Corn took precedent over all other seeds. They dropped the kernels close together, planning to thin them later, which appeared unlikely since squirrels and crows would claim a share. For fertilizer they caught and cut up fish, placing large fish chunks by the corn before it was covered with rich dark earth.

For weeks, Liddy and the girls stayed near the corn patch. Other seeds were planted and flourished as wary eyes were always on the corn. It would feed the horses that had pulled the heavily loaded wagon over the rough trails. Their broad backs and heaving flanks had conquered each obstacle. Succulent roasting ears would be thrown into a boiling pot then immediately swirled in butter. There would be cornbread, corn pudding, hominy, succotash, corn relish, corn cakes, popcorn and mush, along with corn syrup.

At night, Morgan kept his rifle handy and many times after being alerted by the two dogs, he rescued their crops from badgers, raccoons, porcupines and possums. Crows and blue jays were their bane. The large birds would swoop in at lightning speed to rupture large tomatoes and tear long green beans from corn stalks. Rebecca's job was to train the pole bean vines around the corn stalks as soon as they were long enough. The bean seeds had been dropped next to the seed corn and both were growing rapidly. They erected several scarecrows and enhanced the vigil by frequent gunfire as Liddy and Morgan banged away with shotguns, and the birds retreated to the forest edge. Sarah was everywhere at once. She loved wading in icy streams that left her feet and legs blue and numb with cold, even in midsummer. She chased both tiny and enormous crawfish as they backed beneath large rocks to escape her fast fingers.

Ellen could well keep up with her, but Rebecca straggled on occasions. When mulberry trees were heavy with ripened fruit, they climbed the large trees and ate to their hearts' delight as long, fat, purple berries bursting with juice dripped dark liquid to their elbows. On one occasion Sarah had inched too far out on a long limb to collect the largest berries and lost her balance, screaming as she plunged downward. Instead of hitting the ground she felt strong arms grip her from behind as she dropped the last few feet.

"That's a good way to break your neck, Sarah," Albert scolded, "You fell at least twenty feet."

Sarah blushed a deep red.

"If you must have all the berries, you just chop the tree down. There are so many around here you won't miss a few."

He preceded to chop the tree down and laughed as the girls swarmed all over it.

"The best ones are always on the ends of the limbs and near the top," Ellen said, as the dark sweet juice dripped from her chin. "Thank you, thank you Albert."

"Me too," Rebecca chimed in.

Sarah pretended to be busy, but she could still feel Albert's strong arms about her waist. Being only ten, she was puzzled as to why. When Daniel related the incident to Ruthie, Albert simply explained, "I was afraid they were going to break their necks climbing out to the edges like that."

His mother smiled, "I'm glad you're looking after the girls." She smiled again when he turned his back.

Morgan completed a bed for the girls, and they giggled when they saw the height of the production. Stripping bark from young pine trees, he planed the wood to sheer smoothness and sealed it with beeswax.

"My girls will sleep high and dry should the cabin spring a leak," he said and accepted hugs from his daughters.

The sturdy posts stood six-feet high, and Morgan anchored slats for the mattress three feet from the floor. "When I finish the upstairs girls, I will build each of you a bed, but this wide one will have to do for now." He could not know it would save their lives.

There was an abundance of natural supplies to work with, and his mind constantly played over the enormous possibilities that he could create for his family. Game was so plentiful, he had only to step from his front door and take aim.

Sarah rushed into the cabin one afternoon with her long braid flying behind her to announce to Liddy that she had heard the stream singing. "When I was catching crawdads, I could hear different sounds as water flowed over rocks and then swished along the sides of the banks."

Liddy smiled at her daughter, "You are so like your father, Sarah."

***

Ruthie took Liddy under her wing immediately to acquaint her with the medicinal plants that covered the mountains. Liddy was astounded by the knowledge Ruthie imparted to her as they tramped through the creek beds and dark woodlands. The only intrusion into the ancient forest had been the infrequent traveler whose journey left no mark behind. It simply closed ranks after him. The humus-rich woods and deeply shaded surface gave rise to lush ferns that climbed steep banks, limey rocks, and moisture-laden mosses.

Sarah loved to tag along and help Liddy pull short-legged Ruthie over large fallen trees that often blocked the paths.

"Ruthie, what is this plant?" Sarah asked.

"That's poke weed, and let's get a whole bunch of that. The small, green shoots are really good when you kill them with piping hot grease. When it grows bigger through the summer, it can poison you though."

"We should gather lots of these, as they will stop a cold in its tracks. We will make a tea from the leaves," Ruthie said, as she stripped lush leaves from deep red-brown stems and placed them in the large homespun bag by her side.

"You should add at least two tablespoons of moonshine to each jar of tea to keep it fresh and to be sure you won't poison your family," she said as she peered at Liddy through the gloom.

They bypassed huge buckeye trees towering at least one hundred feet high. In July, large blossoms would decorate the trees in flowing clusters up to a foot in length. Hazel alder trees, producing a strong pleasant aroma, appeared occasionally in the damper spots. Liddy was informed that she should collect and chew the bark of this tree and use it to treat wounds and ulcers. The tree reached no more than twenty-five feet in height and was dwarfed by the giants of this forest. Dan had fashioned a sharp, short-handled shovel for Ruthie to use in collecting her medicinal plants. She stopped abruptly and dug into the earth to uncover roots from an Indian root shrub.

"These roots are very good for a backache," she said, as she divided the treasure with Liddy.

She wound a younger, more limber root around the bundle, and Liddy followed her example.

"Dan likes this tree because he makes beer from the sap and gives me a little to make into vinegar." Liddy's eyes traveled upward along the dark reddish-brown bark and tremendous height of the sweet birch Ruthie indicated. "We don't need any squaw root just now, but keep in mind where it is and what you do with it. The squaws first used it to help in childbirth. It helps to push the babies right out. Are you in the family way?" she asked, as she eyed Liddy's loose- fitting dress.

Liddy laughed at the frankness of the question and assured her friend that she was not. They passed by a large black snakeroot shrub and mentally marked it in order to harvest the rhizome and its roots come fall.

"Best thing in the world for a sore throat," her guide announced as Liddy scrambled over a heavily mossed log.

Ruthie jabbed her shovel into a thicket and gathered the roots of a coral shrub. The spike-like stem would bear no flowers until late July, but they were not her quest. She sought only the roots.

"Sometimes when you can't get to sleep no matter what, you just chew on a bit of root and you will doze off. I've tried it many times. I've heard of a lot of consumption in these parts, and this agueweed is one thing you need to hang on to. Some folks call it wild sage, but again others say agueweed. We'll gather just the leaves come late summer."

Wild strawberries appeared on low growing vines in any area that allowed a few rays of sun to filter through the dense growth. The small green berries would ripen soon, and the girls would descend upon them with nimble fingers. The two women stopped by a towering white ash. The furrowed bark sustained a dove-gray color that glowed warmly in the meager sunlight that penetrated through its long leaves.

"This is a very important tree, Liddy, and don't you ever forget it. A tea made from these buds will cure a snakebite. Two times, I gave it to Daniel and Albert and both times they were cured. You use chewed bark as a poultice on sores and especially for fever sores on the lips. It can take care of when your bowels won't move, and it can run a headache right out the door." Ruthie finished her description of the tall tree, and Liddy almost laughed out loud.

She could see that Ruthie really liked this tree. She would later remember Ruthie's lecture and pray for the cure it promised. By late June, the mountain abounded with luscious blackberries, huckleberries and wild strawberries. Every day was a feast.

Low growing huckleberry bushes were loaded with juicy, dark fruit, and the girls plucked them by the gallons.

"Girls, I think you are eating more than you are collecting," Morgan said, looking at half empty pails and their blue lips.

"Mama, we want to bake a huckleberry cobbler for Ruthie," Ellen said. "She does so many things for us."

Liddy smiled at their eager faces. "I'm sure Ruthie would like that, and if you need me I will help."

Not only did they bake a delicious cobbler but also picked three pails of berries for their friend. Ruthie was delighted.

"I was just telling Daniel this morning that I needed huckleberries to make jam and jelly. You must have heard me."

"Girls, why don't you take those empty pails and go back down the lane to that large patch of berries we just passed," Liddy said, and the girls were on their way immediately.

Albert and Daniel were just coming in from the fields and decided to help. Laughter floated back to the two women standing in the doorway, while watching their children.

"Liddy, you and your family have brought life into these hills," and Ruthie hugged her friend.

Albert caught his breath as Sarah dived into a bunch of berries crowded against a large boulder. Moving toward her, he saw a huge rattlesnake, coiled and ready to strike. Leaping through the air, he threw a startled Sarah aside and brought a heavy-booted foot down against the snake's head. The thick body of the snake writhed and rattled trying to escape his boot. Daniel quickly drew his hunting knife and sliced through the snake close to Albert's foot, completely severing the loathsome head. Albert kept grinding the snake's head into the soft earth as the headless body continued twisting and turning.

The girls screamed in horror as they watched the gruesome spectacle. When they finally calmed down, Albert instructed them in how to look for rattlesnakes and copperheads around bushes.

"You take a long limb, stand back a way, and poke about the vines, and you can bet they'll strike if they are anywhere close. They like berries even better than we do. It's what they live on. Just remember, rattlesnakes will rattle a warning, but the much faster copperheads strike without a sound. And watch out for the little snakes, they are just as poisonous as the big ones."

The two young men examined each bush before allowing the girls to fill their pails.

Liddy was shaken when the girls told her of Sarah's brush with the snake.

"Don't worry, Mama, Albert and Daniel showed us how to look for snakes," Ellen said, "and it was strange watching the snake flop all over without its head."

"Ellen, you are making me sick," Liddy said.

Through the summer, Ruthie pointed out the green plants that were nourishing and non- poisonous. Watercress abounded along the streams, and although Liddy and the girls plucked it by the mounds, they barely dented the supply. The corn patch, so carefully cultivated, exploded into huge stalks with extremely large ears. Never had their crops produced so abundantly in Ohio. Sweet potatoes, Irish potatoes, tomatoes, green beans and carrots grew to mammoth proportions. Wildflowers of every description erupted throughout the mountains, so profuse the aroma could be almost dizzying. Mountain laurel poured forth blue and white blossoms of incredible beauty. The glistening splendor of the succulent blossoms rested against huge, deep green leaves of equal beauty.

In late summer, Ruthie and Liddy again roamed the woodlands looking for plants to add to their medicinal hoard. Ruthie stopped by

a plant about a foot high with a solitary stem. The leaves were pal-
mately lobed around the outer edge, and they bloomed in early spring.

"We'll dig this root, Liddy," she said, "but you must always keep
it out of reach of the children. We'll powder the root and only use a
very small amount for pain. It's called by the name of bloodroot."
Their medicinal knowledge did not include the name "morphine."

In August, Sarah helped Morgan rob bees of large stashes of honey,
being careful to leave enough for the bees to winter on. A lean-to
fashioned of small logs was used to store the honey. Morgan and
Liddy had very carefully hollowed out large sections of the walnut
logs to use as containers.

Fruit had been gathered from the bayberry wax tree for candles
and other uses, lending a delicate fragrance to the cabin. They were
both filled with joy as they watched the storage bins swell with bounty
for the coming winter. Red sage had been gathered by the bundle and
hung upside down in the cabin, lean-to, and the hollowed-out storage cellar. The plentiful sage leaves would be used to flavor turkey
and dressing, and it was especially flavorful in seasoning venison sau-
sage. An embankment adjacent to the cabin had been a natural place
to dig out and roof over with logs. Through the summer, even when
their bodies ached, they would take time to gradually increase the size
of the storage cellar.

***

By September, Morgan decided it was time to secure the dugout
and make ready to store their harvest. A bin was made to receive
potatoes, and it was quickly filled as the girls dug diligently. Huge
potatoes were rolled from the loose, black loam, and the girls vied to
see who had brought forth the largest one.

"Papa, they cheated because they knew where the biggest taters
were," Rebecca wailed as Sarah and Ellen always found the largest.

Morgan hoisted her into his arms and swung her about to lighten
her mood.

"Rebecca, my sweet, you don't have to get the biggest potato to
be the most important. You carried the largest pail to the bin this last
trip," Morgan teased her into a better humor, and she scampered
back to the potato patch.

He had felt fear and unease in bringing Liddy and the girls to such isolation, but their joys and discoveries had brought relief and a sense of well-being. The one problem that remained with him was fear of poisonous snakes that slithered about. Dan Edwards had warned him they were everywhere. The girls barely missed being bitten on several occasions even though they were careful where they stepped.

Morgan had his own harrowing escape from a huge, striking rattlesnake. He had immediately limped back to the cabin after telling Liddy he would be away for a couple of hours. "Liddy, I need a cold, wet towel to wrap around my knee."

"Good Lord, Morgan, what happened?" a concerned Liddy asked.

"I was hacking away at our coal outcropping by the creek, standing in low bushes, which was a stupid thing to do. The minute I heard a rattle I dropped the pick and sailed over the bushes as the damn thing struck. It was the biggest rattlesnake I have ever seen, and it didn't miss me by much. I banged up my knee when I hit the ground, but I managed to find a big limb and kill it. I'll have to clear out all those bushes to get to the coal that we will need soon."

Morgan built large wooden boxes for each side of the fireplace. One box held wood for the fire and the other held coal. The coal outcroppings were numerous, and Morgan knew it would produce tremendous heat. This particular type would later be called "cannel coal." It was highly volatile in chemical makeup, and its heat-producing qualities would never be equaled by any other high-grade coal.

By September, the girls were gathering chinquapins, chestnuts and black walnuts by the bushel. The nights were much cooler, and the morning crisp lasted longer each day. Corn had been stripped from huge stalks and stored for winter. Morgan cut the stalks and fashioned teepee-shaped bundles around other anchored stalks, securing the top, and half way down, with long, strong blades peeled from the plant. The girls loved parting the lower sections to produce their very own hideaway. When the snow came, Morgan would simply hack the bottoms loose and feed livestock.

Dried corn had been stripped of its husks to make new mattresses. With great patience and strong hands, Liddy slit the husks many times while cutting off the knob at the end. She stitched three sides of a mattress cover together and, with great gusto, the girls stuffed the open side. It was stitched immediately to produce a soft, cuddly and warm mattress. They were delighted that it didn't smell like pee.

Rebecca had a way of never getting awake enough to use the slop jar tucked just beneath the bed.

Though Liddy had been totally awed by the enormous trees surrounding their new home, she was now completely overwhelmed as October arrived, and a breathtaking beauty began to unfold. The mountains were becoming encased in their age-old ritual of changing guard. Rich spring and summer growth of succulent green leaves gradually gave way to colors that left one breathless with wonder. Huge giant oaks spread their enormous limbs with brilliant red. Maples by the hundreds were woven in and out of the mass with golds glistening and sparkling. Birch trees added a lighter golden tone, and their silver trunks could occasionally be spotted through the mass of color. Beautiful weeping willows lining streams and ponds dipped boughs across moss strewn rocks and logs, dotting them softly with gold. Dogwood that had dazzled the girls with lovely pink and white blossoms in the early spring, blazed with a stunning red. So vivid was the hue, leaves appeared to be made of wax, totally uniform and glistening. Spruce pine, the king of the enchanted forest, rose heavenward to as much as two hundred feet. The soft bluish needles distinguished it from other pines and added a striking contrast to the gigantic bouquet of unsurpassed beauty. Its long, cigar-like cones fell beneath the smaller white ash that crowded against the huge trunks of the noble trees. Beautiful balsam poplar, many measuring six feet in circumference, wedged their trunks into the fray and spangled yet another shade of gold. Striking reds of every shade marched up the mountains and along streams. Morgan stood spellbound by the rushing stream each morning to watch the first rays of the sun awaken the hills to their full beauty. As the morning mist gave the mountains one last lingering kiss and rose to oblivion, the full scope of colors unfolded, and he was filled with wonder.

It was delightful to watch squirrels and chipmunks busily gathering the small triangular beechnuts, chestnuts and acorns for their winter stash. Raccoons were busy hoarding black walnuts, which were much too large for the smaller animals to collect. So abundant were the nuts that Morgan did not try to shoo the little animals away. There was enough for all. The chestnuts were delicious when thrown into the fire to roast. After supper, they would rake them out of the hot coals, and the family would feast on them for dessert.

Indian summer was in its glory as October drew to a close. The girls could hardly sit through their lessons in the mornings. Liddy had to insist they do their reading and writing. When released from their studies, they tumbled through the door and the woods resounded with their laughter. The beautiful foliage was beginning to drift to earth and rustle with every footstep. Dan and Ruthie Edwards were sure it was going to be a hard winter.

"Just look at the extra fur all the animals are growing," Dan said, as they circled the cabin looking for cracks or leaks. "We are mighty glad to have you and Liddy for neighbors. It sure gets lonesome when you're bogged down in winter," he said, clapping Morgan on the back to reinforce his words.

Morgan felt great relief knowing Dan was near. Albert could handle a horse and plow on an even par with his father and was just as sober, while Daniel would always be the prankster.

At night by lamp light, Morgan sketched a large upstairs bedroom for the girls and hoped to have it roughed in by Christmas. In early spring he would begin to add two rooms to the cabin with timber he would cut and leave to season during the winter months.

Morgan planned to broach the subject of Albert riding a raft downstream with him in the spring and hoped Dan would give his consent. He would bring horses and cattle back to the hills from his family's farm. He and Dan could fill these valleys with prize livestock. Liddy was excited with the plans and never ceased to marvel at her husband's ingenuity. Sarah, who fell asleep later than her sisters, was privy to their plans, and she was also excited. She could have her own horse to explore the mountains.

***

November had hardly arrived when fierce winds from the north dropped freezing temperatures on the area as fine snow filtered through barren trees. Needles on the ever-beautiful pine trees drooped lower as they were powdered by the drift. Morgan and the girls kept the large boxes by the fireplace filled with wood and coal. By mid-month, ice had begun to form on the outer edges of streams and ponds.

Dan Edwards rode by one day on his frisky horse to assure Morgan that winter was upon them.

"I could hardly get the saddle on old Belle here," he said, as he held onto the reins of the prancing horse. I have never seen the likes of her when it first starts to get cold, and I'm thinkin' we're in for a big snow tonight. Better bank the coal well in your fireplace. You don't want Liddy and the girls to catch their death of cold," Dan said, as he blew warm air into his hands.

Morgan looked at his friend with gratitude.

"I'm mighty beholden to you, Dan. I don't know what me and my family would be doing without you. I've got a spare quart of moonshine if you're short on toddy medicine."

Dan laughed and thanked Morgan.

"We've already laid in a good bunch. Nothing like it for the flu or a bad cold. Just heat up sassafras tea as hot as you can stand it and then you slug it good with moonshine. You'll really break out in a sweat and get better."

Morgan assured Dan that Liddy and the girls had dug sassafras roots by the bunch after Ruthie had extolled its many virtues.

The girls were busy during the day collecting sycamore balls that measured at least one inch in circumference and hung from a long pliable stem. Tomorrow they would use the juices extracted from berries and barks they had collected during the summer to dye their collection. Early in the fall, they had chosen a lovely red cedar for their Christmas tree and they could hardly wait to decorate it. Periodically, they had visited their chosen tree to be sure it was as beautiful as they remembered and still stood. Ruthie had drawn their attention to this particular tree as they gathered herbs and barks.

The frigid cold kept a grip on the region for several days, and, on November twenty-fourth in late afternoon, the first large snowfall of the season began. Huge beautiful flakes floated down at first, adding a softness and insulating sounds. The girls giggled as they held their mouths open to receive the large flakes. Their eyebrows and long pigtails soon turned white, and Liddy ordered them inside.

"Girls," she chided, "we can't have you coming down with colds with our first big snow, so in you go."

They argued at first, but trooped into the cabin to shake off the white fluff. Liddy's freshly baked cornbread beckoned them to the table where they proceeded to crumble chunks of the bread into bowls of cold milk, devouring it immediately.

"Pa, can I throw the chestnuts into the fire?" Ellen asked, plunging her hands into a heavy wooden pail bulging with the fat chestnuts.

"You sure can, honey, but stand back a way. I have never seen coal burn so hot," Morgan answered.

He had used coal in Ohio, but he had never felt such intense heat projected from it. With a heavy stick, he moved the chestnuts closer to the front of the fire. Within minutes, they had charred. Morgan was amazed.

"Ellen, let's try the chestnuts just in front of the fire," he advised. Twice Morgan moved the nuts further from the blazing fire onto the stone hearth as the shells began to blacken immediately. The girls sat cross-legged on Liddy's scatter rug in front of the fire and peeled pipping hot nuts. "These are for you, Papa," Ellen said, dropping the steaming nuts into his outstretched hand.

Morgan opened the door to check on the snow and was confronted by a world turned white. The flakes no longer floated but peppered down with intensity. He had hacked lower limbs from a grove of thick blue spruce and added a log shelter beneath them for the livestock, and they were bedded down beneath the canopy for the night.

The cold that managed to seep through in a few places in the cabin was counteracted by tremendous heat from the fireplace. He and Dan Edwards had checked the hardened clay between the stones, and it appeared to be fireproof.

By bedtime, the girls had checked several times to see how much snow had fallen. They could hardly wait to get up in the morning and frolic in their newfound playground. Rebecca returned to the fireplace to retrieve her heavy woolen socks from her shoes.

"Sarah and Ellen are wearin' their socks to bed so their feet will stay warm, and I want mine," she said, as she sat on the edge of the rug and pulled them over her long, slender feet. When she arose, Morgan pulled his youngest daughter to him and kissed her on top of her head. During many sleepless nights, Rebecca would remember the loving gesture.

When the even breathing of the girls indicated their sleep, he stood up and took Liddy into his arms. New lines had become etched into her face in the last few months, but also a new strength. It had been a long, hard, backbreaking summer and fall, but God had been so good to them. They had friends and a larder stuffed with food for the months ahead. He kissed her as he stroked the smoothly brushed hair that flowed almost to her waist. Liddy had lost weight during the summer, but the angles uncovered in her face were even more beautiful than the former fullness. Her agility and quickness had increased with the many chores that had to be done, and Morgan felt his wife had never looked so radiant. As Liddy warmed the backside of her nightgown, Morgan added several more lumps of coal to the red embers to stay the night cold. They drifted off to sleep in a world of contentment. Morgan never dreamed that before this night ended he would have traversed into an unspeakable hell.

Howling winds masked the slight noise as the hairline crack across the cabin floor began to widen. Tremendous heat from the heavily stoked fireplace continued to open the fissure. A slight and different sound penetrated Morgan's deep sleep. Groggy and half awake, he arose from the treasured brass bed, and by the time he had taken three steps, he was horror-stricken. His bare feet and legs were immediately struck by numerous fangs. In one hideous moment, he knew what had happened as the light from the fireplace illuminated the grotesque scene. Dozens of snakes were pouring through a wide crack in the stone floor into the warmth of the cabin. His reaction was instant.

He screamed to Liddy and the girls, "Stand up on the bed! Do not get out of the bed. Snakes are everywhere."

Before Liddy was awake, he had gathered her, along with a blanket into his arms and headed to the door.

He was shouting constantly to the girls, "Stand up on the bed, girls! Do not step on the floor. I'll be back to get you."

"Open the door," he shouted to Liddy as he held her above the horrible den.

Liddy had snapped awake, and her adrenaline was racing. By the time he carried her across the room, she was unlatching the heavy wooden latch. Morgan practically threw her into the swirling snow. The deadly rattling of dozens of rattlesnakes had completely terrified the girls. They stood screaming and clinging to one another in the center of the bed. His long strides back to the bed were agonizing every inch of the way. Huge rattlesnakes with enormous heads and vicious mouths sank long, curved, poison-filled fangs into his feet and legs with every step. Rapidly striking copperheads added their own poisonous venom to his body. The flailing snakes filled him with revulsion as they rolled and slithered beneath his bare feet.

"Sarah, you first with the blanket," he roared. "Ellen, take care of Rebecca. I will be right back."

"Sarah, run to the Edwards. Tell them what has happened. Hurry," he urged.

He dumped her onto the snow and Liddy dragged her farther away.

"Run fast, Sarah," her mother shouted, as she draped her blanket about Sarah's shoulders.

The long legs of the ten-year-old flew through the woods. She had no time to be afraid. The snow had deepened and was almost to the top of her heavy woolen socks. She kept to the middle of the wagon trail between the two cabins and her speed increased.

Again Morgan entered into the nightmare and rescued Rebecca. "Be brave, Ellen. Your turn is next," he bellowed to be heard above the rising noise as more rattlesnakes poured into the cabin.

Vile, cold, scaly bodies rolled beneath his feet causing him to stumble several times as he prayed he would not fall into the writhing mass with one of the girls.

Releasing Rebecca to Liddy's waiting arms, he made the last agonizing trip through the poisonous nightmare.

"God give me strength," he prayed, as he lifted Ellen from the bed.

Ellen, sobbing, held tight to her father and knew what he had sacrificed for them. A few of the snakes had bitten him as high as his knees. From the knees down, his flesh was almost solid with puncture wounds. Liddy and the girls stood shivering under a large pine tree sheltered from the snow. Morgan lowered himself at last to the blanket that Liddy had spread on the ground for him.

"Oh, Papa-Papa, you saved our lives," Rebecca sobbed over and over.

Liddy dropped to her knees caressing his forehead and covering him with Rebecca's blanket. She was numb from shock and could not feel the cold. She could not cry yet. Her wonderful Morgan was dying, and she could only hold his hand and pray.

Dan Edwards had been awakened by his barking dogs and was just cracking the door to see what was causing the commotion when Sarah slammed into him and the doorway.

"Oh my God, Sarah, what is wrong?" Dan roared, catching her

as she pitched forward, struggling to breathe with eyes wide and wild. A branch had snagged the blanket away, and she stood gasping in her snow-covered nightgown.

"Sarah, honey, what in the name of God," Ruthie screamed.

"It's Pa. Snakes are all over our cabin floor. They came up through a big crack in the rock," she managed to relate between gasps for breath. "He carried me and Mama out over the snakes, and he was barefooted. He was going back for Ellen and Rebecca."

Her terrible words brought shock and disbelief to their faces. Almost instantly, they were galvanized into action. As Ruthie half-carried Sarah to the fireplace and placed her on the warm floor, Dan and the boys were dressing.

"Bridle the horses, boys, no time for saddles," Dan directed, as he grabbed a jar of Ruthie's snake bite medicine.

"Ruthie, you and Daniel bring the wagon and blankets."

Within minutes, Dan and Albert had galloped off with blankets tucked under their arms. Daniel hitched the horse and wagon together in record time and stopped at the door to collect Ruthie and Sarah, and they raced toward the Collier cabin. Sarah had refused to stay behind, and Ruthie understood. Dressed in Daniel's clothes, she huddled beneath blankets in the wagon and prayed for her father.

Ruthie lifted candles from the wagon and, as she lit them, her heart sank. Morgan was drawing his last breath as Liddy and the girls huddled by him sobbing. He was unconscious when Dan and Albert arrived, and his friend knew it was too late to help. Liddy closed his eyes and gently kissed his eyelids as her tears flowed across his face. Ellen clutched his lifeless arm to her and refused to let go.

"Liddy, you and the girls must get into the wagon," Ruthie begged.

Aside from Sarah, who wore Daniel's clothes, the family stood shivering in their nightgowns. Liddy held Morgan in her arms for a moment more, then placed him lovingly back on the blanket. Ellen and Rebecca allowed themselves to be carried to the wagon after they had kissed Morgan's face, bathing it in tears of grief. Sarah had been standing behind Liddy in stoic silence. As the others left his side, she collapsed onto his chest with racking sobs, putting her arms around her father. His legs were so grotesquely swollen, they were the size of tree trunks.

"Oh Papa-Papa, what will we do without you?" she cried.

50

With tears awash on his own face, Albert picked Sarah up and placed her in the wagon by Liddy. Dan Edwards recoiled as he looked through the door of the cabin. Hundreds of snakes with writhing bodies thrashed about the floor. Tremendous heat from the highly volatile cannel coal had reacted with the cold stone floor splitting it apart. The huge rock that had served as the cabin floor was an enormous shelter for hibernating reptiles. The wide crack in the stone had unleashed the nightmare into the warmth of their home. Walking to Liddy, who sat in a daze, he spoke softly, "Liddy, you know what has to be done." She nodded her head. No one would ever be able to go into their home again.

"I will take care of it for you, Liddy, and we will bring Morgan to the cabin when Daniel gets back with the wagon," he said as he signaled Daniel to leave.

The snow had ceased falling, and they traveled through a ghost world to the Edwards' place.

Making torches from pine boughs, Dan and Albert lit them from candles, placing them around the cabin with dry wood chips from the lean-to. The cabin soon became an inferno, coloring the snow red. The hissing and writhing of the snakes were horrific as the flames grew hot and devoured them.

The return trip to the burial site over the snow-packed roads was a sad one. Stately pines were garnered in long shimmering ice crystals as the sun shot rays of brilliant light into tangled branches. A slight wind barely moved the limbs as an ice song twinkled in the stillness. Liddy looked at the smoldering ashes of their cabin with wisps of smoke still curling from the opening in the stone chimney and felt as though her heart had been wrenched from her chest. A tall, gaunt preacher, a total stranger, read from the Bible, and prayed for Morgan's soul.

Morgan was buried beneath a large weeping willow overlooking the gurgling stream that he had so loved. Snow covered the large rocks protruding about the water and muffled sounds that had brought such joy to their ears. The ice had crept from both sides of the bank and only a ribbon of water was allowed to flow. Liddy looked about and wondered from where all these people had materialized. Many she had never seen before. The news traveled fast and within hours, food and clothing began arriving at the Edwards' cabin.

51

For a week, Liddy lived in a world of vague awareness. Dan and the boys had quickly arranged sleeping space and privacy for her and the girls in the loft. He and Ruthie assured them they could stay as long as they liked. Rebecca huddled with Liddy, as Sarah and Ellen took charge. They climbed the makeshift ladder to the loft many times each day to nurture and care for their mother and youngest sister. After several days, Liddy surfaced to a glaring reality and decided what she must do.

She sent a letter to her brothers in Ohio by the young Methodist minister, and two weeks later they arrived at the Edwards' cabin with several extra horses and heavy clothes for her and the girls. Her two youngest brothers, along with two of Morgan's brothers, were horrified by the details of Morgan's death. A saddened and dispirited Edwards family watched the group ride away.

The parting was heartbreaking.

Again, Pine Mountain had played host to "The Dark and Bloody Ground."

CHAPTER 3

Ruthie cried for days after Liddy and the girls departed. "Ruthie, you have to get a hold of yourself, honey. There's nothing we could have done to stop what happened to Morgan," Dan said, alarmed with Ruthie's continuing misery.

"I will never forget the suffering on Liddy's face as she sat holding her dying Morgan. How could God let this happen to such a fine family?"

"Remember one thing, Ruthie, God gave Morgan the strength to carry his family to safety, and it took more than just physical strength to do what he did."

"I know that, Dan, but I love Liddy like a sister, and we all had such good times together. I even forgot that we were in the middle of a wilderness, and now it will be so lonely again."

Dan walked out of the house with Daniel who had overheard the conversation. "I miss them too, Pa," he said, and the son's eyes filled with tears.

After the Collier's departure, Albert spent his days furiously chopping and sawing enormous trees. He had considered Morgan invincible with his mammoth strength and raw energy. The hurt was deep.

Ruthie always had letters ready to send to Liddy, and sent them to be mailed by any trapper or traveler who passed by. Many of the same people returned weeks later with letters back. "I reckon you must have some good friends up North," an old trapper remarked as he handed Ruthie another bundle of mail.

Liddy sent pictures of the girls. "Now you just look at that Sarah. She could almost pass for sixteen years old, and she has just turned twelve," Ruthie said as she passed the pictures to Albert. Sarah was becoming a beauty, and she watched his lingering look of interest.

Albert began to add brief notes to the Collier family and especially Sarah. "Sarah, I thought of you this week when I rode up the mountain to Raven Rock. I can't even begin to describe the flowers that were everywhere, and I remembered how much you loved them. The dogwoods have dropped their petals and the mountain laurels are blooming early. Blackberry blossoms are really big this year, and I can hardly wait to see the size of the berries. I stood at the very edge of Raven Rock and looked at the valley so far below, and it was like I stood next to God himself. I am so sorry I didn't get a chance to show you this spot as I had promised."

Liddy noticed that Sarah put the letter in her music box on the dresser.

Each year the pictures came, and when Sarah turned fifteen, Albert knew what he wanted to do.

"Pa, could I have the meadow over by the head of Elkhorn Creek to build a cabin on?" Dan was completely taken by surprise. "When Sarah turns seventeen, I am going to marry her and bring her back to the mountains."

"Son, Sarah might not want to come back here after the awful thing that happened to her father."

Albert was undaunted, "She will come. Sarah loved these hills as I do." He was remembering her joy and excitement with each new discovery. On one occasion, he had shown her a hidden sulfur spring and watched her face as he gave her a drink of the tangy, icy water in a large, cupped maple leaf.

"Albert, it is so good. Where does it come from?" she asked.

"From way down in the earth, Sarah, and these mountains are full of surprises."

"Will you show me?"

"Not right now, but when it's too cold to work the fields, I will." Albert had first been drawn to Sarah's quick mind and appreciation of the beauty surrounding them.

"I didn't know there were so many flowers in the world," she had said to him after their weekly Sunday dinner when both Liddy and Ruthie always read from the Bible.

On many occasions Albert rode to the Morgan's homestead and there was always an overwhelming sadness when he looked at the blacked chimney where the cabin had stood. He always took time to clear Morgan's grave of weeds and briers, leaving freshly plucked flowers by the headstone.

If Albert had any doubts that Sarah would marry him, he never voiced them to his family. Even though he and Daniel were close-knit brothers, he kept his own counsel. Daniel stood two inches taller than Albert, but he was only the more proud of his little brother. They had experienced their share of fighting and drinking on their trips to the river ports, and Albert was happy to have Daniel's assistance. Black bear pelts were still plentiful, if you were a good trapper, and the two brothers were the best. The bears were increasing each year, and so was the income for Albert and Daniel. Streams and lakes along the Elkhorn and Shelby Gap Creeks supplied them with magnificent beaver pelts and many other hides. The extremely rugged terrain of the mountainsides discouraged most settlers but proved a mecca for the Edwards family.

On frequent trips to the river ports, Albert had closely observed furniture he saw in the towns and how it was constructed. When the days shortened, he worked by lantern light in the barn. Dan was sometimes amazed by the pile of shavings, which attested to Albert's late-night labors, as he painstakingly created furniture for him and Sarah.

Ruthie had given Albert a list of materials she would need to crochet a bedspread. Her fingers had fairly flown through the exquisite thread he had bought in town.

She was excited, happy and apprehensive as she worked on her creation. What if Sarah said "No?" What if she was already married? Would Liddy allow Sarah to return to the spot where the family had witnessed such horror? She voiced her concerns to Dan, whose only comment was, "Let it be, Ruthie."

There was the long, lonely, rugged trip to Ohio for Albert. The beautiful horse he would be riding and the three he would be leading were reason enough to be waylaid and his pockets emptied by worthless drifters. Scores of people were heading farther west from the Carolinas and Virginia, and many unwary travelers in the Big Sandy Valley were paying the price for their passage westward.

Ruthie packed his tailored suits carefully in extra large saddlebags. She had spent days sewing and perfecting the suits, and when Albert tried on the finished product, she was awed. His Swiss-German heritage was evident in the proud way he held his shoulders. He had a confident walk, and appeared taller than his six feet and one inch, with arms that were almost too long. Years of hard physical labor had resulted in chiseled muscles and powerful shoulders.

***

Albert arrived in Ohio in late April of 1846, six years after Liddy and the girls had returned home. Sarah was dumfounded when she opened the door to find Albert on the doorstep. He was much taller than when she had last seen him, and his unwavering stare completely unsettled her.

"Albert," she gasped.

"You must be Sarah," he teased. "Do you plan to shoot me this time?"

Sara doubled over with laughter. "Do come in, Albert," she said, taking his hand and leading him into the large living room. Rebecca, leaving the kitchen, screamed with delight and threw herself into Albert's arms.

"I can't believe it's you, Albert. When did you get here? How long can you stay? Tell me about Ruthie. Mama. Ellen, come quick, look who is here." Rebecca was beside herself with excitement.

Liddy hugged Albert and held him at arms length. "Albert, I am so happy to see you, and you are so grown up. I can't believe it."

Uncontrolled tears slid down Liddy's face, and Albert put his arms around her, patting her back. Ellen was finally able to hug Albert and marveled at how handsome he was.

"I'll bet you are hungry, Albert, and supper is just about ready. Will you stay?"

"Of course," he said, and everyone talked at once.

"Tell us about your family," Liddy said, as the girls filled Albert's plate to overflowing.

"Well, nothing much has changed, except Daniel is taller than I

56

am. Ma is missing you a bunch, and she sends her love to all of you. I have letters in my saddlebags. Pa and Daniel still cut trees with me, and we send them down river, as usual. Trapping and hunting is going good, and we have no new neighbors. We still have the mountainside to ourselves."

There was an awkward silence, and Albert knew what each was thinking.

"I ride by your farm often, and it's just like you left it, still beautiful and full of wildlife."

"I still have nightmares when I think about Papa, Albert. He was so brave, and I really miss him."

"I miss him too, Rebecca. He was the bravest and finest man I have ever known."

"What does his grave look like?" Ellen asked, and Liddy was astounded.

"Ma planted wild flowers on it the first year, and we keep it clean of briers and seedlings. You know those nuts that fall from the trees will sprout all over if we don't watch them."

Many questions later, Liddy was amazed by the things the girls had asked and talked about, things they had never mentioned to her. She was impressed with Albert and his kindness in laying some of their fears to rest as he elevated Morgan to martyrdom for his heroic actions in saving his family.

Sarah sat quietly, saying little. Albert could not take his eyes from her face. She was tall and beautiful, as he had known she would be. Long, flaxen hair swept into a soft bun at the nape of her neck gave her an older appearance, and deep blue-gray eyes adored him. Her dewy porcelain skin extended into her low-cut dress, and Albert felt blood rising to his cheeks.

"Tell us about your trip, Albert," Sarah said in-between bombardments from her two younger sisters.

"I rode my horse to Louisa, and then took a boat to Portsmouth. I have never seen so many people, and they all seem to be heading west."

"They are, indeed," Liddy said, "and I'm surprised you were able to find a horse in Portsmouth."

"He doesn't look like much, but it beats walking."

Liddy was torn between being happy to see Albert and despairing at knowing why he was there. He was obviously in love with Sarah, and Liddy was only too aware of the look in her daughter's eyes.

"Albert, we have just time enough before dark to hook up the buggy and take a quick ride about the farm, if you would like," Sarah said.

"I would like that," he answered while Ellen and Rebecca rolled their eyes at one another.

Liddy watched the buggy leave the barnyard, and her heart was heavy.

"Albert came to marry Sarah and take her back to where those snakes are," Rebecca said.

Ellen was appalled by her gory description of the mountains. "We had a lot of fun there, and it was not all snakes."

Sarah and Albert went to visit Morgan's family the next day, and Ingrid Collier was totally dismayed. The young couple were obviously in love, and Ingrid still considered the Kentucky mountains a nightmare that had destroyed Morgan.

As soon as Sarah and Albert left, Ingrid turned to her husband.

"John, offer Albert a good job. There is lots of land that we can buy to give to them for a wedding present."

"It won't work, Ingrid, but I will give it a try, if it will make you feel better. He speaks of those mountains the same way Morgan did. He is a fine young man, and you only have to look at Sarah's face to know that she is in love with him."

First it was Morgan, and now it was her favorite granddaughter. Ingrid took to her bed with a sick headache.

For three days Albert and Sarah were inseparable, and hand-in-hand they approached Liddy for her blessing.

"I promise you, Liddy, I will always look after Sarah."

Liddy had no doubt that Albert would lay down his life for her daughter, and she knew that regardless of whether she gave her blessing, the young couple would marry. She missed Morgan even moreso at this moment.

"Liddy, I cleared a large meadow by the headwaters of Elkhorn Creek and built a house for Sarah. There is not one rock left in the clearing that a snake could crawl under." Albert spoke with great intensity, knowing the fear that must be gripping Liddy.

She hugged the two young people, and her tears flowed unashamedly. Both families offered Albert jobs and land for him and Sarah to build on, but the generous offers were graciously refused. Wedding plans were made, and whirlwind arrangements were completed within a week.

Albert had never been inside a Methodist church, and he looked about in awe. High ceilings covered beautiful, dark and shining walnut beams that shimmered in rainbow colors as light filtered through tall, stained-glass windows. He wished his family could have been here for the wedding. A plump matron with a heaving bosom attacked the organ with pumping feet and short, stubby fingers. A melodic sound escaped, but Albert was not sure whether it was good or bad since he had never heard organ music before. Sarah's uncle stood with him as he watched her slowly and gracefully glide to his side. The minister, in his long black robe, elaborated on many subjects before he finally pronounced them husband and wife. They slipped away from a very noisy reception in the large church basement and headed for the hills.

The Collier family volunteered a handsome buggy for the newlywed's trip to Portsmouth. They would retrieve the buggy after Albert and Sarah boarded the boat upstream to Louisa, where Albert had left his horses.

***

Late in the day, they arrived in Portsmouth, and Albert stopped the buggy at the front entrance of a rooming house that had definitely seen better days. The white paint had tinged to a dirty gray, and several of the shutters hung askew. The front steps had rotted and large stones had been carelessly thrown in to replace them.

"I'm sorry, Sarah, I spent a whole day going from one hotel to another, and it was the same all over. 'Sorry, we are all filled.'"

"Albert, it doesn't make any difference where we are," she said smiling at him.

They were totally engrossed in one another, and suddenly realized people were staring at them. A brash young man leaving the rooming house removed his hat and offered Sarah his hand to help her from the buggy. He departed immediately, as Albert's large frame stepped forward and fixed him with a murderous stare.

"And I thought I would only have to fight bears on the way home," he said, as he lifted Sarah to the ground.

They spent three nights in the drafty rooming house, and Sarah knew she was meant for Albert. Rugged mountain man that he was, he made tender love to her as she clung to him.

After three days of sightseeing in Portsmouth, they were ready to head for home. Liddy and her sisters had helped Sarah pack new clothes and gifts in flat canvas bags that could be thrown over the horses' backs. Liddy had expressed concern as to how they could manage all the luggage, until she learned that Albert had brought two extra horses to Louisa for just that purpose. Ruthie, no doubt, had helped to foster the idea.

Arriving at the stables in Louisa, Albert left Sarah in the buggy and disappeared for a few minutes. He returned leading a beautiful, shining black mare.

Helping Sarah form the buggy, he said proudly, "This is my wedding present to you, Sarah."

"Oh Albert, she is so beautiful. I can't believe she is mine."

She threw her arms about Albert's neck as the stable boy gawked at them. When she drew away, she stroked the head of the fine animal, and it took Albert's breath away to see her standing so fair and beautiful beside her shining, black mare.

Early the next morning, Albert loaded the two extra horses with Sarah's luggage. They also carried a small tent and food.

"Sarah, we have to camp for at least three nights, but these horse are fast, and we should be home in no less than three days."

Sarah shivered as she watched Albert slide a rifle into a holder on the saddle, and she also noticed he wore a gun belt with a large pistol and extra ammunition.

"I want you to put this small pistol in your pocket, Sarah, and, if the need arises, don't be afraid to use it. Better safe than sorry," he added, seeing a doubtful look on her face.

She felt much more secure as the stableboy led Albert's large black dog out to welcome them.

At the end of the third day, in the last waning rays of light, they arrived at their new home just as the sun was sliding behind the hills.

For two years Albert had worked to clear the dense woodlands in order to create their own meadow, one and a half miles from Ruthie and Dan. He had left a few maples for shade, and several dogwoods were scattered throughout the clearing. The quiet softness of twilight touched the scene with magic. With help from his family, he had rushed to complete a wide porch completely surrounding the large cabin. A long rustic swing hung from the rafters, and finely woven, willow rocking chairs were scattered about. Smoke curled from the large stone chimney, and the odor of spicy food welcomed them.

Ruthie, Dan and Daniel rushed into the front yard as the barking dogs alerted them to their arrival.

The family was awed by their first glimpse of a grown-up Sarah. A white silk scarf trailed on the shoulder of her tailored black riding habit, as she sat proudly aboard her striking black mare. Long, thick, flaxen hair gathered at the nape of her neck was secured with a wide silver clasp, leaving it to hang freely, almost to her waist. Her cheeks, flushed from the long ride in nippy spring air, glowed warm, while her large, blue-gray eyes danced with happiness. They were stunned by her beauty. There was little resemblance to the tall, skinny, long-legged child of eleven they had last seen.

"Sarah, Sarah, I can hardly believe it's you," Ruthie said with tears streaming down her face, "and I know you need to get off that horse."

Daniel lifted Sarah from the saddle and gave her a bear hug. "Glad you dropped by, Sarah."

They all laughed, including Sarah, and she almost lost her balance when Daniel released her. The long hours in the saddle had left her legs stiff and wobbly. She cried as she hugged both Dan and Ruthie.

"My whole family sends their love to all of you, and we have talked about you so many times."

The memory of their long-ago tragedy was suddenly very fresh in her mind. She saw the same strength and security in their kind and loving faces, and now, standing here, she knew she had come home.

"Where the hell have ya' been, Albert?" Daniel asked. "This is the third night we have cooked supper for you."

Ruthie glared at Daniel poking him in the ribs, "Watch your mouth, Daniel. Sarah is a young lady."

Albert lifted Sarah off her feet and carried her into the cabin. He was unabashed as Daniel followed with a sly grin. Sarah was astounded as she looked about her. The cabin had been built with huge, wide logs that had been squared and meticulously notched so that they rested solidly upon one another. The ceilings were high, and the boards just in back of the large overhead beams had been carefully planed and smoothed. "Albert, this is beautiful. I can't believe it."

A long table of white oak stood laden with food, the edges of the table had been rounded and smoothed as was the top.

"Albert did this with turpentine and finished it off with bear grease," Daniel said, seeing Sarah's admiring gaze on the table. "He has worked night and day to get everything in order for you, Sarah, and we're sure glad you didn't say no." The group laughed uproariously, as Sarah threw her arms around Albert's neck.

One long bench and several beautifully carved chairs, finished in the same manner, were placed around the room. They all saw the haunted look in Sarah's eyes as she looked at the floor and knew she must be thinking about another cabin miles away where she had lived before. The logs were completely flat and tightly fitted with large interlocking wedges.

"Sarah, there is another layer of fitted logs just under this one but laid in this direction," Albert said, as he gestured to explain the right angle. Albert put his arms around Sarah and hugged her. She smiled at him through misty eyes, then looked away, trying to regain her composure.

"I know you two must be mighty hungry and bone tired," Ruthie said, as she bustled about. "We've had our supper, we need to be getting home while we can still see. Sarah, we are only one and a half miles away, and we hope to see you often. You always made these hills sing."

"Daniel, you and me just might saddle up our horses when we take Albert's to the barn," Dan said, as he guided a reluctant Daniel to the door.

They unloaded the horses at the front door, and for the first time, Sarah noticed the doorway leading into another room. She walked through the doorway into a large bedroom, and she was speechless as she stared at the bed. It was like nothing she had ever seen. The long headboard consisted of intricately woven willow.

"I saw one like this at the rooming house in Prestonburg," Albert announced proudly.

"Oh, Albert, it is so beautiful. I have never seen anything like it, and look at the bedspread. Ruthie, you must have spent weeks making this, didn't you?" Bending over, she hugged Ruthie and kissed her on the cheek. "I will always cherish it." Ruthie's face lit up with one of her most beautiful smiles, and it stayed in place all the way back to their cabin.

***

For days, Sarah examined every inch of the cabin and each article of furniture. She lovingly traced each curved arm of every chair, and her love for Albert deepened.

It was late spring and the nights were chilly. Albert stoked the large fireplace at night and carried her to the gigantic black bearskin rug in front of the warm fire. She melted into his strong embrace, returning his fierceness as the blazing logs settled into ashes, and they slept at last. Sarah had never dreamed such happiness could exist.

Dan rode by a few days after their return and visited briefly with Albert as he let the horses out to pasture early one morning.

"Was that your father?" Sarah asked, seeing his horse disappear around the last bend.

"It was," her husband answered, "and they want us to eat supper with them tomorrow. I said we would come," he said, looking at her to be certain she agreed.

"I would love to Albert. I have so many things I want to ask your family." A look of sadness crossed her beautiful face, and his heart ached for her.

After two weeks they both decided it would be better to ride by the old home place. Sarah cried when she saw the chimney her father had built six years earlier. Vines had twisted themselves through the stones and ran everywhere. The large flat rock that had been the cabin floor lay blackened, a large crevice running the length of it. The horror of that terrible night blazed again in Sarah's mind. She had thought the memory would be dimmed by now. Her father's grave was clear of brush and briars, and she knew this had been the work of the Edwards family.

"Albert, thank you for caring for Papa's grave. I don't know if I will ever be rid of the horrible nightmares."

Albert drew her trembling body close, "In time, Sarah, they will fade."

The headstone still stood as she remembered. She read the words to herself: Morgan Collier, Born 1808, Died 1840, Loving Husband and Father. Dan had taken them to see the stone he had fashioned for his friend before they left for Ohio.

A few weeks after their return, beautiful flowering dogwoods began to relinquish their blossoms, and the pregnant earth erupted with mounds of flowers of every shape, size and color. Each morning was breathtaking, as Sarah surveyed all before her in the beautiful hills. When she carried Albert's noonday lunch to the fields, they picnicked, and many times made love on the wide-bladed grass beneath a huge white oak. Birds fluttered overhead, and deer occasionally looked on. They were oblivious to the world. She would linger for a short while and watch as her handsome husband threw long, leather reins over his shoulder. He guided the heavy plow deep into the fertile soil as he followed the massive horse. The sweet, pungent smell of freshly turned earth wafted to her on a slight breeze, and her joy was complete.

She was shocked when she realized that she hardly thought of her family back in Ohio. Albert's family was overjoyed to have Sarah back with them. Her beautiful, smiling face was like a ray of sunshine. Ruthie attacked her chores with a new vigor, and Dan smiled more. On many occasions they had to thwart Daniel's trumped-up excuses to linger with the newlyweds.

The cabin now reflected Sarah's touch, and Albert lavished her with praise as she added each crocheted doily and ruffles to the curtains. When Albert worked later into the long evenings, she milked their cow and churned rich, yellow butter, storing it under a rocky ledge on the clear bubbling stream that meandered below the cabin. Icy rivulets, streaming from the headwaters of Elkhorn Creek, swept over the ledge, keeping their food chilled and delicious.

Ruthie was delighted to have another companion to tramp through the forest with her and collect familiar plants. In their searching, they never wandered so far from the cabin to which help could not be summoned, if needed. The mountain was filled with wild animals, and both women had been well-warned of the massive bear traps.

"They could just about snap your leg in two," Albert had worried.

Sarah shivered, "I will definitely look out for the traps."

Albert exploded from the cabin one day when Sarah's hysterical screams reached his ears. She had gone to the creek to collect milk for their supper and a huge, coiled rattlesnake lay in the path on her way back to the house. She barely missed being struck. Albert seized a large limb lying nearby, and within seconds he had killed the intruder. Sarah collapsed into his arms, her body shaking with terrible sobs. The pail lay on its side as white liquid coated the grass. They had both known the time would come when Sarah would have to face monsters from the past, and Albert was thankful he had been nearby when the first encounter occurred.

"Sarah, we are going to go rattlesnake hunting. I am sure it will help you come to grips with some of your awful fears. I know how well you can handle a rifle, and it's time we met this problem head on." She nodded in agreement.

Their fields of corn and gardens were laden with bounty by midsummer. The rain came gently during the growing season, and the family rejoiced. There was no propping corn that had been flattened because of whirling, smashing wind driving it to the ground. They gave Sarah credit for bringing them good luck.

"Sarah, I knew you were a good omen the minute you got off that horse. I could feel it in the air," Ruthie said.

"Ma talks to the hills, Sarah, and she knows about these things," Daniel teased, dodging Ruthie's swipe with a dishtowel.

***

As the advent of fall approached, Sarah discovered she was pregnant. "Sarah, I want us to have a beautiful daughter just like her mother."

"I will accept either, Albert," Sarah sighed, snuggling into his arms.

The Edwards family was ecstatic. Even Dan hovered over Sarah with advice, and Ruthie rocked with laughter.

"That is supposed to be the job for a grandma, not a grandpa," she teased, as Dan looked somewhat abashed.

When snow whirled around the cozy cabin in the dead of winter, Albert held Sarah close, placing his large hand on her broadening stomach as they took joy in the antics of their unborn child. Shortly before their first anniversary, a strong and bawling baby boy was born, and Jonathan Edwards joined their household. Ruthie and Albert delivered the baby, placing him in Sarah's arms as soon as he was wrapped in a tiny blanket. Her wan, exhausted face beamed with pride and happiness as she gingerly touched the small head.

Daniel and Ed Rife mailed a letter for Sarah to her mother on their next trip to Prestonsburg with their pelts. She wrote letters often as Jonathan began to babble and crawl about, giving Liddy details that she knew would make her mother smile.

Ed Rife had wandered into the hills the year before, after losing his young wife and son in childbirth. He was lonely, lost, totally miserable. He spent the first winter with the Edwards and later built his own cabin nearby. He hunted, trapped and farmed with his adopted family. For weeks on end, he would disappear and never volunteer any information on his absence. He was very shy with Sarah but would always bring dressed pheasant, a plump young turkey hen, and occasionally filleted trout from the cold streams. Only on rare occasions would he consent to stay and take a meal with them.

Their rugged and secluded mountain life provided everything they needed. Many families were moving to Kentucky from Northeast Virginia, the Carolinas, and the Deep South, but they shunned the deep ravines, steep mountainsides and narrow valleys of the Pine Mountain range. The Edwards family was left to enjoy the expansive woodlands and revel in its bounty. The few pioneers who lived in the area were as independent and self-reliant as they. If an emergency arose, they helped one another, but these were few, and their contacts were minimal.

A year after Jonathan arrived, Sarah rode her beautiful black mare to Pikeville with Albert to celebrate a second honeymoon in a large, rambling rooming house. Albert looked quite handsome in his suit, and Sarah was lovely in a pale green, silk dress that had been packed away since her arrival in the mountains. Her flaxen hair, piled atop her head, exposed her beautiful long, graceful neck. She turned many heads as they entered the crowded dining room. Albert had never seen her eyes sparkle so and a sudden fear seized him.

"Sarah, are you sorry you came to the mountains?"

"Albert, how could you ask such a thing?"

"It's just that you have been so happy since we've been in town. You look so beautiful in your nice dress, and you can't wear it at the cabin."

Sarah clasped his large, strong hand in both of hers and with a look that almost melted his soul, assuring him her real happiness was with him and Jonathan.

"Albert, you are my life, and I really feel that I must have inherited my father's love for those beautiful hills. Almost every day is a new experience and some wondrous discovery. We have only been here two days, and I miss Jonathan something fierce. We'll leave the day after tomorrow, won't we?"

Albert breathed a sigh of relief and thoroughly enjoyed himself as Sarah continued to dazzle the local gents the remainder of their trip.

They left town with bulging saddlebags, containing gifts for the family and extras, hanging from the saddle horns. Sarah had purchased a new riding outfit, and her bearing was regal. Albert's joy turned to fear as he realized that a lurking group of roughnecks was observing their departure with more than a passing interest. He was trying to decide what course of action he should take as they neared the edge of town and the beginning of the dense forest. To his utter amazement, two figures in coonskin caps and soft leather shirts with flowing fringes materialized from the tree line. Rifles slung from their saddles and their pistols holstered, they rode slowly by the four roughnecks before galloping to Sarah and Albert to exchange greetings. His brother and Ed Rife had immediately sized up the situation, and Daniel's long muscular legs tensed in his stirrups, ready to pounce on a moment's notice. Determination and strength seethed throughout his tall frame. Ed Rife's eyes said everything, the cold, wary, calculating stare of a man who had faced death and misery. He would meet a foe head-on and "beware" to any adversary. Daniel and Ed Rife were the most welcome sight Albert would ever see. Sarah was delighted to see the two, though she had been completely unaware of the danger they had faced.

When Jonathan was two years old, he welcomed a baby brother and was completely awed by him. He had never seen a newborn baby, and Sarah had to watch him constantly. Not only did he try to feed baby Henry, but on a few occasions, his mother rescued the little brother when Jonathan tried to remove him from his crib to rock him, as he had watched his parents do. When Henry was only a few months old, he began to resemble his uncle Daniel — long and lean — where

Jonathan was extremely square-jawed like Albert. Two years later young Martin was born, and the three boys kept Sarah running. In 1852, Luke arrived into the melee and his three older brothers soon taught him to roughhouse. They started him off by bouncing him on the bed when no one was watching.

Sarah's deep and abiding fear of the poisonous snakes was always with her when the children were playing in the yard. She kept a shotgun out of reach of the boys and had used it on several occasions to blast copperheads and rattlesnakes that ventured near the cabin. The Edwards men and Ed Rife had cleared several fields in the narrow valleys, and Albert was out of earshot on many occasions, forcing Sarah to defend their children.

Ruthie was sad that Daniel, at twenty-seven, had not found a bride. There were few women in the area, and Daniel did not care to bring one home from the river port saloons.

"They're fine for company in town, Albert, but I'm not bringing one back here for younguns," he confessed to Albert, on one occasion after Ruthie had brought the subject up again. "Besides, it takes all of us with this bunch you and Sarah are bringin' on," he said, and they both laughed.

Sarah insisted the boys learn to read and write, but Jonathan's greatest love was roaming the mountains and hunting with Daniel and Ed Rife. Albert noticed that Sarah's nightmares were becoming more infrequent, as she discovered she, indeed, could deal with the deadly snakes on her own.

Life was beautiful and calm. The hills remained mostly unsettled, and all they viewed was theirs. Albert added a large bedroom where the boys slept and tussled. It was not unusual to find feathers strewn about after a hard-fought pillow fight. Four sturdy beds stood side by side, and Sarah sometimes found it hard to believe that she and Albert had filled all those beds.

Letters to and from her family were always heartwarming. Both Ellen and Rebecca had married young men from their hometown and started their own families. Sarah had yearned to see them on many occasions, but the time and distance were formidable obstacles. Their farm prospered as Albert added more land and extras to the cabin. Their porch with the willow chairs and swing was the favorite gathering place for the clan. Ed Rife was now considered part of the family and was beloved by all. He never talked about his young wife or the son he had lost years before. Sarah could see a hunger in his eyes on occasions when he was watching the boys in their never-ending roughneck activities. His dark-brown hair and beard were beginning to gray prematurely and, at times, Sarah's heart ached for him.

The mountains continued to supply beautiful pelts, and buyers at the river ports were always happy to reward the Edwards for their efforts. The boys had become adept at spotting ginseng and extracting it from the soil. Each had his own stash, and they could hardly wait to get to the market with their bundles of roots. The mountains were a natural habitat for the plants, so sought after in Europe and the Orient. The roots branched to resemble a human body and were used as medication for many ills. In China, they were used as love potions and talismans. Different countries claimed to have isolated various compounds that had therapeutic values. The roots would remain a staple of the mountains well into the next century and increase in value.

CHAPTER 4

The earthshaking news of civil war finally reached the area, and the Edwards family was astounded. Like most Kentuckians, they did not want any part of the war. There were few slaves in the whole state, and most of the citizens did not hold with the idea of one man owning another. The Big Sandy Valley - with its wide river - was crucial to both the Union and the Confederacy, and both converged on the peace and tranquility of the rich forest. Kentucky tried, in vain, to remain neutral. The statehouse drafted laws restricting fighting by either side on their soil, but it was all to no avail. By 1861, when fighting commenced, both sides had overrun Kentucky.

**

An enormous General Humphry Marshall was first to arrive in the area with hundreds of Rebel soldiers in his regiment. "You are the South," he informed the Edwards family. "We need food and horses, and I will give you vouchers to collect for your contributions. You just take them to headquarters in Knoxville, Tennessee, and you will be paid."

He sat on his huge horse with three-hundred pounds of body spilling over the saddle. His extremely large face, with three chins, pulled the corners of his mouth downward to resemble the face of a bulldog. The loose leash he kept on his men endeared him to them forever, and they followed him into fierce battles for the Southern cause.

It was late fall, and Albert's larders bulged with produce from his harvest. The soldiers emptied corn cribs stuffed with large ears of corn and stashed them onto pack mules and quickly hauled them away. Large, Irish potatoes and sweet potatoes were piled by the corn cribs. The family was dumfounded as they watched the strangers empty a huge, wooden box of chestnuts into bags and sling them over saddle horns. The boys had spent days collecting the fat, delicious nuts to roast at night when they finally closed the door on darkness.

Fourteen-year-old Jonathan was enraged, Albert bent close to his ear and whispered a warning. The young man unclenched his fist and stood by his mother. His uncut thatch of straw-colored hair fell to his broad shoulders, giving him a much older look.

"Oh, God," Sarah thought, as she looked at her oldest son. He was as tall as his father and looked as old as some of the young men surrounding them in their Confederate uniforms.

"We only got enough for our family," Albert objected. "We can't feed no army."

General Marshall appeared not to have heard him as he signaled his men to collect what was available. Albert and Sarah stood by helplessly and watched as their horses were bridled and led away. Smoked deer meat and hams were hoisted from the smokehouse, leaving none for the family. Two of their three cows were driven past the cabin by young recruits who looked embarrassed as they passed the porch, feeling Albert's enraged glare. Several soldiers entered the cabin and cleaned the shelves. Albert had to restrain Sarah when the men lifted the strings of shucky beans from their drying place by the chimney.

The beans had been carefully tended during the summer and plucked from the vines by patient hands. Sarah and the boys had strung the beans by the bushels, later threading them onto long strong strings. When the strings were several feet long, they hung them on pegs along the wall by the chimney. During the long winter, the family would remove the dry, brown, rustling beans from the strings and soaked them overnight in water. Early in the day Sarah would start them cooking slowly in a huge, black pot in the open fireplace, and by mid-afternoon, she would throw in a couple of large, quartered, sweet onions along with several chunks of thick bacon. By supper time, the delectable beans would be tender and mouth-watering.

The boys stood gaping at the strange spectacle before them: Men in heavy boots carrying food from their farm and their parents unable to do anything to stop them. Albert looked at General Marshall with hatred. The large steed he rode would no doubt become swaybacked from carrying him.

"I'll bet that bastard weighs over three-hundred pounds, Sarah, and I bet he eats that whole damned ham hisself." His bitterness was deep and unforgiving. They had both held their breath as the farm was ransacked.

The week before, a violent storm had uprooted a huge oak tree that stood near the root cellar. Albert had been too busy with other chores to hack the large limbs away from the opening. It was filled with potatoes, corn, honey and many other staples that would see them through the winter.

General Marshall rode back to where they stood in despair. "Just be sure you take that voucher to Knoxville to get paid for your goods," he restated. He was looking closely at Albert and Jonathan and fear began to mount in Sarah. "You two are mighty strong and healthy. You should be getting yourself into a gray uniform and protect your country. You could ride out of here on one of your own horses. The Federals will be comin' and they won't leave one last person alive if we don't stop them at the Big Sandy."

"I ain't got no quarrel with Yankees, and I ain't got no slaves," Albert retorted, and Sarah feared for his life as Marshall's eyes filled with a black fury.

Ruthie and Dan fared no better than their children. "Who can ride three-hundred miles with winter comin' on to get money for this no good paper," Dan raged. "They took everything."

Albert had gone to their farm as soon as he felt the soldiers would not return to his place. He arrived as the last remnants of livestock were being driven away. Ruthie was in tears, and Albert had never seen his father so angry. "They took it all. They say we are the South, and we have to help them. Damn them. How are we going to live?"

"It's all right, Paw. Remember that big ol' oak that blew down over the root cellar? Well, I never got around to clearing it away, and they didn't find it."

Dan was delighted with Albert's news. "Just be careful not to move them branches. I'm thinkin' we're in for more plunderin' before winter is over." Suddenly both remembered Daniel, and Ruthie knew what they were thinking when fear sprang into their eyes.

"Oh, my God, Daniel," she wailed. He and Ed Rife were on the trail back from Pikeville today. Earlier in the week Daniel and Ed Rife had loaded two horses with hides to sell at market in Pikeville and ginseng had been stuffed into any available space after the hides had been loaded. Eager customers waited for both. Dan looked bleak as he realized the Army would take the horses, money and the two healthy young men.

"Let's wait and see, Paw," Albert urged. "You know how Daniel and Ed can get lost in the woods. They can out-scout any scout." Albert knew his brother well.

The river port was a buzz with news of the war. "We're thinkin' there's gonna be a big battle right where we stand," an old-timer informed Daniel and Ed Rife. "You'd better shore 'nough watch your step going back into the hills. You could wind up in one army or the other. They all want young men and horses. They are fightin' like hell in West Virginia, and both sides want this here ol' Sandy to move supplies." The Big Sandy River would be fought and bargained for many times, and "The Dark and Bloody Ground" would again play host to a savage violence.

Daniel and Ed had heard enough to convince them to stay off the main trail and carefully weave their way home through the dense forest. When they were within ten miles of home, their sharp ears picked up the first sounds of movement. The two men melted further into the dense foliage and dismounted. Holding their horses to steady them, they watched General Marshall and his men march by and were amazed to see huge cannons being drawn by several horses. Two young scouts rode close by the spot where the two men were hiding, and they held their breath. Both unsheathed their hunting knives, but the soldiers rode on.

Daniel was saddened. "Those boys couldn't have been over seventeen or eighteen years old, and I reckon they don't want to fight any more than we do."

Ed Rife shook his head in disgust. "I can't believe our very own people are killin' one another. Did you see how those poor black souls were loading' supplies on the boats? They just kept their heads down and never looked up. Black as night they are, but they've got a soul just like us. Daniel, it just ain't right to own no other man."

Daniel shook his head in agreement, and the two moved out quietly, even farther away from the trail. Winter was almost upon the land and hiding in the forest would not be easy. Fortunately, the majority of hides, honey and ginseng had been taken down the river a couple of months before, and the cash was safely stashed away. Daniel and Ed wanted one last fling before the snows arrived, and their traps had yielded more than the usual number of pelts, but now the euphoria of their good fortune was dimmed.

"Those horses and cows come from our farms," Daniel muttered as they covered more ground. Just after dusk was settling, the two arrived home. Ruthie threw her arms around Daniel and sobbed.

"Thank God, you are home safe. We were so worried. They took everything, and we thought for sure they was gonna take Albert and Jonathan. A bunch of those boys looked like they ain't even shaved yet. I can't think that God is going to let our children go shootin' at each other. It's not right." Dan patted Ruthie on the shoulder to calm her.

"Maw, these men have to be hungry." He stirred the fire to bring forth big potatoes roasting there with chestnuts.

"They didn't find Albert's root cellar, and that's why we have potatoes."

"Damn them, Paw. They have no right to do that. How come they're taking from their own people?" Daniel said as he hitched a chair to the table with Ed.

"Albert went home to hide his last cow," Dan said.

Ed related how they had seen the Edwards' livestock with the regiment. "There was hundreds of them, and there was no way we could've sneaked in to get our animals. If this is how our own people are doing us, how do you reckon the Federals are gonna be?"

The Edwards family began in earnest to collect and store food for the winter. From the tallest pine near Albert's house they build a comfortable seat near the top with extra-large branches secured in place to further conceal the observer and posted a round-the-clock watch.

Fortunately, the bulk of the potato crop still lay in the ground.

Falling leaves had covered the large area several hundred yards in back of the cabin. It was swiftly emptied of vegetables, concealed in large bins and camouflaged.

The boys set about collecting plentiful nuts by the bushel. "We will always keep some sitting about in order to draw suspicion away from our bins," Sarah said, as she emptied large black walnuts, beech-nuts and chestnuts into containers by the fire. The bell was removed from the cow's neck, and she was hidden in one of the many caves dotting the area. The boys took turns carrying tall grasses and weeds to her. Her milk was still concealed under the rocky ledge of the stream. Wild turkey and rabbits were always on the roasting spit, but deer meat was smoked and well-hidden. They removed the shelled corn and other seeds from the hidden root cellar and stored them in ground bunkers lined with large stones. "This war will end one of these days," Albert assured his family, "and we're going to need our seeds to plant again. If they find 'em, they won't give a damn what we plan to do with 'em; they'll take 'em."

Each time they entered the root cellar, the entry was completely resealed with bushes and branches. The four boys became extremely proficient with their large slingshots. They carefully hoarded ammunition for emergencies and hunted turkey and rabbits with rocks replacing shells. Their bows and arrows had always been put to good use, and now they became larger and more deadly.

Henry was exuberant on one occasion when a deer had fallen with a large arrow driven into the skull through the eye. By the time he turned twelve, he was considered an expert marksman. In the past year, Martin had been gaining on him and the two spent hours perfecting their marksmanship. Henry was all legs and arms and beginning to look even more like his Uncle Daniel.

Their hoard of salt was safely tucked away in the hidden root cellar, and Sarah was thankful the boys loved to visit the salt licks and gather the mineral. They had spent a week at the beginning of spring with Daniel and Ed Rife extracting salt from the laden waters. Sarah and Albert had laughed when they arrived home with numerous bulging bags. "Do you reckon the springs are going to dry up, Boys?" Albert teased. Sarah wondered how she could manage cooking their luscious trout and bass without salt, not to mention curing and drying the game that abounded around them.

November turned warm after an early freeze and the family continued to store food in hidden areas. Sarah and Ruthie still gathered roots and other herbs but always with one of the heavily-armed men in the family.

***

News of fierce fighting between North and South was related by passers-by, some on their way to join Rebel forces and others making their way to the Union line. An uneasy calm came to the area with Christmas. Battles were raging in Kentucky and a horrendous loss of life echoed in both North and South as fighting accelerated in many states.

Sarah and Ruthie agonized over the possibility of the Edwards men marching into the terrible fray. Their plans had been made and rehearsed. The lookout in the well-camouflaged pine would give a warning, and the men would simply disappear until the Army rode by. Jonathan and Henry would go with the men. The recruits would be getting younger as the war continued.

General Marshall and his Confederates were being outmaneuvered by Colonel Garfield in the Big Sandy Valley. As General Marshall retreated to Pound Gap, torrential rain enveloped them and added misery to their trek through the steep mountains. As the defeated group struggled through the dense forest in the steady downpour, Jonathan gave the warning signal from his perch high above the timber. The men melted into safe, sheltered areas to wait out the passage. Sarah and Ruthie stood on the wide porch wrapped in heavy shawls and watched the men approach. General Marshall sat proudly on his horse, and his face showed no sign of defeat, only determination. He was sopping wet as he struggled from his horse, but he asked nothing for himself.

"I've got four men that can't ride any further. I'm asking you to please take care of them until they can travel." Sarah was about to say there was no room but stopped, as two soldiers bore one of the wounded to the porch. He had the gray look of death and his blood-soaked uniform clung to him, dripping with cold rain.

The boy's beds were quickly filled as each appeared to be more mortally wounded than the one preceding him. "Martin and Luke, quick, bring water in the wash pan and rags," Sarah ordered, as they began to remove bloody clothing. Marshall had left his heavy, dripping coat on the porch and paid no heed to his sodden tunic as he attempted to comfort his wounded soldiers. He bent to touch each man's head and to thank him for his heroism in the fight.

The two women gained a new respect for him at that moment. They could see the pain in his eyes as he bade the mortally-wounded men goodbye.

"General Marshall, there is turkey roasted on the fire and chestnuts by the hearth," Sarah offered.

"You will need food for these men and yourself, and I thank the two of you."

Turning back to Sarah, he spoke earnestly. "Mrs. Edwards, you must be very careful. There are gangs of cutthroats roaming all over the state and especially the Big Sandy Valley area. They claim to be first one army and then the other. They are killing and robbing everyone in their path, then disappearing into the woods. We have not been able to capture them. They take everything, even the clothes off their victim's bodies. If the menfolk are even in the home, they are slaughtered, but so far, they have not killed women or children. In some areas, the men of the house have simply hidden out until they take everything they want and leave. I am sorry I cannot offer you any protection. The Federals will be close on our heels, and we must leave."

"General, I thank you from the bottom of my heart for your warning."

Sarah felt great anguish as she watched the valiant and exhausted men shuffle along in mud-caked boots. Many wore makeshift bandages on their wounds, and she was overwhelmed with sadness as she watched them march toward the mountain pass in the cold, pelting rain.

Ruthie obtained the names of the wounded men and their families. "If they die, Sarah, I want you to write their families. If this was one of my family, I would want to know."

"I got a boy about your age, son," one gravely injured soldier said to ten-year-old Martin. "Let me have your hand."

Martin didn't hesitate and took the bloody, dirty hand in his. He finally released the hand an hour later when the death rales ceased, and the man was at peace. "I'm gonna write his boy a letter, Maw," Martin said, as tears flowed for the dead soldier.

It rained through the night, and Elkhorn Creek overflowed its banks, as it roared toward the Big Sandy. Thankful that their cabin had been built on high ground, they watched as milk pails and chunks of butter were swept from their hiding places.

"I have never seen it rain this long and this hard," Dan remarked, as the pelting rain continued through noon the next day.

In late afternoon, there was a slight letup in the downpour, and the men dug two graves. They lowered the bodies of two fallen soldiers into the wetness, and Sarah read from the Bible. Dan shook his head in disbelief as they trooped back to the shelter of the cabin. "We just barely took this land from the English and the Indians, and now we're already killing one another. God can't be too happy with us."

Ed Rife was keeping watch, and the four boys sat with their parents by the blazing fireplace. They could hear the two remaining soldiers moaning from the bedroom, and they were sad in their gathering. Dan and Ruthie had returned to their cabin for the night, and Albert felt great unease for them, but both insisted on going.

"There are some things we need to do. We'll be back tomorrow," Dan said. "Unless you are one army running from another, you're not gonna be out in this weather."

For days, the rains poured down, and the already swollen waterways were roiling with froth and debris. Sarah and Ruthie used their roots and herbs to counteract infection in the wounded rebels, and the powdered bloodroot eased their pain. Potato soup made with cream laden milk gradually added strength to their weak and battered bodies. Roasted, turkey and cold, sweet milk gave them new strength daily. Their gaunt and sunken faces began to fill out, and Sarah was surprised to see them looking ten years younger than what she had assumed them to be.

"I'm beholden to you, Ma'am," the young soldiers repeated again and again, as Sarah and Ruthie fed and nurtured them back to health.

The rains continued during the day, forming freezing sleet at night. Their treetop lookouts were changing every two hours, but Albert made sure it was manned around the clock. The armed gangs roaming Kentucky and the Big Sandy Valley were increasingly bolder, and the occasional passerby would speak of the horror left in their wake.

Luke and Martin were spending more time with the two recuperating soldiers. They showed their visitors their large slingshots and demonstrated their deadly aim. The two young men were impressed and gave the boys pointers that added to their exacting shots.

Two soldiers with extra horses arrived at the cabin after a week to check on any survivors. They removed their hats in the driving rain and knelt by the graves of their fallen comrades to pay their last respects. Sarah and Ruthie insisted on feeding the two young men a meal of roasted turkey and vegetables.

The two newcomers ate ravenously as Sarah packed the meager leftovers of the meal for their trip outward. She watched the young men depart as the rain slowed temporarily to a slight drizzle. She had become fond of the two polite and grateful young men, and she wondered to what dangers they were marching.

"They're not goin' far," Ed Rife spoke softly. His arrival had been so stealthy that Sarah was unaware of his approach. "They have bivouacked in the gap about six miles yonder and build lots of cabins. I reckon we are going to see one hell of a fight close by when the Federals come marchin' in."

Sarah had never felt more comforted by his presence than now. The roving and brutal gangs would be their bane, and she silently thanked God for sending Ed Rife to live with them. For the first time in days, the Edwards family ate supper together by the fire, as it spat and sizzled with large drops of rain falling through the chimney onto the fiery logs.

"Grandma, you reckon this is gonna be like Noah and his ark?" Jonathan asked of Ruthie. She deplored the absence of churches in the area and read the Bible to the boys whenever she could corner them for a few minutes. Martin decided God was trying to drown the cutthroats roaming the area.

"The soldiers told me and Luke how cutthroat gangs are plundering and killing families, and me and Albert are gonna shoot them with our biggest slingshots, and we're gonna use our bow and arrows, too." Luke was excited as he thought more about the venture. Sarah was shocked to hear the boys making such plans and admonished them severely. The soldiers had filled the boys with fear of the Federals, but the Union Army was immersed in bigger problems of its own.

***

General Garfield, ensconced in his headquarters in Prestonburg, watched the rain pelting the countryside day after day, as the water

79

rose steadily around their camp and the current kept rolling stronger. River banks blended into the countryside, as muddy and debris-laden waters roared louder with each passing hour. Farm animals with bloated bodies were riding the muddy crest of the waters as it rushed to the Ohio. Much of the countryside was submerged beneath fifty feet of water with only tops of trees breaching the surface. Leaden and murky skies hovered ever closer, and Garfield wondered if the sun would ever shoot its bright rays onto the sodden land again. Army supplies and stores of food were being swept away. Farms kept losing livestock. The situation became desperate with rapidly diminishing food supplies for the entire area. Garfield decided to take matters into his own hands over the strong objection of his officers.

He left his headquarters with only one aide to assist him and boarded a small skiff. His officers watched in disbelief as the two men steered the small craft to midstream and were instantly whirled away. The trip downstream was harrowing, as they dodged logs and lop-sided buildings flying by. Many were lodged on limbs extending out from huge trees. Garfield had worked as a canal boat boy and river pilot on the Ohio, and he prayed as he pitted his strength and expertise against overwhelming odds on the wild ride. The young aide was in awe of his commanding officer.

Immediately after arriving in Cattlesburg, Garfield wrenched the Big Sandy Steamboat from objecting owners, filled the large boat with supplies, and headed back upstream against a powerful current. It was an agonizing trip with water spreading for miles in every direction. He stayed at the helm for forty-four hours, delivering food as far south as Pikeville. He was lauded for his bravery by both Union and Rebels, winning support for the North from many southerners whose entire food supplies had been swept away. Garfield asked nothing from Rebels, as he furnished food for starving families, leaving them overwhelmed by his kindness.

The beginning of March blasted the area with subzero temperatures, freezing flowing water in its wake, with hundreds of fish staring glassy-eyed through the ice. The cold air came as a blast each time the cabin door was opened. Sarah had to tell the boys constantly to shut the door quickly. Torrential rains were replaced with large flakes of heavy snow that heightened fence posts and peaked the cabin roof.

Before daybreak, Ed Rife shoveled his way to the barn and placed a strong harness on a big reddish roan standing quietly in his stall. Ed had no idea who had owned the horse, or where he came from, but his owner had obviously been gentle and caring with the animal. The Edwards family found him drinking from the horse trough one morning and adopted him.

The sweet, dry, musty odor of hay provoked a peaceful and timeless sense of security, and Ed took his time connecting the single trees between horse and sled. He loaded the sled with longer logs for the fireplace and shorter wood for Sarah's cook stove and clamored aboard. Giving the long reins a gentle, rolling flip, the roan's strong legs plodded in and out of two feet of snow, as he dragged the cumbersome sled to the front porch where Albert waited.

He was barely visible in the waning light from the kerosene lamp glowing through a partially shuttered window. Large flakes of snow were still falling, and Albert knew it would soon be up to the horse's belly. Without a word, Ed passed heavy logs to Albert, who stacked them neatly atop the dwindling stash by the doorway. Silently, Albert hopped aboard the sled and Ed guided the struggling horse toward the towering pines. Stopping by the large lookout tree, they waited for Daniel to drop into the sled.

"You're sure welcome to that damned cold perch, Albert," he told his older brother. "I can't figure any fool out in this mess. Why don't you just set this one out for a spell?"

Albert merely shook his head and grasped a large limb, lifting himself from the sled without leaving footprints by the tree.

"Albert ain't gonna take no chances with his family, Daniel," Ed said, as they continued the circle to the tree line where logs lay sawed, and loaded the sled for the return trip to the barn.

On March fourteenth, Albert was astonished to see the Union Army wading through two feet of snow, as he watched from the lookout. He gave the warning call, and the men melted into the forest. Jonathan and Henry disappeared into the cave that sheltered their one remaining cow to feed and keep her quiet. They carried rifles along with bows and arrows.

Ruthie and Sarah left a large pot of stew simmering on the fireplace and did not try to hide the baskets overflowing with nuts. Again, they watched an army approach as they stood wrapped in heavy shawls on the front porch. Union scouts rode warily near the cabin. Their unshaven faces looked cold in the bitter wind, as struggling horses pushed through the deep snow. Their huge, heavy, bluecoats added some protection for the horses but the penetrating cold along with ever-mounting snow was taking its toll on the weary animals.

Martin and Luke watched the soldiers as they dragged logs from the edge of the forest. Wearing larger boots than usual, the boys covered the tracks of the men as they wrestled with firewood in tow. A dozen or so scouts circled the cabin and nodded to the two women. Sarah stood tall, proud and beautiful even in heavy boots and wrapped to her chin. Cold wind had heightened the color in her cheeks and her skin was radiant. A few strands of flaxen hair had escaped the heavy bun twisted neatly just above the nape of her neck, adding softness to her beauty. The eyes of the soldiers ringing the front porch reflected their admiration and also respect.

"We have to search your home, Ma'am," one of the young scouts spoke in an authoritative voice. "It's regulation."

Sarah stepped forward and opened the door gesturing the young men to enter. They tipped their hats to both women, as they stepped through the doorway. The huge fireplace with its crackling logs and bubbly stew enveloped the men with warmth and craving. After days of low rations and dragging through deep snow, it was almost overwhelming. "You are welcome to the stew," Sarah offered, seeing the look of hunger on their young faces.

"We thank you, Ma'am, but General Garfield does not allow us to take food from people," replied one of the men.

They searched the cabin quickly and trooped back through the front door. Albert held his breath until Sarah and Ruthie followed the soldiers onto the front porch. No one had even glanced toward his lookout, and he dared to breathe again. Sarah smiled and nodded her head to Ruthie as if in agreement to something the older woman had said. It was a signal that Albert waited for, and he thanked God again for the safety of his family.

All-clear was issued to the forward ranks of the Federals, and Albert stared, as hundreds of soldiers began to emerge from the forest. The mounted soldiers gave some relief to those on foot, as numerous horses trampled over the deep snow. Woolen strips of cloth had been tied over the Army caps to protect ears from cold and unrelenting winds that cascaded down the mountainsides. They looked cold, miserable and hungry, but they also looked determined.

Albert hugged the tree closer as the blue uniforms passed directly beneath his lookout. His heart thundered in his chest as horses bumped against the tree and quiet conversation filtered upward between the dense pine boughs. The headwaters of the Elkhorn Creek, so swollen from the many weeks of rain, was frozen solid, offering no resistance as the Army clamored over.

Albert tried in vain to count the number of soldiers but gave up. They seemed to swarm from all directions at once. He knew they far outnumbered General Marshall's men on his last trek through, unless reinforcements had joined him on the mountaintop. Daniel and Ed had quietly scouted the outpost and reported at least sixty log cabins being thrown up and the rebels dug in. Albert felt sick to his stomach watching the young men marching so steadily toward their death. He watched from his perch, as they treated Sarah and Ruthie with respect and carried nothing from the cabin. They are good men, he thought to himself, and very shortly, their blood will cover this snow. "God, how can you let this happen," he thought to himself.

General Garfield rode by on his large chestnut horse and touched his hat to the two ladies. Sarah was awed by his pride and strength as he sat straight in his saddle. Clear blue eyes measured them without any threat. His high, broad forehead formed a slight ridge over his eyes as heavy, bushy brows collected the light snow that had begun to fall again. His large features were framed in dark hair that had begun to gray in streaks adding to his dignified presence. Most of the soldiers followed their commander's lead and touched their hats to the ladies.

Garfield's victory over General Marshall's much larger force at Middle Creek had been the most significant battle fought in the Big Sandy Valley. As a result of his ingenuity and brilliant battle plans, he was promoted to Brigadier General. The same qualities and traits would propel him nine years later to the presidency of the United States.

"If this don't beat all," Ruthie said as the last of the long line of bluecoats disappeared into the tall timber heading toward Pound Gap.

"I have seen Garfield's picture, Ruthie, and I know of him," Sarah spoke quietly. "He comes from my area of Ohio, and they say he is a great man."

The clamor of horses and men had ceased for some period when

Daniel came to relieve Albert of his watch. "I reckon you saw it all," Daniel remarked, as Albert slid from the tree.

"There is sure as hell gonna be a fight," Albert answered. "And I'm thinking they're not gonna get to those Rebels up that mountain through two feet of snow. It's gettin' late, and I reckon there won't be any fightin' until mornin'. What do you think, Daniel?"

"Hell, you never know in this damn, crazy war," he answered his brother.

"You know, ol' Clyde Carter over near Pikeville? Well, one of his boys is fightin' with the South and that young one is fightin' with the North. Now what do you think about that?"

Albert simply shook his head in bewilderment and announced he was going to the cabin to warm his backside that was damn near froze off.

*****

General Humphrey Marshall watched through field glasses as the bluecoats mingled among the trees. Garfield had purposely kept the larger part of his men stationed behind a low rise and defended from view by a great number of very dense evergreens.

"Garfield is a brave man, but I won't give him this mountain," General Marshall stated to his lieutenant. "There is no way they can climb this steep mountain in all this snow. We'll cut them to ribbons. I think they will leave out of here before night falls again and carry their dead." He felt no threat to the rear of the perpendicular mountainside covered with impassable amounts of snow.

"I want my best riflemen posted halfway down this mountain behind the biggest trees and more rifles backing them up. It wouldn't surprise me if the blue colonel tried to pay us a visit in the dark."

The lieutenant shouted orders and Rebels began to take up positions behind shelters. Marshall watched his soldiers move quickly to his command and felt love for each man. They had rested for several weeks in the cabins as supplies and soldiers poured in. Garfield's men would be nearly frozen and exhausted after the long march from Pikeville. "Just let them come at my mountain," he muttered.

The Union Army sought shelter under the large pine trees, offering them some protection from the snow. The heavily scented pine needles supplied a softness for their bedrolls as the cold and weary soldiers sought a brief respite from war. The almost vertical sides of the mountain looming before them were ever-present in their minds. Garfield stood staring at the mountain long after dark, as clouds scuttled back and forth across the night sky. The snow had stopped momentarily, and the massive obstacle before him gleamed in the moonlight. Large pine boughs dipped their needles with several inches of fluff as bare limbed trees extended ghostly arms of snow. The beauty belied the horror of battle that would soon ensue.

His scout returned to camp with heartening news and Garfield knew he had to strike before dawn. Eli Wassom had hunted and trapped in these mountains for years and had agreed to guide Garfield through them. He had visited relatives in the Deep South on many occasions and was sickened by the sight of black people laboring in the steaming cotton fields, being driving by whip-lashing overseers. He loved his home and was saddened as he watched his Kentucky neighbors divide their loyalties between the two armies.

"There is gonna be hell to pay when this war is over," he told his wife. They had tended a small farm near Prestonburg for years, and his trapping helped to supplement their income. His two daughters had married and long since settled in California, and he offered up a prayer of thanks for their deliverance from the madness of this war.

"The South can't win, and the sooner it's over, the better it will be for the men out there fightin' it," he told his wife. Eli had been astonished to find no rear guard for the Rebels. He could hardly believe General Marshall would make such a strategic mistake. He had felt no threat from the vertical mountain, dense undergrowth and deep snow. Eli had crawled to the edge of the encampment and even listened to their conversation. On Eli's return to the Union Army, Garfield mapped his battle plan.

Shortly after midnight, Eli Wassom lead the Union Army to his hunting trails, and the tortuous journey upward began. For every step upward, they appeared to slide back two. Sabers had been left behind to eliminate any sound as men slipped, slid and sometimes crawled on their stomachs. One soldier cursed aloud as he grabbed for leverage and a huge blackberry vine sank long thorns into his woolen gloves. Snow began to obliterate any object more than three feet away with huge flakes gaining momentum and drawing a white curtain about them. Gradually inching upward, they almost appeared to be standing on one another's shoulders, moving in slow motion. Gnarled and twisting grapevines, buried within the snow, wrapped around unwary feet dragging many men to their knees as they fought their way through the dense and almost impassable snow and undergrowth.

Each was grateful for a slight reprieve, as they passed beneath towering pines with heavily needled branches keeping the snow at bay. Fear rose like bile to their mouths helping pump adrenaline into their exhausted and half-frozen bodies. Men of many professions and trades pulled one another over jutting rocks and piles of long, dead limbs. The snow helped to muffle the sound of snapping branches as they crawled steadily upward. Gigantic holly trees crowding beneath great pines crushed their needles against unshaven faces leaving long, bloody trails across cheeks and foreheads. They quietly uttered oaths, pushing the limbs away from those directly behind them.

The yawning, black mouth of a cave suddenly appeared before them as Eli held up his hand to stop. He stepped into the darkness and felt along the stone ledge for his flat bottle and quickly withdrew the cork to drink deeply, feeling the fiery moonshine descend almost to his toes. With the palm of his hand, he smacked the cork tightly in place and returned the bottle to its hiding place. "Just checking my supplies," he stated to Lieutenant Bonham. "I found this cave years ago and camp here on hunting trips. Have to chase a bear or mountain lion out, occasionally, but it's almost like my second home." He smelled of heady moonshine, and Lieutenant Bonham envied him.

The overhanging evergreens had kept the abutment next to the cave free of snow, and as the moon sailed behind the next snow cloud, Bonham scrutinized the black, glistening projections, and he knew what he would do when this war was over. He had been astounded by the large layers of coal veins, as he trooped through the mountains with the Army. As a geologist, he knew what lay beneath the surface, and it boggled his mind.

"How much farther?" he whispered into Eli's ear. It seemed to him they had already spent an entire night clinging to the mountain.

"One hour," his scout answered softly and the slow, agonizing climb continued. Eli stopped and signaled quiet. He whispered into Bonham's ear and disappeared into a blanket of snow. The soldiers had become completely snow-covered and appeared to be part of the forest, as their commanding officer surveyed the mountain in his limited view. Fear gripped him as he stood in the darkness. He had seen so many men drop at his side, he could only wonder why God had chosen to leave him standing. Would this be his last battle, and if so, how would it happen?

Richard Bonham was in his mid-thirties with a family, as were many of the soldiers under his command who were now perched awkwardly on the rough mountain. How many widows and orphans would emerge from the dreaded battle before them? Eli drifted soundlessly to his side to interrupt his thoughts.

"It's just like I thought, Lieutenant, there ain't nobody on rear guard. The far side of the mountain is loaded with fightin' soldiers and artillery, but nothin' in back."

"Jesus Christ," Lieutenant Bonham hissed. "I can't believe this," and his chest churned with new excitement. Word was passed down the mountainside and a white movement began upward. With deadly stealth, the Union Army began to move into position against the Rebels. Garfield could only wait in agonizing anxiety below as the snow continued to intensify and visibility was reduced to near zero. His ears strained for sounds of gunfire and many doubts loomed before him. What if Eli Wassom had missed a scout? What if Eli had simply been watched and a trap set?

He covered his near frozen face with a woolen scarf and breathed warm air into it to restore feeling in his cheeks. The night seemed to stretch into eternity, and his misery increased. Just as a cold and bitter dawn was arriving with heavily-leaden skies, a scout returned to report that all was in place, and the Federals were only yards from the enemy line.

Garfield did not relish what he had to do. He had met General Marshall in Washington a few years back and found him to be a remarkable man. He was fearless and would fight ferociously for his men. Their previous encounters had already established that fact. His ancestors had fought long, hard Indian wars and helped to defeat the English in the Revolutionary War. He was saddened to know their meeting on this brutal mountain, separating Kentucky and Virginia, would render them enemies forever. His cavalry was ready to start the attack and rode within view of the Rebel artillery, firing at the encampment but keeping their distance from return fire.

The Rebels lay down a strong barrage of fire as the Union cavalry circled back to the trees for the second time. The Federals had moved to a semicircle surrounding three sides of the compound under cover of darkness and watched as their comrades drew harmless fire that emptied Rebel rifles. The signal to attack came as a third volley was fired at the feinting cavalry. Lieutenant Nelson Lipps was first to sound the alarm. His initial reaction was disbelief, as he saw a surge of bluecoats pouring into the clearing surrounding the cabins. The valiant Virginian discharged his rifle bringing down the foremost Federal. The gray line met with blue in hand-to-hand combat.

Bluecoats broke through the gray lines as Rebels fought furiously. Lieutenant Lipps fought with superhuman strength. Grasping the barrel of his discharged rifle, he swung the wooden stock with devastating force as bluecoats fell before his onslaught, but then a shot caught him in mid-throat, and his partially severed head lobbed to one side. His huge body stood erect momentarily as several rifle shots smashed into his lifeless body. His blood flowed outward to meet that of his fallen comrades.

Sergeant Hughes screamed to General Marshall, "Run! There are hundreds, General, and we will need you later." The cold and partially clouded sun was just beginning to illuminate the horror of the scene, as Marshall urged his horse into a gallop with tears streaming down his large face. His last look back almost tore the heart from his chest. His brave and gallant troops were fighting against overwhelming odds, as they ensured his escape.

Tom Wright cried, as he held the lifeless body of his childhood friend, Joel Fleming, to his heart. The two had grown up together, and their lives had always been entwined. A rifle bullet through the chest had ended his young friend's life. Thomas placed the hands of Fleming across his gray Rebel, blood-soaked uniform, then rose to brush the snow from the knees of the bluecoat that he had chosen. He had not seen his friend fall, and he did not wish to know which of his comrades had struck the fatal blow. God, how he hated this awful war.

Three young Mead brothers stood shoulder-to-shoulder with bayonets and rage against the enemy. Isaac, Chester and Leon fought beyond valor, as their quiet and well-tended farm lay ten miles into Virginia. In sheer desperation, they refused to fall as they wrecked terrible damage on the Union Army. The tremendous onslaught was too much. Isaac watched through a haze of red as a bayonet welded by a huge Federal soldier disemboweled his youngest brother. The top of Isaac's skull shown white, as he slipped to his knees and lay next to Leon. The brothers died as they had fought, shoulder-to-shoulder.

The remainder of the southern Army fled into the forest with the Union Army in hot pursuit. Several Rebels had been captured and were placed in a larger cabin tied back-to-back, sitting on the rough-hewn floor. Shock and amazement registered on their faces as General Garfield issued his orders. "Take your dead and wounded to their families, and I hope I don't see you in this war again." His clear and steady blue eyes looked at them without malice, but his meaning was clear. General Garfield and his Army spent the night in the captured compound feasting on Rebel supplies.

Early the next morning, with all movable supplies loaded, they burned the sixty Rebel cabins to the ground and started their trek back to Pikeville. They carried their dead and wounded with them, nodding to the Edwards family as they again pushed through the snow and headed north.

CHAPTER 5

The frosts of April receded as May approached and the rich smell of freshly-turned earth scented the air as the Edwards family again plowed their fields. Two more riderless horses had been captured in the nearby woods and hidden in the cave with their one remaining cow. A tiny calf now stood by her side sharing milk with the family. The saddles on the horses bore caked blood and the Edwards men had a pretty good idea what had happened to their owners. The horses were put to the plows, and the family quickly planted a garden.

"I wonder who will reap the harvest?" Dan remarked to his two sons after they had covered the seed potatoes.

"The last time the two armies come by, they didn't take nothing," Daniel said, and each hoped silently the pillage had stopped.

News of bloody fighting between North and South slowly filtered down to them even in their isolation and murdering gangs of cutthroats continued their rampage. Their nerves had become taut on the lookout as they spotted billowing smoke in the distance on several occasions. Ed Rife and Daniel knew which cabins had probably been torched but were afraid to venture too far and leave the family without their protection.

The first day of June was beautiful to behold as the early morning mist lifted to expose blossoms of every shape and color. Excessive rains and heavy snows during the winter had fostered wildflowers in abundance. Creek banks were covered with masses of brilliant red and yellow blossoms, many poking between the leaves of large sprawling ferns.

Sarah and Ruthie walked by the clear stream as it gurgled its way downward, admiring the beauty crammed into every corner. "Would you look at that, Sarah?" Ruthie said, as she bent to lift fern fronds and peek at the clumps of blossoms pushing through. "A body would think the ferns are blooming," and the two women laughed. They hiked their long skirts above the wide bladed grass still wrapped in heavy dew, glistening in the early sun and returned to the front porch.

As they wiped excessive damp from their boots, the pristine stillness was shattered by a warning signal from the lookout. A terrible chill enveloped Sarah as she watched the men spring into action. "It could be the armies again," Ruthie spoke with wide-eyed fear, but neither really believed it would be the armies. The cutthroat gangs had been drawing closer each week as they encountered no resistance. The men had placed a large, flat wagon parallel to the cabin, loading it with numerous stacks of logs for the fireplace, and huge stumps had been rolled beneath the wagon to camouflage a rifle.

Albert quickly slid from the lookout as thirteen-year-old Henry replaced his father, scampering nimbly to the top with his bow and arrows slung across his back. The boys had been instructed by Albert on many occasions that they would not be permitted to use their arrows from the perch. "Your job is to signal if you see others coming through the trees. Do you understand, Henry?" Albert asked each time they had practiced the drill.

"Yes, Paw, I know what to do," the impatient young man had answered.

Sarah felt great unease as she watched his long legs disappear into the dense foliage. Jonathan quickly gathered his rifle and sprinted to a clump of large trees closest to the cabin. Oaks measured at least six feet in diameter sitting amid other huge trees. He was an expert marksman, but Albert wanted more than ample protection for his fifteen-year-old son, and the large trees would screen him well.

For years, Daniel and Ed Rife watched as Jonathan, with unerring accuracy, had brought down deer and black bear. He shared in

91

the bounty collected for the hides as his aim became more deadly. Jonathan checked his loaded rifles again and placed extra ammunition close to his right foot. Sarah quickly carried extra rifles to the wagon for Albert, as Ruthie rushed firearms to a pine grove for Dan.

"Oh God, Dan, please be careful," she rasped as she choked with fear.

"Ruthie, you be brave, honey, and just do like we have planned."

Through the years the family had collected guns and were precise in making their own ammunition. Ruthie had admonished them on occasions because of the great number of firearms the men had accumulated but never again, she vowed to herself, running quickly into the cabin. Albert reminded Luke and Martin to stay in the corner of the cabin, as he held Sarah briefly before leaving them to slide under the wagon and ready the rifles Sarah had placed there for him. Ruthie would stay hidden with the boys as Sarah answered the door. Daniel and Ed Rife would be concealed on either side. Ed quickly climbed to the attic to view the visitors and determine the situation. If it appeared to be either army, the men could simply disappear into the dark woodlands, if not, their stations were manned.

"God help and be with my family," Ruthie prayed softly, as she clutched Luke and Martin close to her heart.

"It's all right, Grandmaw, we can fight anybody," Luke insisted as he wiggled out of her reach.

When the alarm had been given, he and Martin had jammed their pockets with large, round stones. Oversized slingshots protruded from their back pockets. The family spent an agonizing fifteen minutes watching and waiting. Ed Rife spotted the two front riders with his spy glass and didn't like what he saw. He gave a signal to stay put, quickly descending the ladder to take his stance by the door. His rifle and a huge saber were held in readiness.

Two large horses emerged into view carrying two dirty and rough looking riders. As they sauntered across the clearing, several other riders appeared. Albert counted ten in all. A few of the men wore Confederate caps, but their rough clothing did not resemble a uniform of any color. They had encountered no resistance in the few cabins they had happened across in this isolated area, and their confidence had become bolstered. The two front riders dismounted at the front steps, dropping the reins of the winded horses that had been ridden mercilessly up the steep hills.

Rough boots clomped across the wooden porch, and a giant fist hammered on the strong door. The two men expressed no fear as they heard the latch lift, and the door open slowly. Sarah stood tall and very beautiful in her high-necked blouse and long skirt. She was instantly repulsed by the leering faces confronting her. The ruffian who stood closest to her reeked of moonshine, and his filthy clothes were even worse. His bloodshot eyes stared at her above a massive mustache and a matted beard streaked with tobacco juice. He looked Sarah up and down with an evident and undisguised hunger.

"Howdy, Ma'am. We are scouts fer the Rebel Army, and we're lookin' for supplies in this area. You reckon you could spare some eats and horses?" he spoke to Sarah, but his eyes were darting in all directions.

"We have no horses, and the armies have taken our food," Sarah spoke evenly, trying not to show her fear.

"Would your menfolk be about?" Their leering had turned to open lust.

"My husband is away at war," Sarah replied, as his ugly mouth widened in what could have been called a smile.

Without any warning, a huge arm shot forward, grabbing the neck of Sarah's shirt and ripped it to the waist. In an instant, the offending arm lay at his feet and a look of shock covered his ugly face as Ed Rife's saber entered his body just above the stomach and ripped completely downward. Daniel quickly felled his companion with a shot through the brain, as he slammed and barricaded the door shut. A barrage of gunfire erupted as Jonathan, Albert and Dan picked their man and saw him fall. The remaining five wheeled about wildly on their mounts trying to find the source of fire. Two horsemen started toward the wagon, and Henry feared for his father's life. He quickly strung his large bow and let an arrow fly. It went through the neck of the foremost rider who screamed as he fell from his mount. A fellow rogue, looking madly about for the direction of the firing, saw the arrow go flying by and lobbed a shot at the slight movement in the lookout. Albert quickly stopped the charge of the other outlaw bearing down on him with a shot to the chest that lifted him out of his saddle. Bullets from several rifles riddled the remaining three, as Daniel and Ed Rife exiting the rear of the cabin and rounding the corners, joined fire with the Edwards men.

Shocked silence closed in on the homestead, as the family gradually and carefully left their shelters, venturing toward sprawled and bloody bodies lying scattered in the yard. Only four horses remained in the clearing and they were quickly tethered as the remaining six galloped wildly away into the woods. Albert quickly entered the cabin to check on the family and was even more enraged as he viewed Sarah's tattered blouse.

"Sarah, I want you and Maw and the boys to stay in the cabin until we get that mess outside cleaned up. You hear me, Boys?" Albert asked the wide-eyed, frightened children. They merely shook their heads and, for once, had nothing to say. The men commenced to place the bodies together and knew what they had to do.

"That big sink hole over by the ridge would be best," Dan said. "We don't want nothin' washin' out of a holler later on. These bastards just might have buddies somewhere who could come lookin'." The men nodded in agreement and set about throwing bodies across the horses' backs. Daniel and Ed Rife dragged the two bodies from the front porch, and Albert picked up the severed arm, throwing it on top of its owner.

"Ed did that when that bastard tore Sarah's blouse off," Daniel related.

"That son of a bitch," Albert gritted his teeth, as he kicked the body lying on the ground. The men quickly collected all the guns and ammunition stacking it on the edge of the porch.

"A body can't have too many of these helpers," Daniel remarked, placing the last weapon on the pile. One body lay near the edge of the clearing and Daniel walked with Ed Rife as he led a horse to retrieve the outlaw. "We better tell Henry where we aim to be," Daniel said, approaching the lookout.

"I'll get that old rope laying by the tree to tie this son of a bitch to the saddle," Ed said. As he was reaching for the rope, a large drop of blood splattered across the back of his hand. It took Daniel only an instant to race upward on the limbs to where his nephew lay. Henry may well have been asleep so peaceful was his face. The one bullet fired into the tree had caught him square in the chest. His long legs hung limp on either side of a large limb as he lay forward along its length, and his young life's blood soaked into the thick rows of pine needles. Daniel stared at his beloved nephew standing in total paralysis. He rested his forehead against the giant tree as a fog hung before his eyes. Ed Rife climbed the tree after him and, standing on the branch below, shook his friend's rough trouser legs fearing Daniel would fall from the tree.

"Henry's dead, ain't he?" Ed spoke quietly. Daniel nodded numbly, eyes reddened in his waxen face. "You go on back down, Daniel, and let me bring Henry," Ed urged. Daniel very slowly, with stiffened limbs, started his downward descent.

Sarah instructed the boys to stay with Ruthie as she quickly buttoned another blouse. Shutting the door, she walked to the front steps. Albert, Jonathan and Dan had just lead the horses to the forest edge as Sarah surveyed the yard and was thankful the bodies had been removed. Only one body lay sprawled near the lookout and a horse stood close by. Even from the distance, Daniel looked strange standing next to the large tree. As she watched, two long, lifeless legs emerged beneath the lower limbs, and Daniel held his arms upward to receive Henry.

A terrible scream erupted from Sarah's throat as she raced toward them. Ed Rife held her son tenderly under one strong arm, working his way slowly toward the ground.

"Oh God. No, no. Please God," Sarah prayed as she flew toward her son. The two men placed him on the ground and his distraught mother collapsed at his side. "Henry, Henry," she cried over and over as she sat on the ground and gathered him to her bosom, rocking to and fro with his blood staining her chest. The stricken family had rushed to the scene, and the two younger brothers stood sobbing. Jonathan knelt by his mother and smoothed Henry's hair with a big, awkward hand, tears streaming down his face. Ruthie stood crying silently, comforted by Daniel and Dan as Albert knelt by Sarah. Albert looked disbelieving at his young son and could not conceive of his being dead until he saw the vacant look on his wife's face.

"Sarah, honey, you have got to let go now. Henry is gone," he said gently to his grieving wife. She appeared not to have heard him as she continued rocking her son's lifeless body.

"Let her be, Albert," Ruthie spoke. "She rocked him when she brought him into this world, and it's only fittin' she rocks him when he leaves it."

The sun blasted rays straight downward as the men carried Henry to his bed. An eternity had passed since Sarah and Ruthie had hiked by the creek bed in the early morning and their peaceful lives now lay shattered.

Weeks passed, and their lives slowly began to rebound. Sarah visited Henry's grave each morning, pulling weeds away from the large headstone, as Ruthie planted more flowers.

They buried him close by the two fallen Confederates, tending their graves as well. "Young men shouldn't be dyin' like this," Ruthie said, "and God knows how many others are gonna join them." The hearts of both women were heavy. Cumberland Gap, lying some fifty miles south of the Edwards' farm, bordering Virginia and Tennessee, became the passage for both armies in a seesawing battle for the area. Rough trails and valleys were littered with dead and wounded as the bitter struggle held the country in its maw. Destruction of bridges and burning of many buildings knew no precedent as the lifetime work of so many went up in flames. Wild and unabated roaming gangs continued their hit and run atrocities at will. Few were captured by either army, but when they were they were executed immediately. October slid gently over the hills with its ethereal brush of magic, etching and burnishing an array of unbelievable colors. The Edwards family harvested each vegetable immediately as it matured and their hidden bunkers were bulging.

"I never expected to see us gather this crop," Dan admitted as they pulled huge ears of corn from the stalks and hauled them to their hidden storage bins. Their horses now numbered six, and the young calf now stood halfway up the cow's side. The corn would see them through the coming winter.

"I feel as though Henry is here with us watching and helping us with our chores," Sarah said to Albert as they stood by his grave with a descending sun glowing red into a bed of brilliant colors that lay in wait for the first bite of frost. Albert gathered her sadness to him and held her as silent tears flowed for their beautiful son.

Henry's gregarious personality was sorely missed during the summer, and Martin cried at night when he looked at the empty bed next to him. Jonathan had become moody, and Albert knew he was struggling with the bitterness of his younger brother's death.

***

In March of 1863, four young Rebel soldiers who had become separated from their regiment during fierce fighting, stopped by the cabin during a heavy snowstorm to seek shelter. "We don't mean no harm, Ma'am," they said to Sarah, who stood completely guarded by the doorway. "If we could sleep in your barn tonight and beg a bite of food, we will be on our way." Ruthie, hearing a familiar voice, arose from the corner where she had been crouched with the boys and peered at the tall young man speaking to Sarah.

"Lord a mercy, Amos Wright. I can't believe my eyes. You have growed up and put on a uniform."

"I'm mighty glad to see you, Ms. Edwards," he beamed as he clasped her hand in a bear grip. Dan stepped around the doorway still holding his rifle in the crook of his arm to welcome Amos Wright. The little boy that Dan had known now towered over him.

"Amos, it is sure good to see you," he said as he looked at the cold and weary young man. "You just bring these boys on in here to the fire to get thawed out." The four young men insisted on removing their heavy coats after they had shaken the snow from them.

"We've been walkin' for three days, and we didn't sleep much last night. We got to get back to Virginia and find General Morgan again," Amos informed them.

By the time they had settled their cold and weary bodies by the fire, Dan handed each a steaming mug of sassafras tea well slugged with moonshine. They were so effusive in their thanks and appreciation, Dan was embarrassed. Jonathan, Luke and Martin listened eagerly as the Rebels gave details of battles and senseless bloodletting. Amos' father operated a gristmill in Pikeville, and Dan had first met him there years ago.

"It has been burned to the ground, Dan," Amos said sadly. "Our own Army had to do it 'cause Colonel Garfield was movin' in with that damn Union Army, and we couldn't let them have any supples. Bridges are bein' burned all over Kentucky along with courthouses and warehouses. We won't have anything left when this war is over," he stopped long enough to slug heavily from his steaming drink. "The Federals have got a lot more men and guns that we have and ol' Abe Lincoln is callin' for thousands more."

The young men were relaxing with moonshine, and their bodies warmed as they described the battles throughout Kentucky, Virginia and Tennessee. "The worst yet is the bushwhackers and outlaws," Amos stated. "They're a killin' all over." Albert was surprised when

Jonathan's eyes blazed with a fierceness his father had never witnessed.

"They killed my brother," Jonathan grated. The young Rebels offered sympathy to the family without asking too many questions. They knew, without being told, that other family members were nearby and, also without being told, that the bushwhackers had never left the farm. Sarah and Ruthie loaded the table with warmed venison stew containing large chunks of potatoes and carrots. They opened cans of pickled corn and green beans and reheated shucky beans, loaded with onions and chunks of rabbit. The pigpens had been emptied by Marshall's men on their first trip through and the bacon that Sarah loved to use for shucky beans had to be replaced with whatever game happened to be on hand. The family sat quietly and watched as the young men devoured everything in sight. They used large wedges of thick, yellow, steaming cornbread to rake food onto their forks, hardly taking time to chew before they shoveled in the next mouthful.

"I thank you for all your kindness," Rufus said, over and over in between large mouthfuls of food, and his friends were just as effusive. Jonathan and his younger brothers decided Rufus and his buddies should have one night's sleep in a bed. The young men objected but Jonathan steered the four to the bedroom where they slept almost as soon as their exhausted bodies touched the mattress. Ed Rife eased into the cabin after the men were asleep, while Daniel manned the watch. Ed unrolled his pallet by the fire with the boys and slept almost instantly. Jonathan lay awake for hours looking into the glowing embers and thinking. At sixteen, he now stood two inches taller than his father, possessing his father's huge shoulders and very long arms. He had also inherited Albert's tremendous physical strength and a quickness that was akin to a mountain lion. Sarah, watching his growth spurt the past few months, worried about him. He would pass for twenty-years-old, and his restlessness had given way to a new determination that haunted Sarah.

Next morning, the cold winter sun sent bright rays skittering off crystalline snow as quiet enclosed the farm. The stream, barely flowing under ice and whitened rocks, slid silently to far rivers. Several inches of snow had fallen during the night leaving a smooth, unmarked surface. The four young Rebels were busy devouring stoneground buckwheat pancakes with honey and butter when Ed Rife sounded the signal from the lookout. Several men were approaching. Dan immediately informed their visitors of preparations and advised them to head for the cave in case it was the Union Army. The young men hastened to the hidden cave, but Amos backtracked to hide in the trees with Jonathan.

"If I see a blue uniform, I know the way to the cave, and if it ain't, you're gonna need another rifle," he stated and Jonathan was grateful. Albert had sprinted to his station beneath the wagon. Daniel and Ed Rife stood on either side of the front door. Dan was in place behind a sheltering pine grove as three riders moved into view. They were young men and wore the Confederate gray. "Well, I'll just be damned," Amos Wright said, beaming with joy. "That there's ol' Sue Mundy."

Amos Wright rushed from the giant oaks, throwing his hat in the air and giving the Rebel yell. Sue Mundy rode toward his friend and dismounted, each giving the other a bear hug. "These people are friends of mine, Sue. They've fed us since yesterday and even put us in a bed last night," Amos explained and motioned for Jonathan to come forward. "They have been visited by both armies and a gang of cutthroats, so you can see why they are hiding,"

Jonathan came forward first and shook hands with Sue Mundy. The two young men could well have been brothers. Sue Mundy was only four years older than Jonathan but aged and hardened beyond his years. They were the same height and build. Mundy's thick, blond hair was dingy and matted under his gray cap from weeks of riding, while Jonathan's hung clean and thick to his shoulders. Jonathan outweighed him by at least twenty pounds as life on the run kept the other men lean.

"Sue and his men go after bushwhackers and any bluecoat that comes along," Amos explained to Jonathan, and Mundy didn't miss the quick interest that jumped to Jonathan's eye at the mention of bushwhackers. Almost forty young men had entered the clearing and none were more than twenty-one years of age.

"We're ridin' back to the Big Sandy, Amos. You want to go with us?" Mundy asked, but Amos shook his head. "I need to stick with General Morgan. Me and my buddies got separated in a fight four days ago, and I'm figurin' he needs us bad. We took a whipping from the damn bluecoats."

"I would like to ride with you, Mundy," Jonathan announced,

and an instant camaraderie was cemented between the two.

"Maw and Paw won't like it, but the bushwhackers killed my little brother last year, and I would like to rid these mountains of them varmints." Mundy knew Jonathan would be a formidable foe. His strength and determination were obvious, and his reason to fight would carry him beyond the bounds of mere action. He felt a pang of embittered remorse for his lost youth and innocence as he looked at Jonathan and dreaded what the coming struggle would do to him.

"I reckon you can shoot a straight gun," Mundy stated.

Without blinking an eye, Jonathan replied, "the straightest."

Dan and Albert emerged from their hiding places to shake hands with the young leader and invite him into their cabin. Like the other young soldiers, he removed his heavy coat and boots before entering the spotless home. Sarah was immediately struck by his resemblance to Jonathan. She would have guessed him to be at least twenty-five years old. Having joined the Rebel forces at fifteen, he had fought fearlessly, suffering as he watched friends fall at his side, maturing under frightful circumstances. She offered him food, but he declined and was anxious to be on his way. Jonathan wasted no time in saddling one of the best horses that he tethered to the front railing and quietly entered the bedroom to collect his belongings.

By the time Mundy retrieved his boots and coat from the porch, Jonathan stood by him with a bedroll and his rifle. He was wearing his heaviest coat, and his saddlebags bulged with extra clothes. It was a moment before the Edwards family could comprehend what had happened. Sarah's hand flew to her throat, but no sound escaped as her face turned ashen. Albert was shocked, but deep down he knew Henry's death had changed Jonathan. He knew his son's quest would forever be to stop bushwhackers before they hit other families. Sue Mundy tipped his hat and quickly left the porch, so the family could say their goodbyes.

"Jonathan, do you realize what you are doing?" Albert asked, but he already knew the answer.

"Paw, I have to do this for Henry," he answered his father gently, knowing the anguish he was causing them.

"You won't be just fightin' bushwhackers and murderers, son. You are taking on the Union Army, and the South is losing the war," his father informed him. But it was all to no avail.

"Maw, I will come home as soon as the fightin' is over," and he folded Sarah in his strong arms.

"I love you, Jonathan," was all she could say, as tears washed over her face.

Ruthie and Dan, who stood close by, hugged their grandson and wished him well. Ed Rife and Daniel walked with him to his horse where Martin and Luke stood patting the animal. He shook hands with the four of them and promised to be home soon.

"Luke, you and Martin can have my biggest slingshots and arrows," he called back as he galloped to Mundy's side, and the two look-alikes disappeared into the trees. Sarah was brokenhearted as she watched her firstborn ride into the midst of misery and savage upheaval.

In Union-controlled counties, the crime of supporting the Rebels was enough to have one's entire property removed, the person jailed and, in many cases, executed. After capturing Pine Mountain, General Garfield had been assigned to another regiment, and his fairness was sorely missed by the habitants of the Big Sandy Valley.

Union bushwhackers were given full rein by some illicit Union officers. Their robberies, outrages and insults toward any who might even be sympathizers to the Rebel cause were overlooked by the provost guard. For every Union soldier killed by southern guerrillas, four Confederate officers were taken from the Federal prison and shot. Kentucky was in turmoil, and the savage cruelties heaped by both sides on one another were unequaled, even by the bloody Indian wars.

Sue Mundy and his avengers scouted for outlaws and Union bushwhackers, taking out bluecoats as they came across them. Jonathan, with youthful strength and daring, entered the fray with a terrible ferocity to avenge his brother's death. His deadly aim with a rifle awed his comrades. His years of perfecting his marksmanship, with his Uncle Daniel and Ed Rife as his instructors, took a great toll on the enemy. When a distant scout or lookout had to be eliminated, Jonathan would execute his assignment with perfection.

On several occasions, they arrived at farms to find bushwhackers had been there shortly ahead of them, and the scenes sickened the young men. Jonathan's rage increased as he became obsessed with destroying the men who murdered families with no defense. In July, General Morgan was in the vicinity of Louisville when Mundy and his command made contact with the famous general and his two brigades. Jonathan was introduced to Morgan and the general welcomed him to the camp. Mundy and Jonathan were chosen along with thirteen of their fiercest fighters to make a wild and ferocious flying wedge into one-hundred and fifty Northern militia to soften them for Morgan's two-hundred men who would be close behind. Their charge was so frightening and so devastating, the entire militia was pushed back to the town of Salem in Washington County. The deadly aim and slicing sabers of the completely wild and savage-looking young men caught the militia completely off guard. It was Jonathan's first encounter with such a large force, and he was exhilarated by the experience.

Morgan's men scattered the enemy completely, burning bridges on both the Ohio and the Mississippi Rivers. The depot was set ablaze and railroad tracks destroyed. General Morgan thanked the brave young men and encouraged them to remain with his command, but Mundy was anxious to get his men back to eastern Kentucky and into the mountains.

As they journeyed eastward, devastation was rampant. Crops lay destroyed in the fields and citizens in most of the small towns cowered in their homes. Most public buildings had been burned and bridges sheered from their moorings. Approaching Cattlesburg, the forty young men were divided into groups of four and five to approach the town from different directions and rendezvous at their appointed destination. They were now in Union-held territory and every move was dangerous. Mundy led his men to a large, old barn that looked totally unused. Entering the gloom behind the shuttered window, he tapped lightly on a metal post supporting the loft. A movement overhead produced a tasseled head and a large musket leveled just below it.

"It's me, Becky," Sue Mundy announced, "and don't point that thing down our throats." A giggle ensued, and a young girl of seventeen or eighteen slid from the hayloft. She was dressed in men's clothes and boots with straw lodged in her blond curls. Jonathan stared in wonder at the pretty, young girl standing before them. His trips to the river towns had been curtailed by the war, and the sight of a girl after almost three years left him openmouthed. Their flying travels across country left little time for girl-watching.

"Men, this is Becky Lane. Some of you have met Becky and some haven't. She helps to feed and hide us." She smiled shyly at the tired, dirty and hungry young men as she pulled a lever and a large portion of the floor slid back slowly. Jonathan was dumfounded as Sue Mundy led his mount down the steep ramp and the others followed. They traveled through a wide, dimly lit tunnel for at least two-hundred feet before angling upward.

Two heavy oak doors separated as they reached the top of the rise. Men and horses entered an enormous, brightly-lit cavern filled with people busily engaged in many activities. Women of every age and size bustled about. Some were cutting and rolling bandages as others sewed uniforms and patched older clothes. A heavy boot over a large iron foot was being hammered by a hefty, buxom woman in her late forties. Mundy led his men to another large cavern connecting with the first one where several horses were tethered to a heavy railing as they munched on hay.

Kentucky was honeycombed with caves throughout the entire state, some small, some very large and splendorous. Huge stalactites adhered to the extremely high, vaulted ceiling lending an eerie and sparkling beauty to the area. Jonathan was completely awed. He had never seen anything so large and so beautiful. There were numerous caves near his mountain home but none of this magnitude.

On returning to the first cavern, a young and very beautiful woman flew toward Sue Mundy who clasped her tightly in her arms, kissing her hungrily. She returned his kisses totally unabashed by their audience. She finally squirmed from his arms and led the hungry young men to tables laden with food. Mundy and his betrothed disappeared, as his followers indulged in the feast.

It had been months since Jonathan had eaten a freshly-baked biscuit, and he managed to inhale three as he loaded his plate to overflowing. Several elderly women urged them to eat more as they poured large glasses of milk as quickly as it disappeared. The young men slept peacefully through the night on clean pallets spread on fresh straw. A stream ran through this section of the cave, reflecting the long projections that had clung to the high ceiling for eons. The men rested and ate their fill for two days, as they explored the many beautiful rooms throughout the underground chain of caverns.

Jonathan made plans to bring Luke and Martin back to see the wonders he now beheld. The two boys were always finding new caves near their family farm and were always anxious to show them to their big brothers. Again, he felt the pain of losing Henry, who was always exploring newfound wonders.

The soldiers were given clean, gray uniforms, which they donned after splashing clean in the icy underground river. As they prepared to leave, each man was presented with a large bundle of food and a warm farewell.

For the next several months they entered forays up and down the Ohio River, ferreting out many cutthroats and bushwhackers, showing no more mercy than the ruffians had shown the helpless farm families. The atrocities were bloody and barbaric on both sides. Jonathan was sickened one night as a young Cherokee youth returned to their hidden camp with a fresh scalp still topped with a Union cap. He was suddenly very homesick for his family and the quiet solitude of the beautiful mountains. He sorely missed trekking through icy streams, collecting trapped beaver, and shooting bears as they fed on abundant nuts and berries. The Edwards family was stashing the magnificent furs in the hidden cave to sell after the war ended.

Mundy, sensing that Jonathan needed to see his family, urged him to go home for Christmas. His trip into the hills was fraught with hazards, and he barely missed the Union Army and bushwhackers on several occasions. He arrived on Christmas day as light was beginning to outline smoke rising from the cabin. He sounded the signal to whoever was keeping watch when he came within earshot, and Ed Rife waited by the clearing. He rushed forward with a bear hug by the time Jonathan had left the saddle.

"God damn, it's good to see you, boy," Ed declared, holding Jonathan at arms' length to look at him.

"It's mighty good to see you, Ed," Jonathan said. "Is everybody all right?" he asked, almost fearfully.

"They're doing good, Jonathan, and they'll do even better seeing you this Christmas mornin'. You go on in, and I had best get back to the lookout. We've had visitors a couple of times since you've been gone, but nothin' we couldn't handle," Ed laughed as he patted his young friend on the shoulder.

Jonathan clamored back on his horse and rode to the front railing just as Albert opened the door to get an armload of firewood. For a moment, his father was stunned. Jonathan had lost weight and his blond hair was matted beneath the gray cap. For a long second, Albert thought he was looking at Sue Mundy. He left the porch in one long bound and practically pulled his son from the saddle. Sarah, noticing the open door, looked on the porch and then shrieked with delight when she saw Albert hugging their son.

Jonathan sat by the huge, familiar fireplace basking in the attention of his family. Martin and Luke fired one question after another as his grandparents and Uncle Daniel showered him with loving attention.

"I just had to come home and see everybody. Sue Mundy understands. He's got people that love him, too." Snow fell in abundance for the next few days, and the family was content to hold Jonathan to their bosom.

It was a saddened family that watched him depart into a world of brutal violence and mayhem. Albert rode with his young son for several miles, reluctant to let him go. He looked at the grim-faced young man by his side and ached for his son. They finally said their good-byes, and Albert watched until the forest completely enclosed his boy in its depths. Tears streamed from his eyes as Jonathan disappeared from sight, and Albert knew he would lose another son.

In June of 1864, Sue Mundy, with Jonathan and thirty fighters, tracked a large force of Federals, as they settled in for the night at the mouth of Beaver Creek. Planning to swing by the Edwards' farm on their way to the Cumberland Gap, they met General Morgan's scouts and alerted them to what lay in their path. They were heading straight to the Union camp.

Morgan came through Pound Gap instead with twenty-four hundred Rebels under his command and with Jonathan guiding them, slipped by the large Federal forces continuing to Mount Sterling. Jonathan's trip home was aborted as word reached them of atrocities being committed against numerous citizens in another area. The South was losing the war. Kentucky lay trodden and helpless. Neighbor fought against neighbor, and many families suffered a rift that would never be mended. One never knew who could be trusted. Deception was commonplace.

Such was the case in middle December as the young adventurers rode the dangerous highway. A force of one-hundred Union soldiers lay in wait, and many of Sue Mundy's young followers fell to the ambush. Of the thirty young riders, only half managed to escape. Jonathan sat his horse but died in Sue Mundy's arms after they had reached safety. Mundy wept bitter tears for his young look-alike and adopted brother. They had known one another for such a short time, but it seemed as though Jonathan had been there all along. He placed his friend across his horse and headed toward the Edwards' farm.

Daniel, manning the lookout, recognized him even before he cleared tall timber, and he also knew what was enclosed beneath the heavy blanket that was tied to Jonathan's horse. Sliding from his perch, he walked with Mundy to the cabin, both nodding to one another, saying nothing. Daniel opened the front door and motioned to Albert as he stood by the fireplace. Again, a young Confederate with matted, blond hair and lean body sat his horse by the front step. He raised his eyes to meet Albert's with tears pouring unashamedly over his gaunt face. Albert lurched from the steps and placed his hands on the rough blankets covering Jonathan's body as he sobbed. The family came through the door into the midst-shrouded morning, again agonizing over the death of a young man. Sarah stood tall and erect, as if she would not bow to sorrow again. This time, it was she who comforted Albert as he had comforted her with Henry's death.

Sue Mundy left after he had helped the men cover Jonathan's grave, riding toward his own untimely death. In early March, as Mundy and Henry Metcalf gave aid to dangerously wounded comrades, they were surprised and captured by fifty Union soldiers near Webster in Breckenridge County. Mundy wounded four Federals, one mortally, and refused to surrender until promised he would be treated as a prisoner of war. The promise was broken. He was captured on Sunday morning, taken to Louisville, tried on Tuesday and convicted of guerrilla action. He wrote a long and very beautiful letter to his lovely betrothed, then marched to his execution. He was hanged on Wednesday, March 15, 1864, at 4 p.m.

The Edwards family grieved for the young man and were again sickened by the wanton waste of so many young lives. Pound Gap was again used by both armies as they fought furiously for southern soil in the waning months of war. Early October of 1864 brought hundreds of soldiers to the Edwards' homestead.

Dan, along with Luke and Martin, spent the morning raking huge potatoes from the loose, black earth. They planned to load the potatoes into large sacks and haul them to hidden storage bins. Daniel gave the signal from the lookout, but before Dan and the boys could clear the field, several hundred Union troops came tearing through the forest. General Burbidge was close behind his scouts and didn't even glance in the direction of the Edwards family who had flattened themselves against large trees to escape being trampled by the fiercely driven horses. Albert felt as though he had witnessed hell itself as the foot soldiers came in waves.

Half-starved, they grabbed at the freshly dug potatoes, eating any soil clinging to them as they were gulped down in huge bites. The stacks were quickly devoured and soldiers dug in the field with bare hands for more food. Some of the soldiers simply dropped and lay still where they had fallen. Many of the wounded were born by their comrades, but those who had fallen would travel no farther. Shouting and shooting from the ridge by hundreds of Rebels on the heels of the Union Army, explained the quick passage by the bluecoats. To the surprise of the Edwards, the Confederates retreated back into Virginia. Most food had been wrested from the steep mountains and the Rebels needed more supplies. In a few short minutes, the Edwards family field had been cleaned of potatoes, and the earth completely torn up. Death rode the hills and hidden valleys, marking passage with misery and wrath.

Torn between two loyalties, Kentucky reeked with injustice. General Burbidge did not use Colonel Garfield's tactics with the unwilling border state. He served as a tyrant who unleashed monstrous injustices on the people. He ordered executions on a whim and even on unfounded rumors. The Edwards family struggled with their terrible loss and sorrow. All of their plans and preparations had failed to protect their children from the encompassing agony that infiltrated every valley and isolated hilltop. Ed Rife felt he had lost two sons, and his pain was deep. In April of 1865, the Civil War ended, leaving bitterness and more brutalities to come. Hundreds of thousands of men had died.

***

Despite their horrendous loss during the Civil War, the Edwards family faired better than many people in the South, especially Kentucky. It had been one and a half years since Jonathan's death and a great sadness hung over their lives.

Albert spoke quietly to Sarah who was becoming more depressed each week. "We still have our home and two healthy sons, Sarah. Nothing will ever replace Henry and Jonathan and our hearts will always hold a big, empty space. We do have livestock and several able-bodied men to do our farming and timber cutting. It's sad to see the number of widows and orphan children who have not only lost the breadwinner in the family, but their homes have been burned to the ground."

"I am trying, Albert," Sarah said, seeing the concern in his eyes.

"We all are, Sarah," Albert said as he wrapped her tightly in his arms. Albert had just turned forty and lines of bitterness were etched into his face. Somehow, he should have been able to save their two sons. He should have been able to spare Sarah the misery of losing two fine boys, so young they had never had time to taste life.

As if she could read his thoughts, Sarah held him at arms' length, looking into his intense blue eyes that she so loved, now burning with anger for the injustice that had been heaped on their family. His handsome square jaw was clenched, and Sarah began her own recovery.

The skills honed through the years now served them well, and in the spring of 1866 they planted their fields once again and harvested abundant crops. They hoarded beautiful pelts in several caves, awaiting the proper time to sell them. Rogues and bushwhackers still roamed the area, but their isolation sheltered the Edwards to a degree. Along with Ed Rife, they still added to the big sink hole on occasions as they were ever vigilant.

Ruthie and Dan continued to live with Sarah and Albert, and amazingly enough, their cabin still stood. The family did not deem the situation safe enough for the two to live alone. Ruthie was a tremendous source of comfort to Sarah after the deaths of Henry and Jonathan. The two women visited their graves often, praying as well for the young soldiers buried there. The seasons evolved and the horror of war began to ease.

**

In 1869, to the surprise of the Edwards clan, Sarah gave birth to a beautiful baby girl. She was thirty-nine years of age and had not expected to have another child. Her childbearing had simply ceased after the four boys.

Ruthie was ecstatic. "It's a sign from God, Dan. He knows we need young life in this home again."

Dan gave her a sly smile, "I don't think God had anything to do with it, Ruthie."

"Dan Edwards, you old reprobate," she answered with her eyes twinkling.

Sarah was delighted. Her step quickened and spontaneous laughter was again her companion. Baby Amy was long-limbed with red-gold curls. She had dark-blue eyes that sparkled above a perfect nose, and a small rosebud mouth was the sweetest.

Luke at nineteen, and Martin, eighteen, were enthralled by the beautiful child. When Sarah gave the baby to the boys to hold for the first time, Ruthie rocked with laughter. "She won't bite, boys," she said to the rugged, young men.

"Gramma, was I ever that little?" Luke asked, looking at the tiny form barely taking any space at the top of the crib.

"You were all about the same size, Luke," and her grandson shook his head in amazement.

The loss of their two older brothers had been traumatic for Luke and Martin. Daniel and Ed Rife kept the two boys busy cutting timber, hunting, trapping and building bigger and better barns all over the meadow. Luke was especially proficient in fine carpenter work.

A room was added for Ruthie and Dan while a small cabin close by sheltered Daniel and Ed Rife. The two men had built the cabin just after the war started and it was a favorite hangout for Albert's boys.

Amy was lavished with constant attention, and she awarded her admirers with beautiful smiles and gurgling. Ruthie and Dan found new meaning to their lives, keeping watch over their ever-moving and beautiful granddaughter.

"Amy looks like her Grandmother Liddy," Ruthie informed Sarah one day as they sat on the front porch sewing and watching the long-legged child racing about the yard.

"I do wish my mother could have seen her," Sarah said as tears came to her eyes. Liddy had died in an outbreak of influenza just after the Civil War ended.

"I can still see your mother just stepping over logs when we looked for medicine plants. I had to find a toehold and climb." They both laughed at the memory, and Sarah's mood lightened.

The family had hoarded ginseng roots for years and finally took them to market. The prices had increased dramatically, and the family continued to gather the much sought-after herb. Numerous stacks of pelts and furs were purchased by European buyers and the Edwards family prospered.

Sarah and Ruthie agonized over trips from the hills into the river ports. Robbing and thievery was widespread and trappers were waylaid going into town with their wares. The Edwards family devised a defensive system along with Ed Rife. They rode in a diamond-shape formation, each man with a pack horse carrying hides and ginseng. A front man would precede the group, while each side was covered and the rear was guarded. One signal from any direction would bring the men to bear on that position. The attackers would be eliminated, and the slight mounds in the forest went unnoticed.

***

Turbulence with animosities was running amuck, again promoting the legend of Kentucky as "The Dark and Bloody Ground." Those who had lost friends and family members to the Rebels and Rebels who had lost loved ones to the North were all too eager to right the wrongs. Each nuance was weighted by former friends, neighbors and family members, and many times, blood was shed senselessly for some assumed or vague insult. Feuds erupted that would last through a century. The Edwards men and Ed Rife encountered many dangerous and hazardous situations on their trips back and forth to the river ports. The single ambusher in the dense forest was their greatest fear. Albert was the only one who had not been shot out of his saddle, but they all managed to survive. The diamond formation worked well.

Beginning in the late 1860s, reconstruction and new building abounded. Much of the South lay in ruins and Kentucky faired no better. Lumber was in great demand and buyers swarmed into the mountain area to encourage production. Sounds of busy saws and axes resounded in the quietness as giant trees were felled and hauled to the river by strong oxen. The Edwards family placed their brand on both ends of logs before floating them down stream to market. Luke and Martin followed the logs to port, collecting payment when the trip ended.

CHAPTER 6

Richard Bonham, true to the promise he had made to himself during the Civil War, now stood at the Breaks of the Cumberland Mountain watching Russel Fork Creek, swollen by the usual heavy spring rains, hurtle through its channel. The year was 1871, and he hoped the bitterness and agonies of the Civil War had lessened here in the mountains. In early March of 1862, he had stood on this exact same spot in bitter cold and deepening snow with the Union Army under the command of General James A. Garfield. They had stopped for the night before continuing their march to Pound Gap and an encounter with a well-fortified Rebel force. None had any doubt that General Humphrey Marshall would defend his stronghold at any cost on the top of Pine Mountain. Richard and several scouts had journeyed through the five-mile channel of the Breaks to the Virginia side, checking for any possible Rebel infiltrations. They had been awed by the incredible passageway towering sixteen-hundred feet above them. The narrow gorge was even more impressive now than he remembered.

Richard had been preparing for this journey since his first day home from the Civil War in 1865. He had kept his excitement and discoveries from everyone but his wife, Elizabeth. His first duty had been to pay off debts incurred by his family during his service in the war. Working long hours in extra surveying and always looking for extra fuel sites, he scrounged every dollar possible.

Elizabeth shared his excitement, knowing that with his expertise in geology he had truly stumbled upon great treasures. Their savings grew rapidly, but at the end of six years he needed more. The venture he was planning would require every penny he could raise. In the last year, he had borrowed from their families and mortgaged their home in order to buy up quietly as many mineral leases as possible in the Big Sandy Valley.

Elizabeth had been dead set against his coming back to the mountains alone, but Richard had a great sense of urgency to complete his survey and needed to do it by himself. His appearance had changed in the past several years, and he doubted anyone would recognize him. He now sported a heavy mustache and beard, well-streaked with gray. His dark brown hair had thinned, and his wife had managed to put twenty pounds on his undernourished body within a few months after his return. Pennsylvania was booming, and Richard knew what he had to do.

His survey through the Big Sandy Valley had already produced findings beyond anything he could have imagined. During the Civil War, as his unit had seesawed back and forth in battles through the valley, he had come to believe the area held uncommon treasures. He had managed to collect several samples of coal to take back to Pennsylvania for testing. Some of the ore proved to be so highly volatile it could be lit with a match. Never in all his years as a geologist had he found anything so exciting. He knew the best part was yet to come. The area in and around the headwaters of Elkhorn Creek was extremely rich in visible outcroppings of coal and he had a gut feeling the coal seams would prove to be enormous. With heavy spring rains, he was forced to travel and survey only on the west side of the Big Sandy River. The stream was roiling with runoff water from the steep mountains, and numerous logs riding the crest made crossing impossible. He had climbed higher on the mountainside after nearly being crushed by a log that had been propelled from the crowded waters like a cannon. Young mountain men following their logs to market barley gave him a scant acknowledgment but stared at his pack horse with strange instruments protruding from the saddle bags. Richard found himself touching the heavy service revolver snuggled close to his body, concealed beneath his coat. He knew feuds had erupted in the hills and that cutthroat gangs still roamed about, but this job had to be done. Huge steel mills in the northern states required gargantuan amounts of coal to fuel the giant furnaces that forced rivers of fiery, molten metals into molds of every description. The Industrial Revolution was in full swing and the urgency to collect volatile fuel was growing by the day. Richard knew where the coal lay buried. The treasure had lain undisturbed for millions of years guarded by the hulking shoulders and precipitous sides of Pine Mountain.

In 1869, Richard became almost frenzied in his efforts to get back to Kentucky. On May tenth of that year, two locomotives rested nose-to-nose on a stretch of track in Promontory, Utah. A solid-gold spike was driven into the track, marking the completion of the nation's first transcontinental railroad. An iron road now connected the nation. Richard knew that thousands and thousands of miles of new rails would be laid throughout the northern and southern sections of the entire country.

In the early 1860s, an amazing discovery by Henry Bessemer, a British inventor, was to catapult the country into an unprecedented period of industrial growth. He had discovered that a blast of hot air directed at molten iron would greatly reduce the impurities, creating a superior steel. The "Bessemer Process" was off and running. It meant that steel was now cheap enough to mass produce, and the American steel industry grew at a staggering rate. The brittleness of iron had required frequent replacements and excessive cost. New and stronger rails were now pouring off the assembly lines in steel mills and high-grade coal was sought after to fire the gigantic furnaces. Endless uses for steel abounded. Bridges would last for decades and skyscrapers could be built. Steel was replacing iron in industrial machines and improving objects like hammers and stoves.

The beauty of the mountains in early May was nothing short of splendorous, but Richard could only concentrate on his goal. He looked at large stands of enormous trees, but they didn't register. Still, he could not deny the aroma of millions of blossoms and inhaled deeply as he finally came to a large cabin nestled in its own meadow. Suddenly, Richard remembered this cabin at the foot of Pine Mountain. His first impulse was to turn around and backtrack, but it was too late.

Watching him closely from the front yard by the hitching rail were two tall mountain men, and he noticed another in the side yard. Martin, in the lookout, had spotted the lone rider with a pack horse and signaled as much to the family, that was still wary of brutal gangs. Richard decided to ride directly up to the group.

"Howdy," he said, approaching the two men.

"Howdy, stranger," Albert Edwards answered in a friendly tone.

"Richard Bonham. Been riding up along the Big Sandy doing some surveying."

Albert sized him up and felt no threat. "You're welcome to water your horses and rest if you like."

"I thank you, my horses drank their fill from a creek we just passed, but we could use a rest. It has been a long ride," Richard said, as he dismounted and tied both horses to the railing.

"This is my son, Luke," Albert said, and the young man towering over his father shook Richard's hand with a clasp that made Richard cringe.

Ed Rife sidled over to the group, measuring Richard with a cold stare that sent chills down his back. "What are you looking for in these hills?" he asked.

"I'm checking out coal deposits that I have found all the way along the Big Sandy River. I just kept following the trail, and I'm wondering just how far this line will go." It was only a small lie, and he prayed the penetrating stare of the other man could not pick up his discomfort.

"We are just about to eat our supper and any peaceful traveler passing through is welcome to our table," Albert said.

Richard remembered the open and sincere hospitality of the mountain people after Garfield had shown them kindness and consideration. If they felt comfortable with strangers, they would open their doors to them. He also knew they could turn deadly when threatened. He was relieved to be invited into their home, and he was especially happy to sit down to his first home-cooked meal in several weeks. He was taken aback at seeing Sarah again and up close. He remembered seeing her, years before, standing tall and composed surrounded by Union Scouts.

"Sarah, this is Richard Bonham, and I told him he could share our supper if that is alright with you."

"Of course, Albert, and welcome to our home Mr. Bonham," Sarah extended her hand to Richard, as he tried to mask his great surprise at hearing her northern accent.

"Thank you, Mrs. Edwards, but I must warn you, I am one hungry man, having camped for several weeks."

Richard was glad his face had been wrapped in a heavy woolen scarf that day, as he rode next to General Garfield in the bitter cold on their way to Pound Gap. He now counted six men in the household, as Luke disappeared, and Martin joined the group. Both Dan and Daniel were cordial to him, and his instinct had been right. He was being watched by other eyes when he stood talking to Albert in the yard. He willed himself not to stare at Sarah's long, lithe body as she gracefully circled around the table seeing that everyone was fed and offering second helpings. Two-year-old Amy sat next to her adoring grandfather. When Sarah finally seated herself next to Albert, Richard did stare openly at her beautiful face, flushed from the heat of a hot stove and steaming food.

Her first question stopped his fork in midair. "Mr. Bonham, could you tell me what has happened to General Garfield since the war. He comes from my area of Ohio, and his many kindnesses to the people here in the mountains will not be forgotten. We get little news of what is happening outside Kentucky."

Richard dared to breathe again. "I come from Pennsylvania, Mrs. Edwards, but I have heard that General Garfield is knee-deep in politics in Washington."

"I hear that can get you killed in Washington," Martin said.

Silence fell at the dinner table, and Ruthie gave a lengthy compliment to Sarah's stacked apple cake.

"Albert, I plan to camp somewhere along the creek bank if that is alright with you folks. I'll just pitch my tent beneath some of those big pines and try not to be a bother. I will need to be in these parts for at least two weeks or maybe more."

"You can bunk in the cabin out back with me and Ed if you like," Daniel said. "We have extra cots for when the boys get kicked out of Sarah's kitchen," and the family roared with laughter.

Richard moved into the cabin and became a very grateful fixture at the dinner table.

Martin and Luke were extremely interested in how he measured the depth of coal and spent several days carting his equipment up hillsides and into ravines. The morning after his arrival, Richard was told about the deaths of Jonathan and Henry, as the two brothers guided him past the graveyard.

"Henry was killed here on the farm when he was only thirteen years old by a band of thieving cutthroats, but Jonathan was killed in northern Kentucky, right next to the Ohio line, by the Union Army," Luke said.

Richard breathed a sigh of relief. For one awful moment he had been afraid Jonathan might have been killed by his troops, or even himself, in the Pine Mountain battle nine years before. He was surprised that the Edwards had not asked him about his part in the war before offering their warm hospitality. He admired them even more, knowing what they must have suffered with two young sons buried nearby.

"So, what are you going to do with all these figures?" Luke asked a few days later, as he peered over Richard's shoulders, watching him record his findings.

"I hope someday to mine this coal, Luke." Suddenly, he decided his young helper could help even more. "I plan to buy up mineral rights in the area, and I would like to have you help me, what do you say?"

"You mean you would pay me?" Luke asked.

"You bet I will. Would five dollars a day be alright?"

"Sure would, and I sure am glad Martin wandered off."

After the first few days, Martin had lost interest, and Richard still needed help in carting his equipment up the steep hillsides.

"It will take about two weeks to complete all the testing, Luke, and then we will have to find a courthouse. I need to know who owns all the land I have been testing, so I can make them an offer for what is beneath their property."

"Shoot, I could do that easy. Not that many people, and I know most of them. I can start writing down all the owners when we do the tests, if you like."

Richard cursed himself because he hadn't thought to ask the boys before. In his eagerness to test, everything else had been pushed aside and with good reason. He was staggered by what he had discovered. In the last few days, he had found that two seams alone would produce one billion tons of extremely high-grade coal. He was disbelieving at first and retested, but the first readings had been correct.

"This will be well worth mining," Richard said to Luke after several more days of testing.

"Do you plan to do it with an ox cart up those steep hills?"

"No, we will have to build a railroad through these mountains, and it will take time."

"Well, I'll tell you Richard, I will have to see it to believe it, and I think you are wasting your money."

Richard laughed to himself. "I still plan to spend my money, Luke, so we may as well get started."

The mountaineers were astounded that anyone would want to pay good money for something that lay beneath their land, and yet, the land would still be theirs to use as they chose. Richard paid the landowners one dollar per acre for their mineral rights, and Luke shook his head in disbelief.

"For such a smart man, Richard, you are doing something just plain dumb."

When Richard had purchased as many mineral rights as possible, he packed his equipment and made ready to leave the mountains. "Mrs. Edwards and Albert, this is to pay you for my room and board for the past few weeks," and he placed a fifty-dollar bill on the well-worn kitchen table.

"We will not hear of it, Richard. You have overpaid Luke, and we did nothing more for you than we do for any decent, law-abiding traveler," Albert said, and Sarah agreed with him.

"It has been good to catch up on news about the country, and you gave us too much money for the mineral leases," Sarah insisted.

In the end, Richard left the money on the table and carried with him a guilty conscience. He had bought several hundred acres of mineral rights from the Edwards clan at one dollar per acre, much below the northern prices.

Waving goodbye to the family, Richard left the Elkhorn Valley with the knowledge that unfathomable riches lay in the area. The barriers to mining the coal were formidable. Mountains would have to be breached and sizable towns constructed for large numbers of miners and other personnel to oversee the mammoth operation. It would take at least a century to mine the unbelievable motherlode.

His survey had yielded findings beyond belief. The area contained at least one-hundred and sixty-seven billion tons of the highest grade coal known to man.

His next step would be to convince monied moguls on the East Coast to buy his mineral leases and begin to mine the rich deposits.

***

Richard Bonham returned to Pine Mountain in 1875. He was encouraged by the fact that conglomerates were impressed by his discoveries but dismayed that no one would attempt the difficult task of bringing railroads into the area. The monied moguls had sent scouts into the region to assess the situation, but backed away after reading their reports. The cost of bringing railroads and highways through mountains into narrow valleys was a formidable project, even though the rewards would be great. Richard knew it would happen, eventually. The cavernous jaws of the mighty furnaces within steel mills were devouring thousands of tons of coal each day and the available supply would eventually dwindle. Again, he had managed to raise more money to invest in mineral leases. He brought with him a young man who had attended some of his classes at the University of Pennsylvania, but had eventually majored in history. Randolph Adams had stayed in Pennsylvania during the Civil War, but returned to Kentucky to teach in Lexington. Richard had contacted him, hoping to secure his help in developing the mining industry.

"It would propel Kentucky to the top of the industrial world. Randolph, just think of the factories and businesses it would promote for your state." Richard spoke, not knowing that he would not live long enough to view the catastrophe that his vision and venture would bring to the enchanted forest.

He knew Randolph had an innate love for his state. He had agonized as he watched an extended family fight on both sides during the Civil War. Slavery repulsed him, but he could not bring himself to fight against the South.

Kentucky was struggling with Reconstruction, and he agreed to accompany Richard to Pine Mountain. If it would help to open up new industry for his state, he was happy to help. He even envisioned steel mills and factories that would create numerous byproducts from coal. Kentucky could become a land of great opportunity. Randolph had never

118

been to this area of the state, and he was overwhelmed by its beauty. The warmth of June had fostered mounds of brilliant blossoms, and he could easily imagine the tons of fruits, nuts and berries that would soon be harvested. They arrived at the Edwards' cabin at noon, and Richard knew they were in for a treat. He could smell Sarah's biscuits.

"Welcome to our home, Mr. Adams," Sarah said, "and this is Amy."

Randolph was taken aback by Sarah's beauty and her gracious greeting. It was not what he had expected here in the middle of the wilderness.

"It's good to see you again, Richard," Albert said. "We were beginning to think you had gotten lost back up there in the North."

"Just working to make a living, Albert. I don't have the resources you have," he said, indicating a large kettle of venison stew bubbling away in the fireplace.

Luke pumped his hand, and Richard could see the dollar signs in his eyes. "I guess you're going to throw more good money away."

"Right you are, Luke. You up to climbing more hills?"

"I've been picking up more names down the river when me and Martin run our logs to market. Thought you might want them."

"You bet I do, and I really appreciate it."

The two men would have Daniel and Ed Rife's cabin. The two were away for a few days, checking their traps for beaver and bear skins. Their pelts were still sought and the stealth of the two men equaled that of their prey, enriching them by the year.

"Do these people know you fought with the Union Army, Richard?" Randolph asked as soon as the cabin door was shut.

"No, they have never asked, and I think they are just glad to have it over. Sarah is from Ohio and admires General Garfield. They lived in the same area." Richard went on to explain Sarah's background and her return with Albert, the death of their two sons, and his own trip to Pine Mountain in the war.

"Good God, they have been through so much, and yet, they seem to harbor no ill will toward anyone," Randolph said.

"They have plenty of ill will toward the cutthroat gangs that prey on these isolated farms, and I'll bet they have buried more of those bastards than you can count."

"Good riddance," Randolph said and promptly went to sleep. As he slept, he did not dream that six-year-old Amy would play a great part in the life of his unborn descendants.

In ferreting out the landowners downstream, Richard bought more mineral leases, and Randolph bought fifty acres near the "Breaks of the Mountain." Randolph was overwhelmed by the fantastic wonder of nature, and he could hardly wait to build a cabin on his property. He and his young wife, Cynthia, could spend their summers there.

Richard headed back to Pennsylvania with more leases and determination to twist more arms.

***

Randolph Adams was unable to get back to the land he had purchased at the Mountain Breaks for five years. Another baby had been born to him and his wife, Cynthia, who struggled with six-year-old Joel and the energy of one-year-old Dorothy. Randolph maintained a year-round teaching schedule and corresponded frequently with Richard Bonham. He had come to believe, as Bonham did, that Kentucky was, indeed, blessed with the richest raw resources in the world. He was astounded when his friend had told him of his survey in the Big Sandy Valley and the extremely rich veins of coal at the headwaters of Elkhorn Creek. He had talked to legislators, governors and other monied groups about the feasibility of developing the huge oil and coal deposits lying in the southeastern mountains, but the obstacles were daunting and interest in developing the mammoth project waned.

His stories about the awesome breaks and unbelievable game had eager friends ready to help construct a cabin they could visit periodically. Finally, in 1880, with a good carpenter in tow, Randy set out for the mountains. Three friends and several pack horses carrying building supplies made up the procession. Arriving at their destination, his friend, Wade Anderson, stared at the majestic spectacle before them.

"Randy, old boy, I thought maybe you were exaggerating this place, but now, after seeing it, there is no way you could adequately describe it," and the others nodded in agreement.

On their trip into the mountains, the group had no problem finding game to cook over their camp fires at night, and their greatest decision was choosing between large fish, turkey, quail or bringing down a young deer. It was a hunter's paradise. The trip had taken two days, but no one objected.

"We could live here all summer without going out for supplies," Patrick Green had surmised, and the group cheered.

"I have a second-semester teaching job starting in July," Randolph said.

Patrick answered, "We will miss you, Randy," and the hills rang with laughter.

With an expert carpenter directing them and even bullying them at times, the cabin began to take shape. At the end of three weeks, a large structure was completed. Abundant rock and clay were crafted into a handsome fireplace, and Doc Wingate congratulated the four novices on their abilities. They forgot their sore muscles and blistered hands when the group viewed their sturdy project.

They stayed on for another week, hunting, fishing and swimming in the cold streams. Deep ponds had been formed by large boulders that had been dislodged from the sides of the breaks, and the five men felt like kids again, as they dove into the icy depths, scattering the multitudes of fish.

The pack horses were loaded with smoked game, and the men left their retreat, already planning a return trip.

Randolph could hardly wait to bring Cynthia and Joel to the cabin. Dorothy was a bit too young for the trip, but eager grandparents could be counted on to keep her in tow for a couple of weeks next summer. The family spent several weeks in their retreat each summer and each was more glorious than the last. Young Joel became part beaver, playing in the cold creeks and ponds.

CHAPTER 7

"What did you bring me?" was always Amy's first question when her brothers returned from running logs downstream. Martin gave Amy a large box on one return trip and she tore into it immediately. "It is so pretty, Martin," the seven-year-old said, holding her new, ribboned dress next to her body.

"Anna helped me pick it out. I told her what you looked like, and she knew right off what you needed."

"Who is Anna?" Amy asked.

"A very pretty girl that I know in Prestonburg." Sarah and Ruthie raised eyebrows and asked for more details.

"I met her several weeks ago. We are just friends. Her dad is the sheriff, and they even invited me to supper on Friday."

"And where was Luke?" Sarah asked.

"Luke and Susan came to supper, too. She's Anna's best friend."

In 1876, with savings from their logging business and trapping, Luke and Martin were able to begin their own construction company, which flourished as the two parlayed their energy and strength into the building boom. In 1878, both married their sweethearts and settled in Central Kentucky. Daniel and Ed Rife did the log runs but preferred trapping and timber cutting.

When Amy was eight, Dan happened to come across a young

palomino, and he knew Amy had to have the beautiful animal. He spent months training the mare, and it was everything he had hoped it would be. The golden horse, with its near white mane, was the perfect mount for his granddaughter. Her long, slender limbs, and her heavy, red-gold braid hanging to her waist brought tears to his eyes as he watched the two race about the homestead. The first time Amy touched the filly there was a special bonding.

"Oh, Grandpa, she is so beautiful. Thank you, thank you," Amy said as she clasped her thin arms around his waist. Anytime she was near the animal, it would nuzzle her hand, her back and even her face. The entire family watched the show of affection and delighted in the antics.

"Grandpa, I know what her name has to be," Amy announced one day after spending the afternoon with the young mare. "I'm going to call her Kissey, because she really is trying to kiss me."

Dan laughed in spite of the serious look on Amy's face. "A horse doesn't know how to kiss, Amy," he chided her.

"She does so know how to kiss, Grandpa, and besides, when I sat by the horse trough today, she lifted her hoof and put it in my lap." And Dan had no doubt it had happened.

"I think Kissey would be a good name for her, Amy." He was not about to disagree with her.

She would arise early in the morning and spend hours feeding, currying and combing Kissey's mane. Afterward, she would climb onto her back and ride without a saddle. She had no need for a bridle but guided the beautiful young mare with gentle, loving hands entwined in the freshly combed, white mane.

Amy missed her older brothers and was determined to ride the log runs with her father, knowing that at the end of the journey, both Martin and Luke would be waiting with presents and open arms. By the time she was eleven, she had enlisted the support of her grandfather, Dan, who could never resist her coy schemes. After much hassling and arguing with Sarah and Albert, Dan convinced them that he and Amy could well ride the river road and be of great help to Albert.

Before the last log was placed in the roaring waters for the trip downstream, Amy was aboard her horse streaking toward the river with Dan at her heels. At almost eighty years of age, Dan was as thin as a rail and looked years younger. His strength had diminished considerably, but he could still carry his own load and sit a horse as long as his sons.

Albert admitted that it was nice to be able to toss his reins to Amy or Dan when he had to leap from his horse in a hurry. A small log jam was much easier to correct than a large and dangerous one. He no longer had to trek back upstream to collect the animal or have him meander away when there was no time to tether him immediately. Running logs downstream could be an extremely hazardous situation, but the rewards were great.

Amy traipsed through the woodlands with Sarah and Ruthie collecting abundant herbs and gathering bunches of ginseng for market. Sarah encouraged her daughter to read the books she had brought from Ohio and many others bought at the river ports.

Luke and Martin were urging Sarah and Albert to let Amy come to Louisa to attend high school, and Sarah knew the time would come. Amy's arithmetic was very good, and her reading ability was increasing daily.

***

The Cantrell family lived several miles from the Edwards' farm, and Albert liked it that way. The parents were hard-working people, but the seven boys ran wild. Their moonshine was the best in the country, and the boys drank almost as much as they sold, which was plenty. The Cantrells lost four sons to the Civil War. They fought with the Rebel Army. The remaining three sons loved nothing more than a fight with a Union sympathizer. Levi was the youngest, and as far as Albert was concerned, the wildest.

As a small girl, Amy had watched Levi race recklessly by their farm on his great roan and fell in love with him. His longer black hair flew as free and as wild as he on his large mount. His wildness was in stark contrast to her reserved father. When Amy was eleven and Levi twenty-one, he had stopped by on one occasion to visit momentarily with her father. Amy came forward to pat the horse's nose as it drank thirstily from the horse trough. Levi lifted her gently and placed her on his broad saddle. She blushed furiously and fell even further in love with him. He left her to sit aboard until the horse had satisfied his thirst and then galloped away without even a goodbye. She watched through the years as his exploits infuriated fathers of many of the girls who admired him.

Levi came from a mixed heritage of French, Indian and German. The combination lent itself to courage, cunning and a striking appearance. He stood six feet, five inches tall with his huge frame enclosed in massive muscles. His dark brown eyes held the phantom promise of paradise, and his heavy, black mustache gave sparkle to his strong, even white teeth.

***

In 1881, Daniel took his father to Prestonburg as they collected money for timber, hides and their ever-popular ginseng. Dan was amazed to see a large town rising from the ashes of war. He hardly recognized the place he had last seen some twenty years ago. Business was flourishing and lumber buyers from around the world swarmed over the loaded docks. Beautiful hardwoods from the hills were in demand for building throughout the South and the world.

The Japanese were obsessed with large, cherry logs and watched with fretful eyes as they were lifted from the water and placed aboard large wagons to be hauled to the nearest depot. They would be shipped to Japan intact in their protective bark. The Japanese would use every fragment, even the bark, to produce medicinal products. Their famous Yamaha pianos would be created from the exquisite lumber. Tender, artistic hands would design the instruments into world-renowned treasures. The deep, red wood with beautiful, dark, elusive grains, polished to a satin finish, reflected ivory keys that would increase in value for centuries to come.

Talented artisans from France, Italy and Scandinavian countries gathered huge walnut logs and vied for the desireable burls. White oaks and ash would dazzle furniture buyers throughout the world as gifted artists produced furniture that would grace castles, private homes and businesses. The mountains would not miss their beautiful products yet, as massive limbs from crowded splendor unfolded into the newly available space, but the reckoning would come.

Unfortunately, visitors from so many faraway places brought disease with them, and Dan was dying of cholera before he arrived back home. Ruthie recognized the symptoms immediately and insisted on returning to their cabin.

"I'm so sorry, Ma. I saw some of this at Prestonburg, but I thought it was just a flu. Pa has been vomiting all day and his bowls are really running off. His fever is a lot worse than it was this morning, and he is cramping something fierce. I tried to get him to stop and let me go for help, but he wouldn't hear of it."

"Daniel, don't blame yourself. You and Pa did what he wanted to do. You take off those clothes right now and burn them, then get yourself in that creek with a big bar of lye soap and scrub from head to foot now," Ruthie commanded and Daniel could not remember her ever speaking so forcefully. "Get the horses and saddles under the lower waterfall and then stake them off to themselves for several days."

Amy was distraught with the news. "Mama, grandma told me that cholera nearly always kills people when they get sick with it. You won't let Grandpa die, will you?"

"Amy, we will do everything we can."

"Let me go and help them, Mama. I am strong and healthy," Amy begged.

"No, Amy, you must not. Your grandmother does not need to worry about you, too. She needs all of her strength for Dan."

Albert, Daniel and Ed Rife kept a close watch on the house from a distance. Ruthie was adamantly opposed to any of the family coming near them. She kept Dan alive for almost two weeks, then they practically died in one another's arms.

It was a crushing blow to the family and Amy missed her grandparents terribly. She kept watch by their grave for several days while gathering wild flowers from the creek banks to adorn their final resting place.

Daniel and Ed Rife rode the huge logs downstream one last time in 1882, a year after Ruthie and Dan died. A wagonmaster, heading west with a large wagon train, spotted the two men in Prestonburg. At 60 and 63 years old, they both looked years younger, projecting strength and fierceness. The wagons were in great need of shotguns and guides, and the two were promised a large tract of land in California.

"We're gonna have railroads into these hills and right up to our front porch," Daniel told Albert, after hearing the plans in Prestonburg. "The trappin' is just about done for, and I'm hankerin' for a big spread of my own."

Sarah, Amy and Albert stood with heavy hearts as Daniel and Ed

Rife bade them farewell in the early morning mist. They understood the unfettered spirits of the two fearless men, even though a large part of their lives had been torn from them by their departure.

Sarah and Amy helped Albert with the fields, and the usual crops were gathered again. Amy was a joy to both parents, filling a lonely void left by all the departing family members. She loved the songs of the streams as pure, crystalline water rippled from mountain top springs. On warm afternoons, she would sit on lush grass, dipping her bare feet in cooling water, watching miniature waterfalls wreathed in rainbow colors. Plucking daisy petals, she would singsong, "He loves me, he loves me not" and think of Levi. Pa will kill me, she would think, but continue to throw petals into the swishing water.

**

In 1883, Randolph Adams and nine-year-old Joel traveled to the cabin alone to hunt and fish for a few days.

"Joel, do you think you could stay out of the ponds long enough to take a little trip with me in the morning?" Randolph asked.

"Sure, Dad. Where do you plan to go?"

"There are some very nice people about twenty-five miles south of here that I would like to see. I met them several years ago, and I thought you might enjoy seeing that area. It's the headwaters of Elkhorn Creek, and an enormous cliff juts out from the mountain above it."

"That sounds like fun. Do they have any children?"

"Their youngest child was a very pretty six-year-old when I saw them last, so she would be about fourteen by now."

"Oh," Joel said and lost interest.

Sarah and Albert were delighted to see Randolph again. Joel liked them immediately. Randolph missed the activity from the previous trip. The absence of Daniel and Ed Rife, along with Martin and Luke, left a hollow echo of livelier times. The greatest change was Amy. She was extremely tall and very beautiful, and Joel was instantly smitten. She was happy to have company and immediately walked Joel to the pasture to see "Kissey."

"That's a strange name for a horse, Amy. How come you call her Kissey?"

Amy's laugh was delightful, and her perfect, white teeth gleamed in the sunlight. "The first time I saw her, she nuzzled up to my face and still does."

Leaning over the split rail fence surrounding the pasture, Kissey obliged by brushing Amy's face with her mouth, and Joel was impressed.

"Could you and Kissey ride with me and my dad up to Raven Rock tomorrow? We're gonna camp out tonight, and we'll have the whole day."

Sarah and Albert were again the gracious hosts and insisted Randolph and Joel use Daniel and Ed Rife's cabin. Amy led the way to Raven Rock the next day, and Joel was amazed to see Kissey side step the large rocks lying in the path. While Randolph and Albert chatted, Amy and Joel explored the surrounding area. He was fascinated by the many places and things Amy showed him. The headwaters of Elkhorn Creek, bubbling unbridled from the earth completely, amazed him.

"Probably from an ancient volcano eruption," Randolph said, when Joel pressed him for information on the sudden appearance of water from nowhere.

"Can we come back next year, Dad?" Joel asked.

His father smiled, knowing his son was having his first schoolboy crush and promised him a return trip.

***

Sarah was acutely aware of Amy's dreamy look as Levi galloped by on his way to God knew what. She remembered well the ecstasy of the young love she and Albert shared their first summer, as they lay on sweet smelling grass in the warm sun of the meadow. They were their only world, and nothing else mattered. A siege of fear gripped her heart.

It was only a matter of time until Levi would see Amy as she really was, fifteen, no longer a little girl but rapidly becoming a woman. Sarah, though tall herself, now looked up at Amy and admired the flawless, beautiful skin she had passed along to her. Albert was the ever-adoring father as he watched Amy brush her heavy, red-gold hair at night. Her quickness and effervescent personality gave sparkle to very dark blue eyes. In the last six months, her body had rounded, and Sarah began to make plans for high school in Louisa in late August.

"I haven't seen Levi Cantrell in some time," Sarah remarked to Albert as they milked two cows in the musty-smelling barn one early morning in March.

"I hear he's off selling his moonshine down river," Albert said, and Sarah prayed he would stay down river until Amy was well out of the area.

Albert had been chopping and sawing trees for several months, and it was time to send them downstream. He was hoping for heavy spring rains in April, and he was not disappointed. The water came in torrents. By the end of April, Albert's logs were on their way.

Amy was preparing to ride out with her father and was astounded when he refused to allow her to go.

"But Papa, I want to go down the river with you. Kissey even knows the way," she argued. "Besides, everyone is gone, and I want to see Luke and Martin."

"The weather is much too bad, Amy, and you could catch your death of cold. When I'm down by the river, under some of the over-hanging banks, I wouldn't know what was happening to you, and it is just too risky."

Amy stomped off to her room and closed the door.

Sarah watched Albert ride out after the logs in a driving rain storm, trying to hide her fear from Amy.

"Mama, I know Papa is in great danger, but you can talk to me about it. You know I am not a child."

Sarah looked at her beautiful, young daughter with surprise and relief. She did something she had not done in years. She broke down and sobbed. Amy held her mother in her arms, comforting her.

The rain lessened to a cold drizzle with leaden skies hovering at the top of huge pines. At least Albert would not be riding in a drenching downpour.

Sarah checked the rifles and shotguns to be sure they were working and loaded. They were two women alone in the wilderness, and she would do anything to protect her daughter. Through the years, she had been forced to master knowledge of firearms, and now alone with Amy for the first time, she was grateful to the men in her family who had trained her in self-defense. Theirs had been such a large, comforting clan, and now the stillness lay like a blanket.

She and Amy talked for hours, as they rocked in front of the blazing logs, and Sarah gave her details about her lost brothers, Henry and Jonathan, small enduring remembrances that still lingered, their happiness and their endless antics. Amy listened with rapt attention, feeling loneliness and yearning for the two young men she had never known. She finally grew sleepy and carried a lamp to her bedside where an ever-open book awaited. After a short period, she placed her hand atop the globe, blowing out the flame and darkening the room.

It was long past Sarah's bedtime, but she could not sleep. Adding another log to the fire, she wandered about the large room that now seemed so empty and forlorn. Logging was an extremely dangerous job, and Albert had tackled it alone as the menfolk gradually left the mountains. He was just past his fifty-ninth birthday, and it seemed to Sarah that he was stronger than he had ever been. Constant, physical work had hardened his muscles and their hardships through the years had steeled his resolve. So many unexpected things could happen along the riverbank, and if the logs piled up, Albert would have to try to release them. Therein lay the great dangers. A swollen river could suddenly rip logjams apart and send them shooting downstream with ferocious speed, which had mangled many loggers.

Sarah rocked gently in the huge, old rocking chair Albert had carved for her before they were married. She finally dozed, and nightmares filled her light sleep. She was awakened by the barking dogs, and rain was again pelting the cabin. Carrying the rifle to a shuttered window, she lifted the latch to peer into the darkness.

Both dogs were backing to the front porch barking fiercely, as something moved toward the cabin from the edge of the trees. A large flash of lightning illuminated the yard for a split second, and Sarah saw two horses but only one rider. The dogs had retreated to the front door and were bumping against it, as they snarled and took a stance to protect the home.

Sarah quickly slid the bolt across the window and was heading for Amy's room to arouse her when she heard her name being called above the roar of the storm and the snarling dogs. Levi Cantrell was shouting at the top of his lungs.

"Ms. Edwards, it's me Levi Cantrell. Albert has been bad hurt, and I got him here on his horse."

Sarah threw open the door and stood with a rifle in her hands.

Calming the dogs, she moved just outside the door and saw Albert lying forward on his horse. A sodden Levi Cantrell dismounted and lifted Albert, unconscious and limp, from his saddle.

"He's alive, Ms. Edwards, but he sure is banged up, and we had better put him by the fireplace cause he is mighty wet and really cold."

Sarah flew to get a heavy blanket and quickly spread it close to the crackling fire. A bloody rag had been tied around his head and Sarah's heart almost stopped as she looked at the white face beneath the makeshift bandage. She quickly untied the rag, gasping as she saw the huge, ragged cut from Albert's temple to the back of his head.

"Amy," Sarah screamed to her sleeping daughter, as she gently removed matted hair from the gaping wound.

Amy was aghast at seeing her father lying wounded and sopping wet by the fire.

"Quick, Amy, water and clean rags," Sarah ordered. Within an instant, Amy came running with both and knelt by Albert. She was terrified by his blue lips and gray pallor.

"Is he dead, Mama?" she asked fearfully. His breathing was so shallow it was hard to detect.

"He is alive, Amy, but it is a terrible wound." Levi stood by, helplessly watching the two women bending over Albert trying to save his life. He placed his soaking hat, coat and boots on the porch, backing into the cabin as the two large dogs growled menacingly and low in their throats.

Albert's skull gleaned white as the two women washed and cleaned the deep wound but Sarah could find no fracture in the bone and her spirits soared.

"I'll get his boots off, Miz Edwards, so we can get him warmed," Levi offered, and Sarah murmured, "Thank you." Albert's bare feet were like ice and Levi quickly removed the rest of his dripping clothing. Sarah now worried about a fever as his chilled body appeared lifeless. Amy quickly wrapped the warming rocks in heavy woolens and placed them close to Albert after Sarah and Levi had gotten him into a long flannel nightshirt. Sarah gently spooned hot sassafras tea, well-laced with moonshine, between his lips as Amy added more blankets. Levi piled the fireplace high with logs and shooting sparks jumped forward as long fingers of fiery flames enveloped the dry wood. The brightness of the fire illuminated the room, and for the first time,

Levi really looked at Amy. She stood before him, extending a steaming mug of hot apple cider spiked with moonshine.

"I know you must be very cold, Levi. Your clothes are so wet," she smiled shyly, and Levi was taken aback.

He remembered seeing a little girl playing in the cabin yard over the years as he rode by, but this was no little girl standing before him now. Sarah was busy tending to Albert, but glanced up in time to see the look on Levi's face.

"I'll get Amy out of here next month," she thought to herself.

As warmth began to return to Albert's body, he stirred slightly and moaned. Sarah placed her hands on his face to keep him from turning onto the large wound on the left side of his head.

"It's all right, Albert. You are safe at home with me and Amy. You are going to be all right."

He appeared to sigh and color began returning to his face. He slept peacefully.

Levi changed into dry clothing and combed his wet hair back from his face. Amy handed him another drink and thought he was the most handsome man she had ever seen.

"Levi, what happened?" Sarah asked as there had been no time to talk until Albert's condition had been stabilized.

"I was ridin' back from way down the river about dark, and I saw Albert's horse tied to a tree. I know his saddle, and I was sure Albert had to be about so I hollered and hollered, but he didn't answer me, so I started looking down by the river, and sure enough, there he was. He was half in and half out of the water with his head cut open and bleedin' like hell. Excuse me Ma'am, he was bleedin' somethin' fierce. I tied that rag around his head and got him here as fast as I could. I think he must a' been unplugging logs because two big ones with his brand on them were stuck between some trees." Levi sipped from his mug and shook his head. "It's not safe for one man to work loggin'. It can kill you fast."

"I will never again let Albert go down that river alone with logs," Sarah vowed, and she suddenly realized how late it was and how tired Levi must be. He offered to stay with Albert through the night, and Sarah was touched, but she showed him to the bedroom that had been Ruthie and Dan's.

Levi lowered his tired body into the encompassing warmth of a thick feather bed, smelling the crisp, delicious odor of wind dried sheets. He did not sleep immediately but dreamed with his eyes open. Later when he slept, he dreamed the same dream. A very tall, beautiful maiden came to him. He saw the fire in her dark blue eyes as their limbs entwined and he tasted the sweetest mouth. He slept only a few hours and arose, ready to travel. He found Sarah talking softly to Albert by the warmth of the fireplace where he had left them earlier. Albert was weak from the loss of blood but was lucid, and Sarah had explained to him what had happened.

"I'm beholden to you, Levi, for pulling me out of the water," he said wearily.

"I was just glad to get you home, Albert," Levi answered.

"It sounds like the rain has let up, and I plan to get my brothers and chase those logs down to the river port. How many do you reckon you had?"

Albert tried to object, but Levi shook his head and headed for the door. Albert had slipped a total of one-hundred and fifty logs into the water, and Levi was hellbent on collecting the money for them. He left without seeing Amy who was still asleep, but he would be back.

***

Levi came back often. He helped with the chores until Albert could be up and about, though he was aching to be on his way to Virginia. Levi had new reason to purchase the land of his dreams. He planned to take Amy with him.

He was hurrying back from the river port with his money when he found Albert. He had not ridden by the Edwards' farm since he discovered the cave, as his every hour had been obsessed with earning enough money to buy the land he had discovered. When Amy stood before him in the bright firelight, he had been speechless. The little girl he remembered had grown into a very tall and extremely beautiful woman. Her soft nightgown draped over two beautiful, firm breasts, and he had wanted desperately to touch them. He did not miss the look Sarah had given him, and he had also noticed she didn't want him anywhere near Amy. Albert, he could deal with it, but he knew Sarah would fight him to the end, because she had made it quite clear he was not good enough for Amy.

It had been two weeks since Albert's accident, and he was gradually regaining his strength. Levi had never worked so hard and so long in his entire life. He was up before dawn each morning, plowing his father's field as soon as he could see to put the plow in straight furrows. He stopped at mid morning to gulp down a large breakfast as his mother clucked and worried about him.

"You can't tend two farms, Levi," she admonished him. By noon, he saddled his horse and rode to the Edwards' place to plow the fields for Albert. The very sight of Amy waiting for him by the horse trough sent his heart racing. He forgot fatigue and almost felt he could move a mountain if she had asked him to. The high noonday sun wreathed her red hair with dazzling lights and thick, dark, brown eyelashes shadowed her dreamy, blue eyes. Levi thought he would die if he couldn't have her.

"I hoped you would be here waiting for me, Amy."

"I have been waiting for you for an hour, Levi. I was beginning to be afraid you weren't coming."

"Nothing could keep me away," he said, and his dark eyes glittered.

Sarah strolled from the front porch to where they stood. "Good morning, Levi. Surely you have not come to plow again today. This is really asking too much of a friend."

"It's no trouble, Ms. Edwards. I finished at home and felt like Albert needed a few more days to rest up."

Sarah felt a blaze of anger. Levi was too smart for his own good. "He is much better each day."

"I'm glad to hear that, and guess I had better get the horses to the plow," he touched his hat and knew Sarah would find an excuse to take Amy into the house. Levi also knew Amy would be out shortly.

***

He could not believe the turn his life had taken in the past year. It had started when his old hound had chased a raccoon into a hole a few feet beyond a frothing waterfall. Using a large limb to dislodge the coon, he was surprised when the length of the pole easily penetrated a foliage-covered opening. Carefully pushing the bushes aside, he thought he might have found a cave. Picking up a long pine knot, he lit the volatile torch and peered inside at what appeared to be a tunnel. He entered slowly and cautiously, keeping an eye out for the sharp-clawed coon who was nowhere to be seen.

He was able to walk upright a few feet beyond the opening, and the tunnel almost immediately became high and wide. His hunter eyes darted back and forth constantly. Wild animals and precipitous ledges could lay in wait with fatal results from either. He suddenly found himself in a huge cavern and his "I'll be goddamned" echoed back to him. Levi's excitement mounted as he slowly and very carefully circled the huge cave. "God," he thought, "what a place to make moonshine."

As he explored the high-vaulted room, he counted four tunnels leading off in opposite directions and his joy knew no bounds. Holding the blazing pine knot high above his head, he entered the largest opening leading from the first room. The tunnel widened almost immediately beyond the entrance, as the path gently sloped downward. Levi moved with extreme caution. He had grown up exploring caves and knew well that one step over an unseen ledge could mean instant death.

By the time he had traveled fifty feet, his ears picked up a slight sound that brought joy to his heart. The sound of running water underground was a moonshiner's dream. His greatest urge was to run toward the sound but he curbed the instinct and traversed cautiously. Another fifty feet, and he was upon the scene that would rule the rest of his life. A room slightly smaller than the first cavern with a much lower ceiling was illuminated by his torch.

He could not see the far side from where he stood, but what he really wanted most to see was the water falling gently over a great limestone ledge into a beautiful dark stream that softly whisked its way across the cavern, disappearing from sight. Levi was astounded with his discovery. Carefully edging his way along the stream, he checked for dropoffs and other hazards. Walking the circumference of the room, he found other tunnels leading further back into the mountain and let out an Indian whoop that resounded back at him, as he laughed like a madman.

The flaming pine knot reflected in the dark stream and suddenly he felt heat on his hand. Cursing himself because he had brought only one torch, he quickly retraced his steps to the outside, marveling at his stupendous find. He very carefully closed the entrance, and his treasure was again invisible to the outside world.

"It will be mine," Levi vowed, beginning to formulate his plans.

135

In the waning light, he hurried down the mountainside but managed to shamble nonchalantly into his parents' cabin. He didn't dare tell anyone, even his father, about the cave.

In the months following his discovery, he stacked loads of dry, volatile pine knots throughout the cave and its meandering tunnels. He lived in the cave for days at a time and his habitat took on the look of home. A large coffee pot on a neat rock grate and plentiful wood was stashed nearby. Heavy blankets lay straightened on a thick, straw mattress, and Levi honed his plans. The mountain top would cost money, and he didn't have any. His share for the moonshine he took to Pikeville for Pa was usually spent in whorehouses and carousing all night with the shiftless that hung about. That would have to stop. He needed money.

His father was delighted that Levi started the spring plowing earlier and began clearing more space for growing corn.

"I declare, Floy. I do think that boy is gonna amount to somethin' yet," he remarked to his plump wife, as she squeezed fat biscuits from the mass of dough she had kneaded in a huge wooden bowl. She quickly filled a heavy black skillet with the biscuits and popped it into the oven. Levi had asked her to make extra biscuits for a hunting trip, and she thought idly that he was doing a lot of hunting.

The crops were laid by and Levi wanted a couple of days in the cave before he returned to his timber cutting. His excitement threatened to overtake him each time he crossed the rushing stream on stepping stones. The Indian portion of his heritage took over in cunning he didn't know he possessed. He placed large stones just below the rippling surface of the stream so scuff marks from his boots would be invisible. In warm weather, he simply waded through the water that remained extremely cold throughout the summer, as splashing water from the waterfall sprinkled his rough shirt and beaded on his heavy mustache and hair.

Searching diligently for clues of any intrusion, he carefully pushed aside the low-growing bushes, crawling cautiously inside the hidden opening. Once inside, he began his ritual of placing large stones in the opening, camouflaging his treasure. Before leaving the entry, he again checked it to be sure the opening he had just crawled through was totally invisible. He secured the tunnel and lighted one of his abundant torches.

Traveling through the first large room, he ignited well-placed torches and again his whole being soared as he watched his new world looming high and wide above him. Lighting the torches by the waterfall, he stood watching several minutes, as beautiful sheets of crystalline water slid over smooth boulders dropping the motherlode several feet before entering the waiting stream. Levi could see his copper still sitting on a bed of hot coals with the worm crossing under the cooling falls to the waiting barrels on the other side. He traveled several feet along the stream, which had cut a deep gorge in the rock, crossing and traveling back toward the falls. Levi formulated plans for a wide bridge just below the falling water. Watching the stream flow through the cavern and disappear mystified him. It simply vanished through stone walls, and where it emptied was its very own secret.

He had explored the mountainside around the large cave and its tunnels, but could find no area in which it had surfaced. Picking up several pine knots, he again made his way through the long tunnel that afforded the only other entrance. It was the larger of the four tunnels he had explored. He had crawled over them all, inch-by-inch, but the solid rock was intact. His feet crunched on brittle bones of small animals, and he scuffed them to the side. He approached the largest section of the tunnel and lit a well-placed torch protruding from the small crevice in the rock and checked his catch of pine knots. Before he left the area, he would have added greatly to his stock of torches.

Levi knew the cave was his from his first entry, and he constantly built toward his dream. From the wide area of the tunnel, the walls moved inward until they reached the small opening he had discovered. He guessed the total length to be one mile, and he smiled to himself, more room and space to absorb smoke. Placing the torch between cracks in the stone, Levi inched upward several feet, checking the small opening. He slowly eased the large boulder he had balanced on the jutting stone wall to reveal an oblong cavity in the solid rock. Extremely dense growth allowed only meager light to penetrate the mass. Nothing appeared to have been disturbed and Levi breathed a sigh of relief. It took most of his massive strength to replace the large boulder, completely covering the entrance.

Months before, he had placed markers through the opening to

guide him to the spot outside. It was an area he had traveled many times, totally unaware of the huge cave and the water below. The steep incline was covered in a volcanic flow of black rock and through the eons, trees and shrubs had grown through it in many places. Several evergreens stood near the small opening to the cave, and he nodded with satisfaction. Carefully parting the dense foliage, he viewed only the large boulder he had placed on the high ledge inside the cave.

His crafty mind was at work again, and he decided to place an even larger boulder just in front of the heavy growth. Finding what he needed was no problem and using a strong pole, he maneuvered another large boulder to that part of the entry. Laying in another stash of pine knots, he decided to call it a day.

Exiting the cave, he traveled several yards downstream from the waterfall to a lovely pond formed by debris and rocks. Levi had collected fish from these depths for years and now he appreciated it even more. Huge bass and rainbow trout circled the pond in profusion. It seemed as though they had to line up in order to swim, so great were the numbers. Somehow, he would buy this whole mountaintop, and he would even own a well-stocked pond. Using a large wooden pail, he dipped into the water and hauled forth several flapping trout. Within minutes he had filleted two of the largest, throwing the others back to continue their swim.

Animals had left tracks along the soft banks, and Levi smiled to himself. Hell, he could even get a bear, he decided, as he viewed large heavy imprints among those of raccoon, deer and the scrambling scratches of squirrels. Twilight was deepening, and Levi decided it was time to head back to his cave. He didn't want to stand in the way of a hungry bear or panther that, no doubt, feasted on the plentiful supply of fish. Numerous sightings had been reported of sleek, black, seven-foot panthers tearing trout lines apart and devouring the fish. Even the bravest mountaineer was known to retreat in the steady amber glare of this formidable foe.

Suddenly, Levi froze. Panther tracks so near the edge of the water, he had almost missed them, and so fresh, water was still seeping into the indentations. Levi had seldom known such fear. He had left his rifle in the cave, and he stood defenseless knowing the huge cat was watching him from the dense forest. It was not dark enough to see the glow of its eyes, but he knew it was there. He could feel it. Noting the length of the stride in the muddy tracks, he knew it was enormous. He also knew he must move very slowly, and it taxed his willpower to the utmost not to race toward the safety of the cave opening.

Slowly, step-by-step, he moved upstream turning his head every so slightly trying to decide which direction an attack would come from. When he finally reached the entrance of the cave, he practically dived into the opening throwing the pail of fish before him. He immediately rolled the largest boulder into the entrance and in record time, he had secured his safety. At the same instant, he heard the wild, angered scream of the huge beast as it resounded in the quiet forest. The damned thing had been just behind him. The distant scream of a panther had been likened to that of a woman. This one wasn't distant. It was clawing at his front entrance, and it was the most terrifying sound Levi had ever heard. He slumped against the wall of the cave as his legs gave way beneath him.

Finally recovering from his shock, he placed two heavy logs in back of the large boulders, securing them to both sides of the tunnel. Only then did he feel completely safe. Even the strength of a giant panther could not dislodge the barricade. He was glad he had left several torches burning, as his eyes darted about the well-lit cave. He walked rapidly to where his large rifle rested on the table and felt great relief when he held cold steel in his grip. Levi sat on his thick straw mattress and slugged heavily from his jug of moonshine. He had abstained from drinking since finding the cave, and the fiery liquid burned a quick path through his empty stomach.

He sat with the rifle across his lap, and as his courage began to return, enhanced by the potent moonshine, he looked at the situation and roared with laughter. "I aim to kill that goddamn son-of-a-bitch," he howled, and laughed with delight when the echo came back to him. Starting a fire to cook his dinner, he watched with joy and amazement as the dark, flowing stream drew the smoke into the outlet deep in the stone walls. Just after discovering the cave, Levi had shed his clothes and braved the icy water long enough to explore the opening that allowed water falling freely from the falls to disappear so quickly. He had discovered a jagged four-foot opening, only about a foot in height, with a lot of suction. The water had to be falling a great distance he decided and the mystery intrigued him.

He cooked the trout to perfection in a cast-iron skillet with popping hot grease, and a handful of cornmeal over the fillets. Still watching with satisfaction as the last of the smoke from the fire disappeared into the stream, he knew his moonshine business would forever be safe in his cave.

CHAPTER 8

Levi's greatest chore was to drag his two sodden brothers out of bed each morning, still reeking of moonshine, and bleary-eyed. He persuaded the two to join him in cutting the abundant timber, and the wild three delighted in the dangerous ride downstream on the heavy logs.

When they were paid for the logs, Levi carefully hoarded his money. His brothers were so intent on raising hell they didn't notice that he was no longer throwing his cash around. He volunteered to carry the new runs of moonshine to buyers and placed sacks of ginseng roots across the pack mules bulging with jugs. He had thrown the roots aside as they felled the large trees but after second thought, had gathered them. He knew several mountain people sold ginseng at the river ports, but he had never bothered until he started hoarding every penny.

He needed as much money as possible and as quickly as possible. The moonshine always garnered a good price, as the Cantrells were known to make the best. He was truly amazed at the price paid for ginseng and on the return trip back into the mountains, he made a mental note of the plants he passed along the way.

The only time he aroused his family's suspicions was the day he declined to go drinking with his brothers on another wild spree with several buddies. Levi usually led the pack. He had not been to his cave in several weeks, and he still lived with the fear someone would find it.

"You found some ol' girl you're a courtin' with," his brother Nade teased.

"Wished I was," Levi countered. "Just want to get my rifle and run about."

Shaking their heads in disbelief, they whooped loudly and galloped off. By the time snow was flying, Levi had managed to obtain the name of the man who owned the cave site. He would have to travel one hundred miles into Virginia to meet the man, and he made his plans. Winter was upon the land, and he would have to bide his timing for travel. His dream mountain lay just across the Kentucky line into Virginia. It didn't matter to Levi that he would have to leave his beloved Kentucky hills, as his whole being ached for the land with its unbelievable cave. He would have to wait until spring, and he prayed no one would stumble upon his secret. Cold winter mornings were no deterrent to his timber cutting, as he arose early and waded into the waiting forest with his huge double-bit ax. His two brothers would meander into the woods shortly before noon, having waited for warmer weather, and wonder what in the hell had gotten into Levi.

"You're sure actin' strange, little brother," Nade said, as he peered at Levi through bloodshot eyes with breath that spoke loudly of moonshine from the night before.

"I'm just tired of being lazy and drunk," Levi answered, and the three of them bellowed with laughter. The soaking April rains found Levi with a mountain of logs waiting for market. With their brand on both ends of the large logs, they started the treacherous trip to market. He had managed to sober his brothers long enough to enlist their help, and again, the three daredevils rode the logs mercilessly downstream.

The riverport was alive with activity, and his beautiful logs were snapped up immediately. After he paid his brothers for their help, he stashed his money into a strong pouch, well-secured around his waist and hidden under his huge, heavy shirt. They visited the usual waterfront saloons but neither noticed that Levi held the same drink all evening. He watched the jaded ladies rolling the drunk loggers, and he knew his brothers would arrive back home broke again. He left the next morning, rousing his brothers long enough to tell them he was leaving and supplying them with a few extra dollars. Little did he know, as he pulled Albert from the water, that their lives would be linked forever.

***

Levi told Amy he would have to be away for a few days and was elated with the look of dismay on her face. "I will be back soon, Amy. I have something I have to do, and someday I will tell you about it," he said softly. He wanted desperately to kiss Amy goodbye, but Sarah was watching, and he didn't dare touch her. It didn't make any difference where he and Amy were, Sarah was always there. With one look back at Amy, Levi climbed aboard his huge roan and headed toward Virginia.

Horse and rider fairly flew along the ridges and low-lying valleys stopping only late at night to eat and sleep beneath any available shelter. He arrived in Bristol, Virginia, tired and dirty with a near-winded horse, but he found his way to Arthur Stenson's house before he stopped. Stenson was only too happy to unload a faraway mountaintop that was almost inaccessible. He had come by it as part of another land deal and was glad to be rid of it. Levi had expected to be paying for the land for years and now, though it all but emptied his money belt, he was astounded. He had bought and paid for the dream! Outwardly, Stenson could not even begin to guess what was going on beneath his stoic appearance, as Levi's dark brown eyes did not waver.

"You are welcome to spend the night in our home, Levi, and rest your horse," he said, eyeing the drooping horse.

"I thank you kindly, Mr. Stenson, but I need to be headin' back to the hills," Levi said, turning his face toward home and his future.

He stopped early in the day at an empty, dilapidated shack. His horse was badly in need of rest, and its flanks quivered as the heavy saddle was dragged from its back. The roan immediately headed for a nearby stream eyeing tall, succulent grass on his way. Levi sprawled beneath a huge oak planning his next move. He needed money before he and Amy could build a house on his mountain. Tall stands of trees would have to be cleared for the necessary corn crops, and there would be horses, cows and oxen to purchase. He envisioned the sunsets and the early morning sunrise from their own domain. It would be at least a year before he could ask Amy to marry him.

As he felled the giant white oaks, he would cut barrel staves to soak in the streams, then bend them into proper shapes to hold and age his moonshine. His thoughts returned again to Amy, and he smiled as he thought of her. He knew she would marry him but what would Sarah do? The thought chilled him.

He arrived back home in the dead of night, greeted by yapping hounds and his two brothers still awake slugging on a jug of moonshine. Nade leered at his younger brother, wagging a drunken head.

"I saw why you've been runnin' over to help the Edwards family," he drawled. "That Amy is just about the prettiest filly I have ever seen. I took that single tree back to Albert, and there she was. Her maw sure as hell didn't like me, and she took Amy in the house by the time I said howdy." Even drunk, he spat a streak of tobacco juice into smoldering coals in the large fireplace with exacting aim.

"You plannin' on getting hitched to that little gal, Levi?" Jack asked. He wasn't nearly as drunk as Nade and being the oldest of the surviving brothers, he felt a keen interest in his youngest brother.

"That's what I plan to do, and I have a farm to take her to as soon as I get money enough for stock. It's gonna take time, but I can do it." He proceeded to tell his brothers about the mountaintop farm he had just bought and the two were flabbergasted. They both shook their heads in amazement.

"That's why you've been working your ass off this past year, ain't it?" Jack asked, and Levi nodded.

"Mrs. Edwards ain't gonna let you take Amy," Nade informed him. "I hear she's from up North and got some schoolin', too."

"I will marry Amy," Levi vowed and headed toward the bed with his exhausted body.

***

The next day at noon he found Amy standing by the horse trough, hair, loose and flowing to her waist. He knew the pale blue dress was new and no doubt from her brothers in Louisa. Amy blushed under his stare and twirled around to show him the bow in back.

"Did you miss me, Levi?" she asked shyly.

"Amy, I miss you every minute I'm not with you," he answered with dark eyes blazing.

"Mama and Papa say I have to leave soon to go to school in Louisa. Albert and Luke already have a room at both their homes and have placed my name in the school office."

Levi felt like he had been hit by a bolt of lightning. Goddamn you, Sarah, he raged inwardly. He knew exactly what she was doing. She wanted to get Amy as far away from him as possible. He could not let her tear Amy from him.

"I can't bear to have you leave, Amy."

"Levi, I don't want to go," she answered.

He wanted to crush her to him to taste her mouth, but that goddamn Sarah was standing on the porch watching.

"Let's walk down to the creek and get some flowers for the graves, Amy."

He had to get her out of earshot, he knew Sarah was listening. Amy's favorite pastime was to gather myriads of abundant flowers to place on her beloved grandparents' graves next to those of her two fallen brothers. Levi was in turmoil. He knew Amy was very close to her parents, and yet he knew Amy loved him. He dreaded the coming confrontation.

"Amy, when I left here several days ago, I went all the way to Bristol, Virginia. I bought a farm just in back of Pine Mountain there," he said gesturing upward with his head, and Amy turned to look. "You can't see it from here, but it's even more beautiful than this side of the mountain." Levi could not tell her about the cave. That would have to wait.

"Levi, why didn't you tell me what you were going to do? You were gone so long, I worried about you. Your brothers didn't seem to know where you were when they brought the single trees to Papa."

"I couldn't tell anyone, Amy. I wanted to be sure I could buy the land." He had planned to save more money before he asked her to marry him, but he knew if she left these hills now, she would be lost to him forever.

"Amy, will you marry me?" he asked, and to hell with Sarah, he thought, as he took Amy's right hand between his large hands completely engulfing it.

"Oh, Levi, of course I will marry you. I have wanted to marry

145

you for a long time," and she reddened to the roots of her hair. Levi felt like leaping into the air and giving his Indian war whoop.

"What do you think your folks will say, Amy?"

"They will understand when I tell them how much I love you."

Levi knew better. And what would Amy do when she had to make a decision?

Albert's strength had returned and he was again busy planting the large field Levi had plowed for him. He watched as Amy gathered flowers for the family graveyard with Levi walking beside her.

In the past month Sarah had become rigid and ungiving. Levi Cantrell was not the man for their bright and beautiful Amy. She tried with great patience to explain this to their daughter, but it was all to no avail. Amy followed Levi to the fields as he harnessed huge horses to the plow and ripped the earth apart. At the end of each row, from across the field, Amy could feel his dark eyes on her, as he drove the plow horses to their limit to where she stood waiting. She watched with adoring eyes as he finished the large fields in record time. Sarah saw it all. He had been away for several days, and she had hoped he was gone for good.

As Albert was tethering his horse to the front railing, Sarah walked to the edge of the porch looking totally miserable, which was unlike his wife.

"Albert, you have to do something," she said to him, but her eyes were on Amy and Levi who were completely engrossed in one another.

"Just what do you have in mind, Sarah?" he answered with a defeated look, as he watched Amy and Levi.

"We'll send Amy to Louisa tomorrow. Luke and Albert want her to come now and be ready for school in August. I thought we would be rid of Levi when he could no longer use the excuse of doing your chores, but he keeps coming back."

Amy and Levi walked hand in hand to where the two stood, and as Sarah looked at them, she knew what was coming. Amy gave Levi an adoring look and the confidence he needed badly. Sarah grudgingly had to admit he looked somewhat better. He had trimmed both his hair and mustache and wore clean clothes each day. He didn't even smell like a horse anymore.

"Albert, Mrs. Edwards, me and Amy want to get married. We

love each other, and we want to be together." Levi finished talking, and his dark eyes were intense.

Sarah suddenly turned sick. Albert spoke quietly but forcefully. "Levi, I thank you for saving my life and all the help you've given us, but Amy is only fifteen years old and much too young to get married. We want her to go to Louisa to be with her two brothers and go to high school. I'm asking you to wait until she has had some schoolin'."

"Papa, I will not go to school. I am going to marry Levi," Amy informed both her parents and could not believe the stern unyielding look on both their faces.

"I would like you to leave, Levi, so we can talk to Amy," Albert said.

Levi would have taken Amy with him, but she flew sobbing into the house.

"I'll be back, Amy," he called as he mounted his horse and galloped from the yard. Amy shut the door to her room and refused to come out. The next morning she still refused to come out after Albert had pounded on the door.

"Go away, Papa. I don't want to talk to you."

Sarah had never seen Albert so frustrated and so angry.

"I will not allow that goddamned whoremonger Indian to lay claim to Amy. Better that I had died than have Amy beddin' down with that bastard."

***

For three days Amy cried and refused to eat. In the end her father finally despaired of trying to change her mind and gave in. He took Levi aside and informed him that if he ever hurt his little girl in any way, he would kill him.

"You are a wild one, Levi," Albert said bitterly. "The fault is ours. We should have sent Amy away two years ago, but we couldn't part with her just yet. You saved my life, but I don't hold with you and them drunken brothers of yours."

"I know what I have been, Albert, but Amy will be my life, and I promise you my brothers will not be a part of our life."

When Levi took Amy into his strong arms and close to his heart, he needed no instructions. He would be true to her and love her to the end of his days. Sarah and Albert offered the young couple Ruthie and Dan's cabin, and they were grateful.

"Amy, I don't want you to bend your back carrying' water from the creek," Levi said the first time he saw Amy leaving the cabin with a large pail.

"I've always carried water for our cabin," Amy said, but Levi playfully removed the pail from her hands and lifting her with one arm, kissed her soundly before rushing to the stream for water.

Sarah and Albert could hardly believe their ears when Amy and Levi told them of the mountaintop farm Levi had bought.

"I need to send as many logs as I can down the river, Albert. I need stock and money for our farm."

Albert nodded in agreement to his son-in-law.

Levi set to work immediately with ax and saw to clear more land and send more logs downstream to market. Albert, though still distant with Levi, was amazed to see the number of trees he felled each day. Levi encouraged Albert to cut more timber, and soon the two of them were frequent visitors to the river ports. Luke and Martin were eager to have as much timber as possible from the hills, and the four of them profited from the business.

"The damned distilleries want all the white oak to make whiskey barrels, but we want it in our construction," Luke said, which was welcome news to both Albert and Levi. Almost by the time they returned home, Levi was heading for another oak grove.

As he held Amy at night, he told her of his dream. "I will build us a home on our mountaintop one day, Amy, and I'll make the best corn whiskey a man has ever tasted. It has caves and limestone water that will give us everything we want. The fish have to swim around in circles they're so thick in the ponds, and the rainbow trout are so pretty you almost hate to eat 'em. One day I'll saddle up the horses and show you where it is, but you can't ever tell nobody about the cave. I have never even told my family."

Grudgingly, Albert began to like Levi, in spite of himself. Sarah was still aloof with him, and Albert wasn't sure she would ever give in. She was even more distressed when Amy told her she was pregnant.

"Sarah, you were only two years older than Amy when you had Jonathan," Albert reminded her gently, as Sarah cried and turned away.

Shortly before their first anniversary, Levi came riding hard on his large horse and in such haste, he almost rode over the barking dogs.

"Sarah, come quick. Amy says the pains are comin' close," he urged, and her parents were on their way immediately.

A large, full moon hung overhead as the three rushed to Amy's side. Pine Mountain loomed high into the sky, and Sarah was suddenly reminded of her terrifying race to the Edwards family so many years ago.

"Oh, God, please let Amy be alright," she prayed silently. How could a place so beautiful witness so many tragedies? Amy was only a child herself and would soon hold a little one of her own. At this moment, she hated Levi, as she watched his large frame and horse outdistance them. Their beautiful Amy should be in high school in Louisa, not giving birth to a child in a rustic cabin.

Levi leaped from his horse, leaving the reins dangling and the front door stood wide open.

"I'll tether the horses and be right in," Albert said, as Sarah ran toward the cabin.

As she entered the bedroom, she was relieved to see a very calm Amy, as if this was an everyday event. Levi knelt by her side, her hand clasped in both of his, and his face portrayed enough agony for the two of them.

"Good," Sarah thought to herself. Two hours later, Levi held a large bawling son in his arms as Amy lay exhausted.

"Oh Amy, he is so beautiful," Sarah said softly, and her heart ached as she remembered their firstborn son. She looked at Albert. Their eyes locked as tears ran down his face. He quickly turned aside. This moment was for Amy and Levi.

Sarah felt such joy as they watched baby Hiram grow larger and stronger by the day. Both Luke and Martin had children, but they rarely saw them, which made her and Albert very sad. The distance was too great for them and their sons.

Levi was the doting father, and his love for Amy increased by the day. After a long day in the field or cutting timber, he would rock Hiram to sleep at night and help Amy with the chores. He milked the cows, carried wood for the fire, and kept pails of water at hand.

***

It was a year before Amy saw their farm. Levi's race to send numerous logs downstream and tend large fields of corn left no time during the summer. He would not hear of Amy riding a horse after she became pregnant. He hovered over her like a mother hen, but when baby Hiram was three months old, they left him in the care of his doting grandparents and headed for their high mountain farm.

Amy was delighted to be back on Kissey again. She had missed riding her beautiful mare. She stood atop the mountain and was totally awed by the expanse spreading before them. It was early September, and in another few weeks, the glory of autumn would descend upon the land, coloring the brilliant greens rolling from hill to hill in unbroken continuity. They stood in a clearing wrought by lightning and once a raging fire. Amy felt as though she stood at the top of the world, and if she lifted her feet, she would float away.

Mountain ridges rose and dipped for miles in every direction. High peaks sheared downward into steep narrow valleys, flowing outward as far as the eye could see. The waterfall chimed its own music, and the surrounding forest teamed with life in many forms. Light-footed deer faded into tall timber, while squirrels and rabbits romped over their playground. Birds sailed through branches twittering and calling constantly. Large and small, they shared perches amidst constant movements.

To Amy, the forest appeared to be a living thing. Levi led their horses to the stream to quench their thirst after removing saddles and loaded saddlebags. He staked them out in knee-high grass and walked back to where Amy stood, still gazing about in wonderment.

"Amy, you stay right here, and I'll be back in just a few minutes," Levi said, his dark eyes dancing with excitement.

She watched his huge form disappear behind the waterfall with two saddles and bulging saddlebags over both shoulders, as if they were weightless. Amy looked toward Kentucky and smiled. She had expected Virginia to look different, but they were of equal beauty. Their farm was barely across the state line, and they would forever be Virginians.

"If I miss Kentucky, I can always put my foot on the other side of our border," she thought idly to herself.

Levi came splashing through the stream beneath the waterfall, and Amy flew into his outstretched arms. He crushed her to his body so fiercely she could scarcely breathe. Picking her up as if she were a feather, he carried her to the cave opening. Releasing Amy, he very carefully concealed the entrance to the outside world. The month before he had spent hours placing torches throughout the cave, and now Amy walked through a well-lit interior. Levi had raced through much of the cave, lighting the way for her, and she was dazzled. She had been in small caves with her parents, but there was no comparison. The ceiling was too high to be illuminated by the blazing pine knots bracketed to the walls, and she was astounded.

"Levi, I had no idea," she said, and he practically danced with joy. The vastness of the cave was overwhelming. The complete silence was the next shock. There was no sound, and there was no movement. A musty odor prevailed as the pine knots blazed brighter. Levi had long since swept the floor of his cave to remove bones and small debris, and now, they walked on a smooth surface. His unexpected loud "hello" came back at them in waves, as Amy reacted in surprised agitation.

"Levi, you scared me," she admonished him.

He circled her waist in a tight clasp, and they journeyed through the tunnel into the room containing the waterfall and the dark gurgling stream. Weeks before, he had practically lined the room with large pine knots in anticipation of Amy's visit. He had lit each and every one on his trip into the cave, and now they blazed brightly in all their glory. Amy was speechless. The beautiful waterfall reflected the flames, as it poured a fiery deluge over an ancient ledge and into a crimson stream flowing past the multitude of torches. For several minutes, she could only stare at the beautiful and shimmering waters, throwing forth a vision of liquid fire. As Levi had told her, the river simply vanished into the walls of the cave. Gradually, she began to see the rest of the surroundings, smiling when she saw the rustic table and four chairs placed nearby in an orderly fashion. Farther downstream, a low stone circle, complete with pine kindling and a large metal grate, stood with cooking utensils and a big coffeepot. A long, wide, neatly made pallet lay halfway between the wall and the shifting stream.

"Oh, Levi, how could I know," she said, turning to look at her husband and warmed when she saw his face. His elation was without bounds. Amy, the cave and the farm belonged to him. He began to unbutton her high-necked blouse, and Amy started with the lower buttons.

Her long, beautiful limbs glowed in the light of the blazing torches, as tongues of dancing flames played over her body, painting it with fiery, flickering reflections. The fire in her eyes was her own, and Levi was electrified. He knelt above her on the soft pallet by the musical stream, and the world closed about them.

Amy awakened to the smell of fresh coffee brewing from pure limestone water. The cave was dimly lit and Levi had disappeared. Snuggling deeper into the warm nest, her mind strayed back over their night of wild lovemaking. She stretched her long naked body and decided she wasn't ready to put her clothes on. Wrapping herself in the warm blanket, she slipped her feet into moccasins, heading for the boiling coffee pot.

Levi emerged through the opening of the first part of the cave carrying a lighted torch. His face softened as he looked at Amy in the dim light. He had lighted only a few torches by the stream so Amy would sleep late. The blackness of the cave was immune to light and sound, and it was easy to lose track of time. Levi always slept later in his cave. Amy could well have been an apparition, standing so tall and beautiful, clasping the blanket loosely draped about her body, her hair rumpled and hanging low.

"I thought you had deserted me, Levi," she teased, as he neared her.

"I wanted to light the first room so bright you would have to shade your eyes," he laughed.

"I barely remember seeing it last night," she admitted as Levi gathered her in his arms.

"I'll never forget last night," he drawled, kissing Amy's upturned face tenderly. "If you want, we can walk down to the pond and pick up our breakfast." He was anxious to show Amy their treasure.

"I would like that," Amy said, "and guess what, Levi. I'm going to take a bath in that beautiful waterfall by our front door and wash my hair." Amy had never felt so free and unfettered. This mountaintop was their world, and they could do as they pleased.

Levi threw his head back and roared with laughter. "You're gonna freeze your butt off. That's what you're gonna do. That damned water is ice cold."

"I've always taken baths in cold streams," Amy answered.

Levi filled her large mug again with steaming coffee. "Then you're sure as hell gonna need this," he said. He steered Amy through the

152

wide tunnel and into the huge front room of the cave. Amy was flabbergasted. She truly did not remember this room. The walls appeared to be on fire with numerous torches Levi had spent the last hour lighting. The cavern was enormous. Levi had spent months building long ladders to lean against the rock wall in order to light the entire ceiling. Amy was overwhelmed. The fifty-foot ceiling embellished a tremendous circumference.

"Levi, we could live here," Amy exclaimed, looking around in wonder. "It is several times the size of our whole cabin."

"This will always be our secret place, Amy. Promise me," he demanded.

"Of course, Levi," Amy answered, with puzzlement clouding her eyes.

"With this clear limestone water, and the waterfall so handy, I can turn out hundreds of gallons of moonshine in no time a'tall, and it will be the best. The law will never find it and neither will some thief."

This Amy could well understand. "Besides," Levi continued, "I plan to build you the biggest damned cabin you'll ever see. The trees are standin' right there, and all I have to do is chop 'em down and stack 'em as high and as wide as we like." His eyes blazed with excitement as he planned their future, and Amy knew it would come about. She felt as though she had been transplanted into another world. The vastness of the cavern and Levi's meticulous planning further increased her adoration for her handsome husband. Exiting the cave, Amy blinked in the bright sunlight reflecting off the waterfall.

"Good Lord, Levi. What time is it?" and Levi laughed at her astonishment.

"It's after ten o'clock," he answered to Amy's amazement.

She slipped out of her moccasins, and Levi lifted the blanket from her.

"I'll hold it close and keep it real warm for you," he leered, and his body hardened as it always did when he saw her undressed. Amy giggled and stepped under cascading water catching her breath with the initial shock of the icy spray sliding over her in clean sheets, laughing with wild delight.

"Amy, I'm hungry as hell. Get out," Levi called, when he felt she was doing overtime. She emerged pink and dripping as Levi wrapped her in the blanket taking time to squeeze some of the cold water from her heavy hair.

"I'll get my rifle and bucket, and we'll walk down to the pond yonder," he said as he re-entered the cave. He had left his rifle on the table by the stream and had to search for his favorite fish bucket. Amy decided to walk along the beautiful stream flowing from the waterfall to the large fish pond. Even at ten o'clock in the morning, the tall, succulent grass was still heavy with dew, and her leather moccasins were soon squishing, but everything about their mountaintop fascinated her. Small fish darted about the stream, flipping tail fins as they barely skimmed over large, flat rocks in the water. She was totally absorbed in wonderment watching the unbelievable number of fish swimming slowly and beautifully around the large pond. It was as though they swam to some secret music.

Levi emerged from the cave entrance looking around for Amy. She stood spellbound by the pond with long, wet hair clinging to her back and shoulders. He always smiled when he looked at his wife, and this morning was the most joyous of all. He knew Amy loved their mountaintop farm as he did. He had lived for this moment from the night he first fell in love with her.

Suddenly, Levi was racked with terror. A large oak tree stood near the fish pond with long, strong limbs spreading in all directions. Along one such limb and directly in line with Amy, an enormous, black panther was stealthily making its way toward her as she stood mesmerized by the beautiful fish slowly circling in the water. The cat's massive haunches and powerful shoulders moved in terrifying, purposeful unison as sunlight glistened on its sleek blackness. Levi could feel the amber eyes intent on the back of Amy's neck and knew it would snap it like a twig. The panther's wide, soft feet moved without a sound as it gradually closed on the distance to Amy. It's long, razor-sharp, deadly claws would remain sheathed until the attack. Amy heard no sound except the gurgling stream.

Levi thanked God he was upwind from the big cat as he quickly lowered the pail to the ground, praying the waterfalls would mask any sound. Quickly, he raised his rifle and sighted on the huge head. A stillness suddenly enveloped the hills. Small animals ceased their scurrying, and not one bird twittered. Fear of the giant predator, as it stalked its prey, paralyzed all vulnerable life.

Levi saw its muscles tensing for the attack, and with deadly calm, he fired. The panther's rigid head exploded in mid-air, as its body left the long limb. Amy heard the loud crack of the rifle and was knocked to the ground in almost the same instant. The shoulder of the big cat hit her a glancing blow as it fell from the tree, slamming her onto rocks and thorns.

Levi hurtled down the steep incline at break neck speed to where Amy lay, dazed and covered in blood.

"Oh, God, Amy. Oh, God," he bellowed, wildly wiping blood from Amy's face and arms. He could find no wounds, and he suddenly realized she was covered in the damn cat's blood.

"Amy, it's alright, honey. You're not hurt. It's the cat's blood."

Amy, in a semiconscious state, looked at the huge beast lying next to her and screamed. Levi quickly carried her to the waterfall, washing away cat blood that had mingled with Amy's blood from deep thorn scratches. He stood beneath the icy falls with her, making sure all of the blood had disappeared. Amy was sobbing and shaking uncontrollably.

"Amy, honey, it's alright. You're not hurt," he repeated over and over.

Levi carried her into the cave swathing her in blankets on the soft pallet and quickly stoked the low burning fire with dry logs.

"Amy, I'll be right back," he promised, as he raced to the front of the cave in sodden clothes to retrieve his rifle and secure the entrance.

***

Exactly nine months later, Ben was born. Sarah wrapped him in a soft blanket and gave him to Levi, who beamed with happiness as he looked at his beautiful son.

"He's another spittin' image of you, Levi," Albert said, peeking at the baby's dark hair and his father's features. Finally, baby Ben stopped screeching as Levi rocked him gently in his arms. Little Ben finally opened his eyes and looked at his father. Levi was so shocked he almost dropped him. The baby's eyes were the pale, amber eyes of the panther.

Levi kept his distance from the others as he cradled Ben to him. Finally, Sarah and Albert left the room to dispose of soiled laundry and empty water pails.

He placed Ben next to Amy, "Amy, I wanted you to first see Ben's eyes when we were alone. What do you think?"

Amy turned her head and peered into the large eyes looking at her. "Levi, he looks so strange, what's wrong with him?"

"He isn't strange, he is strong and handsome, and he has the eyes of a panther."

"Oh, my God."

"It's alright, Amy, and I'm sure he is going to be special. I think we should keep this to ourselves for Ben's sake. Do you understand?" He knew she was still groggy, but she nodded her head yes. Ben cooperated by going back to sleep before Sarah and Albert returned to the room.

Levi was thankful he and Amy had decided not tell her parents about the panther attack, fearing Sarah would be afraid to have Amy move to the mountaintop.

Ben's prowess from the time he could crawl, walk and run was amazing. He could far outdistance Hiram who was a year older, and Hiram was no slouch. Levi's greatest fear for his son, once he had seen his eyes glowing in the dark, was that some hunter would shoot him between the eyes.

When Hiram was three and Ben two, Amy give birth to another son, and Sarah's heart lurched. Baby Samuel looked just like Jonathan, dark blond hair and blue-green eyes, a direct opposite of Ben and Hiram. Amy loved being a mother. The youngest child, she had never been around small children, and she adored them. Levi never seemed to stop. He was up before daybreak to stoke the fires for Amy, and by the time she arose, he was bringing fresh, foaming milk into the cabin.

Amy loved her huge husband without reserve, and Levi would always believe he had married the most beautiful woman God had ever created. He loved to touch her long, slender neck and watched in wonder as her long legs and lithe body moved with grace.

CHAPTER 9

Full summers with seminars and extra teaching kept Randolph Adams busy for several years, and in 1888, he and Cynthia were blessed with another son. Long-limbed Wesley with dark auburn hair, demanded time and patience. At the end of the summer, he and fourteen-year-old Joel made a quick trip to the cabin but did not have time to visit the Edwards farm. Albert had run numerous logs to market due to unexpected, excessive rains, which were rare in late summer. Seeing smoke in the distance and assuming Randolph was in the cabin, he and Levi rode by to speak to them. Randolph was shocked when Albert introduced Levi as Amy's husband and especially surprised to know that Amy and Levi had three small sons. Watching the two men depart, Joel turned a disappointed face to his father.

"I don't like Levi."

"Why not, son?" Randolph asked.

"He looks too big and rough."

"Actually, Joel, he is a very striking man, and I wouldn't care to cross him." His father stifled the urge to tease Joel about Amy, realizing the hurt a young boy could experience when his first love was no longer available.

***

Freewheeling women in the river ports tried to hang onto Levi when he took his logs to market, but he pushed them aside. As soon as he purchased presents for Amy and the boys, he was ready to head home.

"I tell you, Sarah, Levi is a changed man. He only thinks of Amy and the boys. I never thought I would see the day," Albert said to Sarah after the return trip home. "He just throws them sluts away from him."

Sarah could not deny the happiness that radiated from Amy's face, and the children were such a joy to her and Albert.

In 1890, another son arrived, and Sarah was practically living with Amy. Little Carl, with light brown hair and dark brown eyes, was a cross between the three older boys.

Even with all the chores of a growing family, Levi had managed to continue helping his father and two brothers with their moonshine production, and his horses were the talk of the country. As quickly as new colts were on the ground, they were spoken for. He kept the best of the lot for his farm. He wanted only superior stock when he made his move. His oxen were huge beasts that could haul mammoth loads once they were encased in cumbersome yokes and hooked to traces. Hiram and Ben loved the large animals. They spent long hours currying, caressing and talking to them. They chose a name for each animal and were ecstatic when the very young steers would follow them to the corn crib, nibbling fresh shelled corn out of the boys' outstretched hands. As the steers grew into enormous oxen, they continued to eat proffered treats from the boys, ambling after them as docile as puppies.

"They are the strongest animals in the whole world, Hiram," Ben said, as he placed his arms around the neck of his favorite ox, swinging to and fro while the docile animal paid little heed to the small boy swinging from his neck.

"Try it, Hiram. It's fun," Ben urged.

"I don't think I want to do that," said Hiram who had long since discovered his body would not do the same things Ben's body did, and on one occasion, he had learned a very painful lesson.

Levi had shown the boys how to test the large grapevines to use as swings. "First, look to see how many trees are hooked to the vines and jerk them several times to be sure they won't slip." Levi had not intended for the boys to swing out over deep ravines, but Ben's curiosity was always traveling.

"Look, Hiram," he called, as he swung out over a deep gulch, holding the large vine with only one hand. Hiram, not to be outdone, tried the same maneuver and, fortunately, fell before he reached the deepest part, suffering only a sprained ankle.

Baby Floyd arrived in January of 1892, another carbon copy of Levi. Their cabin was becoming crowded, and Levi began in earnest to square and notch logs for their new home.

Many nights after Amy slept, he would slip from the cabin with a lighted lantern to cut barrel stoves from the best of white oak sections stacked just outside the barn. Albert had helped him enlarge the old barn, and the new section was snug with close-fitting notches, requiring little need for chinking. Blowing snow and freezing winter winds could not breach the walls, leaving Levi to work in comfort through the long winter months. With strong hands, he removed soaked and pliable barrel staves from a large water trough, quickly shaping and bending them to desirable forms. His moonshine would age in the best because it would be the best. Gradually, through the years, he transported numerous barrels into his secret cave.

Three years earlier, Levi had finally told Albert about the cave. On several occasions, the two men had traveled to the mountaintop and began cleaning space for a home and corn fields. He had planned to enlighten his father-in-law of its existence but had not quite gotten around to the subject. On one occasion, a ferocious storm suddenly arose, and Levi headed through the stream, instructing Albert to follow him to safety.

"God almighty, Levi. What have you got there?" Albert spoke in awe, gazing about the huge cave. He was taken aback as he looked at Levi in the light of the blazing torches. His dark brown eyes glittered with an excitement he had never before seen in his son-in-law.

"You can't ever tell nobody, Albert," Levi said. "Amy is the only other person on earth who knows about this place."

Albert nodded in agreement and was not at all surprised when Levi led him to an underground waterfall with its dark, disappearing stream.

"You're gonna have your own moonshine kingdom," Albert said, as the other man laughed, still in a heightened state of excitement. The two men had long since come to respect and trust one another. Levi trusted Albert as he could never have trusted his own family. He knew Albert would tell Sarah, but she sure as hell would never say anything that might upset Amy or the boys. Her love and loyalty ran too deep. Albert roared with laughter, as they traveled through various rooms and tunnels happening upon Levi's large stash of beautifully crafted oak barrels.

"You sure fooled the hell out of me, Levi. I thought you were taking all these barrels to your father," and both men laughed uproariously.

Sarah couldn't believe how anxious Albert became to leave for the mountaintop with Levi. Levi's excitement had spilled over to him, and the cave became a second home to both men. His respect for his son-in-law increased by the day.

"Sarah, our place here is just about as good as it can get, but I want you to see Amy and Levi's farm. So help me, God, Virginia is even prettier than Kentucky."

Sarah laughed at her usually noncommital husband. "You just want to move into that beautiful cave you told me about," she teased.

"Well, I'll tell you, Sarah, it would make a mighty fine home, but Levi sure has other plans for it. He's got oak barrels stashed all over the place and three fine copper-pot stills."

She turned to face Albert with flashing eyes. "You know who will be helping him, don't you? Our grandsons are going to grow up and become bootleggers, and I don't like it one bit."

"I never thought I would either, Sarah, but his liquor is better than what the distilleries put out in Louisville. Luke and Martin brought us a bottle of Kentucky bourbon the last time we went down river and Levi's is better. The only difference being, he won't have a license for it."

Levi had not exaggerated when he told Albert of the large sparkling pond where fish swam in profusion. His grandsons would love playing in the waterfall and would, no doubt, simply catch the abundant fish with bare hands.

***

When Hiram was eight-years-old, Levi decided it was time to move to the mountaintop. He loaded most of his equipment the day before, and, as usual, he arose long before daybreak to add further provisions. Sarah and Albert spent the night with them. Albert awakened even earlier than Levi and set the coffeepot boiling on the wood stove. Together they added last minute supplies that would be loaded onto the oxen at first light. Levi's father agreed to come and stay with Amy, Sarah and the boys. The two milk cows would have to be tended and the pigs slopped. Amy was pregnant again, and he didn't want her doing rough chores. He would take Hiram and Ben with him. Both were large and strong like their father, possessing an unerring aim with big slingshots that could bring down squirrels and rabbits to supply food for the four men erecting the huge cabin. Levi's two brothers would spend a few days helping to lift the long logs into place, but they would not be privy to his cave. He had fashioned a lean-to for shelter into a hillside, and Albert laughed, knowing why Levi was building it.

"Hell, Albert, they could get drunk and tell anybody about this cave," and his father-in-law agreed.

Boys and men slept soundly through the night after the long and toiling trip up the steep mountain, prodding heavily laden oxen and horses upward at a slow pace. The boys awakened early to the sizzle of fresh fish in a heavy black skillet placed over red hot coals. Albert had scooped enormous trout from the pond in a makeshift net, and he marveled at their size.

Rolling out of their warm blankets, the boys shivered in the crisp morning air and crowded close to the open fire. Albert smiled at his husky grandsons, while loading their large tin plates with sizzling trout and baked potatoes rolled from the fire.

"Feels like I'm on top of the world, Grandpaw," Hiram said with his mouth full of food.

"Well, I would say you just might be right," Albert answered. "You are now in the state of Virginia, and right up the path, and not too far, is Kentucky." The three viewed the far- reaching horizons with many peaks and deep valleys, as the enchanted forest sparkled and came to life in the first rays of a large, crimson sun appearing over the hills. Mammoth trees crowded about the clearing, playing host to a countless number of birds. Crows and black birds sailed through dense foliage dotted with bright red birds and noisy blue jays. Huge horned owls with drooping eyelids snuggled closely to large tree trunks to rest, after hooting and watching through the night. The boys knew the woodlands well, but their new farm was awesome. Large, fat squirrels with wide, bushy tails scampered all over, curious and unafraid.

"The rabbits are awful fat, Grandpaw," Ben said, and Albert laughed. "When you see all the chinquapins, walnuts and chestnuts on the ground, you can see why, and there are still acorns by the pile."

"Boys, you are gonna have to play another day," Levi said, leading two of the large oxen. "The sooner we get the cabin done, the more you can roam about."

Numerous rows of hewed and squared logs lay about the clearing with precise deep notching to ensure a close fit. Nade Cantrell looked at his younger brother with disbelieving eyes.

"What in the hell are you gonna do with all these fifty-foot logs, Levi? Build a damn castle?"

Levi simply stated, "It's for Amy."

***

With oxen hooked to the logs and makeshift pulleys, walls of the new home rose quickly. Levi was everywhere doing everything. With his superior strength, he moved logs to fall into proper notches. In the early morning he stood atop the rapidly rising wall, gazing momentarily about the surrounding forest. Heavy dew still weighted and clung to lush succulent grass, but warmth from the sun would soon send it steaming. He nodded with satisfaction, as his mind envisioned the practicality of his location.

Here on top of this mountain, he could see in every direction, and the two elevations jutting above the cabin would be excellent lookouts for any unwanted visitors. He had scrimped, saved and bargained for this paradise, and he gloried in it. The springs and waterfalls would be their mecca.

There would be no more lugging pails of water up steep inclines. He would ditch the land and use hollowed out logs so water would flow to his back door. The cabin was being built just below the waterfall. The large, honeycombed cave was perfect. Smoke from the fires needed for moonshining operations would mostly disappear with the dark stream, leaving the remainder to dissipate in many meandering tunnels and rooms.

"My God, it is perfect," Levi murmured. At times, his excitement almost overcame him.

A sleek herd of cattle, oxen and numerous horses would share remnants of the corn crop, but the largest and superior grains would produce clear and superior moonshine. Virgin soils, pampered by eons of time with decaying leaves and plentiful rainfall, would send gigantic corn stalks soaring skyward, and the corn itself would drip with sweet juices.

Hiram and Ben outdid themselves at suppertime. Two large rabbits and one fat squirrel were roasted slowly over hot coals during the afternoon. A large, black skillet was brimming with fried potatoes and another with crispy corn cakes. Quart jars of corn and beans were dumped into two battered pots to be heated. Mostly, they were too tired to talk. In one day the four men had almost completed raising enough logs to begin the apex of a roof. Plodding oxen worked steady all day, dragging fifty-foot beams squared to a perfect eighteen inches. With abundant timber crowding and towering above them, Levi had been able to pick and choose.

Over the years, Levi's frequent trips to the mountaintop had been busy ones. He kept several large double-bit axes in the cave along with numerous saws. The tools were kept in razor-sharp readiness, and he chose his trees carefully. Each tree would have to be big enough to supply heart wood from the center that would give him eighteen inch beams. That meant sawing and cutting away several inches of sappy outer wood, and it was a time-consuming chore. The supply surged ahead greatly when Albert joined him in his endeavor. It was a joy to Levi as each beam emerged from a fallen tree, and he was closer to his dream for Amy.

"I'm just glad we didn't have to skin all them damn trees," Nade announced, as they stopped for the day, and Levi's stockpile had hardly been dented. They could all imagine the number of hours Levi had spent bending over the large, mounted grindstone sitting next to the hoard of beams.

"How many axes you wore out on that contraption?" Jack asked, indicating finely powdered steel surrounding the much-used grindstone.

Levi merely shook his head. Bushels of wide chestnut shingles lay in heaps ready to attach to the cabin roof. Albert had come full circle with his son-in-law, and long since admitted to Sarah, he wouldn't have to kill him after all. He knew in his heart that Amy would al-

ways be Levi's only love and his very life. He did not relish the idea of
Levi going full-time into the moonshine business, but there was money
to be made when you produced the best, and Levi could produce the
highest grade. Here, on the border of Kentucky and Virginia, with
sparkling ponds and streams, a man could create his own kingdom.
Albert knew Levi would never deplete the magnificent fish supply
nor the abundant game moving freely about.

The newly-opened pink and white dogwood blossoms sallied forth
into every nook and corner, standing beneath a gigantic forest in prime
display that was breathtakingly beautiful. Albert could see nothing
about the location that wasn't beautiful. By the time the dogwoods
shed their blossoms, wildflowers would cover the entire area.

***

Levi's house for Amy included a kitchen and living area, a fifty-
foot square, with two large bedrooms of equal size attached. A huge
room upstairs would be sleeping quarters for their brood of boys that
would shortly be added to.

Amy was as big as a house, and Sarah was sure it would be twins.
Albert had measured and cut prime oak for a table that would seat
sixteen people.

The wood had been polished to a high sheen and waited in the
cave. It was his present to Amy for her new home. Holes had been
bored for wooden dowels that had been honed to perfection, and he
could hardly wait to see her face. The boys had long since eaten their
meals sitting on the raised hearth in front of the fireplace, and now
each could have his own place on matching benches surrounding the
long table. Albert remembered the cabin he had built for Sarah with
such love and care, and the happiness they had shared in their new
home. A great sadness came over him as he thought of Jonathan and
Henry, now lying in the well-tended cemetery next to their home.

How would Sarah and Amy ever be able to be separated by the
distance between them? Amy had filled the void in their life after
Luke and Albert left, and her growing family had again filled their
lives with laughter and joy. It seemed the same thing had been on
Levi's mind, as he broached the subject to Albert the next morning as
they sat by the open fire, sharpening their axes together. Levi drove
straight to the point as he offered Albert land to build a home on.

"I just don't know what Amy will do without you and Sarah."

"I'll talk to Sarah about it," was all Albert said.

***

In early May of 1893, Randolph Adams decided to take his two sons to the cabin for a few days. Eighteen-year-old Joel had just completed his first year of college, and Wesley at three, wanted to go to kindergarten. Joel couldn't take two steps without his younger brother at his heels, and Randolph knew that, with Joel returning north to school, it might be sometime before they could get back to the Breaks.

Wesley loved riding his own horse but tended to forget the bridle and let the horse decide which way to go. He was completely captivated by animals along the way, and he bombarded Joel with numerous questions about each one. Randolph felt slightly guilty that Joel was bearing the brunt of his little brother's care.

Grateful friends had left a very clean and well-stocked cabin in return for being allowed to use it on their hunting expeditions, and the usual clean up was minimal. "Boys, why don't we ride over to the Edwards' place day after tomorrow and see how things are going there. I saw Luke and Martin a few weeks back, and they asked me to look in on them the next time we came here."

"You didn't tell me you had seen them, Dad," Joel said.

"Sorry, son. They have excelled in building and have gained quite a reputation for themselves in middle Kentucky. They were in Lexington to meet with a new client."

"Did they say how Amy was?" Joel asked.

Randolph was surprised. He has assumed Joel had long since forgotten about Amy.

"Yes, I asked about Amy, and it seems she is partial to boys. She now has five and is expecting again. They are moving to a mountaintop farm very soon now, and her brothers think their parents will probably move with them."

There was no reaction from Joel, but Randolph knew Amy's image would always be with him. She was a beautiful and striking girl, who had for a few days given a nine-year-old boy her full attention, treating him like a peer.

Hiram and Ben had just arrived at Sarah and Albert's homestead on an errand for Amy. Albert was delighted to see Randolph and his sons, and he immediately introduced them to Hiram and Ben. Joel could see no trace of Amy in the boys and was somewhat disappointed. Wesley was intrigued by Ben. He was a very large seven-year-old, and his eyes fascinated the young child.

"Saw Luke and Martin in Lexington a few weeks back, Albert, and they said to tell you hello if we happened to see you. Hear you are moving way up into the mountains," Randolph said.

"Yes we are, Randolph, I came back with the boys yesterday to pick up a few more supplies. We should make the final move real soon. The house is just about finished, and the cabin for me and Sarah is well along. You and the boys come on in. Sarah will want to hear all about Luke and Martin, and dinner is just about ready."

Sarah gave Randolph and both the boys a warm embrace and immediately set their places at the table. As they ate, Randolph gave her the details on her sons.

"They are really doing well, Sarah. Their work is respected, and I think they are going to be even busier. They said to tell you that your grandchildren are growing up fast, and you need to come visit them."

Sarah's still-beautiful face lit up in a delighted smile. She looked much younger than sixty-three years, and her graceful movements were still filled with purpose. Joel saw a strong resemblance to Amy, and he wondered how Amy would look now after several children, but he could only believe she would still be beautiful.

As Randolph and his sons traveled back to their cabin two days later, Wesley was still talking about Ben. "Ben has cat eyes," he said. Joel laughed at the announcement.

"What do you mean he has cat eyes, Wesley?"

"Well, they are yellow, but they are not yellow, and I'll bet he can see in the dark like old Tommy." Old Tommy had been with the family since before Wesley was born. He slept at the foot of the bed but always looked at Wesley any time of the night with eyes that never seem to close.

"I really liked the way he jumped into his saddle." Joel had to agree that he was also astounded to see the seven-year-old spring from the ground with only a slight touch on the saddle.

"I guess he has had a lot of practice, but you should not try that,

Wesley. You could wind up under your horse's hooves," he said seeing the look in the young boy's eyes.

***

Nade and Jack Cantrell could only admire the log house as each phase was completed. Levi had vexed them to the point of exasperation with his relentlessness in marking and cutting, exacting deep notches at the end of each perfectly hewn log. The dwelling could no longer be deemed a cabin. It was a house with solid walls. Each nine-inch notch meted into the opposite one. Levi's obsessive attention to each minute detail had achieved his goal. The apex of the roof peaked at thirty feet, giving the boys a high and wide space to cavort in. A huge rock fireplace anchored each end of the long living and kitchen area, and the chimney rose several feet above the roof. Jack was concerned about the younger boys wandering into the huge open fireplace.

"It's a big house, and I want Amy to be warm. And besides Sarah and Albert are gonna be here." Levi explained, "I gave them land to build on."

His two brothers had long since stopped being surprised by anything Levi hatched up. Levi, giving them a sheepish look inquired, "You two wouldn't want to hang around and give me a hand with a porch would you? I'll give you a bunch of my best corn this fall," he added hopefully.

"What kind of porch you got in mind, little brother?" Nade asked.

"It won't take long. We've already got all those big trees down."

Nade had just about had all the building he wanted, but Jack volunteered their help as Nade sulked over to the outdoor fire pit and settled down for the evening with his jug of moonshine. "At least we can sleep in the damned house if it rains, can't we, Levi? I promise I won't spit tobacco juice on Amy's floor," he jeered.

"Then I reckon I'll have to let you sleep inside," Levi answered, and the two brothers laughed as they pried the jug away from Nade for a short snort of moonshine.

Again, Levi fretted with each log, making sure it was perfectly squared. He took great care in fitting the heavy logs extremely close for the floor. Levi was sure Sarah would go screaming from the mountain if a snake crawled through a crack onto the porch, and wood shavings from extra planing to ensure a close fit were deep through-out the area. Albert had smoothed the railings on the stairs leading to the large upstairs bedroom and taught Hiram and Ben how to add the finishing touches with bear grease and turpentine.

"Damned if that ain't somethin'," Nade said, as he backed off to view the finished porch and house after several days.

A wide porch, fifteen feet high, surrounded the entire house. Chestnut shakes covered the sloping roof of the porch, supported by huge squared beams, sheltering the closely wedged flooring that matched the inside floor. Levi's tribute to Amy would become a land-mark in the hills.

Shortly after Levi settled Amy and the boys into the new home, work began on a cabin for Sarah and Albert. Sarah watched with great interest as the sturdy foundation was laid for their home. Both Albert and Levi saw the anxiety on her face and knew she still struggled with haunting memories from the past. Though a half-century had passed, the terrible tragedy was indelibly etched in her mind. She still had screaming nightmares of teaming, monstrous, reptiles pouring through the cabin floor. The awful dreams had become less and less frequent, but they were still there.

"Sarah, honey, the logs in the floor are so tight not even an ant can crawl through," Albert assured his wife, placing a protective arm about her shoulders.

The faraway look in her eyes disappeared as she focused on him and smiled. Sarah's tall frame was thin but very strong, and her thick flaxen hair was becoming streaked with soft silver strands. Small lines were beginning to appear around her eyes and mouth.

Though Nade grumbled, cussed and slugged heavily on the moon-shine, he finally consented to help with Sarah and Albert's cabin. Levi had promised him more prize corn, and Jack cajoled his younger brother into staying on a few weeks.

Jack was enjoying his stay with Levi and his family. He was com-pletely captivated by Amy and his handsome nephews. He was down right envious of the love and happiness surrounding Levi. He was even beginning to think of looking for a wife. Sarah and Albert's cabin was a smaller version of Amy's house even to the surrounding porch. The logs were fitted so closely, there was little room left be-tween them for clay chinking. The only necessary chore left was to erect a split-rail fence around the two cabins. Levi's herds of cattle, oxen and horses had grown considerably, and Amy didn't want them hanging about the front yard. Levi wasn't about to let the boys tramp manure all over Amy's new floors.

Again Nade and Jack pitched in. Sturdy, zig-zagging oak rails finally enclosed a large area, and both Nade and Jack were impressed with the overall project. It was truly a beautiful setting that time would only enhance. Through it all, Levi had not allowed them to see his cave. He felt a pang of guilt, since his brothers had worked so hard, but he also knew Nade's damn mouth when he was full of moonshine, which was often.

The summer was one of excitement and hard work. After the boys had finished chores, they splashed in the waterfalls and swam in the fishpond. Their happy shouts of laughter with new discoveries was like an elixir for their grandparents.

They planted large grains of corn, and it was a joy to place kernels into rich, black, earth that had never felt the touch of a hoe. Clearing large trees and preparing more fields continued furiously throughout the summer. Hiram and Ben anchored one end of crosscut saws with Albert and Levi, who watched with satisfaction as firewood by the cord was stacked next to the house. Their garden flourished with oversized vegetables, and the boys lay in wait for the next scavenger. Even the elusive crows were dropped by sharp stones from slingshots, as they dove for succulent tomatoes and green beans.

True to Sarah's prediction, Amy delivered twin boys in late fall. Isaac and Owen were identical, with rusty auburn hair and dark hazel eyes. For days, Levi hovered over Amy.

"Looks like we've got all kinds, Amy," he said, as he placed one of the babies back in his crib and brought the other to Amy's streaming breast. He kissed her gently on the forehead, as the baby greedily latched himself to her bosom, and small hands flailed as steady eyes fixed on his mother.

Leaving his wife's side, Levi walked to the large front porch and watched as Albert pulled ears of corn from enormous, thick stalks. Long, dried leaves rustled as the grain was torn away and tossed onto a rough sled. Ben and Hiram worked diligently with Albert, leaving the higher ears for their grandfather to collect. The large ox stood patiently in front of the sled, which was rapidly filled, and another trip was made to the overflowing corn crib. Huge boxes of shucked corn were placed in front of the fireplace at night, and the time-consuming job of shelling the grain from the cob began. Levi finished the stack of ears long after the others had gone to bed, having treated their friction blisters with bear grease. He was up before daybreak to select the grains he would use in producing his moonshine. Only perfect grains would be used to create the malt, which was the first step in the production. He discarded any grains that were even slightly discolored, mildewed or rotten and fed them to the stock. There were few discards, and Levi was elated. He had been carefully selecting his equipment for years and had chosen the best. His large, copper-pot stills were of excellent quality, and he had paid dearly for them.

When the twins were a week old, Levi carried Amy to a rocking chair by the fireplace in the early morning, before anyone was up. He kissed her upturned face before lowering her to the chair he had covered in blankets. "I just wanted you to sit with me for a spell, Amy, before the family gets up and about. I want to show you the prettiest grain you'll ever see." He carried a large wooden pail to Amy's side, plunging his hand into the depths of the grain. He held it up before letting it slide slowly through his fingers. Large yellow grains glistened in the firelight as Amy smiled at him.

"It is beautiful, Levi," she agreed, with an adoring look at her proud and excited husband.

"This will make the best moonshine this country has ever seen," he boasted.

Pushing the pail of corn aside, he knelt down by Amy's feet, burying his face in her lap, placing his arms around her waist, "Amy, I love you so much, and it looks like our dream is coming true."

Amy slid her hands into his thick hair and massaged his head gently. "Levi, my dream came true the day I saw this beautiful house. I had no idea it would be so big, and I know how hard you must have worked. I can never tell you how much I appreciate all you have done, and I love you even more."

"We have it all, Amy, and sometimes it almost scares me, " Levi said as he held her for some minutes, before finally carrying her back to bed.

***

The next day, Levi began the lengthy procedure for his first run. The first step after selecting the corn was placing whole kernels into large wooden pails with numerous holes drilled through the bottom. Having built a slight incline by his underground stream, he now placed the pails in a long line, and began pouring warm water into each. Albert and the boys kept hot, wet cloths over each pail while the water seeped out. As each container relinquished its water, the procedure was repeated over and over. The corn was kept wet and warm with care not to let it sour.

After four backbreaking days and little sleep for Levi and Albert, the cherished corn began to sprout. They were well on their way to producing sugar from the starch contained in the corn. Next, they lighted a long line of brush along the underground stream, and placed the sprouted corn near the fire to begin drying.

Smoke from the flames was drafted to the flowing stream, and Levi, in his joy, moved about the operation with the agility of a large cat. He would have preferred drying the mass of sprouts in the sunlight, but he would never chance discovery by some passerby. Hiram and Ben gently fanned smoke to the stream with some refuse drifting into other parts of the cave dissipating along the way. Bushels of sprouting corn were finally dried, and the grinding process began. Corn grits were ground by the bushel. Coarsely ground, it would have to be kept dry. They placed one bushel of the ground corn in Levi's prized oak barrels, and numerous barrels received the grits. He staggered the process so his production could last for weeks. Years of honing his expertise guided his instinct now, as he added just the right amount of pure limestone water from the cascading waterfall. No other ingredient would ever be more important than sparkling limestone water in producing the best moonshine or the famed Kentucky bourbon. The water was heated to a high degree, and Levi judged the amount for each barrel. It would average about half-full of water, maybe slightly more, maybe slightly less. There would have to be room left for fermentation. The barrel was covered to ensure clean contents and left standing for several days. "Sweet mash" was forming, as the men constantly tended low-grade fires near the barrels. To maintain the "just right" degree of warmth depended on Levi's ingrained knowledge. He knew too little heat would ruin the texture; too much would spoil the fermentation.

After three days, Levi uncovered the barrels, being careful not to breathe the escaping fumes. He knew from experience they could just about knock you off your feet. Again, Albert and the boys carried warm water to Levi as he thinned "sweet mash," adding a small amount of rye malt to seal in the flavor and bring about fermentation. Again he covered the barrels. Levi kept watch, keeping just the right amount of fire going. He and Albert took shifts during the night to inspect and stoke the low-burning fires. During the day, as Albert kept watch over the brew, Levi circled the circumference of the cave on the outside many times, to try to detect any smoke odor that would give away his operation. He sniffed at the one small opening in the far backside of the cave, almost like one of his hounds. Joy and excitement flowed through his tired body. No hint of his other world was exposed.

After several days, he knew his "sweet mash" had become "sour mash," as sugar was changed to alcohol and carbonic acid. A born moonshiner, Levi was ecstatic when he finally heard the necessary and joyful pop-popping sound that meant the mash was ripe and ready to run. He would finally use his beautiful copper-pot still. Trembling, he held a large section of a torn-up bed sheet, as Albert began dipping mash from the barrels and pouring it into the straining cloth. When the still was half-full, the two men lifted it onto the fire, continuing to add more mash. When Levi judged just the right amount had been strained, he quickly mixed a paste of flour and water to seal the lid tightly. A spout on the large copper container was immediately connected to a copper coil, and the "worm" was threaded through the waterfall and into the barrel on the opposite side. Levi was totally drenched by the cascading water as he trudged thigh-deep in icy water. Making sure the end of the worm was well sealed into the barrel, he quickly crossed the footbridge back to the other side. He had long since constructed the small bridge in anticipation of this day. The stream was too wide to jump, and he might need to get to the other side in a hurry.

Hiram and Ben looked at their father in awe, as he bent to check the fire beneath the still. In his excitement, he was totally unaware of his dripping clothes, or even the fact that his large overalls and thick shirt must weigh several pounds. Albert, like the boys, had never seen moonshine produced, and they watched with great interest, as Levi knew exactly what to do next. Changing clothes swiftly, he continued his constant vigil on the fire, lightly touching the sides of the copper container and checking temperatures. Too hot, it would scorch his precious mash, and even worse, it could explode. His obvious look of satisfaction relaxed the group as Levi crisscrossed the small bridge several times to be sure the "worm" was well secured into the waiting barrel. After what seemed an eternity, the alcohol began to cook, with vapors seeping into the copper worm embedded in the waterfall. Levi raced across the footbridge to the barrel and placed his ear on the top to hear the first drippings from the hot still. Cold water from the waterfall rushing over the hot copper tubing changed alcohol vapor into a watery whiskey that soon ran in a small, steady stream into the barrel. When the copper-pot still had emptied its contents through the worm and into the waiting barrel, it was quickly removed from the fire and the next copper-pot still was ready to put in place.

The first run, or "singlings," was full of excess water, impurities and even poisonous substances. A second run, which Levi called "doubled," was soon in process, and the anxiety was high. As the last few drops dribbled into the waiting barrel, there was complete quiet in the cave, as Levi made ready to sample the first run in their cave. He had washed and polished several flat bottles, and now he performed the final test. Using a long-handled, metal dipper and holding a bottle over the barrel, he filled it two-thirds full with the new moonshine. Placing a strong stopper in the top, he shook the bottle soundly, then in an anxious moment, held it high beneath the blazing torch. Bubbles, small and round, arose, and the bead was exactly right. Levi gave out with one of his war whoops, and the four of them danced with joy. There would be hundreds of runs over many years to come, but never would there be the excitement and joy of the first one.

***

As the century turned, Levi's moonshine business was booming and requiring more corn. Acres of tall trees were felled and large fields began to ring the mountainside. The industrious family carted tons of rocks and stumps away, exposing the rich earth. The fields could now be rotated and nurtured with manure from droves of livestock and wagon loads of decaying leaves mounded over the forest floor. When Levi and Albert deemed the fields ready to be planted again, long, fat grains of corn were planted next to the usual and ever-plentiful chunk of fish. Rain showers that hovered over the mountaintops most summer afternoons soon sent the corn shoots bursting from the soil and shooting skyward.

Levi's young foals were sold by the time they were weaned, and the oxen were always in demand. The boys had gentled and burnished the horns of each ox, and the magnificent beasts were always eye catchers.

Hiram and Ben spent hours with the large animals still proffering treats as they curried their sides and even polished their hooves. Ben was always saddened as he watched his favorite ox led away by a new owner. Levi, taking note of Ben's unhappiness, gave him an ox for his own, and promised he would be the only one who could sell it.

Ben and Hiram loved exploring the mountains, always finding new places and hidden wonders. Albert taught both boys gun safety, and the family felt secure when the two set off on another expedition with their rifles. By the time they were ten and eleven years of age, they had become seasoned hunters.

Levi was not surprised by Ben's night vision. On the blackest of nights, he was able to guide his father stealthily through the forest with ease and sureness that was uncanny. His sense of hearing was also extremely acute, and he could sense the slightest change in bird calls when aroused and the excited chatter in small animals when danger approached.

Two lurking strangers had watched Ben and Hiram on one of their forays some distance from the farm. The boy's fine horses drew their attention, along with the two rifles they carried. They held their mounts in quietness as the boys approached, thinking merely to take the horses and guns. Ben smelled the horses and sensed the danger before they reached the ambush. Turning his horse quickly, he shouted to Hiram, "Run!" Knowing Ben's astounding senses, Hiram didn't argue, and they disappeared almost instantly into the forest. When moonshine was delivered at night, Levi counted on Ben's special senses.

On one occasion, the boys had leaned their rifles against a tree as they collected huge, fat, sweet blackberries and meandered away from their guns. Spotting a large bird nest high in a horn bean tree, Ben quickly climbed the tree hoping to find eagle eggs to hatch on their own. A large, black bear was also intent on the blackberries, and a startled Hiram screamed "Ben" as the bear chased him around the tree. Ben quickly dropped to the ground, giving out with a wild scream. The bear hesitated, and then galloped off into the forest. The boys quickly retrieved their rifles and headed home.

Levi saw the boys coming down the mountain trail at breakneck speed, and knew something had happened.

Eleven-year-old Hiram started relaying the story before he reached the porch. "I was being chased around a tree by a big, black bear, and I was only one step ahead when Ben dropped all the way from the top of the tree and let out a scream. He sounded just like a panther, and the bear took off."

Hiram stopped to get his breath, and Ben merely shrugged his shoulders, "He just wasn't hungry, Pa."

Amy looked at Levi, and somewhere in the dark depth of his eyes, a light ignited momentarily. He well remembered the outraged screams of the panther when he barely escaped with his life, and later, the ordeal of rescuing Amy and washing the panther blood from her body that had marked their son.

When Ben was fourteen, he meandered into the dense woods in hope of bringing home a wild turkey, and suddenly stopped dead in his tracks. A large black panther was sitting in a tree, giving Ben a long look of interest, it then leapt gracefully into the thick forest and disappeared. Ben had felt no threat from the huge beast, and strangely enough, didn't even consider shooting the fleeing animal. In relaying the incident to his father, he looked away and did not see the look of awe on Levi's usually stoic face.

Albert, at seventy-five, still worked hard each day at the moonshine site with Levi and kept the fires at low temperatures for proper drying. Levi craftily shifted the heavier chores to Hiram and Ben. At fourteen and fifteen, they both stood six-feet and two inches tall with strong, hard muscles. Isaac and Owen were still identical at seven years and tried in every way to emulate Hiram and Ben. Samuel, 12 years, Floyd, 10 years, and Carl 9 years, carried their share of the many farm chores. It was also their job to keep the cave stocked with pine knots for lighting the large cavern.

Sarah spent more time in Amy's kitchen than she did in her own and always laughed as the boys pounded down the stairs at mealtime.

"You sound like a damned herd of horses, boys," Levi said on one occasion.

"They're hungry, Levi," Sarah said, and Levi laughed.

"Never seen them when they wasn't hungry, Sarah, and who polished off the blackberry cobbler after we went to bed last night?"

Each boy pointed to the other.

***

Albert waked in the predawn hours with an excruciating pain in the left side of his head, and attempted to rise from the bed. His right side was totally numb, and he rolled to the floor instead. A vile odor arose from his body, and he was mortified. His bowels and bladder had released themselves. He tried to call Sarah, but could utter no sound except a low growl as his tongue rolled back into his throat.

The sound penetrated Sarah's sleep, and the abnormal stench immediately accosted her senses. She immediately recognized Albert's stroke and dragged bedclothes with her in her haste to get to the medicine stashed in the kitchen cabinet. Running back to Albert, she knelt by him, pulling his tongue out from his throat. She quickly poured the elixir into his mouth and watched fearfully as it slid down his throat. Slightly elevating his head, she continued to pour small amounts of the lifesaving liquid into his mouth. Sarah knew he was in great pain though he could not speak. His eyes projected agony, and his right side lay completely limp. After several minutes he appeared to relax slightly, and she eased his tongue back to the center of his mouth and waited to see if it would roll backward again. When she finally decided it was safe to leave him momentarily, she rushed to the front door and rang the large cowbell hanging there with all her might. When Levi had finished their cabin, Hiram had driven a large nail near the front door and hung a cowbell on it so Sarah and Albert could summon them in time of need. It was the first time she had been forced to do so. Rushing back to Albert's side, she saw his eye lids beginning to droop and knew her medicine was beginning to take effect. A weak thready pulse barely beat beneath her fingers, and she prayed for a miracle. Levi and Amy rushed from the house, with Levi still pulling overalls over his long underwear and Amy in her night gown.

"Papa," Amy cried, kneeling at his head smoothing his hair.

"It's a stroke," Sarah said, and for the first time saw fear spring into Levi's eyes. "Levi, we will need to clean him up very carefully, he seems to be resting right now. The medicine I gave him is taking effect."

After Levi and the boys had placed Albert on clean linens, Levi gently held his head while Sarah spooned more medicine into his mouth, and he appeared to be sleeping peacefully. Amy's eyes were wide with fear as she sat by the bed holding her father's limp hand.

"Mama, will Papa be alright?"

"He is alright for now, Amy," was all Sarah could say.

Albert was a strong and healthy eighty-years-old, but Sarah knew another massive stroke could possibly strike within a few days. Two days later Albert died in his sleep. A slight sound awakened Sarah, and she knew it had been his last, rattling breath. She held his still warm body and cried silently.

"Rest well, my Albert, my love and my soul," she whispered, as she smoothed his shock of silver hair back from his forehead. She remembered the first sight of an alarmed Albert as he saw her rifle pointed at him from their covered wagon and his strong arms about her when her father died. He had picked her up and placed her in the wagon with tears streaming down his handsome face. She well remembered their joy as newlyweds in the beautiful, flowering meadow that he had created for her and his support and loving tenderness when their two sons had died during the Civil War.

Six months later, twenty-year-old Hiram brought pretty, raven-haired Jeannie Alcott to the mountain as his bride.

Sarah moved into the extra bedroom at Amy and Levi's, insisting that Hiram and his young wife take her cabin.

***

Randolph Adams threw the heavy saddle over his horse's back with the ease of a much younger man. He was sixty-seven years old, hale and hardy, and still teaching a full schedule of classes. He had just bullied his two sons into a quiet hunting trip to their mountain retreat.

Wesley would enter law school in a few weeks and planned to graduate early so his next three years were already full. Joel had become busier each year with his engineering firm, and Randolph knew this would be their last hunting trip together for some period.

It had been four years since their last trip to the "Breaks," and he craved this short time with his sons. Their trips to the cabin had always been filled with fun and adventures, and Randolph had missed them sorely.

Wesley rode ahead of him through tall timber, his long legs loose and relaxed as thick foliage slapped his feet, planted firmly in the stirrups. Joel brought up the rear, and Randolph was grateful to be with his two fine, handsome sons.

Deer, bear, elk, rabbits and numerous fowl of every description appeared to have increased since their last trip to the area. Huge beavers with large flat tails disappeared into their habitats, as horses hooves trampled the edges of their ponds. Numerous new wood chips scented the air where sharp teeth had recently whittled saplings and larger trees to rebuild homes, washed away by the usual spring rains. Wesley breathed deeply of the heavy, pungent odor of dense pines, as water rushing over rocks in the swollen stream produced the only sound around them.

Randolph was excited about the prospect of a large conglomerate that was on the verge of purchasing Richard Bonham's mineral leases. A railroad and highways would be built into Elkhorn Creek area, but he had begun to have disquieting thoughts about the eventual outcome. All of the owners and investors would be absentees, and he was anxiously awaiting the first movements to see future advantages for the whole state. He knew what money in the hands of politicians could accomplish.

"I know there are tremendous fortunes to be made in this area, Dad, but it seems a shame to totally disrupt this paradise," Joel said.

The three men were busy salting and curing the game they had collected.

"I doubt that it will disturb our acreage here. The focus seems to be in the area around the head waters of Elkhorn Creek at this time. I talked with Luke and Martin Edwards recently, and they had been contacted about the family land in the area. Land agents have been circulating through the hills and plan to buy thousands of acres of land if the deal with the mineral leases goes through. The company will have to build an extended town that will be needed for the removal of massive amounts of coal. Word is, it could take up to a hundred years."

Wesley closed the shutters and replaced a covering on the large chimney before climbing from the roof to help Joel load the pack horses with the game they had cured. He took one last look about the cozy cabin before he padlocked the front door. His next visit to this cabin would be a far cry from the peaceful and leisurely visit he had just shared with his father and brother.

CHAPTER 10

In late 1911, the mist-shrouded stillness of the mountains was ex
ploded as an announcement by Ransome Coal echoed throughout
the region. The conglomerate had purchased one hundred and one
thousand acres of land at the foot of Pine Mountain where mineral
rights had previously been obtained by the company. A massive building project was to be launched immediately that would produce a
model-mining town to showcase to the world. Richard Bonham's
dream had finally been realized, but the end results would not produce the outcome he had promised Randolph Adams. Eastern moguls, including the Fords, Delanos, Roosevelts, Rockefellers and many
others came together to form Ransome Coal. The company had purchased many of the leases from Richard Bonham and others who
were scrambling to cash in on the bonanza.

Franklin D. Roosevelt had also traveled into the area to buy up
leases just after graduating from law school. His grandfather, Delano,
accompanied him, advising and bankrolling the quest for the precious mineral. Millions of dollars would be parlayed into the gargantuan project, and their investments would catapult the investors to
incalculable riches. No expense would be spared. The billions of tons
of high-grade coal that lay within would require at least a century to
remove. Hundreds of officials, teachers, attorneys, doctors, accoun-

tants and managers on every level would be required to live in town and oversee the mammoth undertaking with hordes of workers from around the world. Schools, homes, entertainment, transportation and the best of available amenities would be required to entice top-level personnel into this remote and isolated area. Richard Bonham's initial survey in the 1870s had been tested and retested several times, and each testing had proven his original survey to be completely accurate. There was, indeed, at least one-hundred and sixty-seven billion tons of the highest grade coal known to man in and around the Pine Mountain area. Two seams alone would produce one billion tons of coal as Richard Bonham had predicted. Samples of the ore had been tested numerous times, and its volatility was anxiously awaited by homogenous steel mills in the North.

By early January, even with snow still on the ground, the few trails leading into the valleys were filled with men, some on horseback and some walking. Loaded with bedrolls, axes and saws, they convened at the foot of Pine Mountain, as news of extremely high wages spread like wildfire. Lean-tos were quickly erected beneath giant pines whose lower limbs and needles were used to cover the frozen ground inside the shelters. Foremen rushed to choose their crews, and the forest rang with the sounds of axes and saws. The dense forest covering Ransome's land would be cut and used to build homes and businesses. By the time the equipment needed to erect sawmills arrived, they would have thousands of trees down and sheared of limbs. The bitter cold of winter required large fires that blazed constantly around the clock. Those who kept the roaring fires going and the hunters, who procured game to feed workers, were paid wages equal to the timber cutters. Mine openings were being blasted, and thousands of strong props would be needed. Poplar, oak and hickory timbers would be crowded against the mine roofs to hold the mountain at bay. The area so rich in coal and timber also included large amounts of oil, gas, iron, limestone and silica. Medicinal plants and flowers numbered in the thousands. The hulking shoulders of Pine Mountain had heretofore rebuffed the attempts of intruders to rob her of treasures born through the eons of time. Riches that had lain in benign seclusion would be ripped and torn from the earth in unparalleled, flagrant abandon. Man's greed would erase hundreds of miles of God-given beauty. The high-grade mineral would give rise to phenomenal fortunes and disasters. The earth would rebel when invaded by man to rape her of treasures stored for millions of years. Her jaws would close, and men would die or become mangled beyond repair. She would deprive women of sons, wives of husbands and children of fathers. She would not discriminate.

The first and foremost project was providing a roadway across Pine Mountain that separated Kentucky and Virginia. It was a daunting endeavor, climbing the very steep sides of the Virginia mountain with only a momentary reprieve at the crest before the almost vertical side of the mountain dropped into Kentucky and the future site of Elkinsville. Supplies to build the town would be shipped by rail to the hamlet of Wise, Virginia, and then hauled to the final destination by large oxen-drawn wagons. A railroad was being built on the Kentucky side through Shelby Gap, which would take at least a year. Ransome Coal wanted a town and thousands of tons of coal waiting when the railroad arrived. Monied customers were lined up and waiting for deliveries. David Wilson was chosen to launch the assault on Pine Mountain that would open a passageway. Though only forty-two years of age, David was legendary with his feats of construction.

His greatest accomplishments were forging roadways into and through what was usually considered impossible obstacles. Barley shy of six feet, he appeared to be built of springs infused into his flesh and bones. He moved constantly about the construction areas, giving curt orders but never demanding. He was extremely conscious of the welfare of his workers and also of what they were achieving. Deep lines creased his forehead while salt and pepper hair aged him beyond his years. Les Webster thought he sometimes resembled a wizened old man.

Webster had worked as David Wilson's foreman for eighteen years, and he never ceased to be amazed by his instant solutions to what had appeared to be insurmountable problems. The speed with which the two men could collect their resources and quickly set in motion the intricate details of pending projects was astounding.

Webster, in his middle fifties, had never worked for anyone as fair nor as considerate as his present boss. At first he had qualms about taking orders from a man much younger than he, but those doubts evaporated shortly after their first project together. The wages he paid his workers were always higher than other companies, and there was always a bonus if they finished ahead of schedule.

"This will be our greatest challenge," David said. They met at David's headquarters in Baltimore to discuss the gargantuan project. "Pine Mountain has a deep limestone base so there will have to be a lot of blasting to produce even a steep and winding road."

"We have done that before David. Why is this so different?" asked a puzzled Webster.

"Humongous, low-slung wagons are being constructed that will have to pull two locomotives across the mountain and into Elkinsville. One locomotive weighs in at 40,000 pounds and a smaller one at 26,000 pounds. The weight of the wagons and numerous oxen to pull them will be enormous, and then we start with twelve boilers weighing in at 16,000 pounds each. The pressure on the roadway will be hair-raising. There will be months of hauling tons of equipment for hundreds of men building the town."

"Good God, David, isn't a railroad being built into the area in the next year or so? What's the great rush?"

"I believe it's called money. Ransome Coal is investing millions in a permanent town, and the steel mills are screaming for the much-needed combustible fuel. With all the high-rise buildings being erected and bridge construction, demand for steel is growing by the day. This coal field we're going into is supposed to produce the highest grade ore ever discovered and will more than replace the dwindling supply of fuel."

Webster gave a low whistle and began to collect names of their most reliable workers. Two days later they left for Pine Mountain with one hundred strong workmen in tow.

Ellis Bryant had been briefed by company officials and awaited them at the train station. He had been told that David would want to leave immediately for Pine Mountain to begin staking out the roadway. They would need horses, supplies and eight strong local men. Ellis Bryant hailed from Bristol, Virginia, and was experienced in heavy construction and organizing equipment. He had never worked on a project like this one, and he could hardly believe the enormous amount of equipment and supplies being shipped in constantly. He was also looking forward to meeting David Wilson, the King of Construction.

Bryant was surprised by Wilson's reed thin body and dark hazel eyes that blazed with intelligence and impatience. He had quickly assessed the bulging supply depot and immediately inquired of horses and camping equipment.

"Everything is ready, and I have found two brothers who grew up in the area and will be excellent guides. They are the best of horsemen and can handle any job you throw at them."

Ben and Hiram Cantrell appeared leading horses for Wilson and Webster, as six strong mountaineers followed with packhorses loaded with supplies.

"This is Ben Cantrell," Ellis said, and both men were astonished. "His brother here is Hiram." Both Ben and Hiram towered over the group. Like their father, Levi, they were both at least six-feet and five inches with massive frames. Ben's strange light amber eyes measured both men, and they looked at him the same way Ellis Bryant had on their first meeting. Hiram had Levi's very dark brown eyes with the same stoic expression. Both men wore battered hats clamped over shoulder-length, black hair. Ben's large mustache resembled a broom turned upside down while Hiram's extended into a full heavy beard.

"Do you two have any big brothers at home?" David asked and the group laughed.

"No," Ben said, "but we have five younger brothers catchin' up."

"I'm ready to leave when you are, Ben," David said, and the group started immediately for Pine Mountain towering to the south.

Each day, dynamite resounded throughout the hills, and enormous boulders were rolled down the mountainside. Huge trees were quickly felled, sheared of limbs, then stacked in horizontal walls to accommodate the tons of fine rocks and soil needed to form the roadway. Tall, straight trees were wedged into upright, deep pockets to hold the linear logs in place and form another wall.

David was amazed by the strength and fortitude of the mountaineers. They were huge, hard-muscled men, but only a few equaled the Cantrell brothers. David missed the two men who had helped to stake the roadway across the mountain. Their advice had been solid, and their suggestions had saved time and money. Ellis Bryant had stated emphatically that he needed both Ben and Hiram to continue rounding up horses and oxen that would be needed shortly to pull huge wagons over the mountain road. When Bryant arrived in Wise and inquired of the best horses and oxen in the country, he was immediately referred to Levi Cantrell's stronghold. Not only did he find the finest animals he had ever seen, but he also found Ben. He was intrigued by the way Ben walked among the large herds, touching and talking gently to them. At twenty-five years old, he moved like a big cat, and his strange amber eyes ringed with extremely thick black eyelashes almost gave Ellis a chill.

"Ransome Coal is going to build a road across Pine Mountain, and we will have to move thousands of tons of equipment and supplies on it. It will take months. Think you could get wagons and oxen together for the job?"

"Don't see no problem. Been moving heavy loads about these hills for years. You're gonna need some big low-slung wagons with a lot of wheels."

Ellis immediately offered Ben a salary he could not turn down and then felt a few qualms when he realized he would have to pay Hiram an equal amount. Fortunately, Levi had said he needed the five younger boys to run the farm. Ellis had been informed of Levi's legendary moonshine reputation and warned not to appear too inquisitive. Levi, at fifty-two, was in his prime and powerful. He had sired seven sons in his image and only a fool would cross him.

David was encouraged by the progress being made on the roadway. The mountain men earned the many dollars paid them each day and gave more than full measure.

They arrived each morning just before daybreak on their broad-backed horses and stayed until the light had completely waned. They always carried rifles on their saddles. David's first reaction was to announce there would be no firearms on the project, but within a few hours, he understood why. As huge boulders were blasted with dynamite, hibernating dens of hundreds of angry, seething rattlesnakes and copperheads began striking in all directions, filling the workers with terror. With deadly aim the mountaineers eliminated the poisonous mass, and there was always a great sigh of relief with much handshaking and backslapping. On a few occasions David would see a man slip a deep swig from his flat bottle, as he slid his rifle back in place, but he only smiled to himself. Moonshine was a way of life in these hills he had been told, and unless it got out of control, it was better to let it be.

By the last week of April, the road had crested the top of Pine Mountain, and they began the downward decent into Kentucky.

Ransome had brought so many workers into the area, David had been able to start a crew at the foot of the mountain on the Kentucky side, and the two crews were rapidly closing the gap between them. Spring rains had drenched them on several occasions and washed out several days of hard-earned roadway. Pine Mountain, with its head in the clouds, had brought thunder and lighting down upon them, soaking them to the bone. With cold, driving rains, the workers could only hunker down on the muddied worksite in dripping rain gear to wait out the storm. As feathered fingers of clouds cleared the summit, work began anew. Ben Cantrell rode with Ellis Bryant to view the progress David was making with the road and was amazed to see how fast it was progressing. Workers covered the hillsides like ants, cutting, sawing, chopping and fitting logs together. The road was wider than Ben had anticipated, and he was relieved. The height of the two locomotives and a dozen boilers were going to make the crossing cumbersome and dangerous even on a wide roadway. Forty wagons were already loaded and in place to start the trek over the mountains. Oxen and wagon masters were ready to roll on a moment's notice. Ben's wagon would be hooked to his own two favorite oxen, and he would be the lead wagon on the first trip. He still called Luke and Amos his, even though Ransome had paid him dearly for them. Bets were being placed on how many oxen it would take to pull the larger locomotive over the mountain pass.

Ben was disturbed by the ugly gash hacked into the side of the beautiful mountain. Huge boulders that could not be used on the roadway had been pushed over the mountainside taking smaller trees with them. Large grape and blackberry vines ripped from the earth carried great clumps of black soil, and their petals were strewn like fresh fallen snow. Sticky sap oozed from roadway timbers in the last dying gasps of stately trees. In spite of the excessive money his family was making on this venture, Ben was saddened by the sight.

As the roadway progressed into Kentucky, the men camped on the construction site at night, as did the mountaineers whose nightly treks home were taking longer each day. Workers from other parts of the country were lulled to sleep at night by the hauntingly beautiful music from harmonicas. The mountain men were masters of age-old ballads, and the sweet music seemed to hang in the crisp, still night air. It was not unusual to find a light frosting of snow in the early mornings. Large tracks that appeared in the snow were discomforting to men from larger towns who had followed David Wilson. Large black panthers still roamed the area, as did mountain lions, bobcats and bears. Several fires were kept roaring throughout the night, and David always kept a sharp-eyed mountain man on guard. The screams of the panther kept many of the crew jostling for a sleeping place next to the mountain men and their ever-ready rifles. Webster went to sleep at night watching David lie taunt in his bedroll with eyes wide open. He was beginning to think David slept with his eyes open.

Two young men who helped with feeding the animals and keeping the pens clean were in awe of Ben. Jerry Bentley and Frank Upshaw, having been recruited from the streets of Baltimore, were impressed with his tremendous strength. On several occasions, they had watched Ben move objects with ease that the two of them together had been unable to budge. They had been running from the authorities when they stumbled into the shelter of recruiters for Ransome, and there they stayed. Ben was kind to both the boys, knowing instinctively they had led troubled lives. His impact on them would last a lifetime. They were paid excellent wages, given good food and a tent to sleep in. He complimented them on the way they kept the pens cleaned and food constantly before the oxen. Ben knew they had never seen an ox before, and he could see the sheer terror in their eyes when they first approached the animals. They had quickly climbed the fence surrounding the livestock, and Ben stifled an impulse to laugh, as he watched their thin bodies clamor up the high enclosure.

"There is no need to be afraid of these animals, boys," he assured them. He coaxed them from their perch and gradually pressured them into touching the animal's hides, moving slowly to their heads and horns. The docile oxen paid no heed to the intruders, and their fear slowly subsided. "I have always played with these animals, and you can't have a better friend. By the time I was two-years-old, I would swing from their horns," Ben said, as he hugged a huge white ox. In the following days, he would carefully walk them among the animals, and both began to relax in the open pen.

The two sixteen-year-olds had been on the streets for years, and their stringy, scrawny bodies were undersize for their age. In the next few weeks, with plentiful and nourishing food, their bodies began to fill out, and their height seemed to be increasing by the day.

Ben was making late rounds one night as Frank and Jerry came running to the pens. They were about to slide under the lowest wire when Ben collared them. "Just what in the hell is going on here?" he roared at the two.

At that moment three swarthy, rough-looking workers arrived, shaking their fists at the boys. "We aim to beat the hell out of these damned pickpockets," the larger one yelled and lunged toward Frank.

"Friend, you just let me take care of this," Ben said, stepping between Frank and his furious attacker.

"We were shootin craps, and these two bastards stole our pocket books."

He made as if to dislodge Ben from his stance in defense of Frank, while his two friends were ready to back him up. Ben raised the large pitchfork he had been holding, and his amber eyes blazed in the meager light. They stared at Ben's huge frame with bulging muscles and backed away.

"You two shitheads give these men back their money," he ordered.

Both the boys threw their loot to the enraged men, who counted their money immediately and walked away with no further comment.

Ben turned his blazing anger on Frank and Jerry, as they cowered against the fence. "I should beat the livin' hell out of the both of you right now," he raged. "We're treating you like fine, upstanding men with good wages and good food, and you just go right on stealing. I should kick your ass all the way back to Baltimore and let the law have you."

"Oh God, please, Ben just give us one more chance. We promise never to do this again." Tears streamed down both their faces as they begged for another chance.

Ben's belligerent outward appearance gave no hint of the pity he felt for the two homeless boys. He shoved the pitchfork toward them. "I want every pen cleaned before you turn in," and they scampered away to do his bidding.

The depot was a beehive of activity, and guards were placed on duty round-the-clock as supplies continued to pour in. The first wagons to cross the mountains would be loaded with food and tents for the hundreds of men working to clear the dense forest and construct mine openings.

Ellis Bryant had organized the project down to the last box that would be loaded on the wagons. His battered, sweat-stained, gray, felt hat could be spotted any time of day as he circled the multitudes of waiting wagons and supervised the loading of each. Before daybreak he was in his saddle seeing that all incoming supplies were properly marked and checked to be readily available for loading. His slightly bowed legs and leathered face gave evidence of his years in the saddle. His black and white Appaloosa knew every twitch of his knee, and they moved as one.

The road into Elkinsville was completed much earlier than anyone had anticipated, and there was jubilation as word spread. The wagons would start rolling the next morning.

Oxen were hooked to a long line of wagons that had been ready to roll for days. The wagon masters collected their crew by lantern light in total darkness. As the eastern sky began to show the first gray light between night and day, the procession moved out, and history was made. The immense animals moved forward with ease. The single trees connected to the doubletree clinked in the predawn darkness.

Ben Cantrell walked beside a large, well-loaded wagon with a long whip looped over his shoulders. He would never have to touch the animals with It, but one crack of the long braided leather in the air would keep them moving if necessary. He had hooked Luke and Amos first in front of the wagon. Their combined strength was formidable. He has used them for several years to haul mammoth loads, as they cleared more farmland, and he knew their capabilities. An additional four pairs were harnessed to the wagon in front of them. As the loads grew bulkier, and heavier, more oxen would be added.

As the light increased, Ben looked at Luke and Amos and marveled at their beauty. The hours he had spent currying and combing their beautiful hides was evident. Amos was pure white with dark brown splotches on his left shoulder. The same color darkened half of his head, and three of his legs were splotched with brown from knee to hoof. Ben had always polished their horns, and now they gleamed in the early morning light. Luke was covered with a tawny brown, and large white dots appeared over his entire body. His shining coat of short hair reminded Ben of the first leaves of autumn. His head was slightly larger than Amos', and Ben felt that perhaps he could outweigh Amos by at least one hundred pounds. He resettled the heavy wooden yoke on Luke's neck and walked down the line to do the same for the other oxen. Ellis Bryant riding by simply grunted as Ben passed the lead oxen and circled back to the wagon. He had made sure there were no friction spots under the heavy yokes embracing the huge beasts.

David Wilson rode ahead of the wagon train looking for any sign of weak spots in the roadway. Webster rode back of the wagons checking for any break in the construction, as the heavy wagons rolled over it and upward toward the summit. The wagons were extremely low-slung with eight sets of wide, well-greased wheels. David watched as the strong oxen did not appear to break their stride even when the trail grew steeper. The load today was heavy, but it was light compared to what waited at the depot. Materials to assemble nine saw-mills and two brickyards would be moved after a week of bringing supplies for the workmen. The true test of their construction would come when they moved the locomotives and enormous boilers. He willed himself not to look down the steep sides of the mountain and valley thousands of feet below.

Shouting men welcomed them as the first wagon rolled into Elkinsville, and contents of the wagons were quickly distributed to the many workers. Long awaited food and shelter were a welcome relief to sparse rations. The men who brought the wagons over the pass were amazed by the mountains of logs piled everywhere awaiting the construction of sawmills.

A large section of land had been cleared at the top of the mountain so wagon trains returning from Elkinsville could wait for loaded wagons to pass. The first pass was completed successfully and the roadway held. The weight being placed on the new structure was immense, and David Wilson breathed a sigh of relief at the end of each day.

At the end of two weeks, materials for sawmills and brickyards had been delivered, and some were already in use. Numerous construction crews from around the country had forged their way into the valley to help with the mammoth project. As the voracious jaws of sawmills ejected miles of board feet, it was rushed to hastily constructed kilns to dry quickly, and new homes began to climb the hillsides.

Six of the oversized boilers crossed the mountain pass, and a powerhouse was hastily being constructed. David Wilson and Les Webster felt the roadway was holding well, and it was time to move the larger locomotive. Twenty oxen had been hooked to each wagon to pull the cumbersome boilers, and there had been no problem.

"Ben, how many oxen do you think we need to move the biggest locomotive?" David asked.

Ben had been thinking about the locomotive since the first time he had seen it. "I think you need to put twenty pair of oxen to it, David. That steep grade just before the top of the mountain will take a lot of strength."

"Do you think you can hook that many together and working?"

"No problem, I will harness them to a wagon and do some practice runs around some of the hills here in Wise. They can be ready to roll by day after tomorrow."

"It's in your hands, Ben. What can I do to help?"

"I'll give you a list of the men I want to walk close behind with grappling hooks, just in case. We will really need them when we start down that steep grade into Kentucky."

"If you need anything more, just say the word," David promised.

Ben nodded and headed toward the corral to choose the oxen. Jerry and Frank knew immediately which oxen were rested and ready to travel again.

"Could we go with you on this trip, Ben? We haven't even seen the new road or town."

"Sure you can, boys. Let's get these animals hooked to that big wagon there."

The wagon was equal in size to one of the locomotives that had been loaded several days before. Ben was extremely proud of Jerry and Frank. They had become adept at putting the oxen into heavy yokes and examining the hooves of each animal after the trip into Kentucky. Sharp stones on the new roadway had lamed several of the oxen, and the two boys had learned to spot the problem immediately and begin treatment.

Two days later, forty oxen were hooked to the wagon on which the forty-thousand pound locomotive had been chained in place. By lantern light, Ben and Hiram examined every yoke and checked each animal. Luke and Amos were again hitched to the front of the massive wagon with Ben double-checking single trees and the doubletree.

Hiram looked at the setup with disgust. "This is the craziest damn thing I have ever seen. They don't even have a railroad yet."

Ellis Bryant overheard Hiram's remark to Ben and roared with laughter. "Hiram they have already opened up eight mine entries and several more will soon be in operation. Miners are already digging coal and laying tracks to the tipples so they need these locomotives, pronto."

"By the time the railroads come through, there will be thousands of tons of coal waiting to fill miles of gondolas, and the steel mills will be singing "Hallelujah!" As soon as we take the last boiler across, we start carrying material for a tipple."

"What's a tipple?" Hiram asked with a blank look.

"It's where they wash and grade all the coal. They wash off all the bug dust then run it on conveyer belts, so they can discard bits of rock and any other trash that shows up. By the time the coal is dumped into gondolas, it is pure and clean. They say it will be the largest tipple in the world."

"We don't haul nothing that ain't big," Hiram said, eyeing the locomotive that was beginning to move out.

David Wilson chose to ride in back of the locomotive, and Webster would take the lead. A multitude of men walked ahead of the wagon with grappling hooks attached to strong ropes looped around their shoulders. Heavy metal rings had been welded to the iron framework of the wagon, and numerous thick ropes were attached to the rings. Scores of workers walked on either side to man the ropes immediately, if needed. Excitement ran high as each hour passed, and the huge animals lumbered farther along the winding roadway. The sturdy oxen approached the steep incline and their momentum was constant. There was no sound from the animals, and their brute force was incredible. Ben and Hiram watched closely as each plodding hoof did not miss a beat. Neither saw any indication that might signal a need of help from the hoard of workers watching in amazement and ready to assist. A roar of applause echoed through the hills as the locomotive crested the top of the mountain. David Wilson following closely behind the vehicle breathed a sigh of relief. The roadway had held. Suddenly the sight of a locomotive perched atop the mountain without a track struck him as hilarious. His laughter was one of great relief and release, and the entire group joined in. The steep, winding, downward descent into Kentucky was beautifully executed with brakes set and dozens of men pulling backward with ropes and grappling hooks.

Spring rains stretched into June, and the rich odor of mounds of decaying leaves permeated the air. Black loam beneath the many layers of leaves and pine needles remained wet, and each day late afternoon showers added excessive moisture. The mountains were blooming in splendor, and the many newcomers on the workforce were awed by the beauty of the mountain laurel. The huge shrubs merged into a sea of long, beautiful, elegant, dark green leaves that held forth acres and acres of extraordinary, large, lush flowers of blue and white. They poured through every minute space and encircled almost every tree.

Ellis Bryant had supervised the loading of the last, oversized boiler the night before. There would be months of heavy loads yet to be delivered, but the massive bulk of the boilers had given him a great feeling of unease each time the cumbersome objects headed out. Twenty oxen moved forth in the early predawn. Ben Cantrell walked with Amos and Luke and felt great pride as he watched their strong, muscular bodies move forward.

David Wilson galloped out of the shadows on his gray horse, ready to take the lead again. The crude roadway was holding, but David, like the others, would be greatly relieved when this last boiler rolled into Elkinsville.

"It sure is rainy for this time of summer." Ellis Bryant had assured David early in the week, and he looked especially edgy this morning.

"Something on your mind, Ellis?" David asked.

"I'll just be glad when we get this last boiler across that mountain. There is a stillness in the air this morning, and I don't like it one bit."

David hesitated but shook off the warning. Ransome supervisors were screaming for supplies. Mine openings were rapidly being constructed, and hundreds of men continued to pour into the valley each day. It would be months before the railroad through Shelby Gap would be completed, and he could not stake a delay on an ominous feeling. The enormous amount of supplies needed to shelter and feed the hordes of workers was staggering. The town being constructed in this year, under such primitive conditions, would be nothing short of phenomenal.

The wetness was everywhere. Heavy dew was always visible on leaves until late morning, and incessant late afternoon showers continued.

"This damned road needs to dry out, Ben," Ellis grated as he dismounted and led his horse, testing the huge braces that held the makeshift road in place. He projected rigid tenseness, and Ben felt a great unease.

The ascent began, and Ben waved to Hiram, who walked next to the wagon on the other side. A large grappling hook hung over his broad shoulders.

"You aimin' to drag her up the mountain, big brother?" Ben teased.

"I aim to save your ass, little boy," Hiram shouted back as both men laughed.

In a short time Hiram's prophecy would prove true. Ben resettled the heavy yoke on Luke's shoulders and walked the line to do the same for the other oxen. Ellis simply grunted as Ben passed the lead oxen and circled back to the wagon. Numerous wagons and oxen fell in line behind the lead wagon with the awkward boiler. The pace was slow, but the time would be made up in the downward descent into Elkinsville.

Ellis Bryant had decided to make this trip today at the last moment. He was receiving conflicting orders for material with so many foremen overseeing so many different projects. Some felt they had been shorthanded by Ellis, and he figured the most affective resolution was to get firsthand information. He was a grizzled sixty but extremely strong, with a constitution that could outlast many younger men.

The wagons were rolling every day, and a man could work seven days a week, if he so chose, or he could be scheduled for a day off occasionally. Few of the men asked for that day. The large paychecks lured them over the mountain day after day.

The usual raucous laughter and joking were held to a minimum today. Ellis Bryant seemed to have placed a damper on the whole outfit. By midmorning they were slightly ahead of schedule, but Ellis could still feel a tightening in his gut. He was anxious to reach the crest of the mountain. It was always a relief to look down on the construction and view the rapidly rising town.

Ben circled the wagon again making sure the ropes and chains securing the boiler were holding steady. He continued his circle toward Ellis Bryant and remarked, "They sure as hell want this town in a hurry." He was looking back toward the long line of wagons and plodding oxen.

"That they do, Ben. Never seen so many men and so much money being poured into a mining camp before. This one is mighty different."

As Ben continued his trek to the end of the lumbering wagon, a sudden thought brought him up short. I will buy my own oxen back when this job is finished. He watched in amazement as the huge beasts began the steepest part of the ascent and did not break pace. They worked as one unit each sharing his part of the enormous load. His greatest fear was seeing the ungainly boiler topple backwards, but the heavy restraints held it securely in place, as the perpendicular ride continued slowly up the steep incline.

Hiram looked toward Ellis Bryant, who still walked with the head ox, and was surprised by the look of dismay on his face. "What is the hell is eating on you Ellis? We are making good time, and we are gonna be on top of this mountain in another hour."

He didn't answer Hiram but simply nodded toward the sky in back of the wagon. Hiram looked in the direction of his nod and, his heart sank. The sky that had been clear and sparkling blue only a few minutes before was rapidly being invaded by a monstrous black mass. Hidden by the mountain the clouds were upon them without warning. Thunderheads bloated with huge dark bellows were moving at an alarming rate. "God almighty, we're in for it," he shouted to Ben who was walking toward him.

Ben could sense a subtle change in the animals, and he immediately placed his hand on Amos's broad back. He could feel a slight tightening of muscles beneath his heavy coat of white, which darkened as the clouds began to cover the sky.

As the menacing black clouds began to cover the entire sky, David Wilson came racing back to the wagon and even his usually controlled countenance showed alarm. His prancing horse, feeling the atmospheric change was beginning to look wild-eyed. "Ben," he bellowed, "can you move these oxen faster? We might fair better at the top of the mountain."

Ben responded by cracking his whip in the air, and his beloved Amos and Luke immediately heaved harder. At the very fastest, the pace was slow.

Turning to Ellis, David simply stated, "It looks like we are in for a bad one." Ellis nodded in agreement.

The rain started with large drops, sporadic at first, but the intensity grew steadily. Broad brimmed hats drooped downward with rivers of water as the sky seemed to rip apart and release torrents of wind-driven rain. Ben could only see the wagon directly in back of them.

"It's a goddamn cloudburst," he shouted to Hiram.

Hiram's heavy beard hung sopping wet against his neck and chest as he bent forward into the storm with Ben.

"Keep the team moving, Ben. I have to check on the others," Ellis Bryant ordered as he turned his horse to head back down the wagon-strewn trail.

David rode back and forth checking the roadway ahead, becoming more apprehensive by the minute. The fierce rain continued unabated, drenching men and beast, as they slowly struggled upward on the vertical and unprotected mountainside. Water gushed over the makeshift roadway in sweeping sheets.

"We gotta get on top, Ben. All this water coming off the mountain side is sure as hell gonna take this damn road right out from under us," Hiram shouted.

Just as David appeared at the head of the wagon a tremendous twisting wind drove them into the side of the hill. A huge red oak was ripped violently from the earth and slammed downward across the roadway with outer limbs brushing him and the horse. The terrified horse reared wildly at the edge of the road. Hiram leaped upward barely missing the horse's hooves and dragged him downward by the halter with superhuman strength, barely saving horse and rider from plunging to the depths below. The men with the boiler wagon were stunned. Had they traveled a few yards farther, they would have caught the full brunt of the huge falling tree. The massive root system brought with it tons of earth and rocks, creating a barrier at least one and a half stories high, totally blocking the road in front of them. The towering mass disappeared into a complete whiteout.

David was visible shaken. He had cheated death on several occasions, and this one had been close. "We will just have to sit this one out, boys," he said, knowing the close proximity of the wagons just behind them.

The constant thunder and lightning seemed to hover directly over their heads and shook the ground beneath their feet. Ben was first to notice the slight tilt of the huge upright braces holding the roadway together. There was no let up in the wind-driven rain, and a particularly wide stream of water was rushing full vent beneath the wagon.

"God almighty, Hiram, we're settin' ducks. We can't go ahead and we can't go back," Ben shouted over the cracking of thunder coupled with violent wind and torrential downpour. The rain and constant wetness of the preceding weeks took its final toll as the huge upright logs began to lean further out. The linear logs started to give way, and the wagon hung momentarily on the edge of the mountain. Amos and Luke strained with every muscle in their rain-soaked bodies to pull forward. Ben's heart almost broke as he watched them trying desperately to find a foot hold, their hooves flailing as the logs continued to move outward. He could not bear to watch the horrible crushing death of his beautiful animals. Grabbing a double-bit axe from one of the workmen, Ben jumped between the wagon and oxen swinging demonic blows at the large steel pin connecting the wagon to the oxen. It was pulled taut as the roadway continued to slide, and the oxen were beginning to give ground. The tremendous force of Ben's blows sent sparks flying when metal met metal, even in the driving rain.

Hiram was horrified as he watched Ben battling against overwhelming odds. He would be caught between the oxen and the boiler wagon as it tumbled down the steep mountain. Both David and Hiram were screaming over the roar of the storm, "Let it go, Ben. Let it go."

Suddenly the pin sheared in half, and the wagon immediately flipped on its side. A wide surge of water and sliding timbers carried the wagon and boiler down the mountainside. Hiram's body was taut with fear as he quickly threw his large grappling hook to his trapped brother. David and Hiram dragged Ben through rushing water and rubble to safety just as large boulders and logs filled the recess that a moment before held Ben.

"Ben, you Goddamned fool. I thought you were one dead son-of-a-bitch," Hiram said, hugging his brother as the wild storm lashed about them.

"You won't get rid of me just yet, big brother," Ben said, but his attempt to laugh was a meager one.

By late afternoon the storm moved on and repairs began immediately on the washout. Long timbers were placed solidly across the open space, and David Wilson with his crew and faithful oxen crossed to safety. Ben walked beside Amos and Luke, patting them on their flanks. They would learn later that an unprecedented twelve inches of rain had fallen. Elkhorn Creek had swollen to new levels, and many temporary shanties had been washed downstream. Supplies had been washed away, but miraculously, there had been no loss of life. It was several days before repairs could be completed and the roadway dry enough for the next onslaught of traffic. Week after week, the supplies continued to roll over the mountain pass, and eager hands waited at the base of the mountain in Elkinsville. The wagons were quickly unloaded and made ready for the return trip to the supply depot the next day. Ben would never pass the spot of the washout and near disaster that he didn't offer up a small prayer of thanks.

CHAPTER 11

A powerhouse was placed in operation with the large boilers and two brickyards were turning out bricks. Experienced bricklayers were paid premium wages.

Permanent homes were marching further up the hillsides, standing in the shade of ancient trees. Wooden walkways followed each new house. A large, three-storied, brick office building was quickly structured, and its offices filled immediately. An extensive company store was stocked by the time the last brick was in place. Ransome had promised its high echelon employees the best in available amenities, and it was living up to its promise. Each day the lengthy wagon trains delivered enormous boxes of clothes, furniture and food to the commissary. Long lines waited for the doors to open each morning, and the counters were lined with impatient customers, some who had arrived before dawn. A three-story school building was rapidly being completed for the many children arriving with their parents.

Mine openings now numbered twelve, and the precious ore was being hauled from the mines by mules pulling wagons loaded with tons of coal. Railroad tracks were connected to each mine opening, and the two locomotives drawn over the mountain pass were busy hauling coal from mines to holding pens close to the tipple under construction. As production increased so did the number of storage pens. The large tipple was running ahead of schedule, and thousands of tons of coal would be ready to roll out the day the railroad was completed.

A handsome courthouse and a sturdy jail were a first priority along with a well-equipped, four-story hospital. A huge shelf was dug into the mountainside, high above the town, and the hospital opened its doors to patients even before it had been completed. The push and shove for quick lumber from the sawmills had mangled several new comers, untrained in the treacherous work. A temporary bakery was thrown together, and hordes of workers swept the shelves clean by the end of each day.

Ransome kept police officers constantly circulating through the entire area. Many situations were diffused before they erupted into all-out frays. Some of the overworked and exhausted men tended to have short fuses.

A four-story recreational building was erected across the street from the office building, and it was constantly jammed. Men leaving the night shift would bathe, have breakfast and head for the bowling alley that stretched across the entire basement area of the recreational building. It was much less crowded in the early mornings, and they could sleep in late afternoon while others waited in long lines.

An ice cream parlor with a high-vaulted ceiling sported an enormous, mahogany-framed mirror covering the entire wall behind a well-stocked fountain. The large counter was thronged most days with customers hoping to capture the next empty table.

A large, comfortable theater was overfilled at each showing, with people lining the aisles. The shows changed weekly, and no one wanted to miss a feature. More theaters were already planned for outlying camps, as harried managers were harassed for lack of seats. Pool tables covered a large area between the theater and ice cream parlor, and the noise level could be deafening at times. The mood was one of high excitement, and even those who had wrought the drastic changes in this wilderness were awed.

The skeletal framework for a dam close to the powerhouse was progressing rapidly and would soon be filled with sparkling water from Elkhorn Creek.

Large, beautiful homes continued to be built around the lake site among majestic trees. Ransome planned to exhibit its model town to the world and the foundation for a several-storied, lavish hotel and clubhouse faced the lake. The town would be an uncommon sight in an area where fly-by-night coal operators had left stilted, decaying shanties in order to cut and run with a short profit.

Ransome Coal had entered the richest raw resource area in the world, and it intended to stay. The magnitude of the coal fields, oil, gas and, above all, the fabulous standing timber was without equal anywhere else in the world. The flora and fauna were unparalleled.

Miners' homes were rapidly rising, but they did not resemble the homes for company officials. The average house was four or five rooms without indoor plumbing. The kitchens were equipped with a spigot for cold water only. Company carpenters built walkways to the outdoor toilet and coal houses next to the outhouses.

Ben Cantrell was constantly amazed with the progress being made in the construction of the town. Each week he crossed the mountain into Elkinsville and stood agog as the town practically erupted. He watched in amazement as bricks quickly mounted into buildings. The office building was now surrounded by concrete sidewalks, and men in coats and ties hustled in and out of the offices.

Large crates were quickly unloaded from wagons, and crowbars pried away heavy boards to expose desks, chairs, filing cabinets and numerous office supplies. "I'll just be damned," he said to Hiram. "If this don't beat all." The two brothers had never ventured far from the hills except to visit with their uncle Luke and Martin in Louisville on rare occasions.

"This place is worse than a damn beehive, and there are too many people," Hiram said, as he lobbed a mouthful of foul tobacco juice at the newly constructed sidewalk. When we finish work on these supplies, I plan to take all my money and go back yonder to the top of the mountain. "You're not listening to me, Ben," he said, seeing Ben staring across the street.

Mary Jane Newsome was just entering the bakery, and Ben's eyes watched every move. Her father had packed up his family in Pennsylvania when he heard of the huge undertaking in this coalfield by Ransome and headed South. Having worked as a foreman for years in mining, he was welcomed to Elkinsville with open arms and immediately ensconced in an upscale house almost next door to the new school. The indoor plumbing and a telephone made him grit his teeth. He would be on call constantly.

Mary Jane was devastated by the move, but she was immediately employed by the bakery, and her loneliness didn't last long. Numerous young men pouring into the valley spent a lot of time in the bakery. As she approached her seventeenth birthday, she doled out huge, luscious doughnuts and cinnamon rolls as admiring, would-be suitors lined up to eat more. Ben had watched as young men came streaming from the bakery gobbling up the sweets. The smell of yeast and rising bread beckoned his hungry stomach, but he forgot his hunger as he looked into a pair of beautiful green eyes. Mary Jane blushed under his stare. Her soft skin looked like white petals on dogwoods in the early morning dew, with her long, dark auburn hair tied back from her forehead with a black velvet ribbon. Ben had never seen anything as beautiful as Mary Jane. Her high-collared, white blouse was nipped at the waist by a shiny black skirt. Finally finding his voice, he ordered, "One of them little cakes."

Mary Jane gave him the cinnamon roll and a strange tingle ran through both of their fingers as they touched. She didn't know exactly what had happened, but Ben knew he had found his soulmate. Ben's striking amber eyes held her spellbound. She didn't even notice the rough work clothes nor the battered hat clamped on his unkempt hair. She only felt his huge presence as she lost herself in his incredible eyes.

"Thank you, ma'am," he stammered and left. He had been conscious of the way the blouse swelled above her small waistline, and it didn't take him long to find out that her name was Mary Jane Newsome.

Hiram laughed as he watched Ben's distraction. "You sure are taken with that girl, Ben," he said. "She's got them big tits that are gonna hang like two 'toe sacks' once she's had a couple of younguns."

"I'm just thinking about right now," Ben said, and headed for the bakery.

He had conferred with Jerry and Frank after his first meeting with Mary Jane, and they had coached him. They didn't laugh at Ben or try to tease him. He was their hero and protector, and now they could help him.

"First thing you have to do is get your haircut and mustache trimmed. You look fine for oxen, Ben, but not for courtin'. You can pay one of the workers to let you take a bath and clean up in one of the shanties. The company commissary is already open, and me and Jerry bought some new clothes when we crossed over last week. You can't ask a girl to share a soda in those old worn-out clothes that smell like cow shit." Jerry was encouraged by Ben's attention and added slyly, "I bet you could damn near buy the store out with all the money you've been making and nothing to spend it on."

Jerry and Frank were being paid handsome wages, and they knew Ben's pay must at least double theirs. Ben checked out a shanty on his next trip to Elkinsville. A huge, hard-muscled, young man answered his knock on the flimsy door, and Ben liked the way he looked. Rufus Connley was only sixteen-years-old, and his broad body was barely over six feet. With light sandy hair and blue eyes, that were slightly crossed, he was what the mountain people would call a "fine figure of a man."

"I hope you ain't looking for a place to stay, stranger. We already have ten men in this shack, and there ain't even room to fart," Rufus said. He had already sent two would-be tenants away earlier in the day.

"No, nothin' like that. I'm just wantin a place to take a bath and clean myself up when I come over the mountain with the ox teams."

Rufus gave him a big lopsided grin, "You shore can, feller. I've been hearing all about the work you men have been doin', and I want to see that road. You just tell me what you want and I'll fix you up. The men in this shanty work day shift, and they won't be here before five. They leave early so you can come in anytime after daylight. My job is to keep the place clean and cook. I bring water in from that pump out there and heat it for their baths. They damn sure get dirty in them mines. It ain't no hard job, and I get time to drive delivery wagons around on my own time and make twice as much money." Their brief encounter was the beginning of a lifetime friendship.

Mary Jane had managed to find out about Ben in a very sly way. He intrigued her. His pale amber eyes with the pinpoint pupils had held her spellbound. Her breath caught in her throat today as Ben entered the bakery. His hair and mustache had been trimmed, and his new clothes flattered his huge frame. Ben didn't stutter or stammer but got right to the point. "Mary Jane, I would like to buy you a sodi at the ice cream parlor when you finish here tonight."

Mary Jane smiled at him, and he had trouble hearing what she was saying. Her mouth was beautiful! He had not noticed before. He had been busy sizing up her other attributes.

"I would like that and the new ice cream parlor is as nice as anything we have in Pennsylvania." His enormous height seemed to dwarf her five-foot, five-inch frame.

Ben and Mary Jane were together each time he crossed the mountain, sharing sodas and Ben's first movie.

Andrew Newsome was infuriated with Mary Jane, after meeting Ben for the first time. "Jesus Christ, Mary Jane. With all the young men hanging around the bakery, do you have to choose an old man?"

"He is not an old man. He is only seven years older than I am."

"Mary Jane, I think he looks a bit wild, and he doesn't look like the boys you dated back home," her mother wailed.

"That's why I like him." Mary Jane answered sharply. She smiled secretly as she remembered the way Ben kissed her as they sat on the front-porch swing in the dark. The boys back home had never kissed her like that.

It was late August and the town little resembled the wilderness that had covered the entire region only three months before. The smell of newly sawed timber permeated the air as sawmills continued to rip apart the large trees, and mounds of sawdust had to be hauled away constantly.

The hotel and clubhouse were rapidly being completed to accommodate teachers from across the country. Extremely high salaries had drawn many inquiries. A new school, a new town and a large contingent of students from around the world drew the best of teachers like a magnet.

Mary Jane wondered what her new teachers would be like and was a bit homesick for her old, familiar school. Classes would be held in various locations around town until the new school could be completed. The streets were filled with large wagons hauling bricks and lumber for the next urgent structure.

"Have you ever rode on a horse, Mary Jane?" Ben asked one night as they walked home from a movie.

"Oh, yes," she smiled at the memory. "My grandparents live on a farm in Pennsylvania, and I always stayed with them in the summer. Grandpa gave me my own horse when I was five." "I was kinda thinkin' we could take a ride up the mountain, and you could meet Ma and Pa."

"Ben, I would love to ride up there with you and meet your parents. I'll have to ask my dad." She winced as she thought of the ordeal ahead, knowing her parents strongly disapproved of Ben.

The objections were loud and unpleasant, as Mary Jane announced that she wanted to visit Ben's parents. It was finally decided that her thirteen-year-old brother, Thomas, would accompany them. Thomas was delighted and could hardly wait to see the mountaintop stronghold. In despair, Andrew watched them leave.

"I don't like this one damn bit, Emily," he raged as the three rode out of sight. "I hear their corn whiskey is the best in the whole country, but it is no life for Mary Jane."

"God, help us," Emily choked.

The horses Ben had chosen were well-acquainted with steep and rocky mountain trails. "These horses must be kin to mountain goats, Ben," Thomas said, as his mount either stepped around or over the many rocks lying on the trail.

Ben laughed, and Mary Jane's heart skipped a beat. Ben was not an unhappy man, but most of the time he was serious. He had beautiful, strong, white teeth, and his pale, amber eyes ignited with dancing lights when he smiled.

The unusual amount of rain in the spring had added a succulence to fat pine needles that were extremely long this year, and the aroma was so pungent it lay heavy in the air. Mary Jane and Thomas were awed by the dense woodlands as huge trees and tangled undergrowth threatened to overtake the narrow trail.

The lower limbs on chestnut trees drooped almost to the earth with fat, weighty chestnuts that would soon cover the ground, and Thomas could hardly wait to come back to this spot in the fall to collect them. Black walnuts were abundant, and he could almost taste them in Mary Jane's chocolate fudge. Grapevines, the size of his thigh, wound upward into the trees, looped over branches and descended downward again. The grapes had ripened during the summer, and the same birds now flitting through the trees had no doubt devoured them. Brilliantly colored blue jays pecked at the hordes of chestnuts, impatient to have them on the ground.

Mary Jane gave a startled shriek when her hair tangled in a large sweetgum limb extending out over the trail. Ben leaped from his horse and was by her side immediately. With gentle hands, he untangled her hair from the limb and retrieved her ribbon dangling from the tree. He loved the way her heavy hair fell about her shoulders, and he laughingly put the ribbon in his pocket.

Huge squirrels with arched bodies and protruding eyes leaped about overhead in giant trees. Big-eared rabbits hopped about, and Thomas was sure he saw the fading gray of a bobcat as it melted into the forest. A vague odor of skunk lingered in the air, and he hoped it wouldn't get any closer. Half an hour later, Ben dismounted and plucked shiny leaves from a creeping plant growing near the trail and offered them to his companions.

"These are teaberry leaves. You just chew them," he instructed. The leaves were delicious, a tangy, sweet taste and in summer, their small, red berries were delectable. "They grow all over these mountains, and you can eat them the year round," he said as he climbed back on his horse.

Thomas laughed and chided Mary Jane, "They would be good just before kissing." She pretended not to hear him.

After two hours of steep climbing, they reached the crest of the mountain and Mary Jane gasped as she viewed the wonder of God's own handiwork. The area they rested in had been totally untouched since time began. Evergreens and deciduous trees growing in profusion stood with inner-locking limbs. The earth was soft with eons of layering leaves and pine needles, creating an earthy odor that produced a sense of timelessness.

"It is so beautiful, Ben," Mary Jane said softly.

"How come you're whispering, Mary Jane? You won't wake anybody here," Thomas said.

Her answer was a look of disgust.

Ben dismounted and held his arms upward to lift her from the saddle, then had trouble letting go of her small waist once she was on the ground. Thomas couldn't wait to see what they were going to do next, and his steady stare made Ben uncomfortable.

"I want to show you and Thomas something," he said as he took her hand and led them through the trees. An enormous rock cliff jutted outward over the forest and Mary Jane was dizzy at first. She had never been afraid of heights, but they were so high and the cliff was so steep, her equilibrium was momentarily unbalanced. Ben could feel her tremble, and he placed his arm around her waist to steady her.

Spreading for miles in every direction was beauty beyond belief. They were standing atop fabled Raven Rock, on the border of Kentucky and Virginia. Many, many miles away to the south they could see the blue, hazed mountains of Tennessee and shimmering green leaves waiting patiently for the imminent approach of another blazing autumn. Far below Elkinsville throbbed to the heat and rumble of sawmills with smoke billowing upward. Steam from the powerhouse rose in white clouds as the hectic pace of building a new town never slowed.

"It looks so danged little," Thomas said, keeping his distance from the cliff's edge. "I can't believe we have come this far. How high are we, Ben?"

"I don't know exactly, Thomas," Ben said, "but it is a far piece."

Thomas was disappointed. He had thought Ben would surely know the height of this mountain. He was just going into the eighth grade, but he had always read about mountains. After several minutes of viewing the panorama, Ben was anxious to be on their way again and interrupted Thomas's excited chatter.

"We better get movin', but we can stop on the way back tomorrow, if you want to."

"How much farther, Ben?" Thomas wanted to know, as they wound their way through the ancient forest.

"About half an hour to the house. And watch your heads, the branches here are mighty low." He ducked ahead of them, and they did the same.

A few minutes later, they were shocked when out of nowhere, and completely without warning, two rough-looking young men appeared. One stood by Ben and the other midway between Mary Jane and Thomas. The two large men stood with ready rifles. Their long, matted, dark auburn hair hung beneath battered, black, felt hats, and their loose-fitting overalls gave them an even wilder look. The heavy boots they wore had made no sound as they surprised the group.

Ben slid from his horse and whopped the nearest one on the back. "Where in the hell have you been? I've been on top here for an hour."

"We've been watchin' you," Owen said to Ben, but he didn't take his eyes off Mary Jane.

"I guess you were at that," Ben said as he looked in the direction of the young man's stare.

Mary Jane looked more beautiful than he had ever seen her. She had pulled her long, thick hair to one side and over her shoulder as her green eyes blazed in defiance. Ben quickly introduced his twin brothers, Isaac and Owen. "Bet you've never seen uglier twins. This is Mary Jane Newsome and her brother, Thomas."

"Howdy, ma'am, and Thomas," They both offered politely.

Thomas squeaked a weak, "Hello." He had been terrified when the two wild-looking young men had simply materialized by the path. He had heard stories about the mountaineers in the area, and he had figured they were in for real trouble. Mary Jane, still trembling, looked from one to the other and smiled with relief. They were completely identical, and neither removed his hat when he was introduced. Owen, who stood between the two visitors, said they had been waiting nearly two hours for them to show.

"We made a few stops on the way, and I wanted them to see the hills at the lookout," Ben explained.

"Everybody's waitin' for you," Isaac said, never taking his eyes off Mary Jane.

"If you don't stop staring at her, I'm gonna shake the shit outta you," Ben said softly, bending to Isaac's ear. He didn't want Mary Jane to hear such talk. Isaac was flustered and embarrassed as he headed down the trail.

After several minutes, they topped another bluff and before them spread a settlement. A huge log house was encircled by several smaller cabins with a split-rail fence zigzagging around the entire compound. Just outside the fence, large, spotted cows with bulging udders grazed lazily as bells hanging around their necks produced a melodious and soothing sound. Mary Jane turned in her saddle to look back at Thomas and was surprised to see two more large, young men following them. Her brother looked at her with wide and excited eyes.

"Mary Jane, have you ever seen anything like this?"

She only shook her head in wonder. Another young man appeared from nowhere to open the gate into the yard, pushing a cow aside. Floyd, twenty-one-years-old, looked at Mary Jane with bold, open approval.

"Watch it, Floyd," Ben hissed as he rode by.

***

Mary Jane knew the family consisted of seven boys, and they all lived within the enclosure. Hiram's wife and two sons lived in one of

208

the cabins, and he was off to this mountain at every opportunity. Jeannie loved the many nice things he brought from town each time he came. By the time they reached the front porch of the main house, Sarah and Amy were waiting for them. Amy's red-gold hair had darkened to a shinny, bright-auburn and was pulled back from her face into a heavy bun at the nape of her neck. At forty-three, she was still beautiful, and, like her mother, the years of constant activity with a large brood had kept her slender and strong. Mary Jane was awed by the tall woman and could see no resemblance to Ben. Amy looked at Mary Jane with keen interest and knew, instinctively, that she would take Ben away from the mountains. The thought pleased her.

Hiram, Samuel and Carl had all brought wives to the mountains and started families, but Ben had always been different. Mary Jane looked lovely in her riding skirt, matching blouse and highly-polished boots. She watched as Ben lifted her from the horse and could sense the love they shared. Even after twenty-eight years of marriage and seven boys, she still loved Levi's touch. His strength had carried them through rough times, and his gentleness with her had never ceased. She took Mary Jane's hand and welcomed her to their home.

Sarah held her firm, smooth hand in her rough and worn fingers. "We are so happy to have you," she smiled as she spoke to the young visitor. "Hiram told us last week that you would be coming with Ben, and we have been getting ready all week."

Mary Jane was surprised. Sarah's English was totally unlike some of the mountain women who came into the bakery.

"I hope I haven't been too much of a bother," Mary Jane said and suddenly remembered Thomas. "My brother was happy to be invited, too." Thomas solemnly shook hands with both women. Sarah beamed at the two of them.

"Have you met the other boys?" she asked as the yard seemed to fill with people.

"Only the twins and Floyd." She was made acquainted with Carl and Samuel. The two of them had fallen in behind them farther back on the trail.

Their wives, hearing the commotion, came strolling from their cabins. Samuel's wife was carrying a small baby and leading a little girl of about two. Martha smiled shyly at Mary Jane and extended her hand.

"We are so proud to have you. Hiram said you came from a big city up north."

"Yes, we did, Martha, and we love your mountains."

At that moment, two other women approached, and she met Hiram's wife, Jeannie, and Hannah, the wife of Carl.

Hannah was a striking young woman with very dark eyes and hair. Beautiful, smooth skin with a tint of copper bespoke of Indian heritage, and Mary Jane thought her very beautiful. She was several months pregnant with her first child, and the large folds in her dress were no longer folding.

Jeannie's two handsome, young sons smiled shyly at Thomas. Both boys greatly resembled Hiram.

"Howdy, Jeannie, Martha and Hannah," Ben said. "It's mighty good to see you and lookin' so pretty, too."

"We know now why you stay in town on your day off," Jeannie teased and the women laughed.

He hugged both Sarah and Amy, announcing that he wanted to show Mary Jane and Thomas some of the farm before dark. "I promise to bring them right back."

Ben headed toward the waterfall first, and Thomas was fascinated.

"It just comes out of the ground, Ben, just like Elkhorn Creek."

"I thought that was where all the water comes from," Ben said.

"We have lots of rivers and streams in Pennsylvania, but I have never seen water come out of the ground."

"You will just have to go looking for the source next time we go back," Mary Jane told Thomas, tiring of his questions.

They walked downhill from the cascading waterfall and its rushing stream that poured into an extraordinary, large pond still teaming with innumerable fish. The pond looked exactly the same as when Levi had discovered it as a boy. The family had always taken only what they needed and multitudes of fish still swam in crowded circles. They could always sit near the pond and collect all the game they needed. Deer came for the water and bears for the fish. They dropped fowl of every type with large slingshots, and their smokehouse was always laden. Ben gave Thomas a long-handled net that was kept over a large stump. "Take your pick for dinner, Thomas, and Ma will be happy to fry them up."

Thomas easily brought forth several flopping rainbow trout, and Ben instantly gutted and filleted the catch, throwing them into the net. Mary Jane was quite taken with the water trough system. Large logs had been split in half, then hollowed out to allow water from the waterfall to run by the side door of the cabin. The logs had been worn smooth over the years as sparkling water slid over the passageway of interlocking wedges connecting the logs to keep the water flowing in a straight line. A five-foot square rock pit, constructed just outside the kitchen door, provided easy access too cold, clear water, and a log channel carried excess water back to the downhill stream.

The three trekked back to the house with Thomas clutching his catch. The front porch was filled with people, and all eyes were on Mary Jane. She blushed as Ben's five brothers stared at her with open admiration. Hiram was working with the ox teams on the mountain crossing, and Jeannie missed her husband, but the large group of young people teased and played with her children as she bantered with them. Their laughter resounded through the hills as the young men hand wrestled and roughhoused about the yard.

"Catch, Thomas," Sam called, as he lobbed a strange looking ball to their young visitor.

Thomas caught the lightweight ball and was puzzled.

"That's a pig bladder all blowed up," Sam said, responding to Thomas's quizzical expression. "You just get a hollow weed and poke it in the fresh bladder and blow with all your might before it starts to dry out. Then, tie it hard so no air can leak out."

Thomas laughed and booted the strange object high as he joined the fray.

Collecting Mary Jane's bag, Amy led her into a large bedroom with a willow-woven headboard and a crocheted bedspread that was a work of art. Mary Jane touched the spread gently with an awed look on her face.

Sarah smiled from the doorway, "My husband's mother crocheted it for me as a wedding gift sixty-five years ago. She was a wonderful woman, and she could put any doctor to shame with her knowledge of medical treatments with herbs and roots growing in these mountains."

There was an instant bonding between the two women, and there were so many things Mary Jane wanted to ask Ben about his grandmother. At eighty-two years, she was still beautiful, with a mass of lovely white hair, and her blue-gray eyes were still sharp and alert. Amy and Sarah left Mary Jane to unpack and headed back to the kitchen to complete the feast they had been planning for days.

Thomas was given a bunk in the cabin occupied by Owen and Isaac, and they were busy showing him how to operate a rifle after promising him they would take him coon hunting. He sure hoped Mary Jane wouldn't tell him he couldn't go.

Mary Jane quickly unpacked and headed for the kitchen to help Sarah and Amy and stopped in surprise. Levi had just placed an armload of wood in a box by the black stove, and the two stood staring at one another. Ben was a carbon copy of his father except for his strange eyes. He had the same dark hair and tremendous build. Ben introduced her to his father, and the older man shook her hand holding it carefully in his extremely large and calloused hands.

"I'm glad to know you, Mary Jane. Ben has been telling us about you."

She stood dwarfed by the two men and totally mesmerized by Levi. Her father had told her he was a moonshiner, but beyond that she had not known what to expect. She thought he looked more powerful than Ben, and the slight tinge of white in his hair and heavy mustache only reenforced his aura of uniqueness. Levi could see right off why Ben was so taken with Mary Jane, and he smiled at her with the same even, strong white teeth that Ben had inherited, now beginning to be tinged with yellow. He wore a heavy, rough shirt tucked into a massive pair of overalls, which hung loosely on his large frame.

"I met Thomas on the way in, and you have a fine young brother there, Mary Jane."

"Thank you," she replied. "We were really looking forward to this visit."

Amy announced that supper was ready, and the large table quickly filled. The twelve-foot table that Albert had perfected for Amy years ago was completely surrounded with bodies crowded together on long benches with several chairs added at the ends. Large platters of fried trout, baked ham and tender chunks of beef cooked with carrots sat in the center of the table surrounded by mashed potatoes, pickled corn, sweet potatoes and corn on the cob. Mary Jane and Thomas had never had so much fun. The boys poked raw jokes at one another and teased the young women. Everyone pampered and pushed food at the two visitors, which Thomas gobbled up at great speed.

"What is that?" Thomas asked, looking warily at something on a platter he didn't recognize.

"Those are wild, fried mushrooms, Thomas, and they are very good," Sarah said.

Thomas still looked apprehensive but was coaxed into trying one and immediately devoured two more. Seven layered applebutter cake and gingerbread rounded out the meal, and Mary Jane could not believe so much food had disappeared as she looked at the empty platters.

Levi had built a fire beneath a large, black wash-pot just outside the kitchen door, and he lugged pails of steaming water into the kitchen so the women could wash the stacks of dirty dishes.

Mary Jane was enthralled by the sensuous, soundless communication between Amy and Levi. It was evident in the quiet looks they gave one another and the way their hands touched as he helped Amy with her chores. Mary Jane blushed at her own feelings. She insisted on helping with the dishes, and Levi motioned Ben to the outside.

"Thought we might check out the cattle, Ben."

Watching the cattle move slowly to the woods for the night, Levi spoke to his son. "I reckon you aim to marry this girl, Ben."

"If she will have me."

"She will have you, Ben, I can see it in her eyes. What about her folks?"

Ben was surprised at Levi's question. "Her father has no use for me, and he has let me know it each time I see him. I think Mary Jane's mother would side with her, but she won't go against her husband. As long as Mary Jane wants to see me, I can deal with her parents."

Levi studied his strong, handsome son wondering how anyone could find him unfit for a son-in-law.

"There was a time when Sarah and Albert felt the same way about me."

The statement shocked Ben. "They always seemed to like you, Pa. I never heard them say a mean thing, and I heard grandpa say many times that you were the strongest man he had ever known."

"I was a wild one in my day, son, and they were afraid of the worst. The day I knew I loved your ma was my last day to run wild and go whoring. After several of you children came along, and me and Albert worked together, they came around to like me. Just thought you might like to know," and Levi never broached the subject again.

Sarah awakened Mary Jane early the next morning to tell her Ben was waiting in the kitchen. She dressed quickly and found Ben standing by the huge, stone fireplace with a steaming mug of coffee. He smiled at her, and again, the look in his strange eyes made her knees weak.

"Mary Jane, I thought you might like to ride up to the top of the hill and watch the sun come up. I saddled the horses and even poured you a cup of coffee."

"That sounds like fun, Ben. I have never watched the sun come up from atop a mountain," she said, taking the coffee.

The fog was so dense she could barely see the outline of the fence enclosing the cabins. "Ben, how are we going to see the sun in all this fog?"

"You'll see, Mary Jane."

Mary Jane followed close behind Ben hardly able to see the back of his horse. She knew they were climbing and felt a sense of panic in case she became separated from him. Suddenly, they came out of the fog and Mary Jane was completely overwhelmed. Everything below them was shrouded in misty waves of the softest peach glow, created by the early-morning sun spreading its rays over the entire terrain. She wanted to wade back into the illusive mist, touch the colors and hold them to her. Ben, watching her closely, roared with laughter seeing the look of disbelief on her face.

"I knew you would like it, Mary Jane."

"Ben, I have never seen anything so beautiful. You grew up with all of this?"

"Sure did, and even when I was a little boy, I would climb up here to watch this special sunrise."

Lifting Mary Jane from the horse, he crushed her to him with arms like bands of steel, kissing away the cool, damp moisture from her lips as they stood knee-deep in the swirling mist.

"Mary Jane, I guess you know I love you, and I want to marry you."

Her resounding kiss gave him the answer he wanted.

214

CHAPTER 12

In late fall, Mary Jane sat in class in the new high school, dreaming as she looked through tall windows at the mountaintop. She and Ben decided they would be married as soon as she graduated. She didn't dare broach the subject with her parents before she finished school. Under the best of circumstances, it would be a traumatic experience. They did not approve of Ben and his moonshining father, and she would have to bide her time.

Andrew Newsome had been amazed to see the progress that had been made when he arrived in Elkinsville in June. And it was nothing short of miraculous to view what had been constructed since his arrival. As each new building had been completed, it was occupied immediately, and new homes mushroomed almost overnight. Most mining towns wore a tired, drab and dreary look, but the hustle and bustle never stopped in Elkinsville. He had expected a roughshod wilderness town and had harbored qualms about bringing his family into this wilderness, but his doubts had been quickly laid to rest.

The new movie theater, bowling alley and ice-cream parlor had become favorite hangouts for Mary Jane and Thomas and their new friends. Mary Jane was radiant, and Andrew scowled as he thought of Ben Cantrell. He was hoping Mary Jane would find a new boyfriend in her senior class. He hardly saw Ben any more, but he knew it was probably because the ox

215

teams were working overtime. Enormous amounts of supplies had been moved over Pine Mountain in the past month in preparation for a huge celebration when the railroad was completed into town. He knew Mary Jane was meeting him occasionally at the ice-cream parlor. It galled him to see the two of them together at the small table with Ben's huge body practically hovering over her.

Andrew now had plenty of money, and he planned to send his daughter to college. As soon as she graduated, he would put her on a train to Pennsylvania to waiting grandparents and school.

Late November arrived and the railroad was ready to blast through the last stone barrier into town. The month of November had been spent in frenzied activities. The railroad was expected to be completed shortly before Thanksgiving, and company officials were keeping a wary eye on the weather. Winter could come early in the mountains, dumping snow and freezing streams, but Indian summer was lingering, and those in charge of the celebration offered up a prayer of thanks. Huge tents were erected to shelter the railroad workers temporarily and other tents to house long tables and oversized ovens to prepare the Thanksgiving feast. The ovens were to be used in the new bakery that was rapidly going up to replace the temporary one, now straining at the seams. It had been running nonstop for days, preparing cakes, pies, cookies and breads for the celebration.

It was the last week of November, and the railroad was to be completed by late afternoon of the following day. Shortly after midnight, the stoves had been filled with high-grade coal and the warmth spreading from them heated the cooking tents to a summer high.

"I have never chopped so many onions," Emily Newsome said to another volunteer, as she wiped at water streaming from her eyes. "If you don't mind, Lois, I think I'll switch to crumbling cornbread." Scores of miners' wives had volunteered to mix dressing and were busy loading it into huge turkeys. "I always lay a few strips of bacon across my turkey breasts just to be sure it says moist. What do you girls think?"

It was four in the morning, and the exhausted women had been working since midnight. "What turkey?" one of the volunteers asked, and the group laughed hysterically.

By daybreak, numerous stuffed turkeys had been loaded into the ovens and countless vats with sizzling, liquid lard awaited tubs of frying chickens that was being floured and readied by droves of volunteers. Office personnel along with company officials mingled with miners and other workers as all pitched in to help with the final preparations. An almost impossible task had been achieved, and Ransome was ready to celebrate.

One very large tent housed a rousing band that was beginning to tune up as workers raked and pounded the dirt floor for dancing. Firearms had been restricted inside town, which did not sit well with many of the mountain men, as they reluctantly checked their rifles and side arms at the new courthouse. Moonshine was flowing, and officials had no desire to see tempers ignited by the combination.

Hundreds of workers would be entering the town as they blasted through the final barriers and connected steel to steel. By noon, the first workers were in sight as whistles blew and men shouted. The last mile of creosoted, white oak crossties were hammered into place, and workers tested the rails.

They raised huge sledge hammers high above their heads with both hands and a great roar arose from the crowd. Spirits were so high and rambunctious the burly workmen formed lines on either side of the track for the safety of revelers. The people were ever jubilant as they watched two giant locomotives roll slowly into town with blaring horns and shrieking whistles, while plumes of steam hissed from the engines.

Two Pullman cars directly in back of the locomotives carried company and railroad officials, along with the press from several states. Accommodations at the new hotel awaited them.

The Chesapeake and Ohio railroad has spared no expense to highlight their achievement, and the press was only too eager to accept their amenities.

Flatcars and boxcars in back of the Pullman coach were loaded with workers of every nationality. Huge, black, hard-muscled men from the South came in droves. Most of the mountain people had never seen a black man and stood gaping at the spectacle. They had been hired from cotton fields in the South, and their strong bodies had been the major force in pulling the railroad through the rugged mountains. Dynamite crews left jagged rocks that had to be chiseled out by oversized sledge hammers. Strong, black arms swung the heavy hammers with massive force as solid rock crumbled at the onslaught. As the road across Pine Mountain had been honed for the ox-drawn wagons with brute strength, so it was with the railroad. Thirty miles of rails over

217

deep ravines and through mountains of rocks had been completed in one year. There had been many accidents and men had lost their lives, but the pace never slackened. The wages were stupendous compared to day labor in cotton fields in Georgia, Alabama and Mississippi.

Large boxcars contained items of many descriptions. The first car provided countless kegs of iced beer for the celebration, and numerous volunteers stepped forward to help with the unloading. Cases of Coca-Cola filled an entire car, no doubt advertising the new plant that was beginning to rise in the town.

Behind the boxcars were dozens of open gondolas ready to receive thousands of tons of coal that had been mined, cleaned and were ready to roll. They were immediately eased beneath the belly of the tipple to begin loading the precious black gold. Most of the railroad workers would stay on to fill the many vacancies in mining, timber cutting and scores of other jobs.

For two days, the town danced, drank and feasted. The jail was full to overflowing as the celebration became overheated in some quarters, but the sheriff and his deputies released the battered workers from jail as they sobered and returned them to their jobs. The press was caught up in the gala and managed to capture the spirit and the colossal undertaking of the model town.

Boxcars parked on side rails by the company commissary contained merchandise that would rival any city department store. Nat Baker saw little of the festivities. Most of the wares were snapped up before they were even displayed, and Nat's order sheets were long and detailed before the first coal drag left town. The engineer promised Baker he would see his orders filled for the return trip.

By December of 1912, incoming freight trains supplied the town with tons of food, clothes, furniture and treasured Christmas tree ornaments. Baker had never managed a store that ran out of supplies so fast. Jesus Christ, he thought, Ransome won't even have to sell coal at this rate. The prices were high, and Ransome owned all stores.

The hordes of workers had worked overtime and even double time for months, and their pockets bulged with cash.

*** *

Ben and Hiram carried silk blouses and shiny skirts to their womenfolk, and even Sarah, at eighty-two, was delighted with the beautiful clothes. Memories of her childhood in Ohio flared again as she

218

remembered the excitement she and her two younger sisters shared as they shopped for beautiful dresses. Albert should be here to see their old homeplace erupting into something they could never have dreamed of, and she missed him terribly.

Ransome paid wages every two weeks in silver dollars, and many workers were eager to spend their money as soon as they earned it. Special coins had been manufactured that could be spent in any company business. It was called script and the largest denomination was a large, round, fluted-edged coin of five dollars. A one dollar coin of equal size wore a smooth edge as did all the smaller change. Script cards had been quickly printed, and workers were making good use of them. A small office with a large metal window was situated in one corner of the commissary to serve as a script office. Employees were allowed to charge merchandise from any company business according to the amount of work-time they had on the books. Thousands of workers were on the company payroll and script, flowed back into company coffers. The cash registers overflowed with script at the theaters, bowling alleys and pool rooms. Many housewives would leave the script office red-faced and embarrassed when told by the clerk their husbands did not have enough time on the books for a withdrawal.

"Next, please," the clerk would sing, out and another hopeful would slide his or her card across the window sill. The month's rent would be deducted from the paychecks along with utilities.

Coal houses erected next door to outdoor privies were checked weekly, and coal would be delivered by a lory driver who kept exacting records. No withdrawal could be made until all credit had been satisfied. The worker's homes and walkways, all owned by Ransome, were kept in repair by company carpenters. Their only chore was to dig coal, cut timber or perform any of the numerous eight-hour jobs needed by the company.

A lovely Methodist Church built next to the high school saw well-dressed, hatted women each Sunday morning and on Wednesday nights, they slid into polished pews. A low-key minister who just talked and "didn't really preach," according to some of the mountaineers, surveyed the group and collected his salary from Ransome.

***

The ox wagons were discontinued in mid-December as snow blanketed the area, drifting three to five feet in places, so Ben went to work in one of the sawmills, and his knowledge of timber, plus his

219

eagerness to work long hours without complaint, catapulted him to foreman within two months. Mary Jane was delighted. Ben's long hours during the week kept them separated, but he managed to take time out on Saturday nights to see the latest movie with her. They spent much of their time in line at the bowling alley and ice cream parlor, as a cold and snowy January and February held the mountains in its grip. Ben immediately mastered bowling, sending the pins flying like sparks with his tremendous strength. His catlike stealth and graceful movements were awesome, and each team tried to recruit him. He was soon president of the bowling teams, and Mary Jane helped him with the books, taking up where Sarah had left off with tutoring her grandson.

Frank Upshaw and Jerry Bently had been hired by a pushy mine foreman who promised added incentives. They would always have Saturday nights off, and he would furnish moonshine for a night out. Jerry Bently barely finished a half hour in the pits. He didn't realize he was claustrophobic until he was deep underground, and suddenly the black depths seemed to be closing in on him. The long flame licking out from his carbide lamp attached to his miner's cap sent wild, flickering images dancing over the dark wall, and Jerry had trouble breathing.

"Frank," he choked. "I have to get out of here. I think I might be having a heart attack."

Loading Jerry onto a man car, the foreman rushed him to the entrance. The instant he cleared the tunnel, his breathing returned to normal, and though somewhat weak from his ordeal, symptoms of a heart attack completely disappeared. Color began to seep back into his face that had drained to chalk-white.

"You ever been afraid of closed places before, Jerry?" the foreman asked.

"I don't remember ever being in a closed place before, and I don't plan to go back into one again."

Jerry made a beeline to the sawmill, and Ben was delighted to have his young friend work with him again.

The new churches were filled to capacity at each service as everyone tired of being snowbound. The railways were kept clear at all costs, and the coal drags rumbled through town day and night. Ransome Coal had spent a record forty million dollars the first year to get their operation rolling, and there could be no let-up in deliveries that were eagerly awaited in many cities and ports. Discarded coal dust and small chips were beginning to collect at the tipples and no one seemed to notice. Degradation of the enchanted forest had begun.

April arrived with cold, frosty mornings, but the fog lifted by midmorning and a welcome sun warmed muddy paths. Heavy snows through the winter had left a sodden earth that was trampled by hundreds of people, and unpaved areas became quagmires. Construction crews would remedy the situation by winter, but for now, it would have to be tolerated. Steps leading into the large recreation building were constantly scraped and swept. New theaters and entertainment centers would be constructed shortly in the outlying coal camps to alleviate the long line and short tempers in the only existing one.

Andrew Newsome gritted his teeth and clenched his fist each time he spied Mary Jane with Ben Cantrell. "Mary Jane," he railed, "you are the only high school senior dating an older man, and besides being a hillbilly, he is ignorant and a damned bootlegger."

"Pa, Ben is a foreman at the sawmill, and he is learning very fast," she retorted, standing toe-to-toe with her irate father. "He is already the best bowler in town, and the baseball team is trying to recruit him," she added proudly. "His grandmother grew up in Ohio and has taught him to read and write. His father's illiterate, but Ben can't help that."

Andrew looked at his beautiful daughter and made one simple request. "Mary Jane, please, at least try dating one of your classmates. I have seen them hanging after you at the Rec building."

Mary Jane didn't answer him, and he finally left the living room slamming the door on the way out.

Thomas, sitting slumped in an easy chair unnoticed with his book snickered, "You date one of those city boys, and Ben will wring his neck."

Giving her young brother a withering look, she retreated to her room. Mary Jane was totally miserable because she had made her father so unhappy. He simply could not understand how much she loved Ben.

She watched him toss large logs when she stopped by the sawmill and yet when he held her he was so gentle and sweet. He was anxious

221

to learn new things, and his high wages at the sawmill would provide them with a nice home. Ben had checked out several small farms on the outskirts of town, and he and Mary Jane would soon decide which one they wanted.

Andrew was sullen at the supper table as Emily cast a baleful look at Mary Jane. Mary Jane looked at her plate and ate in silence. "Emily, we got a new bunch of workers coming in tomorrow, so I have to leave early and I'll be late for supper," Andrew spoke harshly, thinking of the danger with raw, untrained recruits. He knew that some of them had lied about mining experience and especially their knowledge of explosives. They had terrified him on more than one occasion with their mishandling of dynamite. The large veins of coal had to be blasted with just the right amount of explosive, not enough to bring the mountain down on top of them, just barely enough to dislodge the black, shining mineral, so the job could be completed with picks and sledge hammers. The large, black lumps would be loaded onto cars continuously, moving the heavy loads toward the giant tipple where the coal would be washed, sorted and dumped into a waiting line of gondolas that were outward bound.

***

The highly volatile fuel far outstripped what customers had expected and orders increased accordingly. Ransome Coal was falling behind in deliveries, even though they had hired every available man. Now, they were dispatching agents to Europe to recruit workers from the fertile labor fields in Wales, England, Belgium, Hungary, Poland, Italy and numerous other countries. The offers of monied jobs and free transportation to the New World sent young, robust men clamoring for a better way of life. They boarded miserable freighters that were poorly equipped for large numbers of passengers, as the price was graded downward, according to the number of people stuffed into the smelly holds. Upon reaching New York harbors, they were quickly herded onto trains that brought them directly to Elkinsville. As the trains roared into town with their human cargo, it was hard to say who was more astounded, the gaping and exhausted newcomers or the mountain people. Word had spread to every hill and valley about the approaching arrival of foreigners, and whole families hiked miles to see the event.

After an arduous trip at sea and miserable overland accommodations in open gondola cars, their arrival into a misty, beautiful valley gave them great hope for a better life and a prosperous future. Unfortunately, it was not a friendly reception. They were not accepted into the mainstream and chose to cling to their own countrymen, forming their own communities. Italians lived in "WOP Town," Hungarians in "Hunky Town," and the blacks were relegated to "Nigger Town." The black children were not integrated into the white schools and were forced to devise their own meager educational systems. Their ingenuity was not to be denied, and the black restaurants with pool rooms and great food were filled with the high school crowds for lunch and a quick game of pool. Hard-working miners respected any nationality or color that worked by their rules, but at the end of the day, each went his own way. Foreign students mingled with Americans in classrooms and sports, helped by eager and resourceful teachers. Much to the chagrin of these talented teachers, the black children were not included.

Prop cutters were in great demand. The mountains would have to be held at bay as they were emptied of their black gold and huge, heavy props were installed immediately as the coal was removed. The ledges of soft slate and sandstone lying above the coal adhered weakly to one another and therein lay the great danger. The mountains could fall without warning. A "coal bump" was the most feared catastrophe in the industry. Nothing would be left alive beneath the massive fall. Black oaks and towering hickories that crowded the forest were felled by the hundreds with the cries of "timber" an almost constant, unbroken chant. Their large limbs were quickly sheered, and the massive trees were loaded onto ox-drawn wagons and rushed to saw mills. The mountains were being assaulted from within and without. Greed for the priceless endowments that had created and sustained their beauty would destroy it. Workers labored under false expectations from the beginning. Large, permanent, brick structures were crowded with a bevy of fussy, white-shirted officials spelling a phantom security.

Ransome had procured the very best of health care and built an exceptionally beautiful hospital, nestled into the mountainside overlooking the town and a tranquil, reflective lake. A winding driveway snaked its way along the mountainside between towering trees to encircle the hospital. It was fully equipped with the latest technology and well-trained personnel. Interns and residents from all over the country sought training periods in the hospital. Battered and mangled bodies hauled from mining accidents offered a unique opportunity for training in trauma and surgery.

May flowered its way into the hills again blending beautiful colors beneath giant evergreens. Hundreds of newcomers beheld the advent, and those from afar looked on in awe as thousands of giant dogwood blossoms opened and preened in the clear, crystal air. They felt it could only be a good omen to be ensconced in such beauty.

New coal camps were beginning to rise on the outskirts of Elkinsville as Ransome constructed more mine openings and planned grade schools for each camp with a large high school in Elkinsville playing host to students in the outlying areas as they completed the sixth grade.

***

Mary Jane nervously awaited her graduation. She dreaded telling her parents that she and Ben would be married as soon as she graduated. They had been lulled by the fact that Ben had not been around as much. Sawmills were whirring around the clock with winter past and construction galloping. Ben worked into the night and weekends, knowing the money would buy the home he wanted for Mary Jane. He didn't want to live in a company house. He wanted his own home with a creek and lots of trees, and he had found just the spot close to town. He knew Mary Jane dreaded telling her parents, and he waited anxiously. He felt sure she would not change her mind, but he worried. His whole life revolved around her, and it was more and more difficult to leave her at the front door as he walked away. He wanted Mary Jane in his bed, her lush, unclothed body next to his and the obsessive thought almost cost him an arm at the sawmill on one occasion.

Mary Jane would never get the chance to tell her father. Hale Potter, a new recruit from England had talked his way into the blasting division, and Andrew felt strongly the young man was embellishing his knowledge of explosives. Eager to get ahead and draw more money for his services, he took chances that left Newsome shaking. They were being rushed from all sides. Time was vital, and precautions were being thrown to the wind. Steel mills running every blast furnace possible, were not the only customers pushing for the prize fuel. Locomotives screaming their way across new territories and new rails devoured tons of coal as sweating firemen lay into their shovels, feeding the hot fires that drove the huge engines. Homes and rapidly rising office buildings throughout the country needed heat from constantly refueled furnaces.

Emily arose at four o'clock in the morning on April twentieth, making biscuits, eggs and gravy. Bacon sizzled as Andrew entered the kitchen, pecking her on the cheek. An experienced and tough foreman, his days stretched from ten to fourteen hours as his paycheck bulged. While her husband ate a hearty breakfast, Emily busied herself packing his dinner bucket. She squeezed in an extra sandwich loaded with roast beef.

"You're working too much, Andrew," she admonished her husband as he attacked the large breakfast.

"I've never made so much money, Emily. When we have saved enough, we can go back to the farm in Pennsylvania and live well."

Having finished his breakfast, he took a small container of carbide crystals from the cabinet and refilled the bottom section of his carbide lamp. Spitting into the small cup, he flicked the tiny, rotary screw on a cupped reflector, sending forth a long, steady stream of fire then adjusted the length of the flame. Satisfied with its performance, he extinguished the fire and settled the lamp onto the catch on his hat, kissed Emily goodbye, and left with his dinner bucket.

His crew waited at the mine entry and each merely nodded or grunted as they entered the blackness and marched to the workplace. The night shift had done its job well. The cut had been completely cleaned, and smooth, black, gleaming walls of coal waited for the next shot. Andrew marveled at the height of the coal. His years of mining in Pennsylvania had not prepared him for the sights he had seen in this area. Twelve to sixteen feet of coal rose above them, and he was awed by the sight. Coal in the Pennsylvania mines averaged five to six feet, and much of it measured only four feet. It would take decades to even dent this supply.

"Make the hole dead center," he told Hale Potter, as he checked the surface for other holes or fissures that could possibly release methane gas into the tunnels.

Satisfied, he watched as Potter loaded black blasting powder into the open cut and turned to walk the crew away to safety. Potter didn't particularly like the way the fuse looked and it felt too pliable, but what the hell, he was sure it would burn. He lit the fuse with the flame from his carbide lamp and scampered to safety with the others. The fire didn't travel along the fuse as it should have, and Andrew was vexed.

"What the hell did you do, Potter, spit on the damned thing?"

Hale didn't dare tell Andrew he didn't like the way the fuse felt because he knew for sure he could catch hell. They waited for several minutes with no sign of fire. Andrew decided he would do it himself and he took the role of fuse from Hale.

"This is the third time this week," he said, glaring at the young man. "I'm beginning to believe you don't know shit about explosives, Potter."

He reached toward the black powdered hole to insert another fuse as a deafening roar engulfed him with tons of coal smashing him into the floor. His men were horrified by the spectacle. Hale headed to the mine opening for help, screaming at the others to start digging.

Men came running through the tunnel with shovels to join the crew already shoveling furiously, each hoping to find Andrew alive but fearing the worst. After hours of digging away tons of coal, their worst fears were realized. The full brunt of the explosion had completely mangled Andrew. After scraping his body from the floor with shovels, the sickened crew made for the outside.

Emily was devastated but showed a strength that surprised Mary Jane. She had always thought of her mother as being completely dependent on her father, but she pulled herself together before the funeral to bid him a tearful but dignified farewell.

Thomas turned to Ben for comfort, which pleased Mary Jane, and Emily was grateful. Friends and many company officials attended the funeral offering help and condolences. Emily had helped friends bury family members in Pennsylvania and knew the extreme dangers associated with mining, and yet, she had always thought of her strong and sturdy husband as invincible. Mary Jane's graduation was a sad one. Her father had been buried the week before. With tearful eyes, she received her diploma and wept for her father who had looked forward to the ceremony. Emily surprised everyone by starting a job in the commissary a month after the funeral. Friends had thought she would take the sizable insurance funds and move back to Pennsylvania.

"I know you and Ben will be married, Mary Jane, and I want to be near you. Thomas looks up to Ben, and he doesn't want to leave his friends. Besides, I can stay on in the company house, if I work in the store." Mary Jane was flabbergasted. She had assumed her mother had been as opposed to Ben as her father was.

CHAPTER 13

Near the end of April 1913, Randolph and Cynthia Adams made the train ride from Lexington to Elkinsville.

"Randy, this is so beautiful, seeing the country from the train. You get a much better view than riding a horse through tall timber," Cynthia said. Her trips to their cabin had been made on horseback. Though always interesting and beautiful, it could not compare with roaring over high bridges then plunging into black tunnels burrowing throughout the mountains. Dogwoods were just beginning to bloom, and the mountains were glorious.

"I'm going to look young Ben Cantrell up and see what information I can get from him. You remember me talking to you about Martin and Luke Edwards?"

Cynthia nodded.

"Well, they are Ben's uncles on his mother's side, and they wanted us to say hello to him. He was only about seven years old the last time we met, so I doubt he will remember me."

The train braked to a screaming halt at the railway station in Elkinsville, jerking both the Adams against their seats. "Glad I didn't have my tongue between my teeth," Randolph hissed to Cynthia.

A horse-drawn, passenger buggy drove Cynthia and Randolph to the hotel entry, and Randolph was amazed. His memory of this area was of the Edwards' cabin in a wilderness area. They had passed several tall buildings, and business establishments were solid for several blocks. The greatest surprise was the number of beautiful homes surrounding a small lake, reflecting a vivid blue sky.

As they drove about town in a rented carriage the next day, the luxurious hotel was only one of the many surprises they encountered. New streets were being paved throughout the town, and wooden steps were being constructed up the hillsides to the miners' new homes. A bevy of carpenters moved about with loads of new lumber for the next project.

Randolph located Ben at the largest sawmill where the hotel clerk had told him Ben would be working. A worker found Ben in the lumberyard, and the huge, handsome man, who gave them a quizzical look, impressed the Adams.

Ben's size and his unique presence intrigued Cynthia. It took her an instant to realize that somehow it related to the most unusual pair of eyes she had ever seen. They were very pale amber and seemed to take everything in at one glance. A thick, black ring of eyelashes gave them even more distinction.

"Ben, I'm Randolph Adams, and this is my wife, Cynthia. Your uncles, Martin and Luke Edwards, asked us to say hello. We live in Lexington and see them on a regular basis. I met you years ago at your Grandfather Albert's home when you were only a small boy. I doubt that you remember me."

"Yes, I do remember you, Mr. Adams, and I'll bet my uncles are workin' hard as usual." Ben smiled and extended a huge, strong hand to both.

"They are, and their company stays mighty busy. Ben, we would like to have supper with you tonight at the hotel, unless you have other plans. If you have a girlfriend you would like to bring along, please do so."

"I'll be happy to come, Mr. Adams, but I will be coming alone. The girl I plan to marry in July buried her father three days ago, and her mother needs her right now."

"I am so sorry to hear about her father's death, Ben. What happened to him?" Randolph asked.

"He was killed in a terrible mine accident. It had to do with blasting. Several other men have been killed by explosives this past year, too." Ben explained, as Randolph shook his head in sadness.

"I don't plan on ever goin' into no mine," Ben said.

After visiting with Ben Cantrell, Randolph kept an appointment with the C.E.O. of the Ransome project. He felt dejected after the meeting. He came away with the distinct feeling that Ransome would jealously guard their interests in the town and resented any reference to sharing manpower with other businesses.

At supper, Ben brought them up to date on his family and delighted them with tales of their mountain compound. Randolph was pleased to know that Sarah was doing well at eighty-three years old. Luke and Martin had told Randy about the death of Albert. He missed his old friend whose wilderness cabin had disappeared into the sprawling town of Elkinsville.

"Ben, I visited with Mr. Aldridge, the C.E.O. of Ransome here in Elkinsville this afternoon. We talked about new industry in town, and he definitely was not interested. I was hoping to see factories for byproducts of coal and even a furniture factory for some of this fine timber, but I hit a brick wall. I must say that I am more than a little bit disappointed. They are developing a beautiful town, but it needs diversity."

"What you have in mind for the town sounds good, Mr. Adams. I had never really thought about it, but I have heard that people pay a big price for furniture made from the big trees in this area. The timber buyers are always bragging about what the foreign countries can do with these hardwoods. Don't see why they can't do the same here. I'll keep my ears open, if you would like," Ben responded.

"I would appreciate that, Ben."

"How is your family, Mr. Adams? I remember you had two boys."

"Our older son, Joel, has an engineering firm in Louisville. We also have a daughter, Dorothy, who is a teacher, and Wesley will graduate from law school in December. He has really been working hard in order to graduate early."

"Well, at least he is going to take a day off and go up to Louisville to see the Kentucky Derby next Saturday," Cynthia said.

"They say that is some race, and I would like to see it sometime," Ben said with a wistful look.

***

Wesley Adams stood near Churchill Downs in Louisville waiting for his friends. Benton Blair and his young, redheaded wife, Elsie, had insisted that Wesley take time out from his studies to come to the race today. Wesley had crammed his schedule to the hilt in order to graduate six months early from law school, and his social life had been at a standstill.

He could almost taste the excitement of the big day. The crowd surged into the stands filled with laughter and high-pitched urgency. Women in gala attire tripped over the grass holding onto large, colorful hats in order to stay them in the brisk May breeze. Some reminded Wesley of floral floats, and he noticed many escorts glancing sideways to be sure they wouldn't be pummeled by the massive creations. The Kentucky Derby was drawing more celebrities each year, with parties and social events starting at least two weeks before the great event.

Waiting near a pasture fence where thoroughbreds munched on succulent grass, Wesley moved closer to the fence to keep from being swept into the arena by the boisterous and overflowing crowds. When his friends finally arrived, he was stunned by the beautiful girl they had brought with them.

Lacey Calhoun leaned lazily against the newly painted, white fence and gazed boldly at Wesley. He thought she could well have been a lovely flower growing from the rich earth.

Her white dress, scooped low at the neck, was filled to the brim with bosom. It was nipped at her small waist by a long, flowing, yellow sash, and she carried a wide-brimmed, white, straw hat ribboned in yellow to match the sash. Her feisty, white ankle-buttoned shoes bottomed out the scallops on exquisite linen. Lacey Calhoun's raven-black hair sheened to blue and hung long, heavy and beautifully loose. Her startling, huge, very pale, blue eyes held Wesley spellbound. He found her beautiful beyond words, and both his mind and body reacted. The race was a blur to him. His eyes were glued to Lacey's face and the luscious mouth he wanted to possess.

Elsie giggled quietly and nudged Benton. "I told you so. I knew Wesley would be bowled over."

"I don't know about this, Elsie," Benton told her later in the evening. "You know how wild Lacey is. Hell, she has been kicked out of a half-dozen schools."

"Only because she is lively and doesn't want to be tied down to silly rules and regulations in all those stifling private schools. Her father should allow her to go to the university here instead of trying to further a pedigree."

"If you don't remember, I do. Elsie, she flunked out of U.K., in spite of her father's large contributions. You do have to go to afternoon classes." Benton emphasized "afternoon classes" because Lacey even slept through those.

"She just hasn't met the right man, Benton, and I think Wesley will be the sobering force she needs."

"Right for her, but wrong for Wesley," he retorted.

Thomas Calhoun was very impressed by tall, handsome Wesley. His daughter's suitors had ranged from those who hoped to buy her to those who wanted her money. Twenty-four-year-old Wesley was the striking image he wanted for his daughter. A doting father and Lacey's incredible beauty placed the pedestal high. The Bluegrass country bore witness to Calhoun's magnanimous contributions. His numerous grants, parks and buildings denoted his generosity. Having profited mightily from oil and railroads, he was always willing to share his good fortune. He was a kind man who had started as a roughneck in the oil fields, with only one shortcoming: He had never been able to deny his twenty-year-old daughter anything. His wife had died when Lacey was nine-years-old, leaving him to hover and protect their only child. Each time she had been shipped home from school, he had chosen to believe her lame excuses.

***

The last of July rolled around and Ben managed to beg a three-day leave from the sawmill. "I was hopin' I could do better, Mary Jane," he apologized, as he broke the news to her. Mary Jane wrapped herself around him and assured Ben she would be there at night when he came home. The ceremony was a quiet one with only Emily and Thomas standing with Mary Jane. Hiram cleaned himself up and stood next to his younger brother. After the Methodist minister pronounced them man and wife, their families disappeared as the newlyweds headed for their new home. Even though his time off was meager, Ben had been able to find a small acreage with a livable house, and he was elated when Mary Jane approved. An icy mountain stream flowed at the bottom of their hill, making bubbly waterfalls over large rocks as mountain laurel limbs hanging low with large blossoms, dipped and swayed. They could have a large garden with enough pasture for a couple of milk cows. Mary Jane had been emphatic about living close enough to town so their future children could go to school. Ben would miss his mountaintop home, but he would have missed Mary Jane a hell of a lot more. After two days, she whispered she wasn't sure she could let him go back to work. Ben roared with laughter and squeezed her even tighter.

"If we're gonna live and love, girl, we're gonna have to pay for it."

September was well on its way when Mary Jane realized her full breasts were becoming gorged, which only made Ben happier. Emily had never talked to her children about sex, and it was several weeks later when her daughter finally realized she was pregnant. Ben was dumfounded at first. He had wanted Mary Jane all to himself for a while, but her happiness and excitement finally filtered through to him as they awaited their firstborn.

Emily and Thomas were frequent visitors to Mary Jane and Ben's new home. When Ben could spare the time, he and Thomas would roam the hills in back of the house. He was surprised at how quickly Thomas had perfected his aim and the ease with which he handled a rifle.

"You're sure this is the first time you've handled a gun, Thomas?" Ben asked late one evening, when Thomas had shot three squirrels from their perch in a tall oak tree in rapid succession.

"My dad would not have a gun in the house, but Isaac and Owen showed me how to line up the sights, then squeeze the trigger, steady and gentle."

"Sounds like Isaac and Owen. The only time they come out of the woods is to eat and help Pa when he swears at them for layin' out and not doing their share of work on the farm," and the two laughed at the accurate description of the brothers.

Thomas had grown several inches in the past year, and, on occasion, the haunted look in his eyes tore at Ben's heart. He knew the boy missed his father and arranged to have his two younger brothers invite him to the farm for an occasional weekend of hunting, which delighted him, but Emily was very uncomfortable with the situation.

"Mary Jane, your father said they were a wild bunch and bootleggers. I just don't think it's safe for Thomas."

"Mom, I hope you will be able to meet Sarah and Amy sometime. They are beautiful women, and I'm sure they will see that Thomas is well-taken care of. I know you would love their farm. It reminds me of a small village with all the cabins, and the waterfall near the house is so unusual. I just wish it was close to town so we could spend more time there. After I have the baby, you will have to ride up there with us sometime."

***

In December of 1913, six months after their introduction at the Derby, Wesley and Lacey were married. The wedding was elaborate, and Thomas Calhoun pulled out all of the stops. The country club had never hosted a larger or more extravagant affair with the most expensive band that could be hired and a gourmet dinner that required seating for several hundred. The dancing lasted into the wee hours, and the society columns required extra space to list the many details. Lacey charmed Wesley's family, and they felt like they had inherited another daughter.

Wesley put a cap of two weeks on their European honeymoon, but Lacey could have romped forever. "Daddy only has me, and why shouldn't we spend another month in Europe?" she pouted. Taking his disappointed bride into his arms, he explained his burning desire to open his law practice immediately. Wesley had always planned to hang his shingle in a small town, but Lacey had other plans. They stayed in Louisville, and, like Lacey's father, he spoiled her. The rewards were beyond belief, and Wesley considered himself blessed. His law practice was busy from the beginning. Lacey's father seemed to leave a never-ending stream of friends who needed legal counseling. Wesley could well stand on his own merit, having graduated number three in his class, and his appointment to various boards was quickly forthcoming. His father-in-law blessed them with a lifetime membership in the country club, and box seats at Churchill Downs was an added bonus. Lacey turned her energies toward house-hunting, as Wesley buried himself in work. One month after their return from Europe, she insisted on taking him to see a dream house. She was dismayed by the stern look on her husband's face as their carriage stopped in front of a high-columned mansion.

"Surely, Lacey," Wesley began as she threw up her hands in disgust, and tears flowed.

"Why do you have to be so stubborn about my father giving us a home?" she sobbed.

"Lacey, as an attorney, I will be able to give you a fine home in a few years. Give me a chance," he begged. "None of our friends have a home like this."

"None of our friends have a daddy like mine," she flared.

They finally settled into an older home that Lacey completely redecorated, and the results were stunning. Wesley bit his tongue and didn't ask how much daddy had bequeathed to the project.

Their first visitors were Wesley's family, and Lacey was truly gracious. His father, so steeped in Kentucky history, had many tales to impart about the area, and Lacey was an avid listener. Wesley's mother, tall with a regal beauty, smiled sweetly at her daughter-in-law, complimenting her on their house and the dinner. His sister, Dorothy, and his brother, Joel, were especially impressed with their brother's vivacious wife. Joel's wife, Kathleen, was away in Ohio, attending to a mother who was quite ill, and he promised to bring her by as soon as she returned.

The weeks flew by, and Wesley worked harder. Weekends were a flurry of parties and picnics, many at the racetracks. He had never dreamed such happiness could exist, and he could hardly wait for each day to begin. He left Lacey asleep each morning but knew she would be at her father's stables before noon.

Most mornings, father and daughter rode together, and her cheerful chatter was what he lived for. His tremendous respect for Wesley was the only barrier that kept them from resenting his son-in-law who refused his money.

Wesley's long-legged, towering frame became a common sight at the courthouse as he raced up and down the stairways. An old time courthouse watcher remarked, "That young feller never walks, he attacks them stairs."

His heavy shock of dark-auburn hair appeared almost too heavy for his long, angular face, as it fell across his forehead. His hazel eyes, that never seemed to blink, could bore into the opposition, and no few were seen to shrink from his sharp stare. He was leaving home earlier and returning later as his client load increased, much to Lacey's dismay. On several occasions she was left to host a dinner party on her own, after which she raged at Wesley.

"We don't need the money, Wesley. It will take us three lifetimes to spend what my daddy has."

"I prefer to spend my own money, Lacey," he replied cooly, "and furthermore, the client I spent the evening with doesn't have any money."

She flew up the wide stairway slamming the door to their bedroom, and Wesley slept in the guest room.

Although Lacey would rant and rave, they always made up, and each time it was sweeter.

***

January of 1914 blustered its way into the mountains and buried Elkinsville beneath two feet of snow. Mary Jane, tired of being indoors, volunteered to work in the high school library to assist students with their reference work. Ben was especially happy for her, since his days at the sawmill were getting even longer. Mine foremen were constantly wooing the mill workers into the coal mines, leaving Ben shorthanded. They had sought out Ben and promised him extra incentives, but he had no desire to dig in the blackness.

Emily cautioned her daughter that she shouldn't spend too many hours on her feet as she began to gain weight. Ben was happy to have his mother-in-law advising Mary Jane. He knew nothing about pregnant women, and with snow continuing to pile up, he couldn't check with Amy and Sarah. He missed his grandfather. Albert always had time to answer his many questions. Nothing was too trite to dismiss.

Sarah sat in her favorite rocking chair by the huge fireplace, knitting booties and a matching sweater for Mary Jane and Ben's baby. She was delighted that Ben would now have a family of his own. At eighty-four, she was amazingly strong. Her thick, snow-white hair appeared to be a beautiful, puffy cloud, framing a still lovely face with fine lines fanning out from the corners of her eyes.

Amy had been restless for weeks, a fact Sarah had credited to being snowbound. Amy loved to hike about the farm, and Levi counted on her to spot new calves and keep correct numbers of all the newborns.

The first of February brought a slight warming trend, and most of the January snow had melted. Amy threw a lightweight shawl around her shoulders and slipped on heavy boots to wade through mud left by melting snow. Waving to Sarah, she stepped through the door into welcome sunshine.

Levi caught up with her before she reached the pasture. He had seen the fear in Amy's eyes when they first learned of Mary Jane's pregnancy. Neither she nor Levi had discussed the baby except to congratulate Ben. It was as though there would be no adverse effects if they didn't talk about or speculate on the possibilities.

"Levi, do you think we should have told Ben about his eyes before he married Mary Jane?" Amy said, knowing Levi was surely thinking about the same thing.

"No, Amy," Levi answered firmly. "It could have changed his whole life. Things are going well for Ben and Mary Jane, and we should let things be." Beneath Levi's calm exterior he was facing the same nagging doubts that Amy had just voiced.

"Ben is special, Amy, and real smart. If the child is anything like him, it will be very lucky."

"I do worry, Levi. What if this child is somehow different from Ben?"

In early June of 1914, Elizabeth Cantrell arrived, and Ben was smitten by his tiny daughter. The raven black Cantrell hair, coupled with Mary Jane's green eyes promised a beauty in the making. Hiram had been in town but cut short his visit to rush back to the mountaintop to announce the birth of the baby, and Amy asked him a dozen questions.

"What color is her hair, Hiram? How long is she? What color are her eyes?"

"Well, she is long, and she sure has the Cantrell hair. It is black as night, and it surely is pretty with them green eyes."

"What kind of green eyes, Hiram?' Amy demanded.

"Well, green eyes kinda like Mary Jane's."

"Are they exactly like Mary Jane's or could they be lighter or darker?' Amy asked.

"Ma, they are just green eyes," a puzzled Hiram said.

CHAPTER 14

Ransome wasted no time in touting Elkinsville as a model and unique mining town. Dignitaries came from around the world to view a modern town carved into a remote wilderness. They came by Pullman cars and viewed with wonder the deep mountain passes and roaring waters far below, as the locomotives whistled around curves and breathtaking precipices. They were awed by the dense woodlands and swift sightings of abundant wildlife. They were royally entertained at the new and expansive hotel and marveled at the delicious wild game prepared by master chefs.

The highlight of the trip was the frosty mint juleps served in silver goblets, well endowed with Levi Cantrell's moonshine and enhanced with large, fragrant mint leaves that thrived throughout the area. Numerous flat bottles filled with white lighting were favorite souvenirs of departing guests. Ransome's officials always arranged a side trip to Raven Rock by horseback or wagon, and visitors stood in reverence atop the jutting cliff, as they beheld the majestic panorama spreading for miles in every direction. Tennessee misted to the far south, and Elkinsville shrank to miniature.

Frequently, happy visitors, highly imbibed, would crowd forward, teetering on the edge of the soaring precipice, while the guides verged on panic.

Chefs traveling with the visitors prepared sumptuous picnics that were feasted upon as they sat almost to cloud level.

It was a far cry from Rockefeller's debaucheries in Colorado mining, but it was setting the stage for a far more deadly and painful outcome.

Foremen vied for the best workers and attempted to keep them satisfied. The men developed a camaraderie over the months, and loyalties were strong. So many mine openings were being constructed that a man could walk off his job in the afternoon, if he so chose, and find another job by morning. Farm products were much in demand. Huge vegetables grown in rich soil were treats to the many foreigners whose land had been overtilled for decades. When farmers had filled company store bins to overflowing, they made rounds in the residential areas, with homemakers converging on the horse-drawn wagons. The area flourished, and independent merchants began filtering into the mountains. Their small stores and restaurants beckoned to those who wanted diversity. They carved their niche into available land between the coal camps, erecting homes for their families and creating their own small towns. The new merchants would not accept company script for its full value, charging a ten percent surtax, which their customers grumbled about but paid. At the end of the month, they carried large bags of script to Ransome offices exchanging it for full value.

Dance halls were springing up on the edges of these small towns. Moonshine flowed at the hot spots, and fighting usually broke out. Those who were jailed for their Saturday night flings were hauled into court on Sunday morning to pay fines and ready themselves for work on Monday morning. Ransome couldn't waste money on a Monday hearing.

Many bootleggers were pulled in from the hills by the law, but Levi, with his crafty Indian heritage, was always one step ahead. His sons were sworn to secrecy, and their wives had no idea where the cave was or even if there was a cave. They produced many farm products that Hiram delivered to town, camouflaging moonshine beneath squawking chickens and vegetables.

The Cantrell fields flourished with vegetables of every description. Their huge sweet potatoes and Irish potatoes were sought by the townspeople, and their roasting ears were the juiciest and sweetest that could be found.

The family missed having Ben and Mary Jane visit the farm. Ben was besieged from all sides at the sawmill, as demand increased for lumber and props for the mines. His fatigue vanished when he arrived home at night and could hold Mary Jane close again. He was completely awed by his beautiful wife and small daughter.

***

Near the end of the second year of their marriage, Wesley sometimes wondered if something was amiss. Lacey would often appear distant, but he would always tease her out of it. Having finished trial earlier than usual on one occasion, Wesley decided not to go to his office, but to go home early and surprise Lacey. As his livery approached the house, he saw Jessie Mulling leaving by the side yard. Jessie was an insolent, arrogant young man that Wesley did not particularly care for. He had worked as the Calhoun's stable boy for some period, and Thomas had mentioned something about him supporting his mother.

"What was Jessie doing here?" he called to Lacey as he hung his coat and hat on the umbrella stand. Being preoccupied with mail, Wesley failed to notice the somewhat breathless reply that Jessie had returned scarf and gloves left at the stables.

Before she descended the stairway, there was a hasty buttoning of dress and smoothing of hair. Her welcome to Wesley was very warm and sensual. He was only pleased.

Many people knew what Wesley never suspected. There was a subtle difference in his family beginning the third year of their marriage. Occasionally, Wesley had been tempted to ask his brother Joel if something was amiss, but it would seem absurd. His only problem was time. Tenacious by nature, nothing escaped his mind in legal matters, and the followup was always time consuming.

It no longer seemed to vex Lacey that several of the couples they had shared many social occasions with were drifting away. Wesley encountered Benton and Elsie Blair while at lunch with two of his clients on a busy Tuesday. They had been a constant foursome since his early dating days with Lacey, and Wesley suddenly realized they had not seen the Blairs in several months.

"Elsie," he chided, "is this husband of yours keeping you under a basket?" It had been a joke between them that Benton had to put

240

Elsie's beautiful and shining red hair under a basket so the sun could shine.

Elsie giggled, but Benton looked evasive and made the excuse of being busy with two small children. Wesley mentioned the meeting to Lacey when he arrived home for a late dinner, as ususal. Raising her eyebrows, she shrugged her shoulders with a comment about Elsie and her babies and more babies.

Long after Lacey slept, Wesley lay thinking. He made up his mind to curtail the late hours. His practice had developed beyond his greatest expectations. Their home life could now take precedence. He finally slept a troubled sleep. Arriving at the courthouse the next morning, he found his case had been postponed due to a death in the family of the opposing attorney. Leaving the courthouse in the brisk morning air of spring, Wesley decided he wanted Lacey and to hell with everything else.

He arrived home and let himself into a still darkened hallway. Smiling to himself, he decided to quietly awaken Lacey and silently mounted the stairway, removing his coat and tie as he went. His long legs cleared the stairs with quickening strides. Lacey would be warm with the sweet smell of sleep, her silken tresses splayed across their pillows, and his body hardened. He stopped in shock and disbelief as the small bedside lamp illuminated a scene that would follow him to his grave.

Lacey and Jessie Mullins were convulsed in the final throes of passion. Her slender arms and legs greedily drew his muscular body to her as she lay with closed eyes and contorted face. Wesley would vaguely remember lifting the Colt 45 from a rack above the chest of drawers. He shot Jessie through the left temple. Lacey's eyes flew open and were wide as she screamed. He aimed the gun again but could not pull the trigger.

Blinded with fury, he dropped the weapon and staggered from the room. He descended the stairway dazed and numbed by his shattered world. Lacey's screams echoed again and again, as Jessie's blood flowed between her heaving breasts, pooling in her navel. His flaccid body slipped from hers, and she fainted.

Wesley could never get drunk enough to wipe out the memory of Jessie Mullins' mother. She had appeared in the courtroom on the day of his arraignment, resting her large body on the first seat of the second row. Heavy, thick stockings rolled over elastic garters bit into her huge legs just below the knees, bulging enormous varicose veins almost to the breaking point. The old and too small dress was hiked to knee level as she sprawled in her seat with fat, flabby arms folded across a large girth. Dark, straight hair, pulled tightly back from her face into a knot, rested on her short, wide neck. Celluloid hairpins were poked at random into the lopsided mass to hold it in place. She had a heavy jaw and a florid face with dark, beady eyes that appeared to be receding into the depths of excess flesh. There was no mistaking the hatred projecting from them.

When the judge announced Wesley's freedom, a tortured scream erupted through the courtroom. In his nightmares thereafter he would remember the scene over and over. Two deputies grabbed her as she lunged toward Wesley. Fists flailing in the air, she kicked and screamed as a barrier was formed between them. The knot of hair had fallen and become streaked about her face, wet with tears and perspiration. Her heavy, heaving body practically moved the two deputies forward.

"You killed my boy!" she shouted over and over. "You and your whore killed my boy! I curse you, Wesley Adams, and I witch you. You will live to see any son you have dead at your feet."

Shaking, Wesley left the courthouse with her hysterical screams following him into the street. Joel and his father almost ran to keep up with him as he headed to his office.

"Hear me out, Dad, and you too, Joel. I have to go away for awhile. I'm going to the cabin, and I want to be alone."

"I think that would be a good idea, son," his father spoke softly; his heart breaking for his son. As they entered his office, the two men watched in desperate silence as Wesley raked unopened mail into his desk drawers and savagely threw a stack of papers lying on his desk halfway across the room.

"I'm just going to lock it up and leave it," he said as his eyes swept the office that had been his life. Randolph and Joel walked to the stables with Wesley and watched with sadness as he threw bulging saddlebags across the horse, and his father was further dismayed when he saw that most of the supplies were bottled.

"I'll be checking on you, Wes," Joel said to him. "Is there anything I can bring?"

"Just be sure it is my favorite bourbon," Wesley answered, and his heel sent the horse trotting. He rode in a daze through the streets, so familiar and friendly in the past. They now appeared to have narrowed with hostility, and he rode faster toward the hills.

Wesley sobered only long enough to reach for another bottle, but not even that could wipe the courtroom scene from his memory. He would pay for the rest of his life.

***

One month later, Joel's trip to the cabin was more disturbing than anything he could have visualized. Wesley's scraggily beard and mustache so shocked Joel that he momentarily didn't recognize his brother. Shaggy, dirty hair was glued to his head and barely parted enough to expose deadened, bleary eyes that refused to focus. He had no doubt slept in the same rumpled, dirty clothes for days on end, and the odor from his unwashed body was repugnant. Only one corner of the cabin had been used, and the rest was in neat stark contrast to the filthy heap of bedclothes where Wesley spent his days and nights.

Joel spent two days cleaning the bedding and changing Wesley's clothes because he was too drunk to object. He managed to get a few decent meals into his brother, who kept telling him he wanted to be left alone. He was afraid if he pushed Wesley any further he would completely shut him out. Joel longed to cut the bourbon off completely, but the hills were full of bootleggers, and he knew Wesley would manage to find them. Some of their concoctions could kill, blind or maim a man for life.

After several weeks, he saw no improvement in his brother's condition, and his clothes were beginning to hang on his tall frame. A diet of bourbon was fast becoming devastating.

"Wesley, many of your clients are waiting for you to return to your office, and Lacey has filed for divorce. She now lives in New York, and I doubt that she will ever return to Kentucky." Joel was even more upset when Wesley appeared not to have heard what he had said.

In Wesley's self-induced, drunken stupors, he had exercised little, and after two and a half months, it was beginning to show. Even walking to the creek to catch his dinner from the teaming fish was beginning to leave him winded. Awaking early one morning with breath like a dragon, he walked to the creek to brush his teeth and eat two of the oranges Joel had left for him. The sun, barely giving birth to day, was silhouetting the eastern side of the Breaks, rimming the hulking mass in liquid fire that almost blinded him. He suddenly had the urge to hike to the top of the mountain towering above the yawning chasm.

In his weakened condition it took him nearly three hours to climb to the top. As a young boy, he had scampered the distance in less than an hour. When he finally reached the summit, after stopping and resting numerous times, his legs felt like yo-yo's, ready to roll up on him, and his muscles twitched painfully. He was suddenly very dizzy as he looked down into the tremendous depths beneath him. The thought of stepping off into the stream so far below played through his mind. His well-ordered life had eroded into the intolerable. He had brought misery and shame to his family and dishonor to his profession. Wesley moved closer to the brink of the canyon, and the loose loam suddenly gave way beneath his weight. He slipped over the edge, and grabbed frantically for a handhold, grasping a large, extended root, and he clung desperately to it.

He had slid forty feet into the opening and was filled with terror as he hung limp against the rough and rocky side of the mountain, watching as rocks he had loosened in his fall landed several hundred feet below. The rough sides of the crevice offered some support for a toehold, and Wesley prayed the rocks wouldn't crumble beneath his flailing feet as he dragged his weakened body, hand-over-hand, toward the top. Huge trees standing near the rim of the canyon extended roots outward, and Wesley grabbed one after the other in a death grip as he inched his way to safe, solid ground. He managed to crawl a few feet to the nearest tree and collapsed.

When he awoke several hours later, the sun was low in the West, and he slid, rolled and crawled to the bottom of the mountain. He managed to stagger into the cabin, falling onto his unkept bed. He slept until early morning and awoke stone-cold sober. For the first time in months, Wesley had not drenched himself in bourbon to allay his misery for a few hours. Turning on his side, his glance fell on the headlines of the paper Joel had left for him, and he realized America was on the brink of war. Wesley knew what he had to do. He knew he no longer wanted to die. The next morning, he saddled his horse and left for home.

Two days later, he arrived at his parents' home and announced that he was going to join the Army. His arrival was timely. Joel had become greatly alarmed on his last visit with Wesley. His brother had dropped at least twenty-five pounds, leaving a gaunt face and hollow eyes. Constantly drunk, his conversation was reduced to mumbling. Joel had talked bluntly to his parents about Wesley's rapidly deteriorating condition, and they had decided he would have to be committed to a hospital in order to save his life. His family was astounded and overjoyed to see him sober and coherent. Though greatly emaciated, he had a determined look in his eyes.

Six weeks later, Wesley was sworn into the Army as a lieutenant. He had gained eighteen pounds, and with constant exercising, he little resembled the man who had returned home several weeks before. His family was loath to see him off to war but accepted the decision, knowing that it had turned his life around. Wesley's quest had begun, to atone for his errant act of madness.

***

In 1916, World War I was beginning to have dire effects on the mining industry in Elkinsville. Many experienced miners from Europe agonized over the fate of families and friends. Belgian men were first to leave the pits and return to their homeland. Their presence was sorely missed. They were rugged men from generations of miners whose skills in the labyrinths of blackness had been honed to perfection. Frenchmen, whose blood-soaked homeland was battling for its life, were not far behind. They traded shovels for rifles, taking up positions in the long trench on the Western front.

By late fall, English miners heeded the call of their beloved British Isles, heading for New York harbors and passage home. Unfortunately, many never arrived at their destinations. German U-boats ruled the seas, sweeping the endless water that lay unprotected from their merciless torpedoes. Their prime targets were merchant ships and their cargo. The ships were the quickest and cheapest transportation for many heading to the defense of their countries, only to be lost at sea.

The United States entered the War in early April of 1917, poorly equipped and undermanned. A draft was immediately imposed, with thousands of young men and women volunteering their services as

Americans rallied behind the Allied cause. Armament and munition factories sprang up throughout the country, and the demand for bituminous coal was never satisfied. Coal mining was hard hit by miners going off to war, and foremen begged for more workers to help the war effort. Many older farmers who had never entered a coal mine responded to the call and entered the black caves. Long coal drags roared through the town, constantly carrying precious fuel to factories turning out materials for war.

Jerry Bentley was one of the first to volunteer, and Frank Upshaw was devastated when the slight limp from a knee injury kept him homebound. Thomas Newsome turned eighteen in January of 1917 and was drafted in May. Emily was beside herself. Mary Jane did her best to comfort her mother, hiding her own misery because Thomas had been snatched from them just as her father had been.

Ben and his brothers had taught Thomas to become an expert marksman, which landed him on a troopship within a very short period. The dreaded telegrams began arriving shortly after the first troops arrived in France. Newly devised flamethrowers and poisonous gas took a heavy toll. Friends and neighbors comforted families in their terrible losses, praying for their own young men who had so quickly and brutally been thrown into the battle. Theaters were even more packed as black-and-white newsreels gave soundless views of war, and families wept for their sons. Evidence of mining accidents became more prevalent. Miners with armless sleeves and trousers with only one leg filled began to appear more and more on the streets of Elkinsville. Legless men in wheelchairs dotted the sidewalks and were given front-row seats at the outdoor band concerts. The long hours and exhaustion played a major part in the increase in accidents.

***

Wesley was on one of the first troopships to head toward French shores. The fog-shrouded vessel crept through murky waters as the soldiers huddled on damp decks, thinking about home and the War. Wesley studied the young men in the meager light and guessed some of them to be as young as fifteen and sixteen years old. Large and well-developed, they had been accepted by eager recruiters without proof of their age. Many looked frightened and apprehensive, no doubt wishing they had stayed on dry land. The young men from Kentucky farms, who had grown up hunting with rifles from an early age, were at ease with their weapons, and Wesley knew they would be formidable foes.

German U-boats searched for troopships, as German forces were desperate to gain complete control on the Western Front before American troops could become entrenched with their allies.

Wesley's depression departed swiftly as he saw near terror on the faces of so many young men. As the huge transport mounted and rode over each new wave, the new troops watched in the blackness for the dreaded periscope and the terrifying thud that would take them down into the depths.

Upon their arrival on French shores, the young and green troops were rushed from the ships and to the trenches that may as well have been hell itself. Wesley saw several of the men heave, until only bile was left, as they struggled over dead and mangled bodies in the grisly trenches. The roar of guns on both sides racked the nerves of the incoming soldiers.

Wesley felt no fear for himself. He leaped first into the firestorm of assaults, screaming orders and fighting like a madman.

His men followed him into battle, and he tread where no officer was required to go. Wesley wept when his men died, and he gave himself no quarter. The soldiers were in awe of their fierce leader who was driven above and beyond the terrible missions asked of him.

The American forces swelled to almost two and one-half million men whose gallant and heroic efforts helped greatly to end the war in September of 1918.

Germany would rise from a resounding defeat and roll toward an unbelievable Armageddon. At the end of the war, Wesley returned to a hero's welcome.

CHAPTER 15

Thomas remained in France beneath a white cross and Emily was devastated. Jerry Bentley returned unscathed from the war, and his first errand was to visit Thomas's mother and awkwardly try to comfort her. Elkinsville was very proud of Jerry and his be-ribboned chest.

Ben would always carry some guilt for Thomas's death. Had he and his family never taught his young brother-in-law to shoot a rifle, he just might still be alive. The young men who were rated "expert riflemen" on entering the Army were the first to be shipped out.

Mary Jane consoled him. "Ben, how could you possibly have known there would be a war in Europe with Thomas winding up in the middle of it?"

Vacancies left in the mines and sawmills by men rushing off to war had stretched manpower beyond its limits. The sawmills needed an all-around, knowledgeable driving force to produce much needed lumber and props. Sloppy work in the mills and poorly chosen timber were creating mammoth problems.

Ben was placed in charge of the entire mill industry. In a forest crowded with innumerable trees, he could quickly spot the hickory and black oaks that produced the strongest props, although occasionally, not even the best trees could prevent a mountain from falling and snapping the strongest of props like matchsticks. Ben's expertise eliminated numerous mistakes and saved valuable time.

His quiet but compelling ways thwarted many dangerous outbursts among workers when overtime and exhaustion, bolstered with moonshine, became explosive. Ben would appear at random to check on the night shift and possessed the uncanny ability to arrive just before a fight. His stealthy approach unnerved some of the workers.

"I don't think he ever sleeps," one worker said. "Those damned eyes of his sometimes make me feel as though a cat is watching over my shoulder."

Mary Jane gave birth to their second child in late 1918. Stephen was a large, rawboned baby who looked a lot like the Cantrell clan. His dark, green eyes were Mary Jane's, but the resemblance ended there. Mary Jane's mother doted on the infant and young Elizabeth, finding a reason to live after the terrible loss of Thomas. Amy and Levi breathed a sigh of relief that Stephen did not have Ben's eyes.

Shortly before noon, a red-faced mining foreman came raging into the mill screaming for Ben. "Ben, I want you to see the shit they delivered to number seven. No two props are the same size, and half of them are rotten. We have one hell of a big room there, and I need props right now."

"You'll have them right now, Clint, and I'll bring them myself."

Ben immediately started loading the strongest props with help from Jerry Bentley. He was greatly relieved when Jerry came back from the war, ready to work in the mills again.

"Why in the hell didn't he get the men out of there, Ben? They have no business digging more coal out of there right now, and Frank is working in that area today. You know how fast a mountain can come down when too much coal has been cleared."

"Jesus, Jerry, move it," Ben said, fearing for this friend's life.

Within minutes, they were racing toward the mine entrance. "The war took so much of our manpower, it's going to take a long time to catch up. Ransome has orders backed up for months, and they're pushing foremen to bring out more coal. They cuss at them, beg them and downright bribe some to sidestep safety measures just to keep stockholders happy. The war changed things at home, too, Jerry."

They rushed the loaded wagon to the mine entrances and quickly transferred the props to man cars.

"I'll drive them in, Jerry, if you'll take the wagon back for another load."

Ben was angry that any worker had delivered shoddy props. "I'll find out who did that, and I'll kick his sorry ass." He spoke to the high, glistening, black walls of the tunnel. He passed through rooms that had been emptied of coal and noted with relief the tall, strong props supporting the ceiling. He could hear the sound of shovels and men talking as he neared the site and cut the motor on the man car. Lights illuminated the work area, and Ben spotted Frank just as his keen sense of hearing picked up a slight cracking sound.

"Run, Frank, run!" Ben shouted.

He saw Frank drop his shovel and start toward him just as the mountain gave a thunderous, angry roar and thousands of tons of slate, sandstone and earth crashed onto the unprotected workers. Ben dove beneath the steel man car as the mountain came down upon them. The deafening roar was like nothing he had ever heard. The man car held, and Ben was completely immobilized beneath it. He was so wedged into the small space he was unable to bring his hands to his face to screen out the dense, black dust he was gagging on. His long legs were cramped in their bent position, and the wall of rock and earth pinning him to the tracks would not budge. He agonized for Frank, knowing there was no way he could have survived the crushing mountain. If only Frank had been able to make it to the man car.

It was four hours before workmen began to dig near the first car. There were four cars, and Jerry prayed Ben had been able to take shelter beneath them.

"This is the outer edge of the fall. Jerry, we just uncovered two props," a workman said, and Jerry's heart leaped into his throat.

It seemed to Ben he had been buried for days when he finally heard the sound of a shovel scraping against rock.

"Help!" he croaked as dust filled his mouth when he opened it. Coughing and gagging, he managed to keep calling.

"I thought I heard something," the foremost worker said as he leaned toward the wall of rock. "Gimme that pipe, and I'll try to get in between these rocks."

After several attempts to push the pipe through the mass of rubble, they were able to thread it around obstacles. Ben could hear scraping sounds for several minutes before he felt pressure on the bottom of his boot. Using all the strength he could muster in his bent position, he pushed hard against the pipe. A cheer went up from the men when the pipe suddenly moved backward several inches.

"Lay into these shovels, men," an overjoyed Jerry Bentley shouted, digging ferociously toward his friend.

One hour later, a blackened and battered Ben was pulled feet-first from beneath his meager shelter. Jerry took a second look at Ben. His amber eyes were like two lights, visible against his blackened face and dark tunnel walls.

"Jesus, Ben, if I didn't know it was you, I would swear you were a damned cat."

"Maybe the only thing that saved his life," someone quipped, but no one laughed at the ludicrous statement.

Hours later, the men finally uncovered the first body, and both Ben and Jerry were devastated. Frank had almost made it to the man car. Ben knelt next to Frank's badly battered body, wiping the black dust from his face, with tears washing a path through his own grime. It would be several days before the twelve men who had died with Frank could be uncovered and removed from the mine. Ben managed to track down the two men responsible for delivering damaged props to the mine and fired them on the spot.

***

Shortly after Wesley's return to Louisville, he was appointed circuit court judge and quickly slid back into civilian life. His sister, Dorothy, invited another teacher for Sunday dinner and Wesley met Jenny. She had shining, light-brown hair that framed her small, lovely face and large, dark sober eyes. It seemed to Wesley that he could almost see her soul in the bottomless depths of her eyes as she surveyed him with admiration. Dorothy had told Jenny about her brother, and she was awed.

"Tell me about your friend Dorothy," Wesley said, the day after meeting Jenny.

"She's an outstanding teacher, Wesley, and our high school feels very fortunate to have her. She teaches French, German and Spanish, and kids clamor to get into her classes."

Wesley gave a low whistle, "Does she have a steady boyfriend?" her brother asked.

Dorothy gave him a sly look. "I think you would qualify," she said, and Wesley was somewhat flustered.

Jenny had just excused her last student in late afternoon when she looked up to see a tall, handsome man in the doorway. She felt her face flush and was speechless as Wesley moved with an easy grace toward her and perched on the edge of her desk.

"I hope I'm not interfering with your schedule, Jenny," he said, smiling into her extraordinary eyes.

"I have just finished for the day," she quickly assured him.

"I would like to take you for a ride in my Model T, and when I asked my mother where I might find you, she rushed to fill a picnic basket." They both laughed.

Jenny's laugh was low and throaty, which surprised Wesley as he looked down upon her petite frame. The day was unusually warm for early January, and Wesley lowered the top on his car. The wind and bright sun soon turned Jenny's cheeks to crimson, but she refused to let him raise the top. She forgot her shyness as she discussed her students, and her animated expressions delighted him.

On their next date he tried to explain what had happened in his marriage, but she stopped him.

"I came to Louisville shortly after you left, Wesley, and the whole town was abuzz with gossip. No one blamed you. The only surprise was that you were so late in finding out what everyone had known long before. If you want to talk about it, I want to listen, but I do know what happened."

Wesley found himself looking forward to each visit with Jenny, and most evenings they had dinner together. Jenny's parents were Methodist missionaries in Africa, and she had her own small apartment in Louisville. She had traveled over most of the world with her family, picking up several languages along the way, and she especially loved teaching foreign languages. Wesley listened intently to her stories of other countries and greatly admired her unwavering faith.

By the end of two months, Wesley knew he was deeply in love with Jenny. Their marriage was quiet and totally unlike the ostentatious affair that had heralded his marriage to Lacey. In early May, Jenny knew she was pregnant, and they were both overjoyed.

In 1919, two days before Christmas, their first son was born. A beautiful baby with red hair, Danny, with the nickname "Red" that would remain with him.

"Just like his father," Jenny said. Wesley stood, looking at their baby in his crib and again the words came back to haunt him. "You will live to see any son you have dead at your feet." God he thought just the words of the anguished mother, but the chill remained. His schedule was a busy one, and he spent time in arranging rehabilitation for any defendant who showed a desire to better his life, especially the young offenders. Jenny, who shared his love and belief in young people, encouraged his activities and never complained about the many hours it took from their time together.

***

Life flowed peacefully for a period, and Wesley put his fears aside. He was asked to fill in for various judges over the state who could not be on their bench for short periods of time. As he boarded the train for one such trip, he could not know that his life would change as a result of his one encounter with the town of Elkinsville.

He had ridden horseback through the area on a few occasions with Joel and his father, but the train ride through the mountains was an exciting experience. The train lurched around curves and labored over deep precipices as the rails shrieked and protested with sparks. The swaying coach almost sent him tumbling into the aisle. Spring rains and melted snow had swollen the usual placid, meandering waters to a wild, frothing avalanche that carried large branches, rocks and debris in the downward rush to the valley. Wesley felt his stomach tighten as the train roared over numerous mountain passes and the raging waters below. The bridges through this area had truly been a feat of unbelievable engineering. The locomotive pulling the passenger cars screamed, hissed and blew plumes of steam as it slid into Elkinsville.

After Wesley unpacked his bags and waited for dinner, he strolled along the large, wraparound veranda that encircled the beautiful hotel, admiring the manicured lawn sloping downward to a lovely lake that reflected the dark, blue sky and a sinking sun disappearing behind the rim of the mountains. Large, lovely homes surrounded the lake and extended upward onto the mountainside.

Wesley walked to the water's edge and perched on one of the

many benches bordering the lake. The only landmark that was still recognizable was Raven Rock, entrenched atop Pine Mountain. It reminded him of a sentinel. There was something mystically beautiful about the area, and his soul felt completely at peace. "I must show Jenny," he thought.

Wesley was intrigued by the people he met at the hotel and throughout the town during his week's stay. There were educators, office personnel, company staff and mining supervisors. Superimposed over the lot were mountain people. Descended from the early pioneers of Kentucky, they were people of incredible independence. The pioneers had trekked over the mountains from the Carolinas and Virginia, while others from the North had poled up the Big Sandy River into the narrow valleys.

Many Swiss, German and French arrived on eastern shores to fight in the Revolutionary War and were awarded large tracks of land throughout Virginia and some parts of Kentucky. They had battled Indians and tamed the wilderness. Their descendants were evidence of that proud and independent group.

With each visit, Wesley became more and more intrigued with the hamlet, a modern town carved from the wilderness. He especially liked visiting with the teachers from various sections of the country. They were offered salaries that were exorbitant compared to other areas.

***

Prohibition was ushered in on October 28, 1919, much to the dismay of most of the country. The government announced a great increase in the number of revenue agents, and bootleggers were put on notice. Levi Cantrell sat on top of his mountain, watching the goings on, calculating the amount of moonshine he could sell to new customers, and it was considerable.

Ben arrived at the jail on an early Sunday morning to bail Jerry out of the clink after a drunken Saturday night brawl. "Judge, Jerry becomes wild when he is drinking liquor, and he thinks he's back in the trenches in France." Ben was surprised to see a softening in the judge's face. "He has nobody except me and my wife. He grew up on the streets of Baltimore, and has helped to build this town and has fought for his country."

"What is your name, sir?" the judge asked.

"My name is Ben Cantrell, and I oversee the sawmills. Jerry has worked for me for several years, and you couldn't find a better, more dependable worker."

"Ben Cantrell," Wesley said. "My father, Randolph Adams, asked me to look you up and say hello."

Ben was surprised to know the judge was Randolph's youngest son.

"Ben, do you think we could meet for lunch down the street tomorrow? My father will want news of your family."

"I would like that, judge," and Ben gave Wesley one of his rare smiles.

"Take care of your friend, Ben," Judge Wesley Adams said quietly.

Ben was impressed with Judge Wesley Adams and his fairness. He nodded and pushed Jerry toward the door. Wesley's mind strayed momentarily to his own nightmares, and he wished desperately his dreams were only of war. Even though he was haunted by the desperate and terrified screams of dying men, writhing in death throes combined with the anguished cries of their buddies who held their bloodied bodies in their arms, his worst nightmares were still of Lettie Mullins. They had only become more oppressive and frightening with time.

Suddenly, Wesley knew where he had seen Ben Cantrell before. It was here in this town. For years he had thought of Ben Cantrell's eyes whenever his big tabby cat had blinked at him during the night. It was a lifetime ago.

***

Ben's mind was running to the months ahead and the dangers his family would be facing. The word in town was that Elkinsville would be crawling with feds. It was no secret the mountains were honeycombed with stills, and Ben knew there would be hell to pay. The bootleggers would go down fighting, and they weren't likely to do so alone. Levi and his boys had developed a keen night sight as they roamed the hills making deliveries under cover of darkness. Owls were their greatest friends. When owls were disturbed at night, their great flapping wings alerted listening ears. The Cantrell family's special hoot owl call could even fool an owl. The family could read signals from numerous furry and feathered friends, and now they would need to sharpen their ears even further to ensure their survival. Ben was sorely missed with his unusual night vision and his incredible ability to hear and monitor every animal sound.

In the early spring of 1920, Sarah died quietly in her sleep. Amy was heartbroken. Her mother had been her constant companion for all of her fifty-one years. Sarah was ninety years of age and still walked with a steady step. Arthritis had bent some of her fingers, but she didn't let it interfere with her daily routines. Daughters-in-law and grandchildren looked to Sarah for answers and endless hours of reading and teaching. Levi had come to love and cherish Sarah years ago. He could never tell her how much he appreciated her being with Amy in her lonely years before the boys began bringing wives to the farm. She had missed her Albert in so many ways, and now she could rest beside him.

Sarah had never been a nagger, always complimenting Amy on her decisions, then fading into the background to leave Amy time with her family.

Levi took time out to walk Amy about the hills, knowing the agony and emptiness that filled her heart. His extreme sensitivity carried her through the miserable days after they buried Sarah.

They hiked to Levi's favorite spot where he had spent so many hours observing all that lay around him and glorying in all that belonged to him. His greatest concern was still the possibility that smoke from fires inside the cave could be detected by someone passing by. Over the years he had planted small pines around and in front of the back opening to the cave, and he continued to add large boulders in front of the trees. An impenetrable wall now covered the outlet. He had carefully sealed the inside to such a degree that not even a small animal could wedge its body into the opening. For the first time he revealed his secret to Amy.

"Even the boys don't know about this back opening, Amy," he said quietly. "Some day I will tell Hiram and Ben about it."

Amy took his large hand and gently kissed the back of it, holding it to her bosom. Levi looked into her navy blue eyes and felt his body grow hard. He laid his beautiful mate back on the soft green moss and made love to her as they lay enclosed in the quiet, enchanted forest.

***

Immediately after prohibition had been signed into law, Hiram began making trips into town two and three times a week. Regular customers were stocking up on supplies, and the family was always eager to know of further government activities.

"They're setting up offices right in the courthouse," Hiram informed Levi, "and the goddamn government is puttin' agents up at that fancy hotel."

"That's good," his father answered. "The folks there use a lot of our game and beef."

"Orville Crabtree won't be able to keep all of them in his sights."

Levi nodded in agreement with his son. "You've already paid the sheriff this week?"

"Sure did, Pa, and with the money he's making from us, he sure as hell will be on our side. Mrs. Crabtree sure does like fresh rabbits," and both men roared with laughter.

"You know, Pa, a lot of ol' boys out there in the bushes makin' their runs are gonna get caught."

Levi smiled in sympathy. "Guess we'll have to take up the slack, son."

Hiram notified customers where to pick up their moonshine when the family decided it was no longer safe to deliver it with vegetables and game. The revenue agents were prowling about town and had stopped a couple of farmers to search through the produce they were delivering to customers.

Other eyes were watching Hiram also. A large, husky, Hungarian had been keeping his eye on Hiram for some time.

"I would like some of da whiskey you sell," he said boldly to Hiram as he was making rounds with vegetables. "Me, Nick and I buy the bunch."

"I have no whiskey for sale," Hiram said.

"You no like Nick," he wheedled.

Hiram glared at the man and walked away. As he started his trek back into the mountains, he spotted Nick following him. Sprinting far ahead, it didn't take long to loose the cumbersome man in the forest.

"Pa, I think we are going to have trouble with a big foreigner in town. He tried to follow me home today. I didn't have any trouble losing him in the woods, but I don't think that will be the end of it. I have seen him around town, and he always seems to be in an argument with somebody about something."

Levi's eyes glittered. "Let him keep you in sight the next time, Hiram," and they made their plans.

A few days later, Hiram allowed Nick to follow him to the mountaintop. Walking by the huge boulder where Levi waited, his father signaled him to keep going.

Nick was brought up short when a voice from nowhere commanded him to stay where he was.

"You are on my land, and I want you to leave." Looking warily about for the source of the voice, Nick was full of bluster.

"I come in peace ta speak ta the Cantrell men. I wanna buy yer likker and make da deal. I be good for you, and you be good for me."

The Hungarian, in baggy overalls, with thumbs hooked in his bib, leered, rocking back and forth with self-satisfaction in having found the homestead.

"We have no likker here. We're farmers, and I want you to leave now."

Nick's face became sullen, and he sneered, "Hokay, I try ta do help."

His thinly veiled threat angered Levi. He had never killed a man, and he didn't relish what he had to do. He knew Nick's next stop would be with the revenue agents. As he slouched away, Levi aimed at the cross in his gallowses and fired, dropping the man in his tracks.

He quickly dug a hole in the soft earth and dropped Nick into the ground, smoothing it flat before covering it with twigs and layers of leaves. He rolled boulders onto the fresh earth, and no sign of an encounter remained.

Levi, with his ingenious and suspicious mind, roamed the mountain daily. He scanned moss-covered rocks, logs, brier patches, the shapes of ferns, small limbs and any growth that would give telltale signs of intruders who had come and gone. He knew their stronghold would eventually be watched closely, and he was leaving nothing to chance. Townspeople were always asking for more squirrels and rabbits. They were considered a delicacy by the varied population in Elkinsville, and the chef of the hotel had turned them into superb feasts. Visitors always ordered the delectable dishes. The boys were constantly roaming farther into the hills, and Hiram was making more trips to town to deliver the game. Levi's cattle herd increased, and new breeding mares were dropping colts all over the place. They covered the mountainside by the hidden cave entrance, chewing on pea vine and wide-bladed grass. One of the Cantrell men always stood guard to protect new calves and colts from mountain lions, bears and large bobcats, always in view of the area surrounding the cave entry. "Pa, if we see somebody poking his nose into our cave, what do we do?" Owen asked.

Levi gave him a look of utter disgust. "You shoot the son-of-a-bitch, and we bury him."

"Okay, Pa," Owen answered, ashamed that he asked such a stupid question. They would have to cut lots of white oak to construct more whiskey barrels and the sooner the better.

Levi had a gut feeling they would be needing lots more. "We need to clear another field anyhow, boys," Levi said, and the family laid into huge crosscut saws as sections of white oak were sawed into the right lengths and were loaded onto sleds to be deposited in the cave under cover of darkness. Several sections were split into firewood and stacked in plain view by each cabin.

"We need a passel of pine knots, boys," Levi ordered. The fewer supplies they toted into the mountain in the months ahead, the better.

Judge Wesley Adams was filling in on a regular basis for old Judge Anderson, who was becoming extremely frail, but was clinging to his job. "I like keeping my finger in the pie," he stated often. Moonshiners knew which pie he spoke of and smirked.

"Damned fool thing for the government to do," he had said when the final Prohibition laws were in place. "Most people have a snort now and then," which included the judge. "It's gonna cost the country a fortune, and it will never work." He was right on both counts.

The Cantrells still emptied spent mash into their underground stream, and Levi was still obsessed with finding the outlet. He spent years checking every stream in the area for their refuse, but never found an inkling.

"Hell, I never even found a drunk fish," he remarked once to his boys as they pondered the mystery.

***

The country was wealthy, and money was being spent lavishly. Speakeasies were springing up all over the country, and moonshine was in great demand. Chicago was loaded with night spots, and

Capone's people were on the prowl for whiskey. Their own stills were constantly confiscated. Traffic into and out of Chicago was stopped and searched by zealous agents, as the government tried in vain to stop bootleggers supplying the swinging speakeasies. Flappers exhibiting their Charleston abilities needed the added zest of smuggled spirits. Women in cloche hats with short, pleated skirts whirled the nights away, and money flowed in all directions. It didn't take the mafia long to contact bootleggers in Elkinsville. A brakeman and an engineer on the C & O were regular Cantrell customers. Clyde Wright related the message to Hiram, and plans were made to have coal drags leaving during the night, make a short stop on the long haul to Chicago. They would bury barrels of moonshine in the gondolas beneath mounds of black coal and carry them to factories. Mafia men were now holding positions as firemen for the factory furnaces where the moonshine would be unloaded.

Levi had never operated on such a large scale, and he was uncomfortable with some aspects of the situation. Delivering such large quantities of whiskey to the trains was risky and extremely hard work. Government agents were roaming the area at all hours, and they could well lay in wait at the point of rendezvous. Hiram and Clyde Wright made a contact point before the train left town, and the Cantrells gave them a signal from a lighted lantern. If there was no lighted lantern, the train would keep rolling. One night, Preston Combs, the engineer, and Clyde Wright made their way to their respective places on the coal drag shortly after midnight in a thick fog that produced an eerie gloom. From out of the murky mists and without a sound, a huge figure materialized. Clyde gasped, and Preston felt the hair on his scalp prickle. Neither of the men had ever met Levi Cantrell but had heard many stories of his strength and daring. Some had absolutely no credence, and others were half-truths as the legend formed. He stood on a slight rise in heavy boots and stared down at the two trainmen. Both were a couple of inches shy of six feet and were awed by the giant. In the meager light, Levi's dark eyes glistened like black coals as he addressed the two in his low-pitched voice. He was quick and to the point.

"I ain't never had no partner in my business, and I think we should get a few things straight at the start. If you are ever caught and sent to jail, you have my word that your families will be taken care of and want for nothin'. If you ever lead the law to me or my boys, you are gonna be two dead men."

He disappeared into the rolling mists as the two men stood gaping after him with pounding hearts. "Jesus Christ," Preston breathed hard. "I reckon that must have been Levi Cantrell."

"Maybe we didn't see nothin'," Clyde answered hoping his eyes and ears had deceived him.

"Bullshit," Preston answered. "We didn't even get a chance to tell him the mafia already told us the same damn thing."

"Wished we never got mixed up in this shit," Clyde said, but they both knew it was too late to back out. And besides, they had never made so much money.

***

The war on moonshine began all over the country. Areas of the country never before involved in making whisky began production, and the government was hard-pressed to cover the entire nation.

Some of the illicit distilleries were huge, with an output of several hundred gallons per day. Purchasing grain, yeast, supplies and sugar became an extremely furtive procedure. Stores and warehouses were closely watched as cunning moonshiners devised ways to outwit the government. Levi didn't have to worry about that aspect of the business. He vowed he would never use sugar. How could you produce good corn whiskey if you were going to add a mess of other materials? Levi continued planting cornfields around the compound, and rich, new ground was planted each year. His animals did well on the dried shucks as more healthy, yellow grains found their way into storage in the caves.

Moonshiners were fighting among themselves, stealing barrels of mash, ready to be distilled from hiding places. Most moonshiners could sniff the fermenting mash for miles, and government agents were learning to do the same. They followed their nose and surprised numerous men at their stills, arresting the men and using axes and sledge hammers to destroy all equipment at the site.

Numerous people stashed stores of liquor as it became certain national prohibition would continue to be enforced. Within two years, supplies began to dwindle, and there was no end in sight on the ban. As demand increased, so did the greed of moonshiners. Any quick fix that would make "alky" was produced, and many of the results were deadly. Poisoning from lethal lead salts was widespread, as customers bought anything that suggested spirits. Paint thinner, ether, antifreeze and rubbing alcohol were only a few of the contaminants used to rush a makeshift batch of white lighting to eager customers, sometimes resulting in blindness, paralysis or brain damage. Moonshiners were running mash for the third time, which resulted in any number of disabilities. Levi would never be guilty of running mash more than once, and his would remain the moonshine of choice. He was nothing short of obsessive with his product, and it came to pass that its own flavor and taste were distinctive, which would finally bring government agents to his door.

Much of the population supported moonshining and embraced judges who dealt leniently with offenders. They felt it was the right of these people to produce a product that had been removed from their reach by the government. Several agents were killed on their way to courthouses to testify against those arrested and supporters of Prohibition were outraged. They demanded the government take action.

By 1921, almost four thousand agents were working overtime, arresting and destroying hundreds of stills. Others sprang up immediately, and most moonshiners were released within six months, returning to business as usual. Every state in the Union was infested with moonshiners, and they were getting rich.

Levi's liquor became a backup to northerners as the feds continued to ferret out many of the large operations in Illinois and New York. One night, Samuel and Hiram survived a close call as they waited in a chosen spot for the coal drag. Hiram's widowed mother-in-law still lived on a small acreage only one mile from the railroad. It was perfect for hiding the kegs of moonshine waiting for delivery to Chicago. The Cantrells paid her well, and she kept watch on their underground storage. The two men waited in thick laurel bushes under cover of black night, stroking the patient oxen pulling the oak barrels full of moonshine. As Preston Combs and Clyde Wright were preparing to leave Elkinsville on their midnight run, agent Jim Harvey arrived with a company official who informed the trainmen the agent needed a ride to Chicago and would be riding in the locomotive with Preston.

Preston paled but gave the agent a pumped up welcome. Feigning an excuse to check one of the cars, Preston climbed from the locomotive and raced down the track, waving the lantern to attract his partner and both men swore profusely.

"Start blowing the whistle several miles before we git there, and they're sure to know somethin's wrong," his brakeman advised. The engineer climbed back into the chuggin' locomotive, chatting amicably with his passenger. They had always kept the whistle quiet several miles before arriving at the designated stop, and Preston prayed Hiram would pick up on the signal and not swing the damn lantern by the track. Hiram's keen sense of hearing picked up the shrill sound long before he could hear the locomotive.

"Listen, Sam," he said to his younger brother.

"I don't hear nothin'," Sam said, straining to catch what Hiram had heard. With the Cantrell intuition, he was instantly alert, and within a few seconds, he was able to hear the sounds, as the fast-moving train came at breakneck speed. The shrill whistle was screaming constantly as Hiram hissed to Sam,

"Don't light that damned lantern. There's sure as hell somethin' wrong." The two men drew further back into thick foliage. Clyde stood by the back railing on the caboose as the train roared by and gave his lighted lantern a swing in their direction.

"I saw two men standin' in the engine," Sam said, and Hiram agreed.

"I'll talk to ol' Clyde this week and see who the extra passenger was. He shore as hell wasn't somebody they wanted to know about the lightin'. We gotta bury this damned stuff before daylight," Hiram said to his younger brother, as the two men turned the plodding oxen toward their hidden bunkers and headed back up the mountain.

In early morning in midsummer of 1921, two government agents made their way to the top of the mountain and looked down on Levi's stronghold. From the time they crossed the Virginia line, they were watched by sharp eyes, and a crow call was quickly sent from one lookout to the next. Levi had periodically sent the boys into town to observe the agents and to familiarize themselves with their attire and their appearance. "I would know a damned revenue agent anywhere," Floyd thought as he watched the two disappear in the direction of the farm. By the time the two reached the farm, Levi was pouring large grains of yellow corn into the hog trough while enormous sows shouldered one another aside to delve into the feed. Hiram and Carl were hoeing tall stalks of corn as Isaac curried and combed a beautiful mare by the gate. The large herd of cattle lay in the shade of huge beech trees, contentedly chewing their cuds. Having grazed most of the morning on dew-draped, tender grass and drinking sparkling water from the streams, they watched lazily as the men approached the gate. Young calves lay grouped together away from the mother cows, their fresh, snow-white markings against the lush green grass awed the visitors.

"Never seen better-looking stock," they both agreed.

"Howdy," they said to Isaac as they approached the gate.

"Howdy," the young man returned.

"I am Gordon Shapiro, and this is Dan McIntosh," the taller of the two men said. "We're looking for horses and were told in town you raise the best."

"We sure do that," Isaac answered and extended his hand to the nearest one. "I'm Isaac Cantrell, and this is my Pa's farm."

Isaac's huge, heavily muscled shoulders were evident beneath his rough work shirt, and Dan McIntosh felt slightly queasy. They watched as Levi dropped the feed pail by the pig pen and sauntered over to the visitors still standing by the gate. He moved with the stealth of a huge cat, and both men gasped. No one had remembered to tell them about the size of this mountain man. Gordon Shapiro quickly extended a hand and informed him of their errand. Levi shook hands with both men.

"What kind of horses you lookin' for?" he asked in a deep drawl that gave no hint of suspicion or acceptance.

"Well, we do a lot of ridin', and we need strong, fast horses," Gordon Shapiro answered, and he was almost sure he saw a faint flicker deep in the depths of those piercing eyes that made him mighty uncomfortable. Jesus Christ, he thought, this damned man is a giant.

"We got several we're breakin', but they've been sold, and the rest are about to foal," Levi responded and stood, staring at the two with folded arms.

"You have some mighty fine stock here, Mr. Cantrell," McIntosh remarked as the two men surveyed the surrounding hills where fine horses and fat cattle abounded. Beautiful oxen, a dozen strong, stood munching hay under a large shed. Chickens of every description pecked about the barn, and two feisty roosters squared off.

Searching vainly for conversation, Shapiro remarked that it was peaceful and beautiful here in the wilderness. Levi's stare never wavered as he answered, "We aim to keep it that way."

"Well, we had better be on our way," Gordon said, vexed that Levi had not even offered them a drink of water. The two bade the Cantrells goodbye and headed back toward the Kentucky border.

"Jesus, I feel as though we are being watched from all sides," McIntosh said quietly to his partner.

"We probably are, Dan," Gordon answered. "Levi has seven boys, and with the exception of one in Elkinsville, they all live in those cabins surrounding the main house.

"You see the size of the two hoeing corn?" Dan asked, and Gordon grimaced.

"I was pretty busy looking up at the two standin' there."

Talking even more softly, Dan informed him that "if you ever decide to take on this family, I will find you a real brave partner."

Gordon grunted under his breath even more quietly, "It would take an army, not two agents."

Levi watched the two men leave without speaking until they were long out of earshot. "How come you wouldn't sell them a horse, Pa?" Isaac asked. "We got at least half a dozen they could choose from."

"Them bastards don't just want horses, they want to see the lay of my land, and they ain't gonna go chasin' no moonshiners on my horseflesh," Levi said, as he walked toward the cornfield, motioning his son to follow.

Picking up hoes, they began working the corn toward Hiram and Carl. Half an hour later, Owen gave the crow call to announce their passage past his lookout and waited for the all clear from Floyd when the two agents continued on into Kentucky.

"Reckon our company has gone, Pa?" Hiram said to Levi, as they hoed within three rows of one another.

"Not till we hear from Floyd," His father answered. He would never let down his guard, and he would never leave anything to chance.

"First, we got a damned agent hitchin' rides on the coal drag to Chicago, and next they are on the doorstep," Carl said, sauntering up to the family. Hiram roared with laughter.

"Preston Combs said he blowed that damned whistle all the way to Chicago, and his arm was plumb tired out."

Samuel stood up on the hillside opposite the field, waving his rifle high in the air. He released the long, lean hounds he had kept muzzled, herding them toward the agents' scent. Sniffing and stopping to howl along the path taken by the two agents, Samuel called them back before their sound could reach the ears of the departed company. The dogs' sharp ears and noses kept the Cantrells alert when they made deliveries at night. With two far-ranging brothers flanking either side of a middleman with the moonshine, ready rifles and sniffing hounds, it was doubtful the Cantrells would experience any surprises.

CHAPTER 16

In early 1921, Wesley arrived in Elkinsville again. Judge Anderson was ailing more and more, but he refused to give up his bench. It was a well-known fact that his demise was near, and several of the officials in the town had talked to Wesley about the upcoming vacancy, urging him to take over the courtroom.

"I will talk to my wife," he promised. Their second child was due the first of April, and Wesley was anxious to be on his way home. Little Alan arrived on time, and Danny was delighted with his baby brother. Alan had Jenny's light brown hair and brown eyes. Wesley watched in awe again as the small body began to fill out and little wrinkles appeared in chubby arms and legs. He loved rocking Alan to sleep at night, holding the soft, cuddly body close to his heart. Wesley dozed and dreamed as he rocked the baby. The mother of Jessie Mullins appeared before him, and her huge, heaving body seemed to have expanded even more. Long, wet hair, clinging in thick strands, was trapped in the fat folds of her neck and chin. Eyes, wild and bloodshot, skewered into his very soul. "I told you, Wesley Adams, your time is coming." The two deputies seemed to have shrunk as they thrashed about with her. Her heavy, flabby arms had become trapped over her head, and long, black, wet hair was plastered in spiky forms beneath her arms. Her odor was repugnant, and Wesley again re-

membered the reeking smell of an unwashed body that had so repulsed him years before in the courtroom. His agonizing moans and
jerking movements awakened baby Alan who screeched because his
nap had been disturbed. Jenny was beside him immediately, and her
wide eyes mirrored her concern.

"Wesley, are you all right? You were shouting, 'No, no.'" Wesley
could not trust himself to speak, but simply nodded his head. He was
drenched with perspiration, and his limbs seemed to have turned to
mush. Jenny took the baby from him, leaning to kiss the top of his
head before going to the nursery. She knew her husband had faced a
nightmare while he dozed. He could only be grateful that she didn't
know the content.

"God," he thought, "whatever possessed me to kill that man?"
His lust for Lacey now lay cindered, but a phantom evil hung over
him. He had been so obsessed by her beauty and sensuous body that
murder had been a simple reaction to anything that intruded on his
mirage.

Wesley spent every spare moment with his two sons. He was in
demand as a speaker for various groups and colleges throughout the
area but never allowed himself to become so engrossed in activities
that it intruded on his family time.

In September, Jenny traveled to Elkinsville with Wesley, as Judge
Anderson was ailing again. She was overwhelmed by the beauty surrounding them as the train clamored over high bridges and around
curves. Each new view was more stupendous than the last one. Rounding one curve, they rode close by an abandoned coal camp that brought
dismay to Jenny's face. Lopsided, vacant houses clung tenaciously to
the sheared hillside that was gradually slipping away. Tall stilts holding the shacks in place were beginning to buckle, and the buildings
would soon slide into the narrow strip of land that was mostly railroad.

"Elkinsville is nothing like this, Jenny. These were fly-by-night
operators who dug what coal they could in a few months, then fled
with their profits. Ransome Coal has built a permanent town. It will
take at least a century to remove the tremendous amount of coal
imbedded there.

"How could they do this to such a beautiful place?" Jenny asked,
and Wesley saw fierce anger on her face for the first time.

The town of Elkinsville fascinated Jenny. "Wesley, it is a town into the trees," she said, noting numerous houses that climbed the mountains with many barely visible through the thick foliage. The area around the hotel was even more wooded than the sections of town they had just passed. "The hotel looks more like an estate, Wesley, and the lawn is so beautiful."

Wesley laughed at the animated expression on Jenny's face. "I tried to tell you how beautiful it was, Jenny, but it is really hard to describe." Jenny nodded in agreement.

Dinner in the hotel dining room was just as interesting and entertaining as Wesley had said it would be. A group of teachers invited Jenny to spend a day at school, and she quickly accepted. She was impressed by the eager, young students from around the world, hustling and bustling through class changes. The native mountain youngsters were a handsome group, standing taller than most newcomers. Classrooms were well-equipped with educational materials, and Jenny felt a pang of nostalgia. Recess was spent in the teachers' lounge, and she was almost envious as the women shared stories of their morning with an easy camaraderie.

Mary Jane Cantrell had continued to work as a volunteer in the high school and was now considered one of the staff. She was introduced to Jenny in the teachers' lounge at recess. "My husband has told me about Judge Adams and his father, and I am so happy to meet you, Jenny," Mary Jane said. She radiated charm and friendliness, and her handclasp was so warm Jenny automatically hugged her.

When Wesley finished at the courthouse and met Jenny at the hotel, she was glowing with news of her day. "I met Ben Cantrell's wife, Mary Jane, and she is a lovely girl. The teachers speak highly of her and the volunteer work she does in the library. Ben must be very proud of her."

"That he is, Jenny, and I'm sure you'll enjoy Ben, too."

Jenny and Wesley were invited to the home of a company official for dinner, and she was impressed with Irene and Lewis Thomas. The living room, with a wall of glass, offered a spectacular view of a moonlit lake. They served mint juleps mixed from the best of moonshine in well-chilled, silver goblets. Jenny had never tasted anything quite like it. They were delicious, and she knew immediately after the first sip she could only tolerate one. It seemed to tingle to her toes, and Wesley suppressed a smile as he watched her closely. The Thomases lovely, white Haviland china from France adorned the dinner table, and a centerpiece of deep red roses reflected in the pristine whiteness of the delicate china. They borrowed the hotel chef for the evening, and Jenny had her first taste of incredible rabbit prepared by a master chef.

The gracious couple made Jenny feel at home, and it was easy to see why Wesley looked forward to these trips. "Who would believe this pocket of civilization so far back into the hills?" Jenny pondered as they walked to their hotel.

"There is quite a cross-section of society here, Jenny, and the output of coal is unbelievable."

"Homes here by the lake are beautiful, Wesley, but what of other sections in town?" Jenny's inquisitive mind never stopped.

"They are comfortable and roomy, but many have outdoor toilets with only cold running water in the kitchens. The structures are well-kept by company carpenters, and the workers spend most of their lucrative wages on fine furnishings for their homes. Many have cars, and their wives spend the rest on clothes at the company stores."

"I think I would prefer a bathroom to a new blouse," and Wesley laughed at his prim and petite wife. "I saw their children at school today, and they are a very handsome group. You can definitely see the Scottish and Irish influence with the number of redheads I spotted in the hallways. Our Danny would feel at home with this group," and they both laughed as they came to the brightly-lit hotel.

"What was your day like, Wesley?" Jenny asked later, as she snuggled close to her husband in the comfortable bed.

"This evening you had a taste of what brings some into court. Moonshine is prevalent throughout the area, and several of the moonshiners are arrested each month, but most of them will never be caught. Their operations are embedded in caves that will never be found, and that type makes the best moonshine. They take pride in the purity and quality of what they produce, and I have no doubt that was Levi Cantrell's moonshine we were drinking tonight. I have been treated to special drinks made with moonshine in many homes here by the lake each time I come to town, and the town officials like to brag that it came straight from Levi. Most people know it is not safe to buy at random. My God, you could be poisoned, blinded or have your nervous system stripped by some of the concoctions being sold these days for a quick dollar."

"Has Levi Cantrell ever been arrested?" Jenny asked, and Wesley laughed.

"Hell no, and he never will be. He is too cagey and too smart. It's a ridiculous law and in time, it will be repealed. Every state in the Union is producing moonshine and draining the government of taxes, plus millions are being spent trying to enforce the impossible. When they are brought before me, I sentence them according to the law, and when they complete their term, they go back to moonshining, correcting the mistake they made the first time. Many of these people are descended from families that have been in these mountains since the early seventeen hundreds. They can track better than an Indian. Some of the revenue agents tell me they can move about the forest without making a sound and never leave a trace. One agent, who barely got away with his life, said he would rather be hugged by a bear than an irate mountaineer guarding his moonshine." They both rocked with laughter, and Wesley gathered his darling Jenny to his heart.

Wesley returned to his office in Louisville on Monday morning and worked into the wee hours to catch up on paperwork that had piled up during his absence. His week was hectic, and by Saturday morning he was wishing he had not promised two-year-old Danny that they would spend the day fishing. By noontime they had settled into one of Wesley's favorite spots when he was growing up. He and his brother, Joel, had spent many afternoons dragging trout and wall eyes from this same creek. Danny's joy and jubilation at catching his first fish wiped away Wesley's fatigue. The boy continued to jump up and down, squealing in delight as he hauled each fish to the banks. The fish pail was filled with large and small flopping tails since Danny could not bear to throw one back. Just when Wesley thought they could head for home, his young son became enthralled with brightly colored rocks lining the creek bed. The day flew by, and home at last, an exhausted Wesley tumbled into bed early in the evening, leaving Jenny with the boys.

His dream began in a mist-filled area he did not recognize. Danny appeared before him saying nothing but looking pale and unhappy. Wesley tried to touch him, but struggle as he may, his son was always just out of his reach. Every nerve in his body was taut as he tried harder and harder to reach him. Danny was moving slowly backward into the mist, and the situation became traumatic as Wesley struggled violently to rescue his son before he disappeared into the rolling whiteness. When he completely disappeared, Wesley heard his voice. "Dad, Dad," he was calling, but his father's feet were rooted to the spot, and his desperation was almost unbearable. Danny's cries became more and more faint as he receded further into the mist. Wesley shouted his son's name over and over. He tried with agonizing force to pull himself forward, but remained immobile and then he heard the terrible sound. Lettie Mullins did not speak, but her heinous laugh sent him into total panic.

"Wesley, Wesley," Jenny was saying as she shook his shoulders. He jerked awake and looked wild-eyed at his wife. His pajamas were wet with perspiration, and his whole body quivered. Danny stood wide-eyed with Jenny as he looked at his father.

"You were calling me so loud, Dad," he said, as his father held out trembling arms to his son. "Dad, you are all wet and smelly. What happened?"

"Your father was dreaming, and he is very tired, so off to bed you go," Jenny said, and Danny squirmed out of his father's desperate embrace after planting a kiss on his damp cheek. Later, Jenny perched on the side of their bed taking Wesley's face in her hands. "It was a bad one, wasn't it?" she said, and he nodded in agreement. "The same nightmare you had when you were rocking Alan?" Jenny asked. Wesley didn't answer, but she knew from the miserable look on his face the two were similar. She felt herself turn cold but dropped the subject. Wesley would tell her when he chose, but she had a pretty good idea what the nightmare entailed.

***

Just after the railroads arrived, the floodgates were thrown open to intense harvesting of beautiful hardwood trees throughout the area. It was in stark contrast to sending timber downstream in early spring on rolling, swollen waters. Prosperity fostered by the industrial revolution created many riches throughout the world, and beautifully crafted furniture from Italy was in demand. The Italians would mortgage homes and souls to lay hands on cherry, walnut and many types of oak still abounding throughout the forest. Entwining limbs simply filled the space left vacant by fallen giants, but continued harvesting would erase the God-given beauty that had taken so many centuries to produce. Enormous chains secured massive mounds of timber to the long cars as screaming locomotives moved the treasures outward to a waiting world. If the miners were a rugged group, loggers were a close second. The ever-expanding demand for the mining props and world demand for timber required hordes of strong and sturdy lumberjacks to weld large axes and long crosscut saws. They frequented the dance halls and roadhouses in the small towns that sprang up on the edge of coal camps. Plentiful moonshine fueled their rollicking Saturday nights. Fists flew and many ended up in jail and filled the hospital emergency room each weekend.

Jerry Bentley and his friends romped through the weekends, nursing miserable hangovers as they trekked back to their jobs on Monday morning. Ben looked at Jerry in the meager light one early Monday morning and figured it must have been one hell of a fight.

"What happened to you?" he asked, looking at his two blackened eyes and newly stitched head.

"I don't care about bein' called a son-of-a-bitch, Ben, but when it gets worse than that, I ain't gonna take it," Jerry stated emphatically. "We were minding our own business and dancing with a lot of girls when this asshole comes up and starts yelling that I'm tryin' to steal his girl and called me a son-of-a-bitch." He stopped long enough to wet his swollen lips with his tongue.

"His friend tells him I was no son-of-a-bitch cause I don't have a mother," Jerry paused, trying to remember exactly what the man had said, and then he remembered. "He said a crow had pissed me upside a tree, and the sun had hatched me. That's when I hit him, and all hell broke loose. We were lucky, we wound up in the hospital. Everybody else went to jail."

Ben wanted to laugh but managed to control himself. "I never heard that one before but wished I could have seen the fight," he said.

The old ox trail used to bring supplies into Elkinsville was loaded with weekend travelers sightseeing in their newly acquired cars. Roadways were hacked and dynamited to Elkhorn City to accommodate increasing traffic into Louisville and Lexington, and moonshiners were among the first to adopt the faster travel. They welded extra tanks beneath cars and under seats to hold gallons of white lightning. Many families, joyriding on the weekends, were delivering moonshine under the noses of government agents. Many agents and lawbreakers alike lost their lives in high speed chases. Moonshiners became expert drivers with heart-stopping antics. Their product was in demand, and the stakes were high. Many young workers who were eager to make more money would hire on for a weekend delivery and excitement.

Jerry Bentley was lured into the setup with the promise of a night on the town in Bristol, Virginia, by two of his co-workers. As they crested Pine Mountain from Kentucky into Virginia, two cars loaded with federal agents blocked the roadway. Alan Baker didn't blink an eye as he gunned the Ford around the federal cars on two wheels leaning inwards as they tilted at a crazy angle above the yawning depths below. Alan yelled at Jerry, "Lean in." After one glimpse downward, Jerry didn't argue but grabbed the overhead handholds and leaned with all his might.

"You bastards!" Jerry screamed. "You're loaded with moonshine, and we'll all go to jail."

"No way in hell, Jerry. They ain't never gonna catch us," his friend shouted over the roar of a hyped-up engine, as he rounded another hairpin curve, throwing Jerry around in the backseat like a sack of flour. A vast cloud of dust rose in back of the flying car, obliterating the roadway as darkness began to overtake them.

"They are gonna have one hell of a time trying to see through that dust after dark," Alan laughed. Jerry was sure he would never see the light of day again as Alan continued to drive at incredible speed, and he was pummeled back and forth constantly.

"They saw the car, and they can still get you," Jerry yelled.

"Hell no, they won't. I took the tag off just before we left, and they couldn't see through these black windows. Besides, we're gonna drive a different car back, and two girls that want to visit kin in Elkinsville are gonna ride with us." Jerry continued to cling to the overhead straps, and for the first time in his life, he had motion sickness.

***

In early 1922, Judge Anderson was felled by a massive heart attack that the doctor had repeatedly warned him about. He had always lived life to the fullest, and he wasn't about to let a little indigestion interfere with his day. He died as he wished, sitting in his judge's chair. In April, Jenny and Wesley moved to Elkinsville, and Wesley started his new job as county judge. They chose a roomy, two-story home only two blocks from the high school. Jenny had decided to return to teaching. By the time they were settled into their new home and careers, the usual fall colors trooped into the mountains with blazing glory, and Jenny was overwhelmed.

"Wesley, I didn't know anything could be so beautiful. The blue-grass country is magnificent, but this is unbelievable."

"I have traveled the world over, and I have never seen anything that would compare to this. It will be a great place for the boys to grow up."

Numerous events on the weekends with other teachers and their families were lively, and the weeks flew by. Jenny and Wesley invited Ben and Mary Jane Cantrell to their home just after getting settled in. Jenny could see why Wesley had been impressed with Ben.

"He is almost overpowering, Wesley. By the time you have recovered from seeing such unusual eyes, you realize how big he is. He is all muscle and brawn, yet you know immediately he is kind and caring. He and Mary Jane are such a beautiful couple."

"I'm glad you like them, Jenny. Mary Jane is in awe of you," Wesley said.

***

Many of the supervisors and office workers ate lunch in the busy restaurants on Main Street. Wesley Adams and Ben Cantrell shared the same table on many occasions, and Wesley's admiration for Ben increased as they shared ideas on many subjects. Many times, Ben was embarrassed when he noticed everyone at the long table had stopped talking and was listening intently to what he was saying.

Revenue agents also had lunch in the restaurant and didn't miss the deference paid to Ben by Judge Adams.

An agent discussing a moonshining situation with Judge Adams in the courthouse on one occasion asked, "You seem to be pretty tight with Ben Cantrell, judge. What will you do when his father is hauled in for bootlegging?"

"I'll throw the book at him just like I do with the rest of the bootleggers," Wesley said.

The agent didn't see his slight smile as he turned to leave. "They'll never catch Levi Cantrell," he was thinking.

Carnage continued in the coal mines, and on the mountainsides as moonshiners fought revenue agents and among themselves.

It was not unusual for agents to receive anonymous notes with the locations of a competitor's still. The leads were always followed up with several agents swooping down on the unsuspecting bootlegger.

The greatest hazard for the agents came from some of the more astute bootleggers, who kept a sharp-eyed guard on duty with a deadly rifle. Several agents had been killed by such lawlessness.

Levi and Amy had more to worry about than just moonshine. In the fall of 1923, Ben was scouting for timber in the area, and rode by for a short visit with his parents. He proudly announced that Mary Jane was pregnant again and expected to deliver in early June. Amy managed to smile and congratulate their son, but Levi could see the fear in her eyes.

As soon as Ben rode away, Levi turned to Amy. "Amy, Mary Jane and Ben have two beautiful children that do not have Ben's eyes. You can't worry about this for the next several months." He knew his words had fallen on deaf ears because Amy had a faraway look.

***

As Mary Jane nestled in Ben's arms one night, he felt tears dripping onto his arm.

"Mary Jane, why are you crying, honey? What's wrong?"

"Nothing is wrong, Ben. I was just thinking about my brother. It has been five years since he died in that awful war, but I still feel as though he is here. If this baby is a boy, I want to name him Thomas."

"I think that would be a good name, Mary Jane."

"Somehow, this baby is different, Ben. I am only three months pregnant, and it moved so early. It seems to crawl all over my stomach, and then it just sort of explodes into action."

"Sounds just like a damned Cantrell," Ben laughed.

"No, Ben. This is different."

***

By fall Wesley cut some of his late hours at the courthouse in order to help Jenny. Pregnant with their third child, she wanted to continue teaching until the birth of their baby. Three-year-old Alan and Danny, now five, kept both parents busy.

276

In April of 1924 Jenny gave birth to Chaney. He was a beautiful baby with auburn curls and dreamy, hazel eyes. He was very long-limbed and well-formed with a sweet, placid personality that marked him as a child to be loved.

Wesley walked Danny to kindergarten on his way to the office each morning as his young son chattered away and ran to keep up with his long-legged father.

"Mom says I can hold Chaney and feed him when I get home from school today."

Wesley smiled at him and was euphoric when he counted his blessings. Three handsome sons and a lovely wife. It was almost unbelievable that eight years ago his life lay in shambles, and he had seriously considered suicide. The torturous nightmares of Lettie Mullins had lessened. Still, sometimes Wesley couldn't help but feel that he stood on an abyss, waiting for the inevitable.

His docket was jampacked each day as the war between the government and moonshiners raged on. Two moonshiners had been shot the week before as they attempted to defend their stills and were in serious condition and under guard at the hospital. Extra guards had been hired to stand watch as threatening families stood vigil.

Ben Cantrell walked down Main Street toward his favorite restaurant to have lunch with Wesley Adams. He passed a man going in the opposite direction and suddenly felt such an overwhelming sense of peril that the hair on the back of his neck stood up. Turning to look back at the man, he found himself following him. When the man approached the courthouse door, Ben's senses screamed with approaching danger. His long legs quickly closed the distance to the man just as he entered the courtroom.

Wesley Adams was just about to leave the courtroom but froze in his tracks. A wild-eyed Enoch Morton leveled a thirty-eight pistol between Wesley's eyes.

As Morton's finger began to squeeze the trigger, a huge form materialized behind him and yanked his arm brutally upward as the shot landed in the ceiling. He fell to the floor screaming with pain from a badly broken arm. Ben Cantrell retrieved the gun and handed it to a very shaken Wesley.

"Maybe you should carry this, Wesley." But his friend shook his head.

Wesley had sentenced Morton's brother to ten years in prison earlier in the day. He had been convicted of a brutal rape, and Wesley thought the sentence a light one.

After Morton had been locked away, the two men walked quietly to lunch.

***

In May 1924, Ben had been tramping through the forest most of the day, selecting prime timber for the saw mills, and was shocked when he returned to his office to learn that Mary Jane had given birth to another son.

"She wasn't due for another month," a worried Ben said.

"Well, you just might tell the little tyke that," his foreman laughed.

He hurried to Mary Jane's side and found her sleeping soundly. Kissing her lightly on the lips, he headed for the nursery. He motioned the nurse to the door and asked quietly.

"Is baby Cantrell all right? He wasn't due for another month."

"I have never seen a healthier baby, and I have never seen an early eight-month baby weigh ten pounds."

Ben viewed his son through the nursery window as the baby slept peacefully. He is beautiful like Elizabeth and Stephen, he thought, with the same dark Cantrell hair. Returning to Mary Jane's room, he found her still asleep and a strong odor of ether wafting in the air. He was filled with love for his beautiful wife and fought back tears as he realized he could have lost both of them in an early delivery. As he sat in the quiet room, he dozed, tired from a long day in the forest. A nurse quietly entered the room, bringing the baby for his feeding and smiled at the sleeping parents. She tapped lightly on Ben's shoulder.

"Mr. Cantrell, would you like to hold your son while I wake your wife and get her ready to feed him?"

Ben held out his arms for the baby and snuggled him into his lap. Thomas stretched the long length of his body like a lazy cat and looked at his father. Ben was shocked when his son opened his eyes. The large, pale amber eyes in the small face was the exact same color of Ben's eyes. The stare he gave his father was not the look of a newborn. In some way it appeared ancient, but also cunning.

When Ben recovered from his shock, he realized he felt an instant, unusual bonding with his new son. He knew instinctively, the baby's eyes had already begun to search. Ben knew why. His own eyes were always searching, seeing things other people had failed to notice, feeling things others had not been able to detect.

"My God," Ben said and the nurse turned, thinking the baby had spit up. "He is so long," Ben stammered, trying to cover his shock.

"Well, just look at his father," the nurse teased.

Ben suddenly remembered Mary Jane saying this baby was different and how he had moved so early and often. For the first time, Ben felt as though his parents knew more than they had told him about his eyes. He had always wondered why they were so different from anyone in the family, but Levi's only remark to this inquiry was, "We had enough of the other kind."

CHAPTER 17

An early summer morning brought the caution call from Floyd, and the extended call indicated four people. Levi tensed and quickly set the boys to their practiced chores. Hiram lay low on the hillside above the cave with two loaded rifles. Deer and wild turkeys roamed the area, and visible tracks abounded. He stationed himself near a fresh group of tracks and watched. The visitors passed the second lookout, and again the signal counted four riders. Levi pitched hay from a wagon to heavily muscled oxen, appearing relaxed and unconcerned as the group approached him. He looked at them with steady, dark eyes.

A heavy-set man riding a large horse was first to approach Levi but never spoke. Directly in front of Levi he cried out and clasped his chest. Before anyone could move, he pitched forward from the startled horse. Levi quickly grabbed the bit preventing the horse from trampling its rider. His shocked companions jumped from their mounts, rushing to his side, greatly alarmed by his purple face.

"My God," Richard Jackson shouted. "Grant is having a heart attack." Stunned, the men stood disbelieving as the man writhed and moaned in pain.

"My wife has a remedy that can help," Levi said and headed to the home. "Don't move him," he shouted back over his shoulder, as he covered the distance to the front door with incredible speed. He was back almost instantly with a quart jar of almost black liquid and a large spoon.

"Raise his head, careful-like," he directed Richard Jackson, who quickly put an arm under his friends shoulder, and Levi spooned the strange-smelling liquid between his blue lips. Levi managed to get several ounces of the medicine into his mouth, and color began returning to his face. Richard Jackson was visibly shaken, as he looked at his longtime friend and co-worker.

Grant had arrived on the afternoon train the day before, and Richard was surprised to see how much weight he had gained in the past two years. They had worked together for fifteen years. Grant had been assigned to the Chicago area for the past two years, while Richard combed the hills and valleys of Kentucky. Not only had he gained too much weight, he looked tired and discouraged. At fifty-five years of age, he looked sixty.

"This whole damned mess is ludicrous, Richard. For five years we have pitted our knowledge and resources against the bootleggers, and we are way behind," he said as the two old friends chatted late into the night. "There is a river of moonshine flowing from Kentucky into Chicago. We plug one leak, and three more spring up. We would be better off with legalized whiskey to stop the whole damned thing. Murder is rampant over profits. People are dying in great numbers from the worst concoctions you could ever think of, and it's getting worse all the time. There is not one state in this Union that isn't producing its own type of moonshine. Most people think they have been sinned against because they can no longer have a legal drink, and they will shelter and protect the moonshiner at all costs. Even the judges are on their side. Most of their constituents sneak a few drinks or two, and they are sure as hell not going to vote for judges who come down too hard on the suppliers," he sighed and sank deeper into the comfortable chair.

"I was really shocked when I first saw this place today. I guess the coal business is booming."

"That it is," Richard answered. "And timber sales are enormous. So far, you can hardly miss what has been cut, but at the rate they're going, it won't be long before these hills will be shorn. Of course, liquor is adding greatly to the area income, but the moonshiners hole

281

up in these damned caves, and there is no way in hell to find them unless a competitor turns one in. We are going to take a ride up and over the mountain tomorrow if you are up to it," Richard said, as he cast a worried look at his friend's tired face.

"Just lead me to the horse in the morning," Grant said, as he heaved himself heavily from the chair and headed toward a beautiful, antique bed. Company officials had spared no expense in producing luxury and beauty in their prize hotel. This was only yesterday, and now Richard knelt by his friend and cursed himself for his lack of good judgment. Grant wouldn't be lying flat on his back in a semi-conscious state had he heeded his gut feeling and canceled the arduous journey over this mountain.

Samuel and Carl left their hoes in the corn fields to see what was going on and nodded briefly to the visitors. Half an hour later, the two carefully carried Grant into the spare bedroom, tucking him into a warm, comfortable bed. A thick, feathered mattress enclosed his weary body in softness, and he slept instantly.

Richard felt alarm and wondered if Grant was dying. He knelt close to his chest, but his breathing was so shallow it was barely detectable.

"Your friend is only asleep. He'll be alright," a low, soft voice informed him. Straightening up, Richard looked into Amy's eyes, which were almost on his level. Her height was his first shock. Few women could look him in the eye. Constant activities with several children and grandchildren had kept her body taut and strong. She wore a long-sleeved, wheat-colored, linen blouse tucked into a rich brown calico skirt. Levi had long since given Hiram instructions to bring the best and latest fashions to Amy. Mary Jane chose the clothes, and Levi had to admit she knew exactly what was best for Amy. Always surrounded by a caring and loving family, Amy's inner peace and serenity reflected in her beautiful face. The three agents stood awkwardly about, and it was Amy who drew the large wicker, rocking chair to Grant's bedside.

"You might want to keep watch over your friend," she said to Richard Jackson. "If he wakes and seems to have trouble breathing, we will give him more medicine."

"Will and Gavin, head back down the mountain and bring the doctor. I want you to ride like the wind," Richard said. The two recent recruits were uncomfortable with their assignment.

"I don't know that we can find our way, Richard," Will stammered. They were new to the area and uncertain about the mountain trail.

"I will have one of my boys go with you," Levi said. He called Hiram to the porch, and the three left quickly. Levi was relieved. He didn't want agents wandering about alone on his land. It was past noon, and Amy carried a large dinner to Richard Jackson as he sat on the edge of the rocker with his eyes glued on Grant. Levi placed a small table close to the chair for the dinner tray, and a surprised Jackson thanked them profusely. Richard spent the afternoon pacing quietly about the large, immaculate room. He bent over his friend numerous times to check his very quiet breathing. In late evening, Levi tapped lightly on the door and entered with a hearty supper for their visitor. Jackson was touched and embarrassed by their kindness. Levi walked closer to the bed and looked at the peacefully sleeping patient.

"His color is a lot better," Levi said, and Richard, with his mouth full of food, nodded in agreement. His guilt was great. Levi must know they were there looking for his stills. At ten o'clock, Hiram arrived from Elkinsville with Dr. Hal Fremont and Ben. Amy immediately steered the doctor to Grant's bedside, and the very grateful friend stepped aside.

Dr. Freemont placed strong fingers over the patient's pulse and frowned. Grant continued to sleep soundly as the doctor checked his entire torso with his stethoscope and then motioned Richard to the outside.

"It is a miracle that he has survived, and there is no way he can be moved for several days. A trip down this mountain, even in a wagon, could be fatal. I want to talk to Mrs. Cantrell. Sounds like her potion is a good one and has no doubt saved Mr. Holmes' life."

Amy had busied herself placing a cold supper on the table for the new arrivals.

"Mrs. Cantrell, I want to compliment you on your home remedy, and I would like you to continue with what you are doing. Since I have been in this area, I have found that some of these concoctions work better than the pills we strew about. The patient cannot be moved for several days, and I'll let you work that out with Mr. Jackson."

"Mrs. Cantrell," Richard began, and Amy stopped him.

"We will do whatever we can to be of help. Mr. Holmes can stay as long as he needs to. We have lots of help here on the farm so that will be no problem."

Levi breathed a sigh of relief at Amy's statement. He didn't want an agent moving in with them. It was time to start another batch of sprouts to ripen, and he didn't dare go near the cave with damned revenuers running around all over the place.

"I'll be leaving in the morning too, Pa. I thought maybe there would be something I could help with, but you seem to have everything taken care of. I just happened to be in Dr. Freemont's office with one of my workers who needed a few stitches when Hiram and the agents came in," Ben said, and the unsaid was silently understood. The fewer agents about, the better.

At eight o'clock the next morning, Dr. Freemont awakened Grant who looked around in amazement with no memory of what had happened the day before.

"Richard, where in the hell am I?" he asked, looking at the doctor and the strange room.

"Levi Cantrell took us in when you had a heart attack and fell off your horse yesterday. Do you remember anything?" Richard asked, and Grant shook his head.

"This is Dr. Freemont. He rode all the way up here after dark last night to take care of you."

"My God, how long have I been out?"

"Since eleven o'clock yesterday. Levi poured a bunch of Mrs. Cantrell's home remedy down your throat, and you have been asleep since then. It's about eight o'clock so you have slept for almost twenty-one hours."

"It's a good thing you were near Mrs. Cantrell's potion. You are very slow in here," the doctor said, placing his stethoscope on Grant's warm chest. "How long have you had this condition?"

"A while," Grant said.

Richard placed his hand on Grant's shoulder and apologized, "You looked totally beat when you got off the train Tuesday, and I should never have brought you on this trip."

"Bullshit, Richard. It is part of my job, and you know it. I don't know an agent that isn't tired."

Dr. Freemont continued to listen to Grant's heart. "Mr. Holmes, you are going to have to stay here for several days, and I believe Mr. Jackson has already made arrangements with the Cantrells. I think you should continue to take Mrs. Cantrell's home remedy twice a day. I have no doubt it saved your life. You need complete bed rest for three days, and if you feel up to it, you can slowly move around for an hour or so each day. I will send Mr. Jackson to check on you in a few days."

Grant was about to object when Amy and Levi walked into the room. "My God, she is beautiful," he thought, but Levi didn't make him feel any better. The huge man had an overwhelming presence, not only his size, but a cold feeling of power that almost bordered on arrogance.

"This is a great imposition on the two of you," Grant said.

Amy's voice was sweet with genuine concern, "We have lots of help, Mr. Holmes, and you are not to worry. Our son, Owen, will be with you, and Levi and I are always nearby. We are just happy that you pulled through."

Richard knew instinctively Amy would be a woman of her word, and he also knew instinctively that Levi was capable of driving a stake through a man's heart if he felt threatened. He was extremely apprehensive about leaving Grant in Levi's home, but he had no choice.

Owen, who had always been attentive to his mother's needs, had volunteered to take care of Grant. As a small child, he had always picked new blossoms for his mother and grandmother, kept the large porch swept, and made sure the wood box was full by the kitchen stove.

Amy continued to give Grant his medicine each morning and night, and he recognized the fine taste of Levi's moonshine in the elixir. It was pure corn whiskey made by a master craftsman.

After three days in bed and weak from his ordeal, Grant was eager to be up and about. Owen practically carried him to the front porch and seated him in a large, comfortable, willow rocker. Amy brought extra pillows for his back, and Grant was struck anew each day by her natural beauty and her willowy, graceful movements. His wife had died, childless, ten years before, and he could only envy Levi with his many handsome sons and his beautiful wife.

He did not remember seeing the place three days before and was awed by its beauty. Beautiful horses and sleek, fat cows covered the hillsides with frisky colts and calves nursing from large-uddered mothers. Levi was walking from the barn to the house, and Grant could only admire the man he was attempting to put in jail.

"Good morning, Mr. Cantrell," Grant said.

"So, how are you feeling today, Mr. Holmes?" Levi asked.

"With the help of your family, and especially Owen here, I am doing much better. Your farm is truly beautiful, Levi. I have never seen anything to match these trees. They must be hundreds of years old. I majored in forestry in college, and the trees in this whole area are without equal."

The skin on Levi's forearms tightened. This son-of-a-bitch was the one person who could figure out where his cave was. It was the only aspect of the cave that had ever bothered him. Humongous trees grew everywhere except directly over the high, front room of the cave. The growth there was low and scrubby, years before Levi had figured out the reason. Huge trees grew roots as deep as their height and as long as their limbs. There was not enough soil covering the cave to sustain such growth. Levi was not an educated man, but he knew what forestry meant. Lack of large trees covering the cave was a dead giveaway to someone who knew woodlands and trees.

Each day Grant sat on the front porch admiring the view and watching water cascade from the waterfall uphill from the house. He marveled at Levi's ingenuity in bringing water to his back door.

Levi was glued to his hiding place in the corn crib. A crack between the logs permitted him to watch Grant's every move and nuance without being seen. He knew Grant was trying to figure out where there was a cave.

On the fifth day, Richard Jackson and Agent Fuller arrived at the farm to check on Grant. They were delighted to see him sitting on the porch, looking rested and enjoying himself as he chatted with Amy and Owen.

"You look as though you're enjoying your vacation, Grant," Richard said.

"Great company, great scenery and great food. What else could a man want? You come to take me back to town?"

"Dr. Freemont says you should stay put for another five days unless the Cantrell's kick you out."

"Of course we won't," Amy answered. "He can stay as long as he needs to."

"I can't tell you how much we appreciate this, Mrs. Cantrell, and the government will pay you for all the trouble you have gone to."

"That won't be necessary, Mr. Jackson. Mr. Holmes has been no trouble at all."

The agents stayed only a short time, and Levi remained at his post in the corn crib. He was extremely uncomfortable with agents coming and going from his farm.

Arriving back in town, Richard Jackson dropped by Dr. Freemont's office to report on Grant Holmes.

"He looks great, Dr. Freemont, and Mrs. Cantrell has really brought him around. He was ready to ride back with us, but we convinced him to stay put for another five days."

"He still has a great problem, Mr. Jackson. I didn't like the sound of his heartbeat, and the most dangerous time and the most misleading is when a patient, who has a severe heart attack, appears to be completely well, then bingo, the second one hits, and most of the time it's massive and fatal."

On day seven, Grant Holmes sat by himself on the slightly moving porch swing, studying the beautiful surroundings in the warmth of June. Suddenly, he gave a start and sat so still the swing stopped moving. Levi could see the revelation on his face. Grant quickly looked about to see if anyone had been watching him, but Levi was well-concealed in the corn crib.

The family was out and about for the afternoon, leaving Amy and Levi to have supper alone with Holmes. At the supper table, he was very congenial, complimenting Amy on her medications and how great he was feeling.

"Levi, could I possibly borrow a horse tomorrow and have one of your boys ride into town with me? I have taken enough of your time, and I really feel well enough to travel."

"Of course," Levi said.

Levi was boiling inside. Amy had just saved his life, and now Grant was hell bent on destroying them. He could see the feds swarming over his farm and rampaging through his cave, smashing his treasured copper stills and barrels of fermenting mash.

Grant returned to his room to rest, and the family convened on the front porch, which was their usual after-supper retreat. Levi quickly emptied a large portion of Amy's sleeping powder into the medicine she gave the agent each morning and night. He also managed to douse Amy's bedtime glass of milk with the sedative. He had to be sure she was sleeping soundly and completely unaware of what he was doing. She would never hold with murder under any circumstance. Close to midnight, he listened to her even breathing, then lifted her hand, and letting it fall without any reaction. He knew it was time to act.

Stepping into a pair of jeans, he remained barefoot as he made rounds to each window, peering into the dark, moonless night to be sure none of the family was up and about. The home place was completely silent and dark. Carefully opening the door to Grant's room, he stood motionless in the doorway for several minutes until he was sure Grant was in a deep sleep. He had dumped such a large amount of the sleeping potion into his medicine, he had hoped Grant might already be dead, but he was disappointed. Amy had insisted on leaving a wide tallow candle lighted in Grant's room at night in case of an emergency, and Levi noticed the curtains were not completely closed on the two large windows. Soundlessly, he crossed the room, closing the curtains and looking at Grant to see if there had been any reaction. Picking up the extra pillow, he stood looking down at Grant with anger because the agent had given them no choice.

Quietly and quickly Levi straddled the sleeping agent, crossing his hands over his head with one hand and pressing the pillow over the man's mouth and nose with his right hand.

Even in a heavy, drug-induced sleep, Holmes' instinct as a longtime lawman surfaced, and he struggled fiercely.

Levi was sickened by what he was doing. Grant had an insatiable will to live, and he was refusing to die. His seven-day growth of stiff, bristly beard scratched roughly on the pillow Levi was holding firmly over his face, and he continued to struggle. He was no match for Levi's massive strength. Slowly, all movement ceased, and Levi held the pillow in place until the agent's body became completely slack.

Checking the pillows for any signs of struggle, Levi placed them in the same position he had found them. Straightening the covers, he dried the drool from the corners of Holmes' mouth and grimaced with distaste as he returned the large handkerchief to his pocket. Closing the agent's eyes, he smoothed his hair, then ran his hands over the still face to remove agitated lines and any trace of the recent struggle. Placing his arms in a relaxed position, he was finally satisfied that Holmes looked as though he had died quietly in his sleep.

Grant had been coming to the breakfast table on his own for the past few days. As the morning wore on, Owen decided to check on their visitor. When his knock on the door went unanswered, he cracked the door to peer in and then stepped to the bedside.

"Ma, Pa, come quick," he bellowed. "My God, I think he's dead."

Amy quickly checked his pulse and any signs of breathing. "I am afraid you are right, Owen. He must have died in his sleep. He looks so peaceful."

Hiram left immediately for Elkinsville and stopped at the sheriff's office to relate that Holmes had died during the night.

For the benefit of all, Dr. Freemont volunteered to ride with the agents to Levi's place to retrieve the body.

"Amy, it might be better that you not mention the agent's plans to go to town today. They know we have stills here on the farm somewhere, and they would like nothing better than an excuse to prowl around. If they can't find our stills, they can't prove that we have them."

"It was not our fault that he died in his sleep, Levi. A second heart attack is not unusual. My mother and Ruthie talked about it many times, but I will not mention his plans to leave."

Levi was grateful that none of the family was present at supper the night before.

Regardless of what Dr. Freemont had said, Richard Jackson had a gut feeling Levi was responsible for his friend's death, and he was determined this would not be the end of the ordeal.

Amy was sincere in her sorrow about Grant's death, but Levi's stoic expression did nothing to alleviate Richard's suspicion about him. Levi knew this man would hound them in the months to come.

Moonshiners were being arrested throughout the area, and one of the revenue agents had been killed as they closed on a large outfit on the outskirts of Whitsburg. A week later, another agent had been gunned down on the streets of Elkinsville, as he made his way to the courthouse to testify against several moonshiners who had been arrested in a well-concealed operation. No one saw the gunman, and there were no arrests.

Outraged citizens supporting prohibition demanded the government mobilize troops to assist the revenue agents who were being murdered in the line of duty. The general population called for a ban on the law, citing loss of life and revenue. Violence in the moonshine business continued throughout the country.

"That damned Jackson is watching me like a hawk, Pa, and he has even been asking people about Ben. I saw him lookin' in Ben's truck the other day while Ben was eatin' dinner in the restaurant. I wouldn't put it past them to plant some moonshine on Ben just to get back at you," Hiram told Levi on a return trip from town.

For days, Levi tread soundlessly through the hills, finally finding what he was looking for. A nest of five men was working their still beneath a deep rock overhang, well-camouflaged with dense foliage. The hideaway was so concealed, he might have missed it, had he not smelled the fermenting mash. There was no lookout, and Levi knew he had found the perfect spot.

A mysterious note, giving the location of the still, was delivered to the agents in Elkinsville, and the next day, Richard Jackson led the foray toward the still. One-half mile from their destination, a rifle shot rang out from the dense forest, striking Richard Jackson through the chest. The other agents opened rapid fire in the direction of the shot, while moonshiners tending the still evaporated into the woodlands.

By the time agents reached the hidden trove, it was completely deserted, leaving a sizeable supply of moonshine that was immediately hacked to pieces by outraged lawmen.

**

In late 1927, the unthinkable was beginning to happen. Orders for the highly sought-after bituminous coal were beginning to dry up. Glistening, black lumps of the volatile fuel no longer tumbled through conveyor belts to be cleaned and deposited into the gaping entrails of gondolas waiting beneath loading chutes.

Oil-well drilling increased dramatically after World War I, with new wells and lodes being discovered in numerous states. Pipelines were being laid throughout the country. The oil offered a much more efficient energy system without the glut of smoke, soot and cinders. Oil barons began to dethrone king coal.

Long lines at the recreational building came to an abrupt halt. The theater no longer had patrons sitting in the aisles and lining the walls. Vacant seats prevailed throughout the auditorium. Bowling lanes were quiet, while the popular ice cream parlor had empty tables. The constant flow of clanging script into the noisy cash registers closed with a deafening silence. An ominous stillness lay over the area, as the usual hustle and bustle gave way to shuffling feet and dismay. The shrill whistle that had sounded the end of each shift for so many years was strangely quiet. For sixteen years the workers had started each day and each week with the same expectations, their eyes on the next monthly paycheck and their next purchase. Now, most were strapped for cash by the end of each pay period. The script office no longer had waiting lines and commissary wares were no longer flying off the shelves.

Optimistic mine managers believed there would be a reversal, but the decline continued each month, and the stock market crash of 1929 cemented a downward spiral. Miners had long since sold their small farms to move to coal camps when the company had decreed they must live in company-owned houses and purchase their every need from company-owned commissaries. Workers with drawn and worried faces haunted the mine office to read signs for available work.

Most of the foreign workers boarded trains and headed for big cities to be with friends and find whatever meager work could be obtained.

As the Depression deepened, so many workers scrambled for so few jobs that daily or hourly wages were discontinued, and piece work was the only alternative. The miner would be expected to clean up a cut that many times required up to sixteen hours to clean away. He was told by the mine foreman that if he did not completely clean the cut, there would be another worker who could replace him. Wages for shoveling coal for sixteen hours were one dollar and seventy cents. The few dollars he earned were withheld by the company to pay his rent and the ever-mounting grocery bills at the commissary.

After years of removing coal, the tunnels extended far into the mountains where many times, the coal was only four feet high. After hours of trudging through low coal in a bent position, the miners were forced to dig coal on bended knees or dig with their backs pressed against the top of the tunnel. The mining company had long since discontinued safety, and props that rotted with age were not replaced. Mine inspectors were dispensed with, and the few who stayed, worked as miners. Numerous men, desperate to feed large families, braved the hazardous situation and paid with their lives. Many lost limbs, and it was not uncommon to see a grizzled miner with both legs missing. Still, other workers took over when the dead and wounded were removed.

***

Ben Cantrell watched with sadness as many of his friends labored endless hours and yet could not make ends meet. The sawmills gradually closed as no new props were used, and repair on the company houses was discontinued when orders for coal had all but stopped. Ben's job as overseer of the nine mills had shrunk to the last and largest of the initial mills that had been established in 1912. He cut his own salary several times in order to keep Jerry, who continued to work for a pittance, on the job.

Jerry had married a pretty girl just shy of his thirtieth birthday, and was now the father of twin boys and a small daughter. He considered Ben and Mary Jane his family, having no memory of his own parents but only the life of hard knocks on the Baltimore streets. He and Ben lived next door to one another on a small acreage, and with Ben's help, he had proven himself to be an adept farmer. Their gardens abounded with vegetables, and their combined four milk cows fed numerous children and adults in the area.

Wesley Adams joined the two in endeavors to ferret out the most needy families and supply them with food, while attempting to find them any meager jobs that could be had. Levi Cantrell would load large wagons with vegetables and any meat he could spare, then send it down the mountain where Ben would distribute the contents to the townspeople.

When an occasional coal drag left town, it was still loaded with moonshine, and even in the midst of the Depression, the price was high. The speakeasies in Chicago continued to roll. Prohibition was still in effect, and great numbers of unemployed men turned to moonshining in order to feed their families.

Scores of empty gondolas were parked on side rails while saddened miners watched them turn to rust. Their era of constantly rumbling through town day and night was now a long lost dream.

Wesley and Ben attempted to organize groups to cart away garbage that was beginning to collect throughout the area, but their attempt was in vain. Company trucks no longer hauled the refuse away, and the miners were slipping into apathy.

Once stalwart and strong, men whose backs had become bent through years of shoveling coal slumped along in baggy overalls or sat immobile on their small, front porches. Many had no jobs and no land to tend. Relatives in far off cities wrote home of the same situations in their areas.

The government began to send tons of flour, beans, salt, sugar and other staples to the mountain people who were beginning to feel hunger pangs. Some of the more independent people refused to stand in line for the handouts at first, but as the Depression deepened, they joined their friends for the free food.

School children were given breakfast and lunch. For many, it was the only nourishing food they would receive for the day. Cafeteria workers considered themselves lucky to have a job, as the line for applicants was long.

***

By 1930, theft became a way of life in the hills. As the Depression worsened, farmers on the outskirts of town kept watchdogs by their chicken coops, which had become a first target of the unemployed, along with baby goats and small pigs. Horses and cows staked further from the houses also went missing.

Levi and his sons had always alternated guard duties at the farm, but a few of the more cunning thieves had managed to make off with some of their prized stock that slept in the open fields at night. Levi ranted and raved at Owen when two of their prized cows disappeared on Owen's watch.

"I thought I saw a shadow, Pa, but I wasn't sure," Owen stammered, shaken by Levi's rage at the missing cows.

"God dammit, Owen, you are too soft. Shoot the damn shadow next time."

Levi would regret his harsh advice to his son many times over.

It was not the first time Levi had found fault with Owen. He could not fault his work because he more than carried his share, and he never shirked the toughest jobs. Owen hunted with his brothers when the family needed game for the table, but he had long since ceased to shoot an animal just for the fun of it. He preferred to read rather than search the forest merely for target practice. He had gradually added to Sarah and Amy's collection of books, and books about the oceans and seas fascinated him. At thirty-seven, he had still not married.

His brothers had long since married, and passels of children ran about the compound, swimming in the streams and sliding through waterfalls. They adored their Uncle Owen who always had time for them, even to sledding down the steep snow-covered hills in winter. But of all, he was closest to his mother. Though Levi made sure Amy did not do heavy lifting, it was Owen who many times helped her set the supper table and wash the dishes. Levi had mentioned helping Owen build his own cabin as the family had done when each son had chosen a wife. Owen simply smiled and shook his head.

"Levi, Owen hasn't met anyone he wants to marry," Amy said on one occasion when her husband had fretted about Owen not finding a wife.

"He is a handsome man, Amy, and he has met lots of girls. He never misses a new picture show in Elkinsville, and Mary Jane says young women are always asking about him."

"He has a full life. He spends time with Ben and his family, and goodness knows the clan we have here keeps him busy." With a twinkle in her eye, Amy added, "He actually spends more time with your grandchildren than you do."

They sat on their wide porch in late evening, watching a brilliant orb light the mountain like the fiery entrails of a blast furnace before sinking from sight and leaving an afterglow that spread the heavens with brilliant reds and gold. The compound was quiet as each family had retreated to their cabins for the night.

Looking at his still beautiful wife, he drawled, "I want all our sons to know a love like ours, Amy."

Levi was a man of few words, and Amy was greatly touched. His blazing eyes set her on fire as they rose and entered their home, closing and latching the door behind them.

Sunday mornings at the compound were always special. Amy and their sons' wives cooked breakfast together, each doing her own specialty, as the numerous grandchildren whooped it up. Occasionally, Amy would see Levi glower when the noise level became deafening. After a large breakfast and settling tiffs with the younger children, everyone gathered around Amy as she read the Bible to the group. After a brief prayer, they sang hymns until the children became restless and ready for outdoor play.

Amy busied herself late Saturday evening. Setting the large table for breakfast the next morning, she dragged two high chairs from the corner for the two youngest grandchildren. It was a gathering she never tired of, and her long legs quickly crossed to the raised fireplace to whisk away dust. Older grandchildren would sit on the hearth with overflowing plates balanced in their laps. Amy smiled in anticipation of the early morning ritual. She lingered momentarily by the kitchen cupboard, trying to decide whether to use a small amount of her night potion. For the past few months, her sleep had been fitful on occasions, leaving her tired and groggy. She knew this was a woman's disposition and, in time, it would pass. Fate had decreed that she would pass the cupboard.

Levi crept quietly into bed by Amy at midnight, dead tired from bringing in another good run.

Amy awakened at three o'clock in the morning and lay quietly. Knowing that Levi must be very tired, she didn't want to wake him. She padded barefoot to the hearth to retrieve her clothes, having made up her mind what she wanted to do. The family loved crispy, corn-meal-coated, fresh trout for breakfast, and a quick trip to the crowded fish pond would produce a nice surprise. Slipping on a pair of trousers and work boots, she scourged in the dirty clothes box for an old shirt. It was going to smell like fish anyhow, so no need to wash two. Opening the front door, she heard a few large drops of rain pepper on the roof, and she retrieved Levi's heavy jacket and hat that were hanging from pegs just inside the door. Though barely shy of six feet, Levi's jacket hung to her knees, and the hat settled down to her eyes. Stuffing her heavy, braided hair beneath the hat, she lifted it to midforehead, and she could see where she was going. Though clouds were low and dark, Amy could easily find her way to the pond.

A battered net with a long handle was still kept anchored over a large stump, and Amy wasted no time in catching the fish and dumping them into a waiting pail. Replacing the net, she scrambled up the incline, lugging the large pail with both hands.

Owen had been roaming the outer fences looking for prowlers and was happy the night was almost over. The few drops of rain had stopped, and the rolling clouds thinned enough to let the waning moon shine a weak light through the wisps. Suddenly, his body tensed as he watched a shadowy figure carry a large object up hill. Had the bastard found the cave was his first thought. Owen was afraid the intruder would get lost in the woods, if he shouted a warning to stop. Remembering Levi's wrath, he raised the rifle and sighted with the deadly Cantrell aim. Racing to the fallen figure, Owen collapsed in terrible disbelief.

Levi was awakened by a wild scream. It was not human, but it was human. Leaping from the bed, he jammed both legs into his overalls at once, snapping one catch as he raced to the door, stomping his feet into boots.

The agonizing screams came from just below the house, and Levi slid down the steep incline. In his haste, he stopped just short of where Owen sat on the ground holding Amy to him while the hills rang with his tortured sobs.

Levi knew Amy was dead, even before he saw the fountain of blood soaking the front of his coat. His agonized roar of shock was wrenched from his soul. "No, Amy! No!"

He finally focused on Owen, and his tormented grief. His rifle lay nearby, and he knew instantly what had happened. The fish pail lay on its side as flapping fish corkscrewed on the ground.

Putting his arms around both Amy and Owen, he tried to calm his son.

"It was an awful accident, Owen."

"I killed her, Pa. I thought she was a prowler. I killed her," he screamed and continued to sob in uncontrollable devastation.

Isaac awakened with a great sense of foreboding. The feelings of identical twins had always been closely entwined. Carrying his boots to the front porch, he saw Levi leaving his house on the run. An ungodly sound reached his ears, and he sped in the direction. Horrified, he beheld the nightmare before him.

"Isaac, oh God, look what I've done!" Owen screamed.

"Isaac, get the boys," Levi commanded in a voice his son did not recognize.

The family arrived quickly in various states of undress with Hiram carrying a lantern. The lighted scene was even more grotesque.

"Carl, get Ben," Levi ordered. Even in a state of utter shock, Levi's mind was working like a steep trap. "Don't let Owen out of your sight," he breathed quietly to Isaac who nodded in understanding. "I'll take Amy to the house now, Owen," he said gently to his son who still clasped his mother to his chest.

Levi lifted Amy for the last time and carried her to their bed.

"Pa, don't you want to put Ma in the other bedroom?" Hiram asked.

"This is Amy's bed. She will stay here for now."

By noon, Ben and his family arrived in a state of total disbelief. The horror of Amy's death combined with great concern for Owen had quieted the entire compound, even to the smallest child.

Amy was buried next to Sarah and Albert in the neatly kept grave-yard surrounded by a split-rail fence

"You can see our house and our mountains from here, Amy," Levi whispered as he kissed her cold lips for the last time.

Ben and Mary Jane conducted a simple service at the gravesite. When Ben asked about a preacher from town, Levi replied, "I don't want no goddamn preacher up here screaming that the wages of sin are death."

Levi left the gravesite and went immediately to Owen who sat motionless in a chair in Isaac and Irene's bedroom. He had neither slept nor eaten since the morning before when he had shot Amy.

"Owen, the fault is mine. I pushed you to shoot. I bellowed and screamed because we lost the damn stock, and I will regret it till the day I die."

"I'm a grown man, Pa, and should know when to shoot."

"Will you come back to the house, son? I need you there."

"I will never walk into that house again, Pa."

Two days later, Isaac rode to Elkinsville with Owen and watched him board a bus for Lexington where he joined the Navy.

For weeks, Levi slept in the cave at night, emerging in the mornings to sit by Amy's grave and watch the sunrise. She had died an early death at sixty-one, and Levi would never let her go.

CHAPTER 18

In 1934, Alan Adams awoke with a severe sore throat and a high fever in the middle of the night. At thirteen years old, he was tall, strong, athletic and rarely even sniffled with a cold. Jenny, a light sleeper, heard his second trip to the bathroom for water. Curious, she slipped quietly out of bed without waking Wesley and tapped on Alan's door.

"Alan, are you alright? I keep hearing you in and out of the bathroom," she said, walking to his bed where he lay in a tangle of sheets.

"I don't feel so good, Mom, and my throat really feels raw."

Jenny flipped his bedside lamp on and was startled by his flushed face. Touching his forehead, she felt a high fever and noticed the damp sheets. "Do you hurt anywhere, son?"

"My head hurts, and my legs keep trying to cramp."

"I'm going to get your dad up, Alan. I want him to have a look at you."

"Don't wake him, Mom. I probably just have the flu. You go on back to bed. If I feel worse, I'll call you."

"Always the independent one," Jenny thought on her way to arouse Wesley.

Wesley, groggy with sleep, stood by Alan's bed before he was fully awake. One look at his son's febrile face cleared his head instantly.

"His temperature is very high, Wesley. His throat and head hurt, and he says his legs are trying to cramp."

As Jenny related his symptoms, Wesley cringed. Polio was rampant in Canada, and numerous cases had been found in the North. Surely to God, Alan couldn't have polio. He made a beeline to the phone to call their friend and family doctor, John Wilkins.

"What should I do, John?" he asked after relaying his son's symptoms and his own anxiety.

"Meet me in the emergency room at the hospital," was his terse reply as he hung the phone up.

A young resident doctor on call waited at the emergency room door for the Adams' family and quickly rolled a stretcher to the car.

"Aw gee, Dad, I can walk," an embarrassed Alan said, but he immediately found himself on the stretcher and into the emergency room.

"So what seems to be the most uncomfortable, Alan?" Dr. Wilkins asked, and the first words out of his mouth sent chill bumps up Wesley's arms.

"My neck is stiff, my throat hurts, and I really feel hot. My legs feel weird and keep trying to cramp."

The two doctors exchanged looks, and Dr. Wilkins spoke to Wesley. "Why don't you and Jenny wait in the waiting room? I will be with you shortly."

A few minutes later, Dr. Wilkins motioned them into a spare treatment room and rocked them with his announcement. "Dr. Lane and I are both sure Alan has polio, and that it is in an early stage. His symptoms indicate that it could be either spinal or bulbar. I'm hoping it is spinal, Wesley, but we cannot rule out either at this stage. I think we should leave immediately for Knoxville General Hospital in Knoxville, Tennessee. They have one of the few treatment centers in the country, and we need to get Alan into an iron lung as quickly as possible. I have just called to see if there was an empty unit. They have only one, and I reserved it for Alan. With an ambulance at top speed, we can be there in four hours. Shall we proceed? Time is critical."

Wesley only stayed long enough to arouse Ben Cantrell from bed and ask him if he and Mary Jane would look after Danny and Chaney until they returned. A stunned Ben assured him that they would take care of everything.

The trip itself was a frenzied nightmare as they careened around hairpin curves in the darkness. Leaving the mountains, the ambulance screamed along the straight stretches of highway at breakneck speed with Wesley practically tailgating the vehicle.

"Jenny, sweetheart, it is alright to cry," Wesley said after a brief glance at his dry-eyed wife who sat coiled like a spring.

"I'm too busy praying for our son, Wesley, and I'm also praying for John Wilkins. How can we ever repay him for making this dangerous trip to be sure Alan gets the treatment he needs?"

"He would do the same for any of his patients. You know how dedicated he is, and there is no way anyone could ever repay him. We will try, though."

Again, the Adams were sent to a waiting room as medical personnel whisked through the corridors in the busy contagion unit. The many-windowed, two story building sat separated from the main hospital with a bevy of doctors and nurses busily commuting on connecting walkways.

Doctors and lab technicians were in and out of Alan's room for over an hour before an exhausted Dr. Wilkins dropped into a chair by them.

"The spinal tap definitely indicated that Alan has polio, but he will have the best of care here. At the first sign of difficulty in breathing, he will be placed in an iron lung that will breathe for him. So far, the right leg appears to be more involved that the left leg, but the next three to four days will tell the full story. They have already started applying hot packs to his legs to relieve the pain and help the muscle spasms. Student nurses are assigned to each patient around the clock, and hot packs will be continuous."

"Does this mean his legs are going to be paralyzed, John?" Jenny asked, white-faced and trembling.

"Jenny, it is too early to say. We just have to hope and pray. Since polio is contagious, you will not be able to go into his room, but you can see one another through the glass cubicles. I want you to meet his doctor and the nursing supervisor for this unit. Dr. George is a polio specialist, and Alan will have the best of care."

Wilkins led them to a small room enclosed in glass. Alan appeared to be extremely groggy and not even aware of the presence.

"He has had a rough night, Jenny, and has been sedated. He will be more alert when you come back this afternoon," Wilkins said, patting an anxious Jenny on the shoulder.

A young student nurse smiled at them from behind a mask that didn't cover her crinkling eyes. She was busy applying steaming packs from an electrical warmer to Alan's very still, straight legs.

Jenny and Wesley paced the streets of Knoxville when they couldn't bear the hotel room any longer.

"Wesley, this can't be happening to our Alan. He was so excited this week because the high school coach approached him about basketball. I can't bear to think of him being paralyzed."

"Jenny, sweetheart, right now I am praying that he will come through this alive. I have read about bulbar polio, and it can be deadly."

Two long rows of cylindrical iron lungs stood side by side in a large room with bellows hissing the breath of life for so many young children. Jenny and Wesley watched as children were taken from the lung with twisted legs and backs. Parents were stricken by the sight, but grateful their children had lived.

The days dragged by, painfully slow. Jenny and Wesley cherished each brief visit to wave to Alan through the large glass window. He looked pale and uncomfortable. Constant hot packs on his legs helped to relieve the cramps and pain, but they could not alleviate it completely. His wide smile at the sight of his parents sent their spirits soaring.

Dr. George met with them at the end of a week and gladdened their hearts with the news that Alan was out of danger and could go home.

"He is very fortunate that only his right leg has been affected. For a while there it looked as though both legs would suffer paralysis."

"Are you saying the paralysis is permanent, Dr. George?" Wesley asked, as both joy and dismay coursed through him.

"It could well be, Judge Adams, but only great care and time will tell. His right leg is going to be somewhat shorter than his left leg. You are looking at years of therapy and a brace. Alan will need a brace to keep his leg straight, and the leg will need lots of gentle messaging and very light exercise, eventually. He should not exercise the leg until after his checkup. I would like to see him again in a month, and if there are complications, notify Dr. Wilkins at once, and we will proceed from there. I am sorry there has not been a complete recovery, but after visiting this ward for a week, I'm sure you are counting your blessings. We have lost numerous young people and children to this terrible disease. Once healthy children leave the iron lung with limbs and bodies so twisted, they will probably never graduate from a wheelchair. Your Alan is a fine and lucky young man."

When the family arrived back in Elkinsville, the party for Alan overflowed the yard into the street. When the stretcher was removed from the ambulance, a cheer went up, and dozens of balloons popped.

Cynthia and Randolph Adams had arrived the day before, and Alan was delighted that his grandparents had made a special trip to see him. The two had always visited Wesley and his family each year, but Cynthia had not felt up to the trip last year. At eighty-four years, she was beginning to shrivel with old age, and her arthritis was becoming more painful, but she would not be denied the joy of seeing Alan return home alive. Both she and Randolph had feared for their grandson's life when Wesley called them from Knoxville with the news of Alan's polio. Randolph, at eighty-nine years, still stood ramrod straight but carried a cane "just in case he became tired."

"I called Ben Cantrell, Wesley, and he met us at the train station yesterday, and Mary Jane brought supper over last night. You and Jenny are really fortunate to have such good friends. Every time I see Thomas, I am still amazed at how much he resembles Ben, and their strange eyes are identical."

Friends arrived daily with food and offered to help with Alan's physical therapy. It was heartwarming for Cynthia and Randolph to see the outpouring of love and friendship for their family.

After discussing his prognosis with Dr. George and his parents, Alan was steadfast in his commitment to walk again. His bout with polio would shape and dictate his life.

Wesley was grateful for more than one reason with Alan's recovery. One, he dared not to mention to Jenny. From the onset of Alan's illness, he remembered his tortuous nightmares and the curse Lettie Mullins had screamed at him. "Wesley Adams, you will live to see any son you ever have dead at your feet." This ordeal was over, but Wesley shivered as he waited.

***

In 1933, Prohibition was repealed, and most of the country rejoiced. Those who had been instrumental in bringing about the law were vociferous in their forecast of wickedness and doom. It had been an albatross around the neck of the government with great losses in revenue and loss of life when brave revenue agents attempted to uphold the law. The repeal had little effect on mountain moonshiners and especially Levi Cantrell.

Levi was kept busy with a constant outflow of moonshine and trying to fill in for his lost Amy. The grandchildren demanded more of him with Amy gone. After a couple of years, his home and kitchen had been commandeered by his daughters-in-law, and Levi found himself looking forward to Sunday morning get-togethers.

He missed seeing Amy's long, lithe body move about the room making sure that each family member was served before she finally sat down. A terrible longing for her would always be with him, and he had never been able to empty her closet. At seventy-five, his long, thick hair and massive mustache were well-streaked with gray, and he wore them like the mane of a lion. His huge frame was still imposing, and his phantom lurking look of total power remained.

Two or three times a year, postcards from around the world kept them in touch with Owen. His few terse sentences were wooden, and each time, Levi's heart cried for his son. He would always carry the guilt and the blame for Amy's death and the loss of his son.

Mary Jane and Jenny began trading babysitting when Thomas Cantrell and Chaney Adams were babies. Being only one month apart, they learned to crawl together, and Thomas began to walk at eight months. Chaney walked at one year but could never keep up with Thomas. They became practically inseparable by the first grade.

The two tall, handsome boys led the pack but never with vehemence nor vengeance. Thomas had skipped the second grade, but Chaney was still his best friend. Thomas' highly acute intelligence was apparent long before he started to school, and Ben had a feeling that, somehow, his eyes played a part in his extreme quickness.

When the boys were ten, Ben had taken the two of them to his mountaintop home, and Chaney was totally fascinated by the enclave. It was July in its glory with huge mountain laurel blossoms and unbelievable, enormous blackberries. There were children of every age everywhere.

"They're all my cousins," Thomas said when he noticed the puzzled look on Chaney's face.

303

"I've never seen so many cousins, Thomas." Both boys laughed and headed for the inviting waterfall.

The two bonded even more as they entered sports, and each was outstanding. Ben allowed the two boys to help out at the sawmill occasionally, with very close supervision. Jenny Adams was extremely nervous with the idea that Chaney would even be near the huge, dangerous saws.

"Ben would never allow the boys near the danger zones, Jenny," Wesley said. "I have been there and watched them," but nevertheless, it did not allay Jenny's fear.

For the Adams' household, dinner was the highlight of the day, with the boys relating events as they stuffed their mouths with food. Jenny sweetly and gently admonished them to swallow before talking. She glowed with happiness and pride in her handsome family. Most weekends they helped her collect food and clothing for the many in need, and it broke Jenny's heart when bright and talented children dropped out of school to work and try to help their families. Thomas Cantrell was almost like a fourth son. Many times he shared their dinner or Chaney ate at the Cantrells.

It was a given fact that Thomas had been blessed with a superior brain. Sometimes it seemed to Jenny that he was old beyond his years with those strange, amber eyes. She and Wesley knew that on occasions Thomas had been able to thwart some of the antics that sometimes landed young boys in trouble, and they encouraged the friendship between Chaney and Thomas.

***

Careless moonshiners were being arrested by the scores. They had wrongly assumed the revenue agents would be leaving town after the repeal of prohibition. Embittered agents lay low for a period, and then swooped down on the hapless lawbreakers, who had been packed into Wesley's courtroom until late evening.

Fridays were always hectic, and today had been even worse. A bootlegger's wife, with five young children in tow, pleaded with Wesley for leniency in sentencing her husband, who had been arrested at his well-concealed still.

"How am I gonna feed all these children, judge, if you lock up my husband?"

304

The agent, who had hauled the man into court, looked away and refused to meet Wesley's stare.

"Come by my office at ten o'clock in the morning, Mrs. Haynes, and I will help you work something out, but your husband will have to serve his time," Wesley said.

Husband, wife and children continued to sob, and the arresting agent made a quick exit from the courtroom.

The day had been a long one, and Wesley was glad to finally get home and partake of a late dinner and then to bed. He slept a fitful sleep, tossing and turning. In his dream he was coming into his home through the front door that had been left standing wide open. Jenny sat across the room in a trance. She had grayed totally and completely. It was hard to tell where the gray began and ended. Her hair, her skin and her dress blended together. Crossing the room to Jenny, he placed his hand on her shoulder, but she remained stiff and unmoving. She did not acknowledge him and continued to stare into space. It was dinner time, but there were no dinner preparations, and a great stillness lay on the room. The boys were nowhere to be seen, no jackets or shoes thrown about the room. No books sitting lopsided on the end tables. There was no good-natured hassling of Jenny and complaining of hunger pangs, as they snatched frying potatoes from the pan. The eerie quiet finally penetrated Wesley's foggy mind. The boys were gone. They were gone for good, and then he heard the terrible laugh. Wesley woke up screaming, feeling as though his heart would burst through his chest, it was beating so hard.

Jenny was just finishing up in the kitchen and was terrified by Wesley's wild scream.

"Wesley, what in the name of God," and then she saw his face.

The color had totally drained away, and a wild look of terror in his eyes shocked her beyond words. She quickly sat on the bed by him and held him while he sobbed uncontrollably.

There was no way he could ever tell her about the unspeakable nightmares. He had to continue to believe they were only nightmares, a figment of his great guilt because he had taken a man's life.

CHAPTER 19

Several of Danny Adams' friends had dropped out of high school to join the Civilian Conservation Corps, and he was saddened. The CCCs gave direction and encouragement to strong, bright, young men. The government shipped them to numerous locations throughout the country that needed new roads or firefighters. It opened new vistas in many fields.

Their discipline and regimented training produced prime candidates for an Army anxious to recruit them. They would be the lead forces for World War II. The young men divided the monthly wages with their families that were in dire straights. They had been the boys whose competitiveness had matched his own. Though Danny was barely six feet tall and slenderly built, his aggressive nature propelled him to the top of the team. He excelled in both football and basketball, and the team sorely missed the departed players.

Danny's younger brother, Alan, was already two inches taller than he, and with a small lift in his right shoe, was proving to be formidable in sports also. The entire family had spent a tremendous number of hours with Alan after his bout with polio, encouraging exercise and massaging the rigid muscles. The doctors in Knoxville considered it a miraculous recovery. Both Danny and Alan took time out to practice shooting baskets with eleven-year-old Chaney. Chaney excelled in throwing long passes to Danny whose skilled fingers would latch onto the football and whip it back to his younger brother. Tall and lanky, Chaney would be the tallest of the lot. Wesley was a constant spectator at the ball games and tried not to show his immense pride.

In the fall of 1936, Wesley drove seventeen-year-old Danny to the University of Kentucky in Lexington to enroll in the fall semester. The year before Danny had decided to attend UK, and both parents were pleased with his decision.

"Dad, I really don't know which field I want to go into just yet. I have thought of law and medicine, but I want to see what else is out there before I make up my mind," Danny said to Jenny and Wesley when he had decided on his school.

"You'll have plenty of time, son. The first two years are pretty much the same in most fields."

"Mom, I know you and Dad do not approve of football, but I would like to give it a try," Danny explained. He had briefly broached the subject several months before, and both parents had been cool to the idea. Wesley had felt it would interfere with his studies, and Jenny had been afraid of injuries. He had very patiently explained to his mother he could outrun the bulky linemen.

"If that's what you really want to do, Danny, then so be it," Jenny nodded in agreement with Wesley.

***

Randolph Adams, though ninety-two years of age, remained extremely mentally alert and even lectured on rare occasions at UK. Wesley felt double relief with Danny and his father keeping tabs on one another. Randolph had become somewhat stooped, but he managed to maneuver by leaning on a stout cane. Millie Smith, a huge black woman, kept his home immaculate and hovered over him. Twenty years before, Randolph had secured a scholarship at his old alma mater in Pennsylvania for her son, and the young man had stayed on at the university. Millie refused to go to Pennsylvania. She would not retreat to her quarters at night until the professor had been made comfortable. Cynthia had died of cancer two years before, and he insisted Millie keep the house exactly as his wife had left it.

Thanksgiving was truly a time of joy for Danny. Both younger brothers hung onto every word and peppered him with questions about college. Alan was leaning in the direction of UK, also, and especially the basketball program. Danny and his grandfather arrived in Elkinsville for the holidays in a large, lumbering Studebaker. Wesley had been apprehensive about Danny driving so far, but Randolph had admonished him, jokingly saying it was his car.

Randolph entertained them with tales of Danny's football games. "I think he might even make the freshman team next year," and the family roared with laughter.

Wesley threw his arm across Danny's shoulder as they were preparing to leave, and his son winced with pain.

"You alright, Danny?" he asked.

"Just a tender spot, Dad. One of my teammates pulled one of those moles from my back in practice, but it's almost well."

Plans were already in progress for Christmas with Jenny promising the biggest tree and turkey ever. Randolph would return with Danny for the holidays, and Wesley's happiness was complete.

When Danny returned to school and football after Thanksgiving his coach sent him to the team doctor. Walking through the locker room, he saw Danny without his shirt and was surprised to see how much the lesion had spread, with red streaks fanning out from it. He had placed a small bandage over it after practice when the mole had been torn away, leaving only a small rupture in the skin.

The team doctor referred him to an internist who ordered a battery of tests that would take at least two weeks. Danny decided not to tell his family. He knew his mother would worry.

Randolph Adams sat in the chilly bleachers, bundled to his eyes, watching his grandson's team play the Ohio freshmen. He cheered loudly when Danny made a touchdown. If he once escaped the huddle, he was long gone. Randolph and Millie made their way to the jubilant winning team and complimented Danny.

"See you for dinner tomorrow, Grandpa," Danny shouted, as the team was hustled to the locker rooms.

Danny called his grandfather at three o'clock on Sunday afternoon to beg off dinner. He was coughing incessantly and complained of chest pains.

"Danny, you probably cooled off too quickly after that great game yesterday. Just wish your family could have seen you make that run."

"Thanks, Grandpa. I hope to see you next Sunday. Coach says I'm to stay in bed today and tomorrow 'cause he wants me to be in good shape for Saturday's game."

"Sounds like good advice, and if you need anything, call me, Danny."

"Will do, Grandpa."

Danny felt even worse the next morning, and his head began to hurt. By midweek his condition had worsened, and Coach Watson took Danny to see Dr. Wallace.

"I want to put Danny in the hospital for a couple of days and get some fluid into him. He is becoming dehydrated, and that will only make matters worse. Better check with his parents. You know how upset some of them get when a hospital is mentioned. His tests will be back in a few days," he added, and Coach Watson had a feeling the doctor wasn't telling him everything.

Dr. Wallace had not told him everything. The lesion on Danny's back had worsened, and he placed a call to the lab to rush the test results.

Gil Watson called Danny's parents and gave them Dr. Wallace's office number.

"He says Danny is dehydrated from the flu and felt you should know he wants him in the hospital for a couple of days."

"I appreciate you calling, coach. Thank you for taking such good care of Danny," Wesley said. "We will contact Dr. Wallace immediately."

After talking to Dr. Wallace, Wesley felt disconcerted. The doctor had assured him Danny had the flu, and proper diet with fluids would bring him around. Yet, there had been something in the doctor's voice he could not quite put his finger on.

Dr. Wallace decided to keep his growing suspicions to himself until he had the test results. Danny's headaches had not improved, and he shivered at what he would have to tell the family.

Randolph Adams and Millie went daily to visit Danny, and Randolph was beginning to worry. It was so unusual to see his grandson so limp and listless. He had always been energetic and lively. Randolph managed to catch Dr. Wallace on his rounds, but the doctor merely mentioned the flu and fluids. Randolph decided to call Wesley.

"I'm sure Dr. Wallace is a capable doctor, and he has a good reputation here in Lexington, but Danny is much worse than he was when he called me on Sunday."

Wesley left at daybreak for Lexington, leaving a very worried Jenny behind. "I will call you everyday, Jenny," he promised.

He went directly to the hospital when he arrived in Lexington. His very worried father sat by Danny's bed, and Wesley's heart sank when he saw his son. He had lost an appreciable amount of weight since his visit home, and dark circles were carved beneath his eyes.

A huge grin stretched across Danny's face when he saw his father. "Dad, what are you doing here?"

"I'm Christmas shopping for your mother." The three men laughed at the ludicrous statement.

"It's just the flu, Dad. I should be able to go home tomorrow. Everyday, Dr. Wallace says maybe in a day or so, and it has stretched out all week. Would you talk to him so I can get out of here?"

"I sure will, son. I'll just step down to the nurse's station and call his office."

Wesley returned to the room shortly to say Dr. Wallace would make time for him and promised to return soon.

Dr. Wallace had just completed reading all of Danny's test results when Wesley called, and he dreaded what he would have to relate to a very caring father.

Wesley was shattered by what a very sad Dr. Wallace had just told him.

"How can a person so young have cancer?"

"No age group is immune to melanoma. It is extremely fast acting and deadly. I cannot give you false hope, Judge Adams. There is no cure, and Danny's condition is rapidly deteriorating. Many melanomas start with a black mole, and I cannot say whether the injury caused it to accelerate. The headaches have gotten worse this week, and his lungs are involved."

"Are you saying that Danny will die soon?" an unbelieving Wesley asked.

"Yes, and God knows if there was anything medicine could do, I would do it. I was highly suspicious of this when Danny came in on Wednesday and checked out various cancer programs, only to learn there is still no known treatment for melanoma. It has already entered his lymph system, which is causing the headaches, and the lungs are becoming more congested."

"In other words, the cancer has spread to his brain and lungs?" Wesley asked.

"I'm afraid so, Judge Adams, and I am truly sorry. This is the miserable part of being a doctor."

"Will Danny have to remain in the hospital?"

"He can stay here in the hospital, or you can take him home. There is nothing we can do except give him something for the pain. Your family doctor could do the same if you choose to take him home. Would you like me to call and talk to him now?"

Wesley nodded and gave him Dr. Wilkins' phone number.

He listened as Dr. Wallace talked to his friend and sank further into his misery when the doctor mentioned six weeks to three months.

"Dr. Wilkins would like to speak to you, Judge Adams," Wallace said and gave the phone to Wesley.

"God, Wesley, I am so sorry. I will do anything I can to help. Does Jenny know?" Dr. Wilkins asked.

"No, she doesn't, John. Dr. Wallace has just told me, and my mind is reeling."

"When you have decided what you want to do, call me, and I will do whatever you need."

Wesley could not dwell on his own misery. He had to think of Jenny and the boys. He would pray for a miracle.

Wesley called Jenny from the hospital as soon as Danny had been sedated for the night. Both were heartbroken and devastated. They would settle Danny into his room and bide their time. As far as Danny knew, he was going home to recuperate from a severe case of the flu. He was placed into an ambulance early the next morning, and they headed for the mountains.

Randolph Adams was shattered by the news. "I will come to Elkinsville after you and Jenny have told the boys. How can this happen to a young man so full of life and purpose? Whatever I can do, Wesley," and tears came before he could finish.

Dr. Wilkins arrived an hour before Danny was due and did his best to comfort a distraught Jenny. Alan and Chaney were both in school, and Jenny, who had never been a crier, sobbed on their friend's shoulder.

Danny was tired from the long ride and, though heavily sedated during the trip, the drugs were beginning to wear off, leaving him in pain with glazed eyes.

John Wilkins took over immediately. "I'm going to put him out till morning, Wes, and he definitely should not have visitors tonight. Marcy and I plan to have Alan and Chaney over for dinner, so you and Jenny will have a chance to talk."

A numbed Wesley could only nod. He could see that Danny had lost ground even in the last two days. He and Jenny sat with their son until the medication kicked in, each holding his hand and not daring to look at one another.

Two days later, Jenny and Wesley asked the boys to stay put after dinner. Hal Wilkins had been by at six o'clock to see that Danny was sedated for the night.

The boys were completely dumfounded.

"Danny can't be dying, Dad, he has just turned eighteen," Alan argued.

Chaney cried softly, and Jenny cried with him.

"Maybe the doctor made a mistake. They told me my right leg would be paralyzed after polio, and now I'm on the track team," a defiant brother refused to accept the unbearable reality. Not Danny. They fought together, they played together, and he suddenly realized how much he loved him.

"Alan, we will have to make every minute count. We must all pray for a miracle and get through one day at a time. You both have to be brave for Danny."

"When are you going to tell him, Dad?" twelve-year-old Chaney was sobbing. Danny had always been his idol. It was Danny who had always taken time to shoot baskets, pass a football, and if he had a problem, Danny understood and listened.

"We'll tell him in the morning, after you have gone to school."

No more had to be said. The boys knew what they would have to do in the afternoon.

The school had hired a substitute to replace Jenny, who refused to let anyone care for her dying son. She wanted to be with him every minute and feel his warmth until his last breath.

Alan and Chaney refused to accept the inevitable, rushing home from school and seeing progress that wasn't there. There was never a minute of Danny's remaining days when a member of the family was not with him.

The entire town rallied behind the Adams' family. People brought food in daily, with Mary Jane Cantrell coordinating the meals.

"Many of these people should not be sharing their food with us, Ben. Is there some way you could gracefully get this across? They can barely feed their own families."

"I would be wasting my breath, Wes. You have given to these people on so many occasions, time, money and kindness, and they are hellbent on finally being able to help you and your family, even the bootleggers you sent up because you had to do your job. You helped feed and find jobs for their families while they were away."

Numerous young people walking past the Adams' house on their way home from school did so quietly with their eyes raised in sadness, as they viewed the drawn window shade in Danny's upstairs bedroom.

After two months Hal Wilkins felt it was past time for any hope for Danny, and the entire family was beginning to look gaunt and ragged. His last injection of morphine to Danny was lethal.

***

By the mid-1930s, outside influences had begun to change the way life for many in the mountains, but Levi continued to prosper on his own. Mining conditions became even more deplorable, and government stores were feeding most of the near-starving areas. Union leaders were pushing the desperate men to join, and John L. Lewis railed against the inhumane condition under which the miners labored.

Miners met in secluded spots to sign up for membership in the United Mine Worker's Union, knowing the perils that would befall them if their oaths were to be discovered. They would be fired immediately from the company and evicted from the company-owned house with their belongings thrown into the street. Even so, miners continued to join the union with pistols in their belts, and when meeting in various homes after dark, they would be hidden behind windows covered with blankets to insure secrecy.

Mine managers, out of sheer desperation, made impossible demands on struggling miners in an attempt to save the sinking company. As a result, the union made greater inroads by the month, with the battered and hungry miner praying for a miracle.

The union prevailed, and miners were euphoric. John. L. Lewis had become their savior, and his word would be their law. Thereafter, when Lewis decreed a strike for better benefits, the miners followed the man.

The United Mineworkers Union did not include sawmill workers, but Ben Cantrell rejoiced with his friends as they celebrated the new status of the union. For years Ben had agonized over the injustices inflicted on his friends, who lost limbs and lives in the black caverns. Dangerous conditions were ignored, and the lack of maintenance took a terrible toll.

CHAPTER 20

S everal of Levi Cantrell's grandsons had grown bored with mountain life, and with urging from friends in town, had joined the
CCCs and were shipped to all parts of the country.

"It's hard to keep up with everybody, Ben," Levi said, as the two
saddled horses and rode about the property. "They write back from
all over the country."

"Some of them had to go sometime, Pa. It was beginning to be a
bit crowded. Not even your barrels of moonshine could keep them
all busy."

"Carl's two boys finished with the CCCs the other day and joined
the Navy. Guess that will give them a good taste of the whole world.
Owen never says much in his postcards." Levi's eyes saddened as he
spoke of his son.

"Mary Jane really misses Elizabeth and Stephen. I reckon Elizabeth is going to marry that policeman she has been seeing in Baltimore, as soon as she graduates from nursing school." Most of the
young women in Elkinsville had chosen to train at Johns Hopkins
Hospital, and both parents had felt comfortable that she would be
with friends in the big city.

Stephen joined the Army just out of high school. His outstanding football record at Elkinsville High School immediately landed

him on the Army football team. Unbeknownst to all, the entire youth of the country would soon be thrown to all corners of the world.

"How is Judge Adams doin'?" Levi asked. Though he didn't approve of the law, period, he had always respected Wesley.

"He seems to be doin' okay, but then he has never talked about his own problems, just ready to help everybody else. Chaney and Thomas are together more since Danny died, and Thomas says Chaney sometimes cries when he talks about Danny."

It always amazed Ben that Levi was still strong and active at seventy-eight. He had been afraid of what would happen to him after Amy died. Levi still spoke of her as though she were there. Never a day passed that he didn't check the well-groomed gravesite, plucking any weed that might appear, and watching the sunset, sitting by her grave.

His brothers had expanded the fields, and the moonshine operation had become mammoth. Numerous people still cherished a superior moonshine to anything that could be bottled in a distillery.

***

A year had passed, and Wesley's pain at Danny's loss had barely lessened. He still saw Danny marching up the sidewalk to the rec building with his boisterous friends at lunchtime. Wesley sat on one of the many benches stationed beneath huge oak trees lining Main Street. He watched the carefree young people laugh and jostle as they passed in front of him, many acknowledging him as they hurried by to keep up with their group.

A saddened Jenny had returned to teaching, and Wesley knew she must be suffering as much as he, when she looked at the young faces before her.

He could speak to no one about his greatest and ever-growing agony. Was the curse Lettie Mullins had laid on him beginning to come about? He had killed her only son when he was only three years older than Danny. "I am being foolhardy," he told himself repeatedly. He found himself watching Alan and Chaney closely and questioned their whereabouts when they were late getting home at night.

"Gosh, Dad, I was only over at the Cantrell's shootin' baskets with Thomas. A bunch of guys came by, and we had a rip-roaring game. Just didn't think how late it was," a puzzled Chaney explained to his anxious father.

After Wesley slept, Jenny slipped into Chaney's room. "Chaney, your father is still grieving for Danny and is so afraid something might happen to you and Alan. His questioning you doesn't mean that he doesn't trust you. He can't help being anxious."

"I know that, Mom. Is there anything I can do? I really miss Danny and so do my friends. Thomas talks about him a lot."

"Just being here is the greatest comfort either of us could ask." Jenny kissed Chaney's forehead and held her tears until she left his room.

Football fever gripped the town in September with both Chaney Adams and Thomas Cantrell excelling. Both boys turned fifteen in early spring but played on different teams. Having skipped two grades, Thomas played on the senior varsity even though he was a junior. He stood six feet and two inches with a body of brawn and extreme quickness. Chaney always followed Thomas' team into the locker room, joining in the fun and frolicking after a hard-fought battle.

The older high school boys embellished on their summer of travel and wild experiences of hitchhiking throughout the South. The younger boys were awed by the tales of near escapes from various encounters, some real and many manufactured.

"Sure sounds like fun, Thomas," Chaney said.

"I think it would have been dangerous if half of what they said is true," Thomas said as he swiped Chaney with his towel.

***

In 1939, as the last day of school neared, Thomas and Chaney approached Ben about jobs in the sawmill during summer vacation. Ben broached the subject with Wesley, as they ate lunch in a crowded restaurant. Thomas had talked to his father about Wesley's concern for Alan and Chaney since Danny's death.

"Wesley, I promise you, the boys will not be allowed anywhere near the saws. They will stack and load lumber onto trucks and railroad cars. I also plan to take them into the forest to help locate the trees we'll need."

"I know he'll be safe with you, Ben, and two strapping fifteen-year-old boys need something to keep them busy during the summer."

At noon, Ben went to the south end of the sprawling lumberyard to take Thomas and Chaney to lunch and was mystified to find the two had not shown up for work at seven in the morning, as they had been instructed to do.

"Ben, I thought you must have found somethin' else for the boys to do," the foreman said when questioned about the two. "I ain't seen hide nor hair of them today."

Ben called Mary Jane immediately only to be told that Thomas had left at six thirty to come to the mill.

Ben suddenly had an eerie feeling that something was wrong. "Mary Jane, check his room. He might have left a note. I'll just hold on."

When Mary Jane left the phone to search for Thomas' room, Ben felt danger for his son, and a fear rose in him that made the rough hair on his forearms stand up. As Thomas grew up, Ben could always sense when something was amiss with him. On one occasion, Thomas barely avoided a fight with an older, jealous teammate, when he was placed on the senior varsity football team at only fifteen years old. Thomas was surprised to find that Ben seemed to know about the near-brawl.

A very perturbed and anxious Mary Jane returned shortly and gave him the unsettling news.

"Did he say who he was going with?" Ben asked.

"It just says, 'Mom and Dad, Chaney and me are going to hitch a ride to Georgia with Len Roberts and Nathan Collins. We'll be back next week, and, don't worry, we have all saved some money, and we will take good care of ourselves. Please do not worry. I love you, Thomas.'"

"God dammit, what a fool thing to do. I can't believe Thomas would do anything so stupid. I'll call Wesley and the other fathers to see if they know anything."

Ben managed to reach two of the fathers but could not locate Wesley. Leaving the sawmill, he headed for the courthouse to try to find him.

He was told by the court clerk that Wesley was busy in his office but would be out shortly. Ben perched on a bench and waited. Twenty minutes later, Wesley escorted a couple from his office and was surprised to see a somewhat anxious Ben waiting for him.

"Could we talk in your office, Wesley?" Ben asked, and the fear that lay just below Wesley's surface threatened to boil over. He had never seen Ben tense, and a foreboding crept through him.

Ben quickly explained the situation to Wesley. "I have just talked to the other two fathers, and they are just as vexed as I am."

Ben watched the color drain completely from Wesley's face, and his eyes shimmered with misery.

The two older boys, Len Roberts at sixteen and Nathan Collins, eighteen, had spent the last summer hitching rides about the South and had only glowing tales about their escapades.

Wesley was little consoled by the experiences of the older boys.

"Nathan Collins just graduated with Alan, and I've had him in court twice for drunk and disorderly conduct. Len Roberts is a fairly good boy, but what they are doing is dangerous as all hell. I just can't believe they talked Thomas into going with them. He is far more mature than the others."

It had not been easy to talk Thomas into the trip. Chaney was eager and ready to go, "It will be fun, Thomas, and as soon as we get back, we can work at the sawmill."

"You know our parents are going to be upset, Chaney, and especially your dad."

"He'll get over it, and besides, we'll be back in ten days."

"I'm not gonna go, Chaney. I have a bad feeling about this, and Nathan always finds a way to get into trouble."

"Well, I'm gonna go anyhow, and just promise me you won't tell on us until we are long gone. We already have a ride lined up for early in the morning. A produce truck that comes in from Kingsport will take us all the way, and Nathan says trucks are always leaving there to get more produce from Georgia. What could be better?"

Thomas was uncomfortable with Chaney depending on the other two.

"Chaney, I'll go for you, and at the first sign of trouble, we'll head back home. Promise?"

"So help me, God," and laughingly held up his right hand.

When they arrived in Kingsport, Thomas almost returned on his own, but Chaney was his best friend. He was even more worried about Nathan who produced cigarettes and a flat bottle of moonshine as soon as the truck left Elkinsville. Chaney barely tasted the moonshine and took only two drags from a cigarette. Thomas flatly refused either, and Nathan turned angry eyes on him.

"You are sure one goddamn stick in the mud, Cantrell. Why did you come anyhow? You know, I could throw you off this truck."

"You could try, Nathan," Thomas said, glaring at the young man that was at least a head shorter than he and without Thomas' muscle.

When Nathan realized he wouldn't get any help from the other two, he sulked and moved as far away from Thomas as possible.

Two days later, Thomas tried again to talk Chaney into going home. They had spent two nights sleeping in the woods on the edge of a small town in Georgia where mosquitoes made life miserable.

"We'll hitch a ride to Macon as soon as we get some breakfast," Nathan said. "They got good movie theaters there and one hell of a big roller rink with lots of pretty girls."

By the end of day five, Nathan was begging money from the other boys who were beginning to run short. Buying moonshine and cigarettes had quickly reduced their meager savings. Thomas had steadfastly refused either and was upset because Chaney had begun to drink and smoke with the other two.

"I say we find a good watermelon patch to raid tonight and head home in the morning," Nathan announced two days later as the group began to pool its last few pennies.

"Chaney, why don't we leave right now? If we get caught stealing, we could wind up in jail," Thomas begged.

"They're not gonna throw us in jail for snatching a few watermelons. We can leave early in the morning."

A black feeling was creeping over Thomas, but he couldn't detour Chaney, who was hell bent on following the other two. He considered leaving on his own, but he still didn't trust the others.

The sun was low in the West, but the heat was unrelenting. Nearing the edge of a small town, they stopped to drink from a gurgling stream only a few feet from a piney forest. Traveling in a straight line by the forest, they came upon a well-tended, neat watermelon field. Whooping, they headed straight for the rail fence.

"No, Chaney, no!" Thomas yelled at his friend. "This field is well-taken care of, and you better bet someone is nearby looking after it."

Nathan and Len cleared the fence with Chaney just behind them. Thomas felt the hair prickle on the back of his neck, and he could not bring himself to cross the fence. The boys were tearing watermelons from vines and then dropping them when they spotted a larger one. Thomas could not believe the destruction they were wrecking in the field.

He felt a burning in his ears and a deafening sense of danger. It was the first time his extra senses had warned him, but it was already too late.

The roar of a shotgun blast splintered the quiet surroundings when a red-faced, furious farmer bore down on the group, shooting as he ran toward them.

"Run, Chaney, run!" Thomas bellowed.

Nathan and Len were closer to the fence and vaulted to safety, leaving Chaney who had wandered farther out into the field. Thomas saw Chaney start to run, but after a few steps, he faltered and began to limp.

Thomas cleared the fence in one high hurdle and ran toward his friend, who was now dragging his right leg and losing ground to the advancing shooter. Thomas was terrified when he saw the blood-soaked leg of Chaney's jeans. Starting at the groin, the entire leg was dripping with blood. He instantly threw Chaney over his shoulder and raced toward the fence. Weighted down by his heavy friend and even with his tremendous strength and quickness, he could not out-run the fast, irate farmer who continued to shoot, and Thomas felt buckshot tearing into the back of his legs.

"Put me down and run, Thomas," Chaney begged. "You have to go for help, or we'll both be killed. Please, Thomas, run for help. He won't shoot me when he sees how bad I'm hurt. You have to save both of us."

Buckshot tore into Thomas' back, and he knew Chaney was right. Placing his friend on the ground, he sprinted over the fence and headed for town ignoring his own blood streaming down his back. He finally reached the police station and blurted out the story.

Sheriff Edgar Lyons was shocked by the huge, handsome young man dripping blood all over the office floor, staring at him with pale, unblinking amber eyes. For a moment, he was speechless.

"Were you hit in the shoulder?" he asked, seeing a massive slick of blood from Thomas' chest and down his back.

"No, I'm full of buckshot from by back to my heels, but the blood on my shoulder is my friend's blood. I tried to carry him out of the field."

"Then your friend is dead by now," he was thinking as he looked at the huge amount of blood covering Thomas.

"Bruce, get out to old Nade's place and check out a young man he caught stealing a watermelon. I think he is bad hurt, accordin' to his friend here. Hurry it up and call me, pronto," Lyons instructed. The deputy left with a screaming siren.

"Sir, I have got to call my dad. Chaney's father is a judge in Elkinsville, Kentucky, and he and my dad are good friends. I have to let them know."

The sheriff's first thought was to throw Thomas in jail and then let him spend some time on a chain gang, but for some reason, he relented and let him make the phone call.

Ben's first reaction was shock and then relief that Thomas was alive, but he was filled with terrible dread for Chaney.

"Thomas, I thank God that you are safe. I will leave as soon as I go by and pick Wesley up. Be careful, son, and be respectful to the sheriff. What happened to the other two?"

"I don't know, Dad," and he stopped before giving any more information the sheriff might hear. "But it's okay there."

"Let me talk to the sheriff, son."

"Sheriff Lyons here," with his usual gruff greeting, but the longer Ben talked, the more subdued he became. His cocky arrogance deserting him, he found himself stammering. There was no open threat from Ben, but the phone line was charged with an undercurrent of immense and hidden strength. He was also shocked to know that both boys were only fifteen-years-old, as he stood there with Thomas towering over his five-feet, ten-inch frame. Lyons was embarrassed and befuddled when Ben asked for his phone number, and he had trouble remembering it.

Thomas noticed a change in the sheriff's demeanor after he spoke to his father and was greatly relieved. Maybe they would get Chaney to a hospital fast.

"Let's get you to the emergency room, boy, and see how much buckshot you've been riddled with."

The phone rang as the two were leaving the office, and Lyons answered, with his face falling after the first sentence.

The deputy had found Chaney dead at the feet of Nade Bates who was still ranting and raving because he had not killed the other three.

"Jesus, Nade. He's just a boy. Did you need to do that?" The deputy, though hardened by years of police work, couldn't help but notice that Chaney was a very handsome boy and probably only hungry.

322

"Them sons-of-bitches done ripped up my watermelon field, and it's a man's right to defend his property," he shouted.

Chaney lay in a large pool of blood that seemed to have drained him dry. The shotgun blast had severed the iliac artery in his right groin, and he was probably dead by the time Thomas laid him on the ground. The deputy knew there would be hell to pay. This was no ordinary young man, who had unfortunately crossed paths with a trigger-happy, bitter farmer who hated humanity in general.

"We'll lay the bastard out in the barn till somebody comes for 'em, and you jest sure as hell need to tell that worthless sheriff how bad my melon patch was tore up."

Thomas knew from the sheriff's conversation with the deputy that Chaney was dead. Collapsing on a wooden bench, he put his head in his hands and sobbed.

Edgar Lyons attempted to console Thomas and dreading an encounter in the morning with an irate judge whose son had just been shot down in cold blood. Before they could leave for the hospital, the phone rang again, and he had to tell Ben Cantrell that Chaney was dead. The group was already on the way.

Two large, black sedans streaked through the darkness and across Tennessee with Ben Cantrell, Wesley Adams and Dave Williams, chief of police in Elkinsville. They sat in grim silence. Five trusted and faithful friends rode with them. They arrived at the Georgia border town by four o'clock in the morning.

Lyons had decided to sleep in his office and warned his two deputies there could be trouble by daybreak. He instructed them to be at his office by five o'clock.

When he answered the pounding on his door, he opened it to confront eight huge men, and he almost dropped his trousers that were halfway on. He knew who Ben Cantrell was. He had those same damned cat eyes that belonged to his son, and, Jesus Christ, he was enormous.

"You Sheriff Lyons?" Ben asked.

"Yes," he answered and hoped his voice didn't sound as shaky as he felt.

"You say my son is dead," the tall man next to Ben demanded. Murderous eyes bored into Lyons as the judge stepped forward. The sheriff knew this man could kill. He felt as though Wesley would spring at him in an instant. Backing up, he prayed his deputies would arrive early.

"I want to see him," Wesley ordered.

"We'll have to go out to the farm where he was killed. He's laid out in a barn out there. We had planned to bring him in at daylight."

Ben knew that Wesley had not accepted Chaney's death until he heard the awful pronouncement that his boy was laid out in a barn. Before Ben's eyes, Wesley changed from the dignified judge he had always known to a man possessed. An unspeakable dread filled Ben. He knew what was in store for his friend.

"You son-of-a-bitch. You left my boy in a barn overnight?"

"It was dark, judge, and like I said, we planned to get him at daybreak."

"We won't wait for daybreak. We will go now. Just give us directions," Wesley thundered.

"Oh, God, that's all I need," Lyons thought. He knew these men were probably armed, and that bastard Bates was all too anxious to shoot.

"I just need to put my clothes on, and we'll go."

"What about my son Thomas?" Ben asked.

"He is alright, but the doctor wanted him to stay in the hospital overnight. He had a bunch of buckshot dug out but no real damage."

Inwardly, Ben wanted to rejoice that his son was alive and apparently only slightly wounded, but Wesley's agony kept his face stoic.

The men swiftly returned to their cars, and the sheriff was completely unsettled when Ben's massive body eased quickly into the patrol car beside him. At that moment, one of his deputies drove up, and he could have cried with relief. Al Johnson hopped out of his patrol car, puzzled by all the traffic. Lyons quickly rolled his window down and filled him in.

"Follow us, Al, and call Dennis on the way."

"Who is Dennis?" a wary Ben asked.

"My other deputy. I hope there won't be any trouble, Cantrell. Let me handle it when we get there. This Nade Bates has a short fuse."

"Guess that's why the judge has a dead son, huh?"

"The boys were on his property, and they were stealing watermelons."

"Watermelons?" Ben said in a tone that left no doubt that Nade Bates would be given no quarter.

The horizon showed a slight line of gray in preparation of day, as the group reached the Bates' home. The second deputy had caught up with them, and the headlights lit up the home place like day.

Bates, an early riser, sat on his front porch in a dilapidated straw-bottomed chair leaning against the wall. Grabbing his shotgun, he bounded down the steps, clutching it.

"Put the gun down, Nade," Lyons ordered, looking at the wild-eyed farmer.

Al Johnson circled in back of Bates and lifted his gun in one easy movement infuriating the farmer.

Ben stayed close to Wesley. He told Dave Williams to stay on the other side. Williams did not need a warning, he was also well-aware of the change in Wesley.

"Take us to the barn, Nade. The judge wants to see his boy," the sheriff instructed.

The headlights produced an eerie glare, and Bates blinked at the group. His sharp, short nose resembled a beak, and his enlarged, protruding Adam's apple jerked up and down when he spoke. Hitching his thumbs in his baggy overalls, he sneered, "He ain't in the barn. We figured nobody was gonna come lookin' for a goddamned thief, so we put him in a big box and buried him at the edge of the field."

An enraged Wesley growled a low, guttural sound, and Ben gripped his shoulder. Glancing at Dave Williams and the others, Ben saw the fury that raged through the whole group. Leaving Wesley's side for a moment, Ben whispered into Dave's ear. "You have to keep these men under control. We don't need another dead man."

Numerous people had volunteered to come to Georgia to help the judge in any way possible, and the five men Ben and Williams had chosen could be counted on to keep a cool head. The farmer's brash, insolent indifference to Chaney's death ignited an almost unbearable hostility.

Daylight was breaking as the group reached the gravesite, and the two strong deputies began shoveling away loose earth covering the box. Dread gripped the bystanders when barely two feet below the surface, they uncovered the top of a large, square, wooden box, much too short to hold the body of a tall man. Dirt sifted through the large crack between two wide, rough boards covering the box. Al Johnson pried both boards loose and lifted both at the same time to reveal Chaney's body.

A gasp of disbelief rose from the group. Chaney lay on his side, clad only in undershorts. His neck and head were bent forward, and knees folded up almost to his chest. Dried, caked blood covered most of his body while black soil had sifted onto his mass of auburn hair.

Wesley's wild scream was that of a man who had lost his sanity. Even with Ben and Dave Williams flanking either side, he sprang at the sneering farmer, slamming him onto the ground and wrapping his neck in fingers of steel, driving the bobbing Adam's apple into the man's throat.

Ben and Dave both tried in vain to pry Wesley's fingers away from Bate's throat. He had a death grip on the man who had so brutally slain his son. Ben quickly eased his fingers around Wesley's throat and firmly pressed against his carotid until Wesley slumped forward and loosened his grip on the farmer's neck.

Two ambulances arrived shortly, one for Chaney and the other one for his father. Ben and Dave Williams would ride with Wesley and administer a sedative supplied by the doctor who had taken care of Thomas.

The massive dose of sedatives would keep him unconscious for several hours, and the doctor insisted that he be restrained for the trip home.

"Your friend has suffered a terrible shock, and he could well wreck the ambulance on your way back, even with the two of you sitting on him. Give him the medication when he starts to wake up and don't wait until he is fully awake. I am truly sorry for what has happened to your families here in Georgia."

The trip back to Kentucky was a nightmare for the whole group, with each friend wishing Ben had let Wesley finish off the farmer.

Ben and Dave Williams knew each time Wesley was about to surface. It was always the same.

"Goddamn you, Lettie Mullins. You waited. You waited."

"Ben, do you know what he is talking about?" Williams asked.

"No, I just wish I did so I could help," a saddened Ben answered.

Ben had made a quick stop in Tennessee to call Dr. Wilkins and gave him detailed information about Wesley's total collapse. Wilkins met them in the emergency room and was shocked by the sight of his good friend. Wesley appeared to have aged twenty years.

A stricken Jenny and Alan stood by the examining table and were even more devastated when Wesley began to wake up, still screaming about Lettie Mullins and oblivious to either of them.

Wesley was placed into another ambulance along with Dr. Wilkins and a deputy to be taken to Lexington and confined in a sanitarium for an indefinite period. Wesley's brother, Joel, and his sister, Dorothy, met the group at the hospital. Dorothy agreed to stay with Wesley while Joel went to Elkinsville for Chaney's funeral.

Chaney was buried next to his brother, Danny. The town mourned with the Adams' family again. Chaney's friends were beyond shock. Families not only consoled Jenny and Alan, but also their own bewildered children.

Joel marveled that Jenny and his nephew had been so strong and so brave. Jenny was pale and so very thin, but yet she appeared to have the strength of Goliath. The absolute horror of Chaney's death had pushed Wesley over the edge, but somehow Joel felt there was something he didn't know.

Mary Jane and Ben Cantrell were by Jenny's side constantly, and both knew she must be on the verge of total collapse. By late evening they managed to clear the house, hoping Jenny could get some much-needed rest. Joel would be staying with her for a few days, and they felt comfortable in leaving her.

"I want us to sit down and talk with your uncle," Jenny said to her son, who had been insisting she lie down. "There are some things I need to ask him and maybe you can help. It is simply not like Wesley to fall to pieces, even in the face of our terrible tragedy. There are some things I need to ask Joel, because we must do everything within our power to help your father."

After the three had seated themselves around the kitchen table, Jenny didn't mince words.

"Joel, what is Wesley's connection to a Lettie Mullins? He screamed obscenities about her over and over. I asked Ben Cantrell exactly what happened when Wesley saw Chaney's body, and though Ben was reluctant to say anything, he did say Wesley had screamed the same thing when his mind seemed to leave him, and each time he was coming out of heavy sedation. Through the years, he has had torturous nightmares, but he always refused to discuss them."

Joel put his head in his hands and suddenly realized the missing piece of the puzzle. The hair stood up on his arms, and he understood how tortured Wesley's soul must be.

"We must know, Joel. It is the only way we can help him."

Joel knew Jenny was not going to be detoured from learning the truth, but he didn't want his nephew to hear it. How could they possibly handle his explanation on the eve of burying Chaney?

"It's alright, Uncle Joel, I can deal with whatever you have to say. I have lost two brothers, and I need to help my father. We can't help if we don't know what we're up against."

"Alan knows that his father killed a man because he found him in bed with his first wife," Jenny said, recognizing Joel's struggle.

He spoke slowly and haltingly in reply.

"The man Wesley killed was Jessie Mullins, a roustabout and a troublemaker. He had been in trouble many times, and it was second nature for Wesley's father-in-law to try to help young people with problems. He gave Jessie a job in his stables, so he could support his mother. She was a backward, illiterate woman, and Jessie was her only child."

"He was a handsome young man and as wild as a March hare. Everyone in town knew about the affair between him and Lacey a year before Wesley found them together in his own bed. Most people seemed to think Lacey would tire of him, and no one wanted to tell Wesley. I have blamed myself so many times, because I didn't have the courage to tell him. Things could have been different, and I will always live with that. At the trial, Lettie Mullins went absolutely wild when Wesley was acquitted and put a curse on him. She screamed that she witched him, and that he would see any son he ever had dead at his feet."

Jenny gave a stricken cry and lurched in her chair. Both men were by her side immediately, and she sobbed on her son's shoulder.

"Poor Wesley, all these years with those nightmares, and now he is blaming himself for the deaths of Danny and Chaney."

"Mom, we will convince Dad there is no such thing as a curse or witching? She was a bitter woman who raised a mean-spirited son, and sooner or later, someone was going to kill him. We can help him through this, now that we know what he has suffered."

The past two years had matured Alan beyond his age, and his uncle thanked God for this boy.

Ben spent most of the night talking to Thomas and gathering all details about the trip. "Dad, I should have told Chaney's father about the trip, but he begged me to be quiet until they were out of the area. I didn't trust the other two, and I figured the only way I could help was to go and keep an eye on him. I failed, and now my best friend is dead."

"Thomas, you laid your life on the line for Chaney, and no friend could ask for more. It's a miracle that you weren't killed." For the first time in his life, Thomas heard Ben's voice quiver.

"Dad, I'm gonna beat the hell out of Len and Nathan the next time I see them."

Thomas would never get the chance to carry out his threat. Len Roberts and Nathan Collins joined the Army immediately, knowing the wrath they would face if they returned to Elkinsville.

A week later, Ben journeyed to his mountaintop home to check on his father. Levi was saddened about Chaney's death and Wesley's collapse. "He was a fine young man, Ben. I always liked having him come here with Thomas." Levi did not tell Ben that Thomas had used up one of his lives. Ben's first brush with death on the mountain roadway didn't occur until he was twenty-five years old. Thomas, at fifteen, had already begun to experience a foretold fable. Somehow, he knew that Thomas would be the one who would be severely tested, time after time. Ben had been sorely tested on a few occasions, but things and places would be different for Thomas.

Jenny spent a week at Wesley's bedside, and he was beginning to make progress. His medications had been reduced to nighttime for sleep, and he was coherent, though quiet, and depressed. Jenny talked to his psychiatrist and filled him in on Wesley's background.

"He has been through the most shocking and heinous tragedy that could be faced by a father," the psychiatrist explained. "He had time to adjust to Danny's death beforehand, even though he, no doubt, felt guilt because he had committed murder, but he was totally unprepared for the horror of Chaney's sudden death. The one positive sign is that his recovery, though slow, has been without shock treatment. When I first examined him, I felt it might be his only way back to reality, but I have been pleasantly surprised."

CHAPTER 21

Early summer of 1940 bore witness to unbelievable atrocities in Europe. Hitler whipped legions of brutal troops into crushing armies that rolled over small countries, one after the other, leaving them bloody and broken. In spite of the massive amount of weapons and arms, America was rushing to countries battling for their lives, they fell before the overwhelming onslaught of German armies. France was overrun, and brave Britain stood alone.

Though the United States was reluctant to enter the war, Roosevelt and many who feared an all-out assault on democracy urged all possible aid to the brave nations embroiled in the fighting. America was equipping struggling countries with ships, tanks, aircraft and other war materials. Roosevelt pleaded to the United States to become the "arsenal of democracy," and battled isolationists who rallied against his aid to warring nations. Their hue and cry denounced shipments of arms, claiming that Roosevelt was leading the nation into a war the country was poorly prepared to fight.

The timber industry in Elkinsville was instantly revived. Beautiful hardwoods were being harvested throughout the mountains for rifle stocks being manufactured by the thousands. Rusted flatbed railroad cars were resurrected from side rails to again haul mammoth loads of logs to waiting factories.

Gondolas, which had not been used for a decade, were rushed beneath the belly of the large tipple, which sprang into action with massive new orders for coal. Shipyards and factories were running around the clock. Elkinsville exploded with new life and purpose.

Ben was working long hours to restore sawmills that had been dormant for years. He had periodically checked the unused mills, oiling and cleaning much of the machinery. He always checked the locks, but even so, thieves had managed to loot several of the boarded up buildings. With Jerry's help, Ben rushed four of the larger and better-equipped mills up and running in record time. Labor was easy to come by, and it gave Ben more time to scout out the favored trees.

The country that had been so mired in the Depression was beginning to go full-steam ahead with new factories opening at a rapid rate. John L. Lewis took full advantage of the situation. His demands for more pay and better working conditions for miners increased. The coal companies writhed with fury. They knew if Lewis spoke the hated word, "Strike," the men would put down their shovels and walk from the pits.

***

In 1940, Thomas graduated from high school at sixteen years old, and Ben had high hopes for college, but Thomas had other plans. Ben knew Thomas was still struggling with Chaney's death, even after talking to Wesley Adams.

"You almost lost your own life, Thomas, trying to save Chaney. Our family will always be grateful to you, and I hope you will visit us often. We miss you." Wesley hugged Thomas when he left and sank into his own misery again.

He dreaded going home at night. Alan was just completing his first year at UK, and the hollow sounds of an utter quiet tore at him the minute he opened the door. The house had been so filled with rowdy boys for so long, and now he and Jenny sat in a strained silence. While in the hospital, the psychiatrist had urged him to talk to Jenny about his dilemma, and for the first time, they talked about his nightmares and his great fears for their sons. His tremendous love for Jenny and Alan and their heart-wrenching support pulled his mind back from the abyss.

Alan came home for the summer, and again, the house was suddenly filled with boisterous boys coming and going into the wee hours.

Instead of going to his job in the mill one morning, Thomas dropped by Ben's office and announced he was going to join the Army.

Ben was dumfounded. "Thomas, you are college material, to say the least. You skipped two grades, and even then you were ahead of your classmates." His skin crawled. Most people felt America would surely go to war. France had fallen, and Britain was hunkered down beneath a blitz, with the Luftwaffe raining continuous bombs on them.

Stephen was just completing officers' training, and Owen was somewhere in the South Pacific on board a ship. Ben had begun to worry about both of them, and now Thomas wanted to jump into the fray.

"Thomas, try just one year of college and then go into the Army," Ben pleaded.

"Dad, this is something I need to do, and want to do. I hope you and mom won't be too unhappy with me."

"When do you plan to leave, son?"

Ben was rocked when Thomas replied, "Tomorrow."

The sadness in Thomas's eyes told Ben why he was going. He would always carry some blame for Chaney's death. In hindsight, Thomas felt it would have been better had he told Wesley Adams about Chaney's plan and risked losing his friendship. Better that than dead.

Ben and Mary Jane rode to the mountaintop to visit Levi the week after Thomas left for the Army. Levi was delighted to see Mary Jane and gave her an awkward hug.

"Mary Jane, don't worry about Thomas. If there was ever a boy who could look after hisself, it's Thomas," Levi said, seeing the strain in her face.

"But Levi, he is only sixteen," she said on the verge of tears.

"Well, who do you reckon would believe it?" he drawled, knowing that Thomas could almost look Ben in the eye.

Ushering her into the house, he placed her bag on the floor and patted her gently on the shoulder.

"The girls cleaned up good for you and threatened me if I tracked up the place."

Mary Jane laughed in spite of her sadness. She never came into this house that she didn't feel Amy's presence. Ten years later, everything was exactly as Amy had left it. Levi would not allow anything to be changed.

Ben and Levi saddled horses and rode over the homestead. The rules that had been set when they moved to the farm still held. The day anyone arrived at the farm, they would not be allowed to enter the cave just in case they had been followed, even though lookouts still manned their posts on the trails leading in. Levi would never let down his guard, and his cave would never be discovered. At eighty-one, he was still ramrod straight, and his cagey mind was always on the offense. He had trimmed his hair and mustache because Mary Jane was coming and even changed into clean overalls. Secretly, Ben had always been his favored son. He felt strongly the love Ben and Mary Jane shared was close to the great passion he and Amy had known.

The two men dismounted and walked about the ancient lava flow. Levi had told Hiram and Ben about the cave outlet after Amy died, but the other boys were not privy to the information yet.

"Hiram and Isaac are finishing up a run and the fires have been burning for days, ain't smelled no smoke. What do you think, Ben?"

Ben sniffed the air and agreed with his father. At fifty-four years, Ben was in his prime, and Levi always felt a sense of wonder when he looked at him. Except for his unusual eyes, they were still very similar in appearance. Levi was becoming somewhat gaunt and had slipped a couple of inches in height but still possessed a great strength.

"I reckon we are gonna be in a war up to our ears, Ben," Levi said. He had long since purchased a battery radio and listened diligently to all newscasts.

"I don't see any other way, Pa. England is the only country left over there, and it is in real trouble. If England falls, Hitler will be over here one way or another."

For the first time, Ben saw a look of fear on his father's face. "A bunch of the family is out there in the service, and a whole bunch more will be goin' when it comes to war."

The thought sickened Ben. Thomas was so young, and Stephen was a son to be proud of. The sea wars would be fierce, and Owen was already in place should it come. Numerous nephews had graduated the CCC's into different branches of the service, and others would be leaving this mountaintop.

Levi was tempted to tell Ben about his heritage, but the time didn't feel right. He knew Thomas would come through. He still had eight lives left, and he would tell Ben when the time came.

***

Thomas came back to Elkinsville in the spring of 1941, before shipping out to the Philippines. Like most of the mountain boys, he had earned his "expert rifleman" on his first trip to the rifle range. At seventeen, he now equaled Ben's six-feet and five-inches, and as his father looked at him in his uniform, he could only think, "My God, what a soldier."

"Several boys from the mountains are in my regiment from hollows I didn't even know existed. Dad, do you remember Billy Lewis? We graduated from high school together, you know, the skinny little kid that carried the water bucket for the football team?"

"Oh, yeah," Ben said, remembering the sad little boy, whose widowed mother had raised her only child on meager earnings as a seamstress.

"Well, he is no longer a skinny little kid. The Army raised him up to six-feet and added thirty pounds of muscle, and he's one tough son-of-a-gun. We are in the same regiment, and we do a lot of hell-raising together when we go into town. I didn't really know him in high school, but we are good friends now and look out for one another."

"Then I reckon he will be going to the Philippines with you," Ben said.

"Oh, yeah, and several more of the mountain men. We don't expect to be doing any fighting there since Hitler is still trying to wipe Britain off the map. Most of us think America will wind up in the war though. The Brits can only stand alone so long."

A chill went through Ben. His young son was so nonchalant about war, but the looming facts were terrifying. His two sons would be on the front lines. Armies could be shifted quickly, and being stationed in the Philippines was no guarantee against action.

Thomas knew he must visit Wesley and Jenny Adams, and it was with a heavy heart that he knocked on their front door as he had done so many times in the past. He almost expected Chaney to fling the door open and greet him with one of his many quips.

Jenny Adams opened the door quietly and stared momentarily at Thomas before he registered with her.

334

"My goodness, Thomas. I hardly recognized you. You are even taller and bigger than ever in the uniform! Do come in. We were just finishing breakfast. Saturday morning is our late morning. Wesley, look who is here," she called.

Wesley, in rumpled robe and pajamas, turned ashen when he saw Thomas.

Thomas crossed the room and into Wesley's outstretched arms. Tears streamed down the older man's face, and Thomas didn't try to wipe his own but let them slide from his chin.

For the next several days, Thomas was a daily visitor to their home with both Jenny and Wesley fussing over him and plying him with numerous questions.

"It will be quite an experience being stationed in the Philippines, Thomas, and we look forward to hearing from you in detail," Jenny said. "Billy Lewis came by the school a few weeks back, and it sounds as though the Army is agreeing with both of you. I do hope the two of you will look after one another."

Thomas laughed, "Billy can well take care of himself now. Have you ever seen anyone change so much in one year?"

"He really looks great, and I know his mother is very proud of him," Jenny stopped, and the tortured look in her eyes tore at Thomas's heart.

In June, Thomas and Billy were aboard a loaded troop ship that sailed toward the Philippines and into a fast approaching, monstrous, maelstrom that would shred and mutilate the island paradise.

***

The battleship Arizona lay at anchor in the San Francisco harbor in July, awaiting the arrival of special-trained personnel. The ship would continue to Pearl Harbor, where she would join a fleet now training in preparation for war in the Pacific. Relations with Japan were rapidly deteriorating.

Chief Petty officer Owen Cantrell checked the roster of new crewmen that would soon be boarding the Arizona. The ship had been his home for the past ten years. He barely visited the ports of call. He always returned to his quarters before his allotted time, impressing his superior officers and gaining their utmost respect. The huge, lean seaman was a physical marvel, and few would have guessed him to be forty-eight years old. He was a loner. No one had ever been able to penetrate his glacial shield. He could not always hide the torture in his eyes that threatened to overtake him on rare occasions. Those, who knew him, held him in highest esteem and would never have intruded into his personal life even when those rare moments occurred.

Owen was shocked when he read the name John Cantrell on his roster. Surely this could not be his nephew John. He loved all his nieces and nephews, but John was his favorite. Like Owen, he had been intrigued by stories of the sea, and the two had discussed their common bond on many occasions. John would be twenty-one years old, and a terrible dread filled him knowing the United States would be going to war in the very near future. Owen had no fear for himself, but would almost welcome a death he had not been able to commit. He had devised means on many occasions but could not bring himself to do the final act.

He stood on deck where he would have a good view of the new sailors coming aboard, and he had no trouble recognizing John, as his long legs cleared the gang plank. He looked exactly like his father, Carl. He followed the young man to his assigned bunk and was thankful they were alone as John dumped his heavy duffle bag on the bunk.

"John," Owen spoke softly.

His nephew turned, wondering who knew his name.

John was rocked. "Jesus Christ, Uncle Owen, I can't believe it's you. I was hoping I would find you when I joined the Navy. You never told us the name of your ship."

He grabbed his uncle in a Cantrell bear hug, and for the first time since Amy's death, Owen allowed himself to cry. The two men found a quiet spot and talked for hours.

"No one knows anything about my past, John, only that I am from Virginia."

"Uncle Owen, they will never know anymore just because I am here. You are still everybody's favorite uncle. It was an awful accident, and Grandpa still says the blame is his because he railed at you to shoot anything that moved. The whole family still talks a lot about you and is always so happy to get your cards, even though you don't say much. I guess you remember that Axel is only one year younger than me, and he is in the Navy, too. We were both always trying to find you. Your secret will be safe with both of us. I reckon I won't be able to call you Uncle Owen on board. How about boss?"

Owen found himself laughing for the first time in years. He had given himself no quarter, and his utter grimness had been self-imposed for so long he had almost forgotten how. Owen was hungry for news of his family and was filled with wonder as he learned about nieces and nephews and how the family was scattering about the world.

"Thomas is in the Philippines, which makes Uncle Ben unhappy because he's only seventeen. Stephen is now an Army officer but still stateside. Me and Axel tried to get aboard the same ship, but it didn't work out, and he is stationed on the battleship Tennessee. Just wait until he hears we are shipmates."

It seemed a lifetime ago that he had sledded down snow-covered hills with his young nephews, and now at twenty and twenty-one, they would be going to war.

"Your records say you are a munitions expert with five years of experience, John. How did that happen?"

"Like you, Owen, I always wanted to be in the Navy, and I guess havin' my own gun and hunting by the time I was six years old just got me interested in firepower. I check everything before, and how it goes into the guns to make sure everything is fresh and ready to fire, but what I really like is to fire them big son-of-a-guns."

The very thought of John standing on board, manning the anti-aircraft guns in time of battle frightened Owen, and suddenly he felt that maybe God had a plan for him after all. He was here to look after his beloved nephew.

The Arizona steamed toward Pearl Harbor the next morning and her rendezvous with destiny.

***

The Cantrell clan was elated that John and Axel had found Owen. The family used Ben's address in town, and Ben always rushed letters to the mountaintop.

Isaac was extremely relieved to hear the good news. He still suffered his twin's agony, and he knew John and Axel would be like an elixir for Owen. He sat with Levi many evenings, listening to the depressing news of war as he worried about Owen and his nephews.

Shortly after the draft had been announced the year before, several of the young Cantrell men had volunteered for service. They chose to enter the branch of service that appealed to them rather than being assigned to one by the armed services.

Isaac cringed for his brothers as war drew ever closer. His sons were too young to go to war at this time, but who knew how long the war would last? He and Della were married for seven years before they were blessed with twin boys, now fifteen years old. Another son and two daughters followed, along with two additional rooms to the cabin.

In October of 1941, the downtrodden town of Elkinsville again prospered with a later generation, and with the same trappings. War materials were constantly rolling off assembly lines with Britain and Russia begging for more.

The hotel had been totally refurbished, and there was rarely a vacancy. Levi's wild game and prime beef were again served to timbermen and company officials, while his prize moonshine endowed their frosty mint juleps. Many visitors added an extra day to their stay as they lounged on the veranda with tall drinks.

John L. Lewis was now the driving force in mining. Laments were no longer taken to the foreman; they were settled by the Union. Lewis knew he held a winning hand, and he played it to the hilt. Even a threat of a walkout brought king coal to the bargaining table. Lewis's mighty roar and pounding fist on the table were heralded throughout the mining industry.

The miners placed him before God and country as the war progressed, and he left no opening untouched. Their savior had taken them from despair to what many thought of as affluent trappings in their new cars and numerous niceties. Their struggle had been long, miserable and without rewards until Lewis blessed them with prestige.

***

Owen and John Cantrell ate an early breakfast in the galley and were topside by seven-thirty in the morning. The Arizona lazed off Ford Island, with the repair ship Vestal moored outboard to begin pending repairs on Monday. The mighty bow of the Arizona extended one hundred feet beyond the Vestal. Owen loved this battleship, and he knew John would come to feel the same way he did. John was eager to get to his gunsite each morning, long before his duty began. The care with which he wiped dew from the machine guns and polished brass pleased his uncle. It was a beautiful Sunday morning even for Oahu, which was blessed by the elements. December 7 would make history for more than its seasonal trappings.

Owen and John waved their caps high, as they spotted Axel taking up his position on the Tennessee, moored only seventy-five feet astern of the Arizona. Both brothers were gunners, and both with the same position on their respective ships.

Owen was very proud of his nephews and reveled in the joy they had brought back to his life. Both tall, with sinuous muscles, were fearless. He knew they would both always fight to the bitter end, and he cringed inwardly. The most dangerous stations on the battleship were the anti-aircraft positions.

As each day passed, tensions were becoming more strained with Japan, and Owen knew the top brass felt that time was running out.

The fleet had been practicing war games and maneuvers in the Pacific waters for several months. Some of the more knowledgeable admirals were opposed to anchoring the fleet at Pearl Harbor within reach of Japan. They felt the West Coast of the United States would give a greater degree of safety, but the war office disagreed, and ninety-four ships were now anchored in the harbor. Eight battleships were lined up in pairs or singly on the Southeast shore of Ford Island. They bore the mark of death as the Japanese were determined to eliminate them.

"Look smart, John. Admiral Kidd just arrived on the signal bridge and Captain Van Valken high on the navigation bridge," Owen hissed.

As Owen spoke, the drone of approaching planes shattered the early morning quiet, and the element of complete surprise sealed their fate. In an instant, a torpedo blasted into the bow of the Arizona just beyond the Vestal. General Quarters sounded immediately throughout the fleet, but it was too late.

Owen and John leaped to the anti-aircraft guns and blazed a murderous arc as their shipmates opened fire in rapid succession. A heavy bomb struck near the second turret and penetrated deep into the Arizona's innards before exploding near the forward magazine. A horrendous explosion blew the Arizona into pieces. Flames shot five hundred feet into the air, with billowing black smoke covering the harbor. The horrific blast blew men off the decks of surrounding ships and threw tons of debris and body parts all over the harbor. Hundreds of men were incinerated above and below deck. Shortly after, a second bomb went down the stack, a third hit the boat deck, a fourth the number four turret, and four more struck the super-structure between the bridge and the tripod mast. The ship settled so fast she did not capsize. A total of eleven hundred and three men died. Many trapped below deck were drowned as she sank into her watery grave. Axel laced the sky with fire from his anti-aircraft gun, despite strafing by the Japanese planes, and two bomb hits. The West Virginia anchored outboard of the Tennessee sheltered her from aerial torpedoes and paid the supreme price. When his gun became too hot to hold, Axel jerked off his shirt, and wrapping the metal, never stopped firing. Screaming obscenities at the Japanese planes, he saw the forward deck of the Arizona explode in massive flames and smoke.

"God be with you, Owen and John," he sobbed unashamedly, knowing that John and Owen could not have survived. They had just signaled one another before the bomb hit where they stood. He was sickened as a severed hand landed at his feet, and he fired even faster.

"Oh, God, Axel, they have killed the Arizona," his buddy Jim Roberts screamed as the Arizona settled into the harbor water.

Sailors rushed ammunition to the gunners as the decks contin-ued to be strafed by low- flying Japs. Axel was exhilarated as he sent one plane flaming into the water. Fire rampaged on the deck and fearless men, unmindful of their safety, fought the blazes that were started by flying debris from the Arizona and the West Virginia. Burn-ing oil spilled from the Arizona, killing many survivors trying to reach safety. Sailors were horrified as they saw Japanese planes strafing the struggling survivors and the small boats attempting to rescue them.

"Bastards! Bastards!" Axel screamed and defiantly stood his ground and never ceased firing. The West Virginia took seven torpedoes on her port side and sank but had saved the Tennessee from greater dam-age. The West Virginia lost one hundred and five men out of a total of fifteen hundred and forty-one from superb and fearless action by all crewmen.

The Arizona took the brunt of total devastation, the worst in the whole fleet. Her casualty list was the greatest, and she was a total loss.

The eight battleships, being the prime targets, were hammered relentlessly with torpedoes, bombs and strafing. Airfields were devastated as were hospitals and numerous other ships in the fleet. When the last Japanese planes turned and flew toward their aircraft carrier, they left a devastated Pearl Harbor in smoking ruins but had opened the door for their own Armageddon.

CHAPTER 22

America was beyond shock by the monstrous, sneak attack on Pearl Harbor. The Japanese had committed an unpardonable sin against the United States of America and its people.

Radios blared day and night as Americans sat glued to the small boxes waiting for more devastating news, and more devastating news arrived shortly. Massive Japanese forces invaded the Philippine Islands.

Anger and complete fury quickly replaced shock in America. From every city, every town and every hamlet to the entire countryside, young men swarmed into recruitment centers. America was at war and at great risk. Both Japan and Germany had been training large numbers of soldiers and producing great numbers of ships, planes and armaments for years. Japan, America's greatest importer of scrap iron, had unleashed the end results on the United States with fury and without mercy.

The Cantrell family was dealt a severe blow with news that both John and Owen had died aboard the Arizona. Axel was heartbroken as he wrote to his family.

"I saw Owen and John just minutes before the awful explosion, and I knew they had been killed along with hundreds of their shipmates. I will fight the Japs with every ounce of my body, and each time I fire my anti-aircraft gun, I will give it double measure for them."

Ben had taken Axel's letter to his father and Carl as soon as it arrived, and he could well imagines his brother's sorrow. Hannah silently suffered the death of her son, and excruciating pain glistened in her black, Indian eyes.

Two days after Pearl Harbor, eleven young Cantrell men boarded a bus for Lexington and were sworn into the Army, Navy and Marines. Ben's brothers and their wives came down from the mountain with their sons, attempting to be brave, as they watched them leave the shelter of their love and march into hell itself. Ben felt his heart lurch. How many more of these fine, healthy young men would die? More of his nephews had volunteered when the draft had been instituted, and then there was his own family. Mary Jane sobbed as she hugged and kissed each of the boys goodbye. Two extra busses had been added today, as the town of Elkinsville rallied to the defense of their country.

Mary Jane was stricken when news of the Philippine invasion reached them.

"Oh, God, Ben, our Thomas is still a child at eighteen, and now he is fighting a war."

A gray-faced Ben could offer his wife no comfort. Their Stephen was still stateside, but Ben knew he could be shipped out any day.

A devastating blow was dealt them when Elizabeth called to say she had enlisted.

"My God, Elizabeth, why?" a shocked Ben had asked.

"Dad, Mike has joined the Marines, and our soldiers will need medical help. It is the least I can do. Over one third of the nurses here at Johns Hopkins have volunteered. I'll be stationed in England, and I hope you and Mom won't worry. I will be safe there."

Elizabeth's twenty-seven-year-old husband, Mike Kelly, a strong and fearless policeman had volunteered immediately. He and Elizabeth had married when she graduated from nursing school, and she stayed on at Johns Hopkins Hospital. Mary Jane had hoped for news of a grandchild coming from their three-year marriage, but instead she got an announcement that both were going to war.

For the first time in Levi's life, he felt helpless. He had always defended his family with his hands and his rifle, but now he watched as his grandchildren marched off to war in distant lands and could only agonize for their safety. In Owen's last letter, he had written that he would be coming home with John and Axel on their next furlough. Levi knew that his son had finally come back to the living only to die by Japan's treachery. He placed headstones for both Owen and John in the graveyard near Amy.

America kicked into high gear as their sons fought gallantly on numerous islands in the Pacific. Old factories were converted to produce planes and tanks, and shipyards were expanded tremendously. Automobile factories began producing planes and tanks.

Though thousands of young men were volunteering, the draft was increased to include all men between the ages of eighteen and forty-five years of age. The 1940 draft claimed only those between twenty-one through thirty-five. Thousands of women enlisted and relieved soldiers in noncombatant jobs.

Shipyards and armament factories pleaded for female workers, and the call was answered quickly by thousands of women from throughout the country. Many women who had never traveled farther than their small towns descended on cities and the many factories begging for workers. They took jobs that had never before been held by women. Assembly lines in plane factories employed more women than men. Many became welders, foremen and handled heavy machinery.

Japan continued to capture island after island in the Pacific and was gaining more ground in China, Burma and threatened India. American troops began arriving in India, and the bloody battle for the Burma Road began.

***

Mine foremen were begging for miners as more and more young men left to fight the war. Old miners, many with partial disabilities were welcomed back into the pits. Most of them had sons and grandsons fighting for the country, and they worked without a day off. War bonds were greatly needed to finance the tremendous arms buildup, and the miners put every extra penny into the bonds.

Alan Adams was devastated when the recruitment center classified him 4-F. Polio had left him with a slight limp, but it had not interfered with track and basketball in high school. The meager lift in his right shoe was no longer even noticed.

"Dad, all of my friends are already in uniform, and some have been shipped out. Is there anything you could do to get me into any branch of the service?" he pleaded.

Wesley was torn. He could not help but be relieved that Alan couldn't go to war, and yet, he could sympathize with his anguish at being left behind. He called John Wilkins and relayed Alan's frustration, hoping his friend could help.

"Wesley, I doubt there will be anything I can do, but I'll try. I'll talk to the doctors in the recruitment center in Lexington and get back to you. I know Alan could handle it, but even in war, there are rigid health requirements."

Alan sat dejected, as Wesley repeated the message to him. It was a cold March in the mountains, and he felt as cold as the snow covering the ground.

"I want to join the Marines, Dad. The news in Lexington says the Philippines will fall shortly, and God knows what will happen to Thomas Cantrell. He will sure as hell go down fighting, and it will be like losing Chaney all over again," and tears streamed down his face.

Dr. John Wilkins didn't call back but appeared at Wesley's door one hour later.

"Alan, I have bad news, but I also have good news. You will not be able to go into the service, but there is a much better way that you can help. Are you interested?"

"Yes," Alan didn't hesitate.

"Medical schools have rearranged their programs in order to graduate much-needed doctors as soon as possible. Your father has told me that you have taken on numerous hours each semester, so it is possible you can graduate at the end of December and enter medical school immediately. You could graduate in three years with an M.D. and work in any number of hospitals trying to put our soldiers back together. Many doctors are being drafted, and this war is going to be a long one, so your service in the medical field would be greatly appreciated."

"Thank you, Dr. Wilkins, I will give my all. I'll double my hours in summer school and even more so for the fall semester. I would like to go ahead and enroll now, if you would be kind enough to write a recommendation."

"That I will do, Alan, and I'll call a couple of classmates that are on the staff at UK so they can get the ball rolling."

Alan's air of dejection turned to one of eagerness and determination.

Wesley walked Wilkins to the door and could barely detain the tears filling his eyes.

"John, again you have come to our rescue. How can I ever thank you for the many times you have been there for this family?"

"And how many nights have you listened to my problems, Wesley?"

Wilkins had only Wesley to unload on when the pressure of losing patients threatened to overwhelm him. Mutilated miners were the hardest to give up, and the terrified faces of their families stayed with him.

***

A pall of desperation hung over the half-starved, disease-ridden troops on Bataan. The food supply, along with their strength, was dwindling by the day. In January, the daily food allotment had been decreased by half, and Thomas Cantrell had begun scouting the surrounding jungle. His upbringing in the mountains of Kentucky and Virginia had taught him what was edible and what was lethal.

Billy Lewis had been stricken with malaria the month before, and Thomas worried about his slow recovery. Medical supplies were close to being completely depleted as malaria and dysentery rampaged through the camp, feeding on weakened soldiers.

The Japanese were relentless in their attacks, but the Americans fought back with every ounce of their exhausted bodies.

Ammunition was running low, so Thomas constructed a large sling shot to bring down ducks, birds and, occasionally, even a deer. Whatever he could scrounge, he carried to Billy Lewis. Billy looked at some of Thomas's concoctions and wondered what kind of varmint they might contain.

"I cooked it real tender, Billy, and I think it tastes pretty good."

There was no way Thomas could disguise the frog legs, but at the insistence of his friend, Billy swallowed them.

General Edward P. King watched in agony as his troops grew weaker each day on starvation rations. The Philippine scouts, well-trained and relentless in battle, fought with the Americans without complaint, as hunger pangs gnawed at their stomachs. They distinguished themselves endlessly in defense of their homelands and families.

On April 9 of 1942, General King gave the order to surrender, knowing that a bloodbath would be the only alternative. Some commanders refused to surrender and were threatened with court-martial unless they followed orders. The American and Filipino forces had beaten back the Japanese attacks for four months with valor beyond description. Food and ammunition were running out, and they were beyond hopeless.

Brutal treatment began immediately after surrender with soldiers being bayoneted and beaten senseless with rifle butts. The march to Camp O'Donnell began at dawn the day after surrender. Several hundred men would begin the sixty-five-mile march each morning that required several days. April in Bataan was very hot, and the soldiers were made to march without water or food. General King requested the men be able to ride in available American trucks, but the merciless Japanese refused. After only a few hours of sleep at night, the soldiers were again headed into line.

By the third day of marching without food or water, men began to drop out of line. Irate Japanese screamed obscenities at the weakened men, ordering them back to the group. When some could not rise, they were either shot or beheaded by sword-wielding guards.

Some of the men became delirious and would fall on fly-infested, muddy puddles of water by the roadside. Many soldiers suffered from severe cramps and dysentery from the contaminated water, with many dying during the march or just after reaching Camp O'Donnell.

On day three, after the surrender, Thomas and Billy Lewis were headed into the starting lineup for the long march. The men were not allowed to wear hats, and the sun reached a boiling point by mid-afternoon. Thomas could see Billy begin to falter on several occasions and urged him on when the guards moved a few feet ahead.

"Billy, you can do it. I know you can. We are mountain people, and we are strong. We will show these damned Japs. Just put one foot in front of the other. Billy, it will soon be dark, and it will be cool."

By the time the group stopped, Billy was walking in a semiconscious state. Thomas walked close to him, so his friend could lean on him momentarily when the guards weren't watching. They were only allowed a few hours of sleep and still no food nor water.

Billy was flushed and feverish as they fell in line again. Thomas was surveying the landscape for any sign of foliage or rocks he could

347

possibly drag his friend into if the guards happened to turn their heads for even a second. As the morning wore on, Billy began to stumble more, and Thomas placed his arm around him for support and was shocked when the beetle-eyed Japanese guard let it pass. As noonday passed, the horrible knowledge of what they were up against was apparent. Headless bodies lay by the roadside. Many had been shot. Those in line who had begun to shamble and stumble walked straighter. Billy was beyond seeing. Thomas had begun to all but drag him, and as the heat blistered down upon them, Billy's legs buckled, and Thomas lifted him and carried him several yards before he was spotted by the guards. The guard was on him immediately, screaming and motioning him to put Billy by the roadside. Thomas kept walking, clutching Billy to his chest. Another guard, hearing the commotion, converged on them, and the two jerked the barely conscious Billy from Thomas's arms. Flinging him to the ground, the newly arrived guard raised his bayonet just as Billy raised a frail hand to ward off the blow. The blade ripped through his hand and deep into his chest. Billy's eyes found Thomas, registering utter shock as he took his last breath.

There was a loud humming in Thomas's ears and the piercing scream of an enraged panther erupted from deep inside him. His huge body sprang at the two guards as his strong hands latched on the backs of their necks like bands of steel, crushing their skulls together like eggs. Numbers of frenzied guards rushed toward Thomas as he grabbed a bayoneted rifle from a fallen guard. He disemboweled the foremost two and, slicing sideways, removed heads as they closed in. A roaring cheer went up from the agonized prisoners, and fear for their own lives was forgotten. A truck full of guards came roaring to the battle, and Thomas continued to rip them apart with the dripping bayonet. At least a dozen Japanese soldiers lay dead as the group finally backed off. Their rifles barked numerous times before a blood-covered Thomas slipped to his knees and keeled over. The entire formation of prisoners wept.

***

The pathetic line of prisoners finally moved out, and the Japanese carted their own dead, leaving the fallen Americans by the roadside.

A dozen Filipino guerrilla fighters rushed from their hiding place just inside the jungle, checking for any signs of life among the fallen. Juan Tecon sprinted to Thomas and knelt by the side of his good friend. Frantically searching for a pulse, he finally felt a very slow, steady beat. He was appalled by the amount of blood covering his clothes. He felt as though he could wring it out.

"He's alive," he whispered to the nearest man, and without another word, several men quickly picked Thomas up and disappeared into the dark tree line.

"He's bleeding to death, Juan," Pablo gritted his teeth, as blood continued to pour from numerous wounds in Thomas's body.

"Into the nearest cave," Juan ordered.

The group ran toward a camouflaged opening in the hillside and placed the unconscious Thomas on the cave floor. With sharp knives the men quickly cut away his blood-soaked clothes and began to wipe blood away from his dripping wounds. They placed wads of clothes from their backpacks over the wounds bleeding most profusely and held them in place with steady hands to stem the flow. His whole body was the color of putty, and Juan expected to hear death rales any second.

Thomas had been shot a dozen times and stabbed repeatedly with bayonets.

"I don't know how he could live through this, Juan, and he still fought on," Pablo said.

"He is a man beyond men, and I have to give him blood right now. He will never make it to the big cave," Juan said.

"We have no equipment. We'll have to send the fastest man to get supplies."

"No, we will have to do something now. He is on the verge of death," and a determined Juan closed his eyes for a few seconds to think and then gave orders.

"Pablo, find me several long, very strong, hollow reeds as fast as you can. Cayento, build a fire in back of the cave and start water boiling. I will give my own blood to Thomas."

"Juan, you will kill him for sure. How do you know your blood will match?"

"Because his blood flows in my veins. He saved my life with his blood, and it is payback time."

His friends were amazed by his revelation.

"But I still don't see how you can give him blood. We have no tubes or needles," Cayento said.

"I will show you. Just keep pressure on the wounds. We cannot allow him to lose any more blood."

A fire soon blazed, and water set boiling. Pablo returned quickly with a handful of various-sized reeds. Juan tested them for the strongest ones and finally grunted with satisfaction. He drew a long string through his chosen reed several times, then blew through it to remove any particles. He poked it through the foliage covering the cave to look for any loose slivers or debris. He did the same with two other reeds to have as backups and poured several cups of boiling water over and through the reeds. He then washed his left arm well and did the same for Thomas.

"You will have to hold him quiet and still, in case he should try to move. He cannot move," he repeated.

Several hands were placed on Thomas's legs, arms and head. The warriors stood in awe of their young leader. Although he was only nineteen years old, he stood several inches taller than his friends. Quick and always with a bright smile, he was fearless and a born leader.

He had joined the Filipino scouts at fifteen years old and had quickly gained the respect of the Americans training them. He always volunteered for the toughest jobs and perfected them. His greatest ambition was to become a doctor, and he knew his ticket to that dream would be through the Americans.

When his duty hours ended, he went immediately to the infirmary to assist in any way possible. He emptied trash cans and mopped the tile floors, even when they were clean. He studied the instruments when he sterilized them and watched each medical procedure. Some of the younger doctors became his friends and even taught him how to start blood transfusions.

He and Thomas were on patrol duty when the jeep he was driving veered over a mountainside after hitting a deer. Juan had been knocked unconscious, and a deep cut on his lower leg was bleeding profusely. Thomas, though groggy, had dragged him from the burning jeep just as fire engulfed the entire vehicle. After tying his shirt around Juan's leg, he had carried him up the mountainside, and a farmer had driven them to a small clinic. The doctor did a quick cross match of their blood, and Thomas was connected to Juan whose vein had been severed.

Juan would stop at nothing to save his friend's life. When he heard Bataan had surrendered, he led his group through the jungle to find Thomas and was horrified by what he had just stumbled onto. Only friends restraining him had kept him from running to Thomas's aid.

He had sharpened the ends of the reed to needlepoint, and as he bent over Thomas, he was steady and determined. A makeshift tourniquet was tied around Thomas' left arm above the elbow and one around Juan's left arm. He carefully threaded the sharpened reed into Thomas's vein and held it downward to be sure he had succeeded. Blood oozed from the opening, and Juan quickly inserted the other end into his own vein without wincing. Leaning over Thomas, he let his blood flow.

Juan was weak the next morning but exuberant that Thomas had a steady pulse and his bleeding had stopped. The men sat quietly in the cave as Japanese soldiers swarmed about the hills and the death marches continued.

***

Thomas was amazed when he awakened in the dark cave with Juan and his friend hovering over him. Pablo filled him in on the details of his near death and Juan's blood transfusion.

"I was only returning the favor, Thomas," an embarrassed Juan said as his friends proudly proclaimed the miraculous feat.

"We buried Billy, and I have his dog tags," Juan said, placing them around Thomas's neck. "We have hidden caves and supplies, and we'll leave as soon as you are able. Thousands of Filipinos and Americans have been killed, Thomas, and the torture is the worst."

Thomas played with Billy's dog tags and waited impatiently for revenge.

By September of 1942 the ranks of guerrilla fighters had ballooned into the hundreds. When surrender had been inevitable, numerous Filipino scouts, American soldiers and sailors had escaped into the jungle to avoid capture. The Filipinos guided Americans to their well-hidden caves, and their forces combined into fierce jungle fighters.

Thomas's superior night vision proved to be a bonanza. Night raids on food supplies and armaments kept the guerrillas well-stocked with both. The darkest of nights played to their advantage, with a stealthy Thomas leading the men over and around obstacles. He had long since lost count of the necks he had snapped in total darkness. "For Billy," he always reminded himself. Upon finding guards with broken necks and their stores completely emptied, frenzied Japanese soldiers would run screaming into surrounding areas with bayonets poking into the surrounding foliage.

The guerrillas and supplies were long since departed and had most effectively covered their tracks. Their numbers had grown so large that supplies were passed along a human chain, and by the time they had completely looted a storage area, the bounty was already being stashed in hidden caves.

Juan had been amazed when Thomas first told him about his night vision. Thomas had kept his secret to himself until night raids had made it necessary to confide in his friend. Gradually, the guerrillas knew he could ensure their safety with his gift, and they were in awe of the huge man who had refused to die when mortally wounded. Now he was guiding them into victories against their vicious enemy.

"Thomas, I thought you had cat eyes the first time I met you, but I was afraid you wouldn't appreciate the compliment," Juan said with a twinkle in his eyes.

"I have been told that before, and my father says he was always teased by his six brothers because his eyes were so different from the rest of his family. Grandpa used him at night to direct moonshine deliveries right under the nose of the law."

"You are mighty agile, too, especially for a big man. Does your father have the same gift?"

"Sure does. He was always getting his brothers in trouble because they tried his tricks and sometimes wound up with broken bones."

"Strange," Juan said.

From a distance, and sheltered by a dense jungle, the guerrillas watched the cruel treatment meted out by the Japanese on their prisoners, and Thomas's blood boiled. They watched as once stalwart Americans, reduced to near skeletons, were forced to dig graves and bury their comrades, who were dying like flies.

"We will have our revenge, Thomas," Juan promised, when he felt Thomas, in his rage, might run firing into the camps.

By mid-1943, so many supplies had been raided by guerrillas that the Japanese Army was sending out large numbers of heavily-armed troops to hunt down the hit and run elusive marauders. They had greatly underestimated the numbers and tenacity of the embittered foe they sought.

A construction company had vacated its site in such haste when the Japanese invaded that they had left behind a large stash of dynamite in a secluded storage bin. The guerrillas were elated when they happened on the explosives and held them in reserve for just the right time.

Guerrillas, totally camouflaged, wrapped themselves around and into tall trees, watching as two hundred Japanese soldiers crept through the dense jungle, looking for caves and guerrillas. The forces were making a thorough and wide sweep. By nightfall, the group had penetrated deep into the jungle. As darkness descended, they made camp and posted guards completely around the outer edge.

Thomas and Juan laid out their battle plans, as the tree watchers reported in after the force passed beneath them. The strongest, quickest and fiercest fighters were placed directly in front of the specific guard he would take out. Two backup men stood with him. The rapidly darkening, thick jungle was their greatest asset. They had long since learned to move without sound, even weighted down with machine guns and knives.

Juan was most unhappy with the job Thomas had assigned himself.

"Thomas, why can't we just take the guards out, then throw the dynamite into the camp?"

"Because they are heavily armed, and we can't get close enough to throw the dynamite into their midst. We could lose a lot of good men. We tested these vines when we knew where they would probably be camping, and I know it will work."

"We have tested half the damn vines in this jungle, and I'm beginning to think you are still ten years old Thomas. What did you do in those mountains in Virginia, except swing on vines all day?" Juan asked, shaking his head in wonderment at his huge friend.

"I'll be on the other side when you land, and for God's sake, don't forget to roll as soon as you drop. That much dynamite will leave a crater big enough to bury a boat."

Thomas checked and rechecked each stick of dynamite that had been tied tightly together and made sure the fuses were well placed in the center sticks. They had cut several strong vines during the day and concealed them in trees. They marked others in case the need arose.

The group was well acquainted with this area, and Thomas could hardly believe the Japanese had stepped into their trap. It was the perfect campsite, but the group had worried all day that the Japanese would miss it, even though they had moved in a straight line toward this end. A tangled jungle had parted enough to let a small frothing stream tumble over a large rock that lay in its path. It only surfaced for several yards and then disappeared into the jungle again. Numerous animals, drinking from the cool stream for years, had trampled and broken new growth leaving a sizeable clearing.

The excited chatter of the Japanese as they stumbled onto the water carried to the waiting warriors.

The strong, long vine that Thomas would need was anchored to a tall tree, and he knew from years of experience the vine would quickly flip back over the small waterfall as soon as it was released. A small, agile scout had climbed the tree at the edge of the clearing adding an extra rope to secure the vine on the last tree the vine was connected to. He hacked away a couple of limbs that could block the vine as Thomas swung out over the encampment.

Wane light from a sliver of a moon was screened out by the thick jungle foliage, and Thomas knew the advantage was theirs. Using the complete stealth of a panther, he circled the encampment, quietly stationing the guerrillas close to the guards. He and Juan had chosen taller men for the job who were expert at noiselessly snapping necks.

When Thomas returned to the dynamite site, he gave a perfect hoot owl call, learned long ago from the Cantrell family, and the group waited. Two scouts quietly appeared next to Thomas to signal the job was completed and well done.

Pablo helped Thomas loosen the strong vine, and two men held it in place. Thomas wrapped his large hand around the ropes, holding three separate bundles of dynamite. Getting a good grip on the vine, he signaled Pablo to light the three fuses in the center of each bundle. The plan had been practiced several times during the day, and the instant the fuses were lit, Thomas nodded the men to let go of the vine, giving him a strong shove on his way. Swinging quietly out over the sleeping soldiers, Thomas quickly flung the dynamite bundles into the encampment and landed in a tall tree on the other side.

Juan was shocked to see Thomas rapidly swinging from limb to limb, away from the dynamite before dropping to the ground. The group that waited to rescue him when he dropped from the vine had to race to catch up and just in the nick of time. They had barely dropped to the ground and tightly covered their ears when an enormous explosion ripped through the forest. When the fireworks ended, the group was up and running through the forest at breakneck speed. Fires were rapidly spreading around the perimeter of the huge crater. The guerrillas knew few, if any, Japanese had survived the earthshattering blast. There was no escape from the large, fiery ring.

CHAPTER 23

B en and Mary Jane were devastated when the Philippines fell and could only imagine the worst for Thomas. Levi knew in his heart that Thomas would survive, though no news of the fate of the soldiers could be learned.

Jenny and Wesley Adams went to Ben's house immediately on hearing the news to try to comfort them. Mary Jane sobbed in Jenny's arms, but Wesley could only offer Ben dry-eyed sympathy. It tore at Wesley's heart to think they had lost Thomas, also. He had practically lived with them for years, and Alan considered him his only surviving brother.

Numerous islands in the Pacific fell to Japanese armies, as did Hong Kong and Singapore. Americans were terrified. Germany and Japan appeared to be unstoppable.

The cry of "Remember Pearl Harbor" resounded throughout the country and the pioneer spirit of Americans exploded into action on every front. When Roosevelt called for an unbelievable 60,000 new planes in 1942, he was presented with 82,000 instead. Aircraft carriers were completed in fifteen months, through Herculean efforts by every worker. Tanks, trucks and all armaments were produced on the same level. America was fighting for her life. Anyone who could lift a hammer was working in shipyards and numerous factories throughout the country.

Elizabeth wrote often from England and worried about Mike who was somewhere in the Pacific. Stephen Cantrell was fighting with Patton, as he faced off with the Germans and their overpowering war machine.

Ben was doing triple-duty in the sawmills as more young men were drafted. Each month, busses rolled out of towns throughout the country loaded with men whose draft numbers had been called, leaving weeping family and friends at the bus stations. Too many would never return.

Mary Jane went to work in Ben's office to replace the forty-year-old bookkeeper who was drafted, leaving a family of four. Ben continued to send his weekly paychecks to his family with Mary Jane's blessing.

Movie theaters were packed to see the latest newsreels, and each was more depressing than the last. In May of 1942, finally there was a glimmer of hope when the U.S. Navy halted an assault on Port Morsby and checked an attack on Australia.

In June, the battle of Midway was a great victory for America as Admiral Chester W. Nimitz ambushed a large Japanese fleet preparing to capture Midway Island. Americans cheered the newsreels and gave vent to anger at the enemy by working harder.

Dreaded telegrams bearing news of American dead flooded towns and cities throughout the country, as thousands of gallant young men died fighting fiercely for their homeland.

The Cantrell clan was grateful at the end of each day when the dreaded news did not arrive at their door. Like many people, they had no idea where their family was stationed. Ben knew Stephen was with Major General Patton, but he got no news until Patton's Army invaded North Africa in November of 1942.

Patton, the formidable warrior, who dared give war the ugly names it deserved, instilled in his men the hate and savagery needed to defeat the most diabolical enemy of all time. His troops entered Casablanca and occupied French Morocco in record time, surprising the world and most of all, Germany. He was Germany's greatest fear, with a speed and surprise that surpassed their own blitzkrieg.

Ben and Mary Jane clung to each bit of news about Patton and prayed that Stephen was still alive. Americans lived with ration books, and few complained. Flour, sugar, meat, gas and tires were in short supply, and they were reminded daily by newspapers and radio that their fighting sons and brothers needed extra supplies on the front lines. Victory gardens replaced lawns as Americans gave their all.

***

Levi sat by Amy's grave, watching another spectacular sunset bathe the rich hills in amber and many shades of red. His family respected his daily visits to the graveyard and kept their distance. Aside from Isaac's four younger children, the compound had been practically emptied of vibrant, young life, and Levi missed his grandsons.

"Amy, our grandsons are fighting all over the world for their country, and I cannot tell our sons and their wives how fearful I am for their safety. Though we have no way of knowing what the damn Japs have done to Thomas, I know he is still alive. Ben and Mary Jane are pretty miserable about him, and yet I feel the time is not right to tell Ben our secret. God, how I miss you right now, Amy." Levi arose and made his way into the cave to relieve Hiram who was watching the low fires drying the sprouting corn.

Their beef, pork and wild game were bringing prime prices, and although Levi could have greatly increased the prices, he would keep them where they were. He had stacks of war bonds, and there would be many more.

John L. Lewis was again demanding more money and fringe benefits for his miners. When the coal companies balked, Lewis called for a walkout, and every miner left the pits. War production was in full swing, and Americans were fighting fierce battles all over the world. The country was outraged that miners would strike when coal was the lifeblood for factories and shipyards where planes, tanks and ships were rolling off assembly lines daily.

John L. Lewis was maligned in newspapers and radios for the lack of patriotism, and the miners along with him, but the miners refused to budge unless told to do so by Lewis. The coal companies finally gave in to Lewis's demand, and miners returned to the pits with a vengeance. Most worked overtime to make up for lost production.

Ben and Mary Jane treasured each letter they received from Elizabeth and Stephen. Elizabeth remained in England. It seemed to Ben that Stephen was circling the world with Patton. Soon, Sicily fell to the Allies, and their son wrote of Patton in glowing praise.

Jenny and Wesley Adams visited each family who received the

dreaded telegrams. The South Pacific, with its numerous islands, was taking a terrible toll on American lives, especially in Elkinsville. So many American boys simply disappeared in the steaming jungles.

The Adams gave their heartfelt sympathy and support to grieving parents, who had stood by them when they lost Danny and Chaney. They made short trips to see Alan in Louisville when they had saved enough rationing stamps to buy gasoline. Alan was totally immersed in medical school and got no vacations, as the students were being rushed through to fill much needed vacancies in the hospitals.

As the year turned to 1944, Americans had gained ground on all fronts around the world. They were reclaiming one island after another in the Pacific, but with a tremendous loss of American lives and an even greater loss for the Japanese. Italy and North Africa fell to the allies leaving the enemy stunned. Japan, especially, had greatly underestimated the Americans, believing them to be soft and easily discouraged. The dormant spirit of the early pioneers rose to the occasion again, with a savagery in battle that was overwhelming the enemy.

The early deaths of John and Owen had shrouded the Cantrell's with fear for so many of their grandsons fighting on numerous fronts.

"I, honest to God, had never expected to outlive any one of my sons, and especially my grandsons," Levi said to Ben when he came to deliver mail from around the world to his brothers and their wives.

"Pa, nothing will ever be the same, and life is not as it should be, but I am so proud of our family. You and Ma raised us to be strong, and to do whatever we had to do to survive, and we have all passed it along to our children."

"I can tell you now, Ben, that Thomas will survive. We have already lost some of the family, and I'm afraid there will be more, but Thomas will come home,"

Ben looked closely at Levi's eyes and saw something he did not quite understand. "Why do you say that, Pa?"

"It's just a feeling I have," but Ben knew there was something more, and he also knew the devil himself would not be able to get it out of his father unless he chose to do so.

***

On June sixth, 1944, in a region of northern France called Normandy, General Dwight D. Eisenhower commanded the largest seaborne invasion in history. Troops from the United States, Britain and Canada stormed ashore into a colossal battle of all time, one that turned the sea red. A young Cantrell died in the first onslaught, and another died three days later.

Hiram's youngest son, Jason, just turned nineteen and Floyd's third son, Lawrence, twenty-two, would remain beneath the sea of white crosses in Normandy with thousands of their comrades.

Mary Jane and Ben were heartsick as they delivered the crushing news to Hiram, Floyd and their wives. They stayed on the mountain for two days, trying to comfort the shaken families. Hiram and Floyd bore the news in stoic, Cantrell fashion, but their wives were inconsolable.

Long after Mary Jane had gone to bed, Levi and Ben sat talking on the wide porch. A shooting star streaked across the heavens as the two men watched.

"That's about how long the lives of our boys were, Ben. They were too young to die," Levi said sadly. The theater in Elkinsville was packed at each showing, and many left with tear-stained faces after watching the horror of war on newsreels. Every family in Elkinsville had either lost a loved one or knew someone who had.

On March sixteenth, 1945, Americans captured the Japanese island of Iwo Jima, as they closed in on Japan. The battle was fierce and bloody with the loss of 25,000 American soldiers. Elizabeth Cantrell's husband, Mike Kelly, was killed in the battle.

Mary Jane and Ben were heartbroken for their devastated daughter. Her letter was brave, but tears had smeared the ink in several places. "I cannot imagine my life without Mike, but I was blessed with his love for three years. I have watched so many young men die here in the hospital with wounds too horrible to describe. I hope and pray that Mike died quickly, and I know in my heart that he died with my name on his lips. I am working extra hours for my own wounds, as well as those of our brave and courageous men who are waiting impatiently to return to the front lines."

Massive bombardments of Germany were nonstop and the country lay in ruins. Factories, refineries, railroads and canals ceased to be. Hitler took his own life in Berlin on April thirtieth, 1945, and on May seventh, 1945, Germany surrendered unconditionally, ending World War II in Europe.

Japan had lost most of its empire but refused to surrender, though its military had been almost decimated. A frail and exhausted President Franklin D. Roosevelt died in April of 1945, and Vice President Harry Truman became President of the United States. Repeated demands by the allies for Japan's surrender fell on deaf ears and the entire Japanese population dug in to fight a bloody home war.

President Harry Truman, a man of great courage and determination, could not bring himself to sacrifice another million American soldiers after four years of barbarous, torturous treatment of Americans. Many were still held in slavery in Japan. The newly completed atomic bomb was dropped on Hiroshima on August sixth, 1945, with disastrous results, but the Japanese refused to surrender. On August ninth, 1945, he directed the second bomb to be dropped on Nagasaki. This time the Japanese surrendered. There was jubilation throughout America and the Free World.

***

Young servicemen returning to Elkinsville were given a hero's welcome, and families were shocked by the changes in their sons and brothers. Scores had left for the war in their teens, and the savagery they had experienced was written on their once innocent, young faces. Many were yellow from recurrent malaria and emaciated from bouts of dysentery over the years.

Thomas Cantrell arrived home just before Christmas. One long scar was barely hidden by the hairline on the left side of his face, and a small scar on his lower right jaw were the only visible signs of his ordeal. Mary Jane was ecstatic and couldn't pass Thomas without touching him. Food lined the tables and every cabinet, and Thomas finally had to refuse another helping. Stephen would return from Europe in June, but Elizabeth was not sure just when she would leave England. Ben felt like crying with happiness, an unthinkable reaction for a Cantrell.

The second morning after Thomas arrived, Jenny, Wesley and Alan Adams arrived laden with food and Christmas presents for Thomas. Alan had just graduated from a hectic three years in medical school and would soon start a rotating internship at the University of Kentucky. Both Wesley and Jenny had aged beyond their years, and Thomas's happiness at being home was suddenly dulled as memories of Chaney flooded back.

His fight for survival the past three and a half years and had pushed Chaney's memory aside, but now the sadness was back, although the acute guilt was no longer there. He had watched so many people die and regardless of what he did, he had not been able to stop it.

He suddenly thought of Juan. He felt as though he was parting ways with a brother when he boarded a troopship for home, leaving a tearful Juan and other close friends standing on the dock. General Douglas McArthur had returned to the Philippines as he had promised. His troops fighting bloody battles across the Pacific as they island-hopped toward the Philippines. The world and the fighting men would never be the same.

Thomas, Juan and other guerrillas had made life miserable for the Japanese but not without a high cost to the Filipino people. Many times after devastating raids on Japanese compounds, civilians were lined up and shot.

"Alan, I need to talk to you about a friend in the Philippines. Could we go somewhere where we can talk alone?" Thomas said.

The two young men hiked to the high school gym that was totally deserted over the holiday season.

"I'm not ready to tell my parents what happened just yet, Alan," Thomas said and proceeded to give Alan an exact account of what had happened in the Philippines, the near starvation of the troops before surrender and the horror of the death march where Billy Lewis had died, and how Juan had saved his life with a miraculous blood transfusion and nursed him back to life.

Thomas pulled his sweater to his chin, and Alan gasped. His entire torso, front and back, was scarred by numerous bullet wounds and ugly scars inflicted by Japanese bayonets.

"My God, Thomas, I can see why you don't want your parents to see this just yet. It seems to me Juan could already pass a medical exam with his firsthand knowledge. I'll talk to my dad tonight about the quickest way to get him to this country, and then we'll contact Dr. Wilkins. He always has strings he can pull at the University of Kentucky. I just don't know how you managed to live through all of this."

"I was luckier than thousands of our soldiers, and the tortures the Japs put them through will always haunt me."

Alan threw his arms around Thomas, and they cried for all their friends who would not be coming home.

Thomas was greatly relieved to know that Alan would start the process of bringing Juan to America. He had come to love and appreciate the Filipino people who had rescued so many Americans, at the peril of death if they were caught. He and Juan had shared their hopes and dreams many nights, as they hunkered down around campfires deep in jungle caves. Juan's burning desire to become a doctor had spilled over to Thomas. He knew he would go to school after the war but was still undecided about a major.

Thomas, along with thousands of other young soldiers, enrolled in colleges throughout the country. He would begin his studies at the University of Kentucky in early June. Alan Adams was elated that he and Thomas would be in the same town.

The Cantrell clan was planning a reunion for the first week of June at the compound, and Levi was busy directing the preparations. Thomas spent a week with Levi, with his grandfather hanging onto his every word.

"Grandpa, is it alright if I sleep in the cave for a couple of nights? I have always had a special feeling when I am there."

"You never told me, Thomas," Levi said as his heart thumped in his chest. "What kind of feelings?"

"It's like I'm in another place, but I don't know where. I'm up high, looking at things beneath me, and I feel so powerful and so peaceful. It's as though I will never have anything to be afraid of, and right now, I need that feeling after what I've been through."

Levi's stoic expression never wavered as deep emotions surged through him. He had been so afraid the cat marking on Ben would be violent and uncontrollable, but the opposite had happened. And now Thomas was following his father's footsteps.

Thomas had related to Levi how his night sight had guided the Filipino guerrillas on night raids against the Japanese and had been invaluable in overpowering the guards.

"Grandpa, I thought of you so many times when we hid in caves in the Philippines. I even pretended at times that I was here in this cave and didn't have to go looking for Japanese the next day."

The two men swept the floors of the caves and constructed long rustic tables for the entrance room. Thomas scampered up and down the long ladders placing fresh pine knots all the way to the ceiling. Most of the young Cantrell men would be home for the reunion except for two, who would have to remain overseas for a period with occupation forces.

As the two exited the cave, Thomas looked around the compound and didn't see any of the women.

"Grandpa, I'm gonna strip down to my shorts and take a bath in my favorite waterfall," Thomas said as he began peeling away his clothes.

"I don't want you to be shocked, Grandpa, because my wounds have healed completely," and drew his undershirt over his head.

Levi uttered a low, vicious growl of rage and horror when he viewed the multiple scars on his beloved grandson's body.

"This one is the worst," Thomas said, as he lowered his shorts almost to his pelvic area. A huge, ugly scar extended from his waist almost to the top of the hip joint. The Jap soldier had evidently meant to disembowel him.

"Them sons-of-bitches, we should have fried their whole goddamned country," Levi bellowed, shaking with rage.

"Other than lookin' like hell, they really don't bother me, and I can't wait to have you meet Juan," Thomas had talked to the family many times about Juan and how he had saved his life.

As icy water pounded his huge body, turning it pink, Levi said aloud, knowing Thomas could not hear him, "Thomas, you are truly the son of the cat," and his silent thoughts turned to Amy.

"Amy, as I watch our grandson beneath the waterfall, I feel as though you are here with me. I can almost feel your softness in my grasp. I remember well the day we stood under the waterfall, washing the panther blood from your body. You were completely covered in it, and you were so afraid. Little did we know what it would come to. I never told you how close I came to drowning Ben as a baby. I really thought he would be as wild as a panther, and we wouldn't be able to control him. My God, forgive me for even having that awful thought, and I could never bring myself to tell you even after Ben turned out to be so special. I must tell you Thomas is even more special. You should see what them Jap bastards did to him but, by God, they couldn't kill him," and he shook with fury.

***

Levi visited the family graveyard two days before his grandsons arrived to be sure there was not even one tiny weed in the enclosure.

The headstones of his three grandsons and Owen always brought extreme sorrow to him.

"Amy, at least you were spared the misery of losing these fine boys but, God, how I miss you. Our grandson, Thomas, will be great someday. I don't know how or when, but he will be. By the end of summer, I aim to tell Ben our secret. I'm eighty-seven, and I feel good but that don't mean I can't drop over like a rock, and he needs to know."

He still hoed corn and pulled his duty in making moonshine, even thought his sons had urged him to leave the hard work to them. He helped with the foaling of new colts and knew the markings of each new calf. His hair and heavy mustache were the color of burnished steel and his dark, brooding eyes could still strike fear into the heart of an adversary. His greatest disappointment had been the fact that he couldn't go to war with his grandsons.

Extra busses had to be added to the bus line to bring numerous soldiers home from war. They arrived daily at the bus stations and into the arms of families who had lived in agony during the war, praying for their safe return.

The Cantrells began arriving in late May in batches of two or three. Mary Jane and Ben meet each of them at the bus station, and Ben would ride to the compound with them, returning the next morning and turning the horses out to pasture to wait for the next arrival.

On the May twenty-eighth, 1946, Mary Jane and Ben waited at the bus station to meet Hiram's son, Jess. He stepped briskly from the steps, quite handsome in his well-fitting uniform and turning, offered his hand to a tall, beautiful soldier with colonel bars on her shoulders.

A scream erupted from Mary Jane's throat and people turned to stare at her. Elizabeth Cantrell Kelly stepped from the bus and into the arms of her family. Mary Jane could not stop sobbing, and Elizabeth held her like a child. Ben was dumfounded and speechless. Jess collected their bags and was ready to hike up the mountain, but Ben wouldn't hear of it.

"It's late, Jess. I will ride up early in the morning with you."

"Please, Jess," Elizabeth said.

"Talked me into it," a tired Jess grinned. Elizabeth had always been his favorite cousin, and they still had much to talk about.

"I wasn't sure I would be able to get here for the reunion, Mom, but at the last minute, I was able to hitch a ride on a DC7, and here I am. I knew you would work like a Trojan getting everything readied, so I just decided to sneak in."

"Oh, Elizabeth," Mary Jane said and cried again.

Elizabeth would not tell them her co-workers had all but bound and gagged her to get her onto the plane. Dr. Erick Newhouse, the surgeon in charge, had been concerned about Elizabeth since Mike's death. She was the chief surgical nurse, and, after surgeries were completed, she made rounds on the wards, comforting the patients and writing letters for many. The circles beneath her eyes had become darker each week, and her sense of humor that had been the glue holding them together in the worst of times was completely gone. When Elizabeth had vaguely mentioned her family reunion to a friend in surgery, the group decided she must go. Dr. Newhouse made one request, bring me a bottle of Kentucky moonshine.

Elizabeth had been so surprised to bump into Jess Cantrell at the train station in Washington, and by the time they reached the bus station in Abington, Virginia, she found herself relaxing as she and Jess traded war stories. It was good to be home.

Elizabeth slept for most of her first two days at home and awakened rested for the first time in months. She was neither shocked nor appalled by the changes and scars on both of her brothers. She had lived with it for nearly four years. She cried the first few times she talked about Mike, but with the love and devotion of the family, her healing began. She considered it nothing less than a miracle that both Thomas and Stephen had survived the brutal battles of the long war.

The day after Stephen arrived, Ben and his family rode up the steep mountainside to the compound. Both he and Mary Jane were so grateful to have their children home, complete happiness radiated from both of them. Ben thought Mary Jane looked ten years younger, and she could not stop smiling at her handsome family. Both Thomas and Stephen were solicitous of Elizabeth, holding heavy, overgrown branches aside that threatened to slap her in the face.

Elizabeth's eye twinkled as she kicked her horse in the side, overtaking them as she crashed through underbrush, shouting back, "I could always outride the two of you," and streaked up the steep incline with both brothers in hot pursuit.

"Dammit, Liz. You haven't changed a bit," Stephen bellowed. "You always had to be first."

"I still outrank you, boy," she called back, and the hills rang with their laughter.

Ben's heart beat with such joy he thought it would surely burst through his chest. His hellish nightmares about his children had kept him awake night after night, as he tried to put up a brave front for Mary Jane, whose anguish threatened to overtake her as the years dragged on with no word of Thomas.

As the group reached the high border of Kentucky and Virginia, Thomas sensed Levi before he saw him galloping toward them. Clasping Stephen's hand he leaned over, hugging him and then rode to Elizabeth. Dismounting, Levi held his arms upward and lifted her from the saddle. She fell weeping into his arms as he stood patting her tenderly. Tears streamed down Mary Jane's face, and none of the men moved until Elizabeth finally wiped her eyes, and Levi helped her back into the saddle.

It was a raucous greeting that welcomed the group as they cleared the tree line and descended to Levi's home. They rang cowbells and hooted while passing flat bottles of moonshine back and forth.

"I never saw anything wilder than this bunch," Stephen said as he tethered his horse and joined the fray.

Tears, hugs and kisses were lavished freely on all the returning warriors. A huge meal had been prepared to celebrate the homecoming, and Mary Jane helped Ben unload the extra food they had carted up the mountain on a packhorse. The three-day festivities had begun. The family would then scatter to the four winds, but this time together was special.

As soon as the reunion date was agreed upon in the spring, Levi decided what he wanted to do. His moonshine for his returning heros would be the best he had ever turned out, and that would be a tall order. He chose the best ears of corn from his storage and spent several hours each morning on his front porch shelling the glistening kernels. None but the most perfect would be used, and he even decided they should be the same size, it just might make the fermentation smoother. He kept watch on the low fires around the fermenting barrels and hovered over the straining of mash into the copper pots. As the last run dribbled into the barrels, he knew it was the best. He had instructed Hiram to buy new pails and dippers in town, and now half a dozen pails sat on the long table in the front cave awaiting the celebration.

After the supper table had been cleared, the family walked to the graveyard as an early summer sun balanced on the high, wooded horizon, casting long shadows over the peaceful homestead.

Axel Cantrell bent and kissed the headstones erected for his brother, John and Uncle Owen. He had sailed with Admiral Nimitz through hell itself, and each time he brought down a Japanese plane, he pledged it to their memory. Hiram and Floyd's sons' markers were close by, and memories of them were related among the group. Elizabeth stopped in her tracks as she came to the fifth headstone. "Michael Kelly, beloved husband of Elizabeth Cantrell Kelly. Born January 10, 1912 - Died on Iwo Jima, February 1, 1945."

Elizabeth was stunned. She turned deathly white and shook uncomfortably, she had no tears left. Ben put his arms around her, and she leaned into him to keep from falling.

"Pa thought Mike should have a place here with the family heros, and we all agreed," Ben said.

"I thank you from the bottom of my heart, all of you. I can't think of a greater tribute to Mike. He so adored my rugged family and loved coming here," Elizabeth said, and Ben turned her toward the house.

The tired and war-weary group of young people slept late the next day, completely lulled by the mountain stillness. They awoke to a cool, early June morning and a dazzling array of wild flowers covering every nook and corner. Heaps of succulent honeysuckle climbed over the rail fences, spinning into the yard, wafting the sweetest of aromas.

Levi and Elizabeth stood on the wide front porch, as she clutched a cup of hot coffee. Her thick, black Cantrell hair was still tousled, and a look of pure serenity was etched on her face.

"I had forgotten what it was like, Grandpa. I was beginning to think everything was death and destruction. I feel as though I have been transported to another planet."

Levi smiled at his beautiful granddaughter, who now stood to his shoulder. Elizabeth had inherited Mary Jane's green eyes but Amy's height and porcelain skin.

Isaac's three young daughters were in awe of Elizabeth and planned to become nurses at Johns Hopkins as soon as they completed high school. Both of Hiram's daughters had married boys from Elkinsville and lived in town with their own families, but none resembled Amy the way Elizabeth did. Fifteen gallant grandsons were home for the reunion, and Levi was counting his blessings. Losing Owen and three grandsons had been a bitter pill to swallow, but he considered it a miracle that so many had survived the bloody war in which they fought in every part of the world. He kept a stack of batteries in the kitchen just in case he should run out and couldn't hear the latest news. Levi, who only knew the names of a few states when the war began, was totally acquainted with every state and country in the world. Ben had brought him maps and, together, they had marked the whereabouts of the fighting Cantrell man.

As the woman busied themselves in the kitchen preparing the first day of feasts, Levi herded the menfolk into the cave. Thomas had climbed ladders most of the morning, lighting torches throughout the cavern. Levi was up before the crack of dawn, as ususal, and had filled the six-gallon pails with his perfect moonshine, placing them in a row on the long table he and Thomas had constructed weeks before. Each pail held two dippers, and Thomas was amazed as he watched his agile grandfather placing roughhewn benches around the table.

"Grandpa, this is a G.I.'s dream, a cave full of great moonshine. We should have invited the regiment," and doubled over with laughter.

"You think they'll like it?" Levi worried.

Thomas gave him a bear hug.

"Grandpa, they'll love it."

The crowd of young men whooped it up as they came into the large cave, blazing with fiery torches. They were young boys again, and their fathers rejoiced with them.

Axel Cantrell was the first to sip the moonshine, and it fired all the way to his toes.

"Good God, Grandpa. I think somebody lit a fire in my stomach. We should've shot this at the damn Japs," and the party began.

The young men wandered through the well-lit rooms, all converging by the waterfall.

"There were times when I thought I would never see this again," Jess said. He had slugged his way along the Burma Road, watching his buddies die or become mangled for life.

The young men exchanged stories as their fathers and grandfather listened with rapt attention.

"Grandpa, there is one warrior missing in here," Stephen said, and Levi agreed.

"I'll get her. Hey, everybody, I'm gonna bring Elizabeth in, our very own female soldier."

"Yeah, Elizabeth. Rah, rah, rah!" The group chanted as the moonshine had begun to spread cheer, and laughter echoed throughout the cave.

Elizabeth had visited the cave only twice in her life, after being sworn to eternal secrecy. She was unprepared for the sight that met her eyes.

Most of the men were slightly drunk and drinking more as they stood in a long line and sang "For She's A Jolly Good Fellow."

Elizabeth burst into laughter as the tipsy group toasted her good health. Thomas brought a glass of moonshine to Elizabeth.

"Didn't think a nurse would want to drink out of their dipper," and gestured toward the group, as he swayed slightly toward his sister.

"Thomas Cantrell, I'm so surprised at my little brother. You are drunk."

"Shucks, everybody else is, too," he slurred.

Ben, standing by Thomas, threw his arm around his son, "I'll see that he don't fall off the mountain, Elizabeth," and again the group shouted with laughter.

Elizabeth, looking at the two of them in the dim light, saw that both their eyes glowed like those of a cat. "My God," she thought, "something is unnatural here, but I don't know what it is."

The group departed the mountaintop three days later, hung over, but beginning to put the war and its horrors behind them. The reprieve had been desperately needed. The young men would be scattered to all parts of the country. Several would be starting to colleges and universities throughout the area. The G.I. Bill had been created to allow returning soldiers to attend schools of their choice in return for laying their lives on the line for their country. Young people who had never dreamed of being able to attend college now flocked to classrooms. Matured beyond their years, their ambitions had changed and taken hold.

Stephen Cantrell, now a major, would leave the service in the fall and head toward law school.

Elizabeth had decided to remain in the Army and received orders to report to Walter Reed Hospital in Washington, D.C. She carefully packed the flat bottle of moonshine for Dr. Erick Newhouse. She knew he planned to return to his private practice in D.C., where his wife and two children were, no doubt, waiting anxiously for his return.

CHAPTER 24

Thomas Cantrell sat in classrooms surrounded by large numbers of returning soldiers, and the instant camaraderie was a special bond. He was surprised to find classes so easy, but, then Thomas would always master most things easily. Upper class female students were delighted with the influx of older men. They had outnumbered male students ten-to-one during the war years, and tall, handsome Thomas Cantrell found himself surrounded by admiring young women.

Weekends were spent in night clubs with blaring nickelodeons and wild jitterbugging. "Boogie Woogie," "Jersey Bound" and numerous swinging tunes by Jimmy Dorsey and Glen Miller kept the floors shaking into the wee hours. Release from war tensions in a generation of young people who had forever changed the country, stoked ambitions and the need to make up for lost time.

Alan Adams joined the group less than half a dozen times during the summer. A grueling routine of forty-eight hours on duty and twenty-four off was standard for interns, which amazed Thomas, but Alan assured him it was only for a year.

"That's because you are dead by the end of it," Thomas said.

"Glad to see you getting back into shape, Cantrell," Alan retorted, rolling with laughter after polishing off a second beer on a rare night off.

Thomas's date was a senior, majoring in education. The student nurse with Alan was dazzling. Alan watched Thomas cover the dance floor in record time with his long legs and an agility that was amazing. Girls lined up to dance with him. "Strange," Alan thought. "How could anyone so big move so fast with total grace?"

Many evenings Thomas would meet Alan in the hospital cafeteria for dinner. "Most people can't stand hospital food, Thomas," Alan said, on one occasion watching Thomas dig into the unappetizing food.

"After three years in the jungle, scrounging for snails and fresh-skinned snake, it's a feast. You appreciate food, period."

"You're making me sick, Thomas."

"Just enjoy your hospital food."

On more than one occasion, Alan was called away in the middle of his meal for emergencies. He knew that before midnight Thomas would arrive with hamburgers and French fries to make up for his lost dinner. Student nurses were always eager to help Thomas find his friend and insistent on taking him to Alan.

"Not everybody gets the guided tour," Alan teased. Thomas seemed totally unaware that he was being ogled.

Thomas was never sure just what emergency Alan would be attending. The night he found him asleep on a stretcher just outside the delivery room, he had not been able to meet Thomas for dinner. Knowing it was the last hitch of his forty-eight hour watch, Thomas knew his friend should eat.

A bleary-eyed Alan sat on the stretcher and devoured a fried chicken dinner. "God, Thomas. What would I do without you?"

"Not nearly as well, I'm sure," and his exhausted friend laughed while still chewing food.

"It's midnight, Thomas. Don't you ever sleep?"

"I'm sleeping better, but it all comes back when I close my eyes. They say it gets better with time."

Alan's heart went out to him. "Anything I can do? I can get sleeping pills."

Thomas shook his head. "If it gets too bad, but so far, I can handle it."

"God, how I wanted to go to war. I stretched my leg like hell and even willed to get it longer."

"You are one hell of a doctor, Alan, and that is the most important, and just what're you doing on this damn stretcher?"

"That's the delivery room through those swinging doors, and the patient says that none of her seven children were born in a delivery room, so I put her on the delivery table to be sure number eight will, at least, be delivered there."

"Dr. Adams," a nurse screamed from the delivery room, and Alan tore through the swinging door. Thomas left in the other direction shaking his head.

Thomas had much to do before leaving for a week at home, as the last summer session ended. Juan Tecon would be arriving in two weeks from the Philippines. Wesley Adams and Dr. Wilkins had pulled out all the stops to get Juan into UK, and Thomas would be forever grateful to his friends. He was moving into a larger apartment he would share with Juan, and he could hardly wait to see his friend. He would spend only one week at home, but he knew Mary Jane and Ben would understand. They were looking forward to meeting the young man who had saved their son's life. Thomas wanted everything ready and waiting, and his excitement grew daily. Juan would love America.

Alan Adams stood on the hospital steps with a duffle bag in hand and waited for Thomas to pick him up. He had insisted on driving Alan to Elkinsville for a few days of badly needed vacation. Thomas and Alan had become even closer friends during the summer, and each felt a brotherhood for the other. Though three years younger than Alan, Thomas felt fiercely protective of him. Alan had just ended another forty-eight-hour shift and stuffed the pillow Thomas had brought along against the window, sleeping before his friend could even start the car.

Looking at his peacefully sleeping friend, an eerie feeling came over Thomas. An ominous echo of fear. He shook it off. He had lost so many friends, it must be an ingrained apprehension.

Thomas had begun an accelerated march toward pre-recognition, a journey that would change his life and lead into realms he had not dreamed of.

He gloried in the beautiful mountains as he roared around hairpin curves and over high bridges. Several times he placed a staying hand on Alan to keep him from falling forward. He swayed with the pitch of the car. Thomas laughed aloud as he watched him sleep soundly throughout the ordeal.

Arriving in late afternoon with a still sleeping Alan, he pulled into the Adams' driveway. Both Jenny and Wesley sat on a shaded front porch, waiting for them. They descended on the car immediately, and Thomas's heart ached as Wesley gave him a bear hug. Deep creases lined his sallow face, and thick, snow white hair fell across his forehead. His body was beginning to stoop, and an emaciated frame did little to hold it up. With one arm still around Wesley, Thomas hugged sprightly Jenny whose brave heart refused to wither. Large, deep brown eyes that threatened to overtake her small face reflected her love for Thomas.

Alan awakened from a near semiconscious sleep and was momentarily confused by his surroundings. "My God, Thomas. Are we home already?"

Jenny and Wesley laughed at his disorientation, as he climbed from the car and into their arms, their faces illuminated with immense love and pride for their only surviving son. Thomas's heart swelled with joy as he watched their heartwarming reunion.

Mary Jane watched the driveway from her kitchen window as she prepared Thomas' favorite foods and readied a near feast. A tortuous three-year wait to learn whether their son was dead or alive, and now he would be arriving home from college in a few minutes. Short, curly, dark auburn hair framed a still beautiful face with worry lines lightly creased into her forehead. Dark shadows beneath her green eyes began to disappear as soon as news of Thomas' survival reached them, and she finally slept through the night. The mill had called with an emergency, and a disgruntled Ben had to leave, but Mary Jane knew he would beat a fast track home as soon as possible.

She flew through the screen door when Thomas' car turned into the driveway, waving a dish towel like a beacon. Her tall son lifted her into the air as she screamed with happiness. By midnight, Thomas was yawning while his parents were still peppering him with questions, and finally relented when it looked as though he might fall out of his chair.

Two days later, Ben and Thomas saddled horses and headed for Levi's homestead. Thomas wanted to see his grandfather before beginning the long fall semester. A swirling canopy of sounds enclosed them as they left town and rode into tall timber. A feeling of complete tranquility and belonging settled over Thomas as the smell and movements of wildlife abounded through the forest.

Ben always chose the largest and fastest horses from Levi's farm, keeping them in shape on the government land surrounding his acreage. Thomas marveled as the big horse he rode attacked the steep mountain trail without breaking a sweat. In the distant forest, Thomas heard the faint scream of a panther and saw his father place his hand on the rifle holstered on his saddle as his horse climbed the vertical trail ahead of him.

"He's a long way off, Dad."

"You never know where his friends might be, but I have never had to shoot a panther. They usually shy away from humans."

"I would like to see one, but I'll bet they are afraid to come near Grandpa. He guards his farm against beasts and humans, and I have no doubt he would kill for that place."

"I think you are right," Ben said, and thought to himself, he has already killed. He remembered the drunken Hungarian who had threatened to go to the law and remembered a very bitter Agent Jackson who was convinced Levi had murdered his partner. He always thought it strange that Jackson had been killed from an ambush just after Hiram warned him he was being watched and his truck searched by the agent.

They arrived at the compound by mid-afternoon, spotting Levi standing by the yard gate, watching the trail. Thomas could feel his intense eyes settle on him and touched the horse's flank to race to his grandfather who responded with a rare, wide smile.

Ben watched with pride as his father and son embraced. There had always been a special bond between the three men, and it continued to puzzle Ben. He knew Levi would not hesitate to give his life for any of his sons and grandsons, but there had always been something different with him and Thomas.

After a huge dinner with all the relatives, Thomas hiked to the highest point above the farm to watch the sunset. He had been so confined at school among so many people, he craved a period of solitude. He watched as a blood-red sun sank low and cloaked the enchanted forest in crimson. Suddenly, a sense of impending danger crept over him, and his body tensed. He quickly looked about his surroundings but found only peace and quiet. "God," he thought, "I must be reliving that damnable war again," but he realized this was something different.

Levi could sense a change in Thomas the minute he stepped onto the porch where he and Ben sat talking quietly.

"You okay, Thomas?" he asked, and Ben was also aware of something amiss.

"I'm just not used to being by myself. So many people at school and no place to get away to."

Levi was not convinced.

The three sat on the wide porch and watched a full moon light up the mountains, as wildlife slipped noiselessly about, preying on the smaller and slower animals.

Thomas was unable to sit still and walked about the illuminated yard listening to night sounds, as calves and new colts scrambled to find their mothers. The men finally retired for the night, and Thomas had the large sleeping loft to himself.

He tossed and turned, even after willing himself to lie still and tame his ranging thoughts. Directly beneath him in his own bed, a worried Levi lay sleepless also. Levi had hunted and stalked animals for years, and he recognized the reaction of animals when they sensed danger and fear. It suddenly dawned on him. Thomas was about to be tested again. He would ask Ben to come back to the mountains as soon as Thomas left for school. Ben must be told the secret so he could help to guide and protect Thomas.

After they left the next morning, Levi wandered down to the fish pond and stopped suddenly. Huge panther tracks along the muddy bands were deeply imprinted, but they had been made the evening before. The cat had followed them home.

***

Several friends decided to treat Thomas and Alan to lunch the day before their return to Lexington. They met at the same restaurant that had been their lifelong hangout on Main Street, and friends that Thomas had not seen since high school joined the group. Thomas was extremely tense even as he greeted old friends and tried to disguise his unrest. Many were just home from the war, trying to put their disrupted lives back together.

Two of the young men were mining engineers who had been classified four-F as Alan had been and had spent years underground protecting miners who dug fiercely for the war effort.

"Did I hear you say you had never been in a mine, Alan?" Jim Ferguson asked.

"No, I haven't, and some of my patients have found that hard to believe. They think all mountain boys start digging coal by the time they are twelve."

"Who else hasn't been in a mine?" Ferguson asked.

Two others confessed, but Thomas said nothing.

"How about you, Thomas? You're being mighty quiet."

Thomas simply shook his head no. "Never figured I was missing anything, though. Been in lots of caves," and the skin around his forehead tightened.

"Well, that's not the same," Ferguson said. "Clint and me are due to check out number four, and I'm inviting you guys who are ignorant about the guts of our hills to go along," and the group shouted with laughter.

"I'm ready," Alan said and thumped Thomas on the back. "You ready?"

An oppressive feeling gripped Thomas. The hair on his arms stood up like hackles.

"Alan, we need to get packed and ready to leave early tomorrow. How about our next trip back?"

"Oh, hell, it won't take more than an hour and a half," Ferguson insisted.

"Thomas, I'll see you later today, if you don't want to go," Alan said.

As the group was leaving, a paralyzing fear assaulted Thomas, and he had trouble moving his legs but turned to go with Alan.

The tunnel into the mine was well-lit. Huge bolts screwed into the ceiling held the mountain in place above. The deeper they traveled underground, the more agitated Thomas became.

"Thomas, you okay?" Alan asked picking up on his unusual quiet.

"I don't like this, Alan, and I think we should get the hell out."

"Ferguson is gonna be pissed if we leave. He just wants to show us his safety measures."

"Go back with me, Alan, now!" Thomas demanded. His senses

had already detected the coming explosion, and he grabbed Alan's arm who had already decided he had to go with Thomas. The two raced toward the entry, with Thomas in the lead. A horrendous explosion fired through the tunnel carrying the two men two thousand feet beyond the entry, dropping their bloodied and battered bodies like rags.

Trees trembled on the mighty Pine Mountain as the explosion erupted. The hulking mass appeared to sigh as it settled back to its former stance and watched as "The Dark and Bloody Ground" usurped another offering and again waited.

Judge Wesley Adams sat in the worn and scarred courtroom that had been his home for twenty-eight years. Totally unaware that fate was riding the crest of a terrible crescendo that would ensnare the last vestige of his being. There had been no warning this time. Lettie Mullins had wrested her final revenge and was at peace.

Hiram Cantrell rushed back to the mountaintop to deliver the devastating news to Levi. He had been in town when the explosion occurred and hurried to the hospital where Mary Jane and Ben sat outside surgery in shocked silence, waiting for word of Thomas.

"They say he might not live through the night, but they are doing everything they can," Ben said with tears rolling down his face. "Alan Adams was dead before he hit the ground."

"Oh God, Ben, how could something like this happen to them boys. You can't let Thomas die, Ben, he has been through too much. I'm goin' to go get Pa," Hiram said.

His horse pounded down the trail at breakneck speed, and Levi knew something terrible had happened.

"Pa, Thomas has been bad hurt in a mine explosion, and they say he might not live through the night."

"Would you saddle my horse, Hiram? I have to go to Ben."

Levi and Hiram found Mary Jane and Ben still standing just outside surgery and knew Thomas was still alive. Mary Jane rushed to Levi's arms and cried for the first time since the horrible accident. She had sat dry-eyed until she saw Levi.

"He will live, Mary Jane," he said empathetically. "Ben, I need to talk to you outside for a few minutes. Can Hiram stay with Mary Jane?"

Ben was hesitant to leave his watch by surgery, but Mary Jane sensed something unusual about Levi's request. "I'll send Hiram if there is any word, Ben."

The two men walked outside onto the wide veranda surrounding the hospital, looking down upon the town of Elkinsville.

"Ben, I'll make this short. Thomas will live. I have never told you how you come to have cat eyes and why you are different."

"When Hiram was three months old, I took your mother to see the farm for the first time. We left Hiram with Sarah and Albert, and your mother rode her horse "Kissey." We were so happy to have our own land, and Amy loved the cave and the waterfall at first sight. Your seed was planted that night in the cave, and we felt like we owned the whole world. The next morning your mother took a bath under the waterfall then wrapped herself in a blanket and walked down the hill to the pond while I went back into the cave for my rifle and fish bucket. When I came out of the cave, I saw her watching the fish swimming around. All of a sudden, I saw the biggest black panther I had ever seen walkin' out on that big oak limb that grows out over the pond. I could see he had his sights set on Amy by the way he was walking slow and quiet, and I could see he was about ready to spring. I damned near died of fright, but I quick sighted on his head and blew it off just when it jumped. Its body hit Amy and knocked her into a bunch of thorns.

When I got to her she was covered all over in blood, and, at first sight, I thought she was dead. I quick carried her to the waterfall and washed all the cat blood away. Scratches from the big thorns were deep and bleeding, and I think that's how she got some of the cat's blood.

We never told anybody what happened, not even Sarah and Albert. We never wanted you to know that you had been marked by the cat when you were growing up, afraid you would test the fact that cats have nine lives. You were tested on a few occasions and still have several lives left. Thomas has used three of his lives, and he needs to be careful. I'm an old man, Ben, and I wanted you to know now, but I hope you won't tell Thomas for a long time."

Ben was stunned by Levi's revelations, and suddenly numerous oddities fell into place. He remembered Levi being uncomfortable when he had asked why his eyes were so different and the numerous times he had been teased about cat eyes, his ability to see at night had always puzzled him, his unusual ability to hear sounds that others had not been able to pick up. He felt a chill remembering the slight cracking sound in the mine accident that had killed Frank, but gave him scant time to dive beneath the steel man cars. He could always understand different animal sounds and instantly pick up on the sense of danger.

Dr. Wilkins was just pushing through the surgery swinging doors as Ben and Levi returned to the waiting room. The doctor's smile and his look of great relief sent Ben's spirit soaring.

"Mary Jane and Ben, we were able to locate and tie off all the bleeders that were threatening Thomas's life. I don't know how he has survived such traumatic injuries. He will heal completely in time."

Ben and Levi locked eyes, and the older man cried.

Printed in the United States
40411LVS00004B/1-78

9 781933 538082